A LITTLE
WHITE DEATH

A LITTLE
WHITE DEATH

John Lawton

Atlantic Monthly Press
New York

First published in Great Britain in 1998 by Weidenfeld & Nicolson,
The Orion Publishing Group, London

Ode on Celestial Music is quoted
by kind permission of Brian Patten

Printed in the United States of America

FIRST AMERICAN EDITION

Library of Congress Cataloging-in-Publication Data

Lawton, John, 1949–
    A little white death / John Lawton.
        p. cm.
    ISBN 0-87113-932-4
    1. Troy, Frederick (Fictitious character)—Fiction. 2. Police—Great
Britain—Fiction. 3. London (England)—Fiction. 4. Physicians—Fiction.
5. Scandals—Fiction. I. Title.
PR6062.A938L58 2006
813'.54—dc22   2005048291

Atlantic Monthly Press
an imprint of Grove/Atlantic, Inc.
841 Broadway
New York, NY 10003

06 07 08 09 10   10 9 8 7 6 5 4 3 2 1

for
Sarah Teale
'An Englishwoman in New York'

Acknowledgements

To Said Aburish, who read and corrected the Beirut chapters.

To Carole Holden, Curator at the British Library, Bloomsbury, without whom several writers would vanish without trace into the BL index.

To Diana Norman, who reads everything I write in typescript and offers good advice.

To Ion Trewin, editor, who has 'sat through' these last three novels from start to finish, and lost nothing more than his pencil sharpener.

To Sheena McDonald, who offered me a cool, Cape Cod bolt-hole just when I needed one.

Ode on Celestial Music

(or *It's The Girl In The Bathroom Singing*)

It's not celestial music it's the girl in the bathroom singing.
You can tell. Although it's winter
the trees outside her window have grown leaves,
all manner of flowers push up through the floorboards.
I think – 'what a filthy trick that is to play on me,'
I snip them with my scissors shouting
'*I want only bona fide celestial music!*'
Hearing this she stops singing.

Out of her bath now the girl knocks on my door,
'Is my singing disturbing you?' she smiles entering,
'did you say it was licentious or sensual?'
'And excuse me, my bath towel's slipping.'
A warm and blonde creature
I slam the door on her breasts shouting
'*I want only bona fide celestial music!*'

Much later on in life I wear my hearing-aid.
What have I done to my body, ignoring it,
splitting things into so many pieces my hands
cannot mend anything? The stars, the buggers, remained
    silent.
Down in the bathroom now her daughter is singing.
Turning my hearing-aid full volume
I bend close to the floorboards hoping
for at least one song to get through.

Brian Patten, *Notes to the Hurrying Man*, 1969

Prologue
December 1962
New York

Not once had it occurred to her to think of him as the kind of man who would bring down a government and close off an era. But at that time – in those days – to whom had it occurred? If she had thought about it, then, of course, he was no revolutionary – he was a sybarite. She knew revolutionaries. Short men, serious men, men who marked their seriousness physically by being bald or mustachioed, or both. She knew. She'd been introduced to Lenin before she was ten years old – in much the same way the devout took their children to be blessed by the Pope. She'd been blessed by Lenin. Fat lot of good it did her.

He was heading for her now. Picking his way through this well-heeled Park Avenue party crowd, intent on her, smiling, charming, exchanging the odd word, the odder kiss, with half a dozen socialites en route to her.

'Signora Troy!'

Always addressed her in Italian.

'Bella, bella.'

Then he kissed her.

'Dr Fitzpatrick. What brings you back so soon?'

He'd been over in August, or was it July?

'The war, m'dear. The war. Had to see if the pavements of New York had cracked or its buildings crumbled.'

'What war?'

'Cuba.'

'You mean October? You call that a war?'

'Missiles piling up among the sugar cane, battleships squaring off in the Atlantic, half England in tears because the world is about to end before they've even lost their virginity. What would you call it?'

'I'd call it diplomacy. I'd call it politics.'

'Well you know what Churchill said about politics and war.'

'War is politics by other means, and I think it was Thucydides.'

'I meant the other way around. Politics is war by other means.'

'No, that we call brinkmanship.'

'Can I get you another drink?'

When he got back with her Martini, she'd make damn sure they changed the subject. She'd all but ignored Cuba. It could not scare her. The panic that had seemed to grip everyone she knew had passed her by. She'd spent her whole life trapped between the USA and the USSR. Bound to get her one day.

'What really brings you here?'

'Can you keep a secret?'

'Absolutely not.'

'Work.'

'Work?'

'I treated the American ambassador in Harley Street last spring. He was kind enough to recommend me to the President.'

'Jack Kennedy's flying in doctors from England?'

'I'd keep it quiet. It's hardly a vote-winner, is it?'

'Is he that ill?'

'Addison's is very wearing. In that sense it's deadly. If he wins next November don't bank on there not being a President Johnson by 1966 or thereabouts.'

Now, that did scare her.

'You know,' Fitzpatrick said, 'we took it very seriously in England.'

'We back on Cuba?'

'We're sort of in the middle. I don't just mean geographically. We none of us, none of the English, think of the Russians as bogeymen. I know some of the London Russians. Perfectly decent people.'

So did she. She'd married one.

'I have a friend works at the embassy. Thoroughly decent chap. Matter of fact I tried telling the powers that be that the Russians are human just like you or I. I wrote to one of the rising lights of the

Labour Party to say as much during the Missile Crisis. If I can talk to the Russians, why can't they?'

She could scarcely keep the incredulity out of her voice. 'You didn't write to my brother-in-law?'

'What? To Rod Troy? Good Lord, no. Rod's not rising, he's risen. He's got as far as he'll ever get while Gaitskell's still alive. No, I wrote to Harold Wilson. He might be Prime Minister in nine or ten years' time. Just wanted to drop the thought.'

'Did he catch it?'

Fitzpatrick shrugged.

'Politicians,' he said simply.

Half an hour later she found herself on the front steps of the building watching packed cabs flash by – up and down Park Avenue. Fitzpatrick followed only minutes later, turning up his collar against the cold, looking up at the rich cobalt blue of a cloudless New York night sky.

'Share a cab?' she said, hoping he would dash out into the throng and find the last free cab in the city. He pointed down the street towards Grand Central.

'I'm at the Waldorf,' he said. 'It's only a short walk. Look, I'm in town for a couple of days. Why don't you give me a call?'

'Sure,' she said. 'Sure.'

He walked off down Park Avenue. She looked again for the elusive yellow cab. Then a voice behind her, calling her name.

'Clarissa. Clarissa.'

She usually had to remind herself that this meant her. She'd added the C years ago as the simplest way of changing her name – Tosca by marriage to Troy, Larissa to Clarissa, a name she'd found on a bogus passport she'd used years ago – but it still sounded odd on anyone else's lips.

A tall young man in a black cashmere overcoat was coming down the steps towards her. It was Norman Somestein – Feinstein or Weinstein, one of the steins – one of the London publishers she worked for from time to time.

'Share a cab?' he said, exactly as she had done to Fitzpatrick. 'I've a room at the Ansonia.'

'Sure. I'll get out the other side of the park, then you can take it on to Broadway.'

Feinstein-Weinstein had better luck than she had had. He flagged down a checker cab and told the driver to take them to 72nd and Central Park West.

Seated in the back, he said, 'I didn't know you knew Fitzpatrick.'

'We ain't exactly bosom buddies . . . but he comes over from England a lot . . . and we always seem to be at the same parties. Asks me to look him up if I visit London. But I ain't been since 1960, so I haven't. Maybe next time.'

'I wouldn't if I were you,' said Feinstein-Weinstein. 'He's trouble.'

'What kind of trouble? I mean. He's very well regarded here. Did you know he's here to see if he can prescribe for Jack Kennedy's problem?'

'Which one – his bad back, his roving cock or his Addison's disease?'

'The last – Fitz is some kind of expert in homeopathy.'

'I'm sure he is – but this is America. The English aren't so tolerant.'

'Of what?'

Feinstein-Weinstein had to think for a second. And when he spoke his tone had changed. He was spinning out something far less tangible.

'Fitz mixes it. Mixes everything. Class and race, sex and politics, perfume and passion, you name it. He's a mixer.'

'So?'

'This time he's concocted too rich a blend. It's volatile. It'll blow up in his face. There'll be blood on the streets, mark my words.'

'Blood on the streets?'

She assumed this was just an image, nothing more. Tears before bedtime.

'And', he added, 'the English can be so unforgiving of a good scandal.'

'Y'know. I think that's kind of why I left them.'

Two days later she phoned the Waldorf.

'Ah,' said Fitzpatrick, 'I thought you'd given me up. I'm leaving for the airport in an hour.'

'I just wanted to ask. Do you ever see my husband?'

'Time to time – perhaps three or four occasions a year. I usually manage to contrive at least one. Freddie's not the most sociable of beasts at the best of times.'

'Could you give him a letter from me?'

'Of course, but you might find the US mail quicker, or a telegramme perhaps?'

'No – seems so impersonal – and he hates telegrammes . . . but a note you could deliver personally . . .'

'Fine. I understand. Now why don't you hop in a cab. We can have one last drinkie before I dash to Idlewild.'

January 1963
England

§ I

When the snow lay round about. Deep. And crisp. And even.
England stopped.

First the roads, from the fledgling six-lane autobahns, known as
'motorways' – a word used as evocatively as 'international' or
'continental' – to the winding, high-hedged lanes of Hertfordshire,
disappeared under drifting snow. Then, the telephone lines, heavy
with the weight of ice, snapped. Then the electricity supply began to
flicker – now you see it now you don't. And lastly, huffing and
puffing behind iron snow ploughs as old as the century and more,
the railways ground to a halt at frozen points and blocked tunnels.

It was the worst winter in living memory, and when and where
did memory not live? It squatted where you did not expect it. And
where you did. Not-so-old codgers would compare the winter of
1963, favourably or not, to that of 1947. Old codgers, ancient
codgers, codgers with no calendar right even to be living at all,
would trounce opinion with a masterly, ''T'ain't nothin' compared
to 1895.'

Rod Troy, Home Affairs spokesman in Her Majesty's Loyal
Opposition, a Labour MP since the landslide of 1945, had reason to
be grateful to his father, the late Alexei Troy. When refitting the
stately Hertfordshire pile he had bought in 1910, as a final refuge
after five years a wandering exile from Imperial Russia, he had
installed electricity and the telephone – the first in the village – and
omitted to remove the gas lamps. Gas was a hard one to stop. It
wouldn't freeze and it had no wires to snap. So it was that, in the

middle of a blanketed white January Rod found himself cut off in Mimram House, marooned in snow, stranded in a post-Christmas limboland, bereft of wife and children, hunched over a traditional English pastime, by the romantic glow of gaslight, facing a short, dark, irritating alien he ruefully acknowledged as his younger brother Frederick.

'How can you?' he yelled. 'How can anyone cheat at Monopoly?'

'That's what it's for,' Troy replied. 'If you can't cheat, I can't see the point in playing.'

'Grow up, Freddie. For God's sake grow up. That's just the sort of attitude you had as a child.'

'It's a childish game, Rod.'

'It's about rules and trust and codes of conduct. All games are!'

Rod should have known better. Such argument had never cut mustard with Troy when they were children and in middle age it was inviting the pragmatic scorn he seemed to store up in spades.

'No it's not, it's about which bugger can be the first to stick a hotel on Park Lane.'

Rod swept the board to the floor. 'Sod you then!' And walked out.

Troy passed an hour in his study, staring at the unchanging landscape, the monotony of white. He put John Coltrane's 'Giant Steps' on the gramophone, but was not at all sure that he was not kidding himself that he had a taste for the music, and he was damn sure it didn't go with England in January. Did Delius write no *Winterreise*? Had Elgar left no *Seasons*?

It occurred to him that he should go and look for Rod before Rod found him. He would only want to apologise and Troy could not bear his apologies. It seemed wise to head him off at the pass. They might, after all, have to spend days cooped up like this, and while the house was big enough to lose a small army within, they would inevitably end up together and if Monopoly brought them to grief, God help them when Troy started to cheat at pontoon.

The cellar door stood open, a gust of icy air wafting up from below stairs.

Troy called out his brother's name and waited.

'Down here in the wine cellar!'

Troy moved cautiously down the stairs, the light dimly orange in the distance as Rod waved his torch beam around.

'I think I've made a bit of a find.'

Troy could not see him, only the dancing end of the torch. Then the beam shot inwards, and Rod's face appeared, pumpkin-headed, in the light.

'Hold this a mo'. I'll get the gas lit.'

A rasp of match, a burst of flame, and Rod reached upwards and lit the gas jet. In the flickering hiss of gaslight Troy found himself framed by vast dusty racks of wine, countless bottles in long rows stretching away under the house. Rod stood facing him, absurdly wrapped up against the cold in the eiderdown off his bed, belted around his chest and waist, looking like the rubber man in the tyre adverts. He appeared to be clutching a solitary bottle of wine.

'What have you found?' Troy asked.

Rod wiped the label with his sleeve.

'The paper's a bit perished, but it says 1928 and I'd lay odds of ten to one it's Veuve Clicquot.'

'Does champagne keep that long?'

'Haven't the foggiest. But there's only one way to find out.'

He unhooked two glasses from the side of a wooden rack, where they had sat untouched since before the war and wiped the dust from them.

The champagne burst into the glass in a healthy stream of bubbles. Troy swigged some of his and pronounced it 'OK'. Rod sipped his gently and said, 'OK? It's bloody marvellous.'

Then the pause, the reflective stare into the glass. The thought so visibly running through his mind and across his features that Troy grew impatient and wished he would speak.

'Whenever I pull the cork on one of these . . .'

Troy knew what was coming. He could see the curve of Rod's illogic arcing between them like static.

'Or whenever I watch you . . .'

He sipped and stared into his glass a little more.

'I think of the old man. Every time. Never fails. No matter what is on my mind or whatever shit you are giving me, as you are so wont to do – and age does not diminish it – it gives me pause. I think of our father.'

'Sort of like unholy sacrament. An atheist communion?'

'Don't piss on it, Freddie. I'm serious.'

'So am I. Has it ever occurred to you that's why he left us this lot, so that we should think of him from time to time?'

'I didn't say from time to time, I said every time. And who else would he have left it to? And I wonder, what else did he leave us of himself? If this is blood of his blood, where is flesh of his flesh?'

Troy was not sure he could follow this.

'Come again?'

'Who the hell was he? Was he the same man he was to you that he was to me?'

'Doubt it,' said Troy.

'I mean . . . I'm his first born, you're his last, the child of his dotage—'

'Hardly dotage. He wasn't that old.'

'There, there's my point. How old was he? Did you ever know? When was he born? Did he ever tell you? Or where?'

'Must've done. Moscow, Tula, I don't know. And if he didn't, his dad lived with us for fifteen years. *He* must have mentioned it. God knows he rambled on enough.'

'Quite. He rambled. His stories never went anywhere. But the old man was a master of precision. He told us everything – at least it seemed like everything – yet when I come to look back on it there are gaps you could drive a tram through.'

Again the pause, long enough for Troy to refill both their glasses. Troy could see his brother's point even if he could see neither the gap nor the tram. Personally he was sure such minor details as the date and place of his father's birth were simply and temporarily lost in his memory; it was not that he didn't know, it was not that he had not been told. But at the heart of the matter, the man was an enigma.

'You're right, of course,' Rod resumed his musing. 'He wasn't the same man to both of us. I got sent away to school before you were so much as a toddler. You hung around the house almost till adolescence—'

'I was at home because I was a sickly child, Rod, they weren't doing me any favour.'

'Nonetheless you were there. He talked endlessly to you. You were his favourite.'

'Rod, this is bollocks. I was the youngest, that's all.'

'Youngest. Hand-reared. Privy to his wisdom.'

'Recipient of all his gags and anecdotes, if that's what you mean?

9

Child corrupted by his view of history and politics, if that counts for anything.'

'Corrupted?'

'OK. That's a bit steep. Let us say I was nurtured into an unfortunate precociousness by prolonged exposure to his didactic asides. He taught me the Theory of Surplus Value when I was seven. Had me on the Second Law of Thermodynamics before I was ten.'

'Bugger me! More booze, I think. I cannot listen to sentences like that and stay sober.'

Rod stuck out his glass again. It seemed a daft thing to be doing, sitting on beer crates in a dark cellar, scarcely above freezing, getting pissed on vintage champagne and pretending not to mind the cold. Rod might not be feeling it, but Troy had on nothing thicker than his Aran sweater. Still, if this was how Rod wanted to spend the last hour of daylight, Troy would humour him.

'Think of it,' Rod went on. 'I mean, think of him. Of what he did for us. I always felt secure in the world as he made it for us. I can't help but wonder if my kids can ever feel what that means. Wonder if they'll ever feel the same security. The world he built around us.'

'Troy Nation,' said Troy softly.

'Eh?'

'That's how I used to think of it. So often I ended up housebound, one damned ailment or another. The house was the world for a time. I used to think of it as Troy Nation. A country entire unto itself.'

Rod looked up at the ceiling. Troy knew what he was thinking. In the mind's eye, he was looking through the ceiling. Stripping away the layers in time and putting them back on in an order of his own choosing. This house, these five storeys of junk-packed, book-lined, history-ridden rooms, looming above them like the edifice of memory, a world of its own through which the old man moved mysteriously even now. The house ought be haunted. It was made to be haunted. Yet they conjured him in words not spirit; he haunted not the structure of their house, but the structure of their minds. Most of the time Troy could take him or leave him. He had long ago got used to being Alex Troy's boy. At forty-seven, Commander of CID, Scotland Yard, half a dozen commendations and an ex-wife to his name, he was still 'Alex Troy's boy'. Doubt caused him little conscience, but such conscience all but made a coward of Rod. Doubting the old man would nag and nag at him, and he could not dismiss it. If there was one gift Troy would have given his brother, it was to free him from such doubt. He had, he knew, probably sown the seed himself.

Away over their heads Troy could hear a bell ringing. It seemed an impossible noise. Logic ruled it out as being simply the doorbell. In households such as this someone else usually answered the door and told the caller whether or not you were at 'ome, regardless of whether you were. And no one had fought their way up the drive from the village in days. Clearly Rod was not going to answer, half-pissed, wrapped up too cosily in his eiderdown, the Michelin man, still sipping the last of the Veuve Clicquot.

'You'd better go and see,' he said, smiling faintly. 'It's probably Titus Oates or Captain Scott.'

It was Driffield the postman. The surliest bastard alive, as far as Troy was concerned. Or – to be precise on the matter of titles – the surliest sub-postmaster, a man in whose eyes Troy was still twelve and simply his father's son, requiring no more in the way of courtesy than a clip 'round the ear 'ole from time to time. He was attired much after the fashion of Rod: at least two overcoats had been added to a layer or more of pullovers and onion rings of collars and scarves obscured most of his face. All the same, Troy could see from the eyes that it was him, and from the expression in them he was, as ever, not best pleased to have trudged up the hill. To do so in several feet of snow had merely refined what was fundamental in his nature. No doubt he missed the days, long gone, when Troy's father would send a donkey and cart to the village to collect the mail.

'I don't know why I does this for you buggers, but I does,' he said. 'Tel'grammes it is, you hev got tel'grammes, the blarsted pair o' ye. Why ye gaht to hev tel'grammes on a day like this, Gahd knows.'

It was, it seemed, deeply inconsiderate of the Troys to be in receipt of tel'grammes of which they knew nothing.

A mittened hand shoved two envelopes at Troy, and then returned to sink into its pocket once more as its owner set off back down the drive, ploughing the trench in the snow he had cut on the way up.

'Aren't you going to wait for the reply?' Troy yelled after him. More often than not the man would tell you what was in a telegramme before you could open it, would stand on the step and recite it to you before you could so much as break the seal, but now nothing, it seemed, would keep him a moment longer.

'Phone it through,' he said over his shoulder. 'There's two blokes from the GPO up a pole in the lane. Ye'll hev phones again in half an hour or so they reckon.'

Rod appeared behind Troy. Troy handed him the small brown envelope and tore open the one with his own name on it. The telegramme meant nothing to him.

HUGH TURN FOR WORST STOP FEAR HE MAY NOT LAST STOP SUGGEST COME SOONEST STOP BILL STOP

Troy read it again, wondering if the author's economy with language and cost had left him to guess at a vital aspect of its meaning.

Rod snatched it from his hand. Stuck another in front of him.

'Dozy sod's put them in the wrong envelopes. You've got mine and I've got yours.'

The new telegramme scarcely made more sense than the last. But at least it was written with scant regard for cost in fully grammatical sentences.

DEAR FREDDIE STOP LONG TIME NO SEE STOP I WOULDN'T BE WRITING TO YOU OUT OF THE BLUE IF IT WEREN'T IMPORTANT STOP I DON'T THINK I HAVE MUCH TIME LEFT STOP I'D LIKE TO SEE YOU ONE MORE TIME BEFORE THE END STOP I'D LIKE TO THINK THAT OUR FRIENDSHIP SURVIVES ON THAT LEVEL AND THAT I CAN ASK THIS OF YOU STOP COULD YOU COME TO BEIRUT? STOP NOW? STOP I'VE RESERVED A ROOM FOR YOU AT THE ST GEORGES STOP COME AS SOON AS YOU CAN STOP I'VE NO IDEA HOW LONG I'VE GOT STOP CHARLIE STOP

It felt as though a ball and chain had tipped softly from the envelope in some sleight-of-hand magician's trick and wrapped itself around him. The old weight, the old friend, the old lie. Was he dying? Could Charlie be dying? Why couldn't he just say so? Troy had not seen Charlie since 1957. He had asked much the same of him then. 'I've taken a job in the Middle East. See me off. Just for old times' sake. It'll be the last time.' Now this was the last time. The last time for what? Could Charlie be dying?

'Gaitskell's dying.'

Rod's voice cut through his reverie. Troy looked up from the telegramme to see Rod suddenly sober, casting off the Michelin outfit.

'I have to get up to London. God knows how, but I have to.'

Gaitskell was the 'Hugh' of the telegramme Rod had just read. Leader of the Opposition and, since it was received wisdom that 1963 would be an election year, the next Prime Minister. He and Rod, of much the same age, class and education, fought like cat and dog and were stubbornly loyal both to each other and to the party. For Gaitskell to die now would be a political inconvenience and a personal tragedy for Rod.

'The phones will be on soon,' Troy said. 'Driffield just told me.'

'Did he say how the roads were?'

'See for yourself,' said Troy, pointing out through the open door at the snowbound drive and the three-foot-deep trench Driffield had carved in it.

Around the corner at the end of the drive, where the curving line of beech trees – resplendent green in summer, crisp brown in winter – shielded the house from the road, a petrol-driven vehicle – Troy could on first sight be no more precise than that – appeared. Preceded by the peristaltic grunt of its engine, it rounded the curve, entered the trench and chugged towards the house in a shower of obscuring and enveloping snowdust, ripping out the slender tracks of human feet into a wide chasm in the white wilderness of Mimram. It was a motorbike. A motorbike with sidecar. A motorbike with snowplough. A motorbike with sidecar and snowplough driven by an extremely fat man in a leather helmet and an old Second World War London County Council Heavy Rescue Squad navy-blue greatcoat.

The motorbike sliced through the drift immediately in front of the porch, and the snowploughing contraption deposited a pile of snow almost six feet high in a V-shape to either side.

The Fat Man pushed up his goggles.

'Wotcher cock,' he said to Troy.

Troy looked down at the contraption from the safety of the porch. He had never seen anything like it. The blades of the snowplough bolted neatly to the front forks of the bike and shot off at a tangent to bolt themselves to the front of the sidecar. A large, round-knobbed lever on the handlebars appeared to raise or lower the device at the Fat Man's whim via a pantograph. He had even put snow chains on the tyres, attached an army-surplus five-gallon jerry can of petrol to the back end, and seemed to be transporting a large hessian sack of something in the sidecar. It was a bike for all seasons, this one in particular.

'What's in the sack?' said Troy.

'Pignuts. I thought you'd be low on pignuts by now.'

'We're low on everything. You wouldn't happen to have a loaf of bread or five pounds of spuds in there too?'

'I'm 'ere to feed the pig, not you lot. You can fend for yerselves. But the pig – she needs lookin' after.'

The Fat Man set his sack on the ground and from the depths of the sidecar produced a pair of snowshoes. The postman had looked like a lone idiot, stepping outside, quite possibly for some time, but this was the full-blown expedition. The Englishman abroad. Man equipped, man kitted out with the best that an army-surplus store could provide. With such pluck and stuff as this, the British had climbed Everest and chugged their way across Antarctica, and that in the last ten years alone. Troy never knew why it was that the army amassed such surpluses and in such quantities – and perhaps mountains were climbed and wildernesses crossed just to diminish the stockpiles – but they did, and without them Sir Edmund Hillary might stand atop Everest in a string vest and half the working men in Britain would be left khakiless and wondering what to wear for the messy jobs or, in this case, how to wade through three-foot snowdrifts down to the pigpens lugging half a hundredweight of compressed dry pig fodder.

'When was you last down there?'

'Yesterday.'

The Fat Man regarded him sceptically.

'Honestly,' said Troy. 'I took her fresh water, a huge bundle of cabbage leaves and a bucket of last year's windfall apples I've been saving.'

'And?'

'And what?'

'And how was she?'

'Fine,' said Troy. 'Happy as a pig in . . .'

He could not quite think of the word. But it was straw. His Gloucester Old Spot sow, the third such he had bred in the last ten years, was happy as a pig in straw, if only because he and the Fat Man had had the foresight to build an insulating wall around her sty late last autumn with twenty-odd bales of straw. Whatever the Fat Man thought, and it was his usual banter to deride Troy's pigmanship, he had looked in on his pig and had thought her sty somewhat warmer than his own house.

The Fat Man hoisted his sack, slipped his feet into the leather loops of the snowshoes and set off for the pigpens under the oaks.

'I'll be back,' he said.

Troy did not doubt it. He had known him on and off the best part of twenty years, and, apart from an increase in his girth, he had changed very little. He was still the committed cockney, determinedly unpredictable, quite the most secretive man he had ever met, and utterly, totally reliable. He had minded Troy's pig, and pigs plural when she had farrowed, at no notice on countless occasions. It had occurred to Troy that perhaps he read minds, for, whilst one could never be at all sure when he would turn up, or from where, he did so exactly when one needed him. Not that Troy needed a pigsitter right now, that went without saying; what he needed the Fat Man had provided almost inadvertently. Transport. A vehicle that could get through snow and ice, something that could get him to London. Something with wheels that did not spin pointlessly on the spot as Troy's Bentley had done when he had tried her a couple of days ago.

He rushed upstairs and began to pack. From his bedroom window he caught sight of the Fat Man cresting a humpbacked ridge of snow like Ahab astride Moby Dick, the snowshoes stuck to his feet like giant leaves miraculously letting him walk on water.

He had no idea what to pack for Beirut and threw an assortment of clothes together. Across the other side of the house he heard the phone ring. The first time in days. Heard the urgent tones in Rod's voice without actually hearing any of his words. Clutching his suitcase, he almost knocked Rod down on the stairs. He was dressed for a journey. Overcoat, trilby, gloves. He was carrying his briefcase.

'I have to get up to London.'

It seemed to be a remark hovering between apology and explanation.

'I heard you the first time.'

JOHN LAWTON

'He has to take me, Freddie. Hugh's dying. Unless you can tell me it's a matter of life and death I'm getting in that sidecar and he's taking me as far as that piece of Heath Robinson machinery will get us.'

Troy did not know what 'it' was – a matter of life and death? A matter of life and lies? It was half-formed or less in his own mind. He would not have dreamt of discussing Charlie with Rod at this point. He said nothing. Just followed Rod down to the front door.

'Are you going to tell me?' Rod said, pulling on his wellies.

'There's nothing to tell. But I do need to get up to town.'

'Secrets, Freddie. Secrets. You're worse than the old man. You play every damn card so close to the chest. Well, I'm telling you now that if you can't tell me honestly that your business is more important than mine, I say sod you for your secrets. I'm commandeering the Fat Man and his motorbike and I'm going.'

Troy said nothing. The very word 'commandeering' made him wince inwardly. This was Wing Commander Troy in fully operational mode. Playing by the Queensberry Rules. Rules that let him hijack the bike, but did not permit him to read a telegramme addressed to someone else.

'Quite,' said Rod. 'Silence.'

When the Fat Man trudged back to his bike Rod made his pitch, plain and simple. A fiver to get him, as he put it, 'to civilisation'. The Fat Man looked to Troy. Troy nodded almost imperceptibly and, as Rod made a racket clambering into the sidecar, leant over and whispered.

'Dump him at the nearest station and get back here. I may need you for a few days.'

The Fat Man tapped the side of his nose.

Rod looked ridiculous sitting in the sidecar. Knees tucked almost to his chin, hat rammed down to his ears, goggles over his eyes, briefcase pressed to his chest. He looked like an owl.

'There is one thing,' he said from his preposterous perch.

'Of course,' said Troy.

'What's the Second Law of Thermodynamics? Is it Einstein or one of those blokes?'

'It's Kelvin.'

'Never heard of him. What did he say?'

16

'Entropy. Everything expands into . . . nothing.'

'Don't quite follow . . .'

'Everything turns to shit in time.'

'And we need a "Theory" to tell us that?'

The Fat Man raised a giant's foot off the ground, slamming down on the kickstart, and brought four 250cc cylinders spitting and roaring into life. He was back in less than an hour.

§ 2

He had not thought Beirut would be cold. It wasn't − it just wasn't warm either. He had so looked forward to being warm. He had somehow seen himself in shirtsleeves, a white sea-island cotton shirt clinging to him loosely as a gentle breeze blew in from the Mediterranean to ruffle his hair. It had been a dream conjured up after a night in a run-down hotel on the Great North Road − where he had finally abandoned the Fat Man's motorbike − another on a bench at Heathrow as his flight was postponed in half-hour chunks − permitting the runways to be swept clear of snow just in time for the next storm, and permitting no one the resolution of checking into a hotel − and a third night on a bench at Orly as his plane was grounded in a blizzard by French air traffic control and much the same stop-go, go-stop policy ensued.

The best part of four days had passed by the time he landed in Beirut. It was pitch dark and the less than gentle sea breeze, whilst hardly a howling North Sea gale that could cut through clothing, was wind enough to cut through expectation, to chill the spirit if not the flesh. It blew across the runway, chased him through the terminal, pursued him to a taxi, raced him the length of the city out to the Ra's Beirut promontory, and was waiting for him fifteen minutes later when he got out. All that could be said was that it was warmer than England.

The taxi dropped Troy in front of the Saint-Georges Hotel, a squat block looming featurelessly over him in the darkness. Sleepless, exhausted, unshaven and unwashed, he felt sure he must stink to high heaven after four days in the same clothes.

'Yes,' said the white-jacketed clerk at reception. 'Mr Charlie instructed us to keep the room exactly one week. Everything is ready for you, Mr Troy.'

All Troy wanted was a bath and a bed, and he was not at all sure he would even bother to take them in that order.

'Fine,' he said. 'Would you get a message to Mr Leigh-Hunt, tell him I'm here and that I'll see him at breakfast?'

'Mr Charlie has gone, sir.'

'Gone?'

'Gone, sir.'

For a moment the same thought passed through his mind that had first surfaced when he read Charlie's telegramme – gone meant dead. A blunt, ineffectual euphemism. But from the look on the man's face that was clearly not the case. There was not a flicker of meaningless public display of regret.

'Gone where?' he said.

'We never know, Mr Troy.'

The man was alone at his post. The use of 'we' was little short of regal.

Troy looked out of the corner of his eye and saw that two men had approached him from the right as he talked. One of them coughed politely and he turned. A short, stout man, well past middle age, who clutched a smouldering cigar between fat fingers, and whose recent meals seemed displayed down the front of his shirt as liberally as his dandruff on his shoulders; and a tall, handsome young Arab with thick black hair and finely chiselled features, wearing a neat Italian black suit and the clean white cotton shirt Troy had seen in his dreams of himself.

'Troy?' said the old one. 'Did I hear him say Troy?'

Troy stared at him and said nothing.

'Would you be one of our Troys, if you don't mind me asking?'

'I don't know. What are your Troys?'

The old one stuck out his hand.

'Arthur Alliss. *Sunday Post.* I used to work for your father. I'm the *Post*'s Middle East correspondent. We'd no idea you were coming out. Nobody told us. We'd've met you at the airport if we'd known.'

The penny dropped. These men worked for his father's Sunday paper. Since his father's death twenty years ago it had been run by his brother-in-law, Lawrence. Troy had next to nothing to do with the family business, with its small empire of newspapers, magazines and publishers. What little responsibility remained for the family, Rod usually handled. It had not occurred to him that there could hardly be a capital city on earth in which he would not find an accredited correspondent or a freelance stringer on one or another of the Troy newspapers.

Troy took the proffered hand, then shook with the young Arab.

'I'm Frederick Troy,' he said. 'I'm sorry, I hadn't thought about it – I mean, I hadn't realised you'd be here.'

Foolish, he thought. Of course they'd be there. Simply hacks doing their job. Why else was Charlie there? When MI6 had discreetly demanded his resignation in 1957, Charlie had asked Rod for a job and Rod had packed him off to Beirut as roving Middle Eastern correspondent for the family's almost defunct journal *American Week*. It had seemed appropriate. Charlie spoke Arabic, and it kept him active and paid, kept him out of England, out of the English papers, and out of harm's way. Only now he wasn't there. These two were, and looking upon him as some representative of the family firm, which he wasn't and would never be.

The old one ruminated a moment on the name.

'Frederick?' he said with a hint of inflection, a question posed more at himself than at Troy.

'Yes,' said Troy.

'The policeman?'

'Yes,' said Troy.

'You've come for Charlie?'

'Yes – he's a very old friend.'

'I think you'd better join us for a snifter, Mr Troy. *Said!*'

The mere mention of his name seemed enough to convey a simple, singular meaning to the young Arab. He headed for the bar and Alliss led the way back to their table. Troy wondered where he'd find the energy to talk to them. He hoped to God all they wanted was to pay their respects and then he could bugger off to bed.

Alliss relaxed into his chair and, finding his cigar out, stuck the wet end back in his mouth and put a match to the other. For a few seconds he vanished into a haze of sucking and puffing. Troy saw the Arab making his way towards them with a tray and three very large Scotches. He'd have one drink with them and ditch them.

'We both worked with Charlie, y'know,' Alliss said. 'Truth to tell I never thought the old firm needed two blokes out here, but there you are, your brother thought different. I file for the *Post*, Said here – this is Said Hussein – he's the local fixer . . .'

Hussein smiled politely at the belated introduction, a cold light in the shining black eyes, enough to tell Troy that at best he was bored by Alliss, at worst probably despised him.

'He's got the local knowledge. Speaks the lingo. And Charlie, Charlie filed for the Yanks.'

Troy noted through the haze of tiredness, and the acrid, repulsive smell of Scotch – he had put the glass to his lips and put it back untouched – Alliss's use of the past tense.

'Do you know when he'll be back?'

Alliss looked puzzled by this, glanced at Hussein, and then continued the same puzzled scrutiny of Troy as if the key were written in his face.

'Have ye not seen the papers Mr Troy?'

'No. I had one hell of a time getting here. I feel as though I've spent four days in a vacuum.'

'He's gone.'

'So everybody keeps telling me. But he's expecting me. I can wait, but it would be useful to know how long.'

'No – I mean gone gone. Defected. Charlie's crossed over.'

On what level had this rippled through his brain to find instant suppression? The telegramme lay crumpled at the bottom of his inside jacket pocket. He had read it over and again a dozen times in the last four days – 'I don't think I have much time left.' Somehow it had been easier – dammit, reassuring – to believe that Charlie's last cry had been a cry of help, that he was in mortal peril, that he had cancer, angina, cirrhosis of the liver. Troy found himself acknowledging for the first time that he had been prepared, had actually preferred, to believe that Charlie was dying rather than believe that his past, and with it Troy's own, had finally caught up with him.

'When?' he said simply.

'Four days ago. Just vanished. Clothes in his room. An article on

Moshe Dayan half-finished, still in the typewriter, cold cup of coffee next to it. Razor and toothbrush on the washstand. He came in here, sent a telegramme from the press room and vanished. We usually lunched together. First I knew was when he didn't show. I asked the boys here, but all they knew was the telegramme and they won't say what was in it or who it was to. Five hours later he boards a Russian freighter in the docks. I reckon all he had was the clothes on his back. Took me till yesterday to find out that much. Bloke in the dockyard recognised him. Came to me for a bit of the old backshish. I filed it, of course. Had to. It's news. Front page of the dailies back in Blighty this morning. If Hugh Gaitskell hadn't died last night it'd be the lead. You can't have a career like Charlie's and not be news.'

Alliss was a pig. The mixture of professional greed and personal pique made for a distasteful fool. Troy was beginning to share Hussein's silent contempt. He feared it might find its voice very soon. Alliss showed no sensitivity to what Troy might be feeling.

'O' course if I could find out who that telegramme was to, I'd really have a coup. That'd stick it to those dozy buggers on the *Sunday Times*. Insight Team my left buttock – more like Shortsight Team.'

He chuckled at his own wit, jowls jiggling, mirth rippling down to his fingertips, Scotch in his glass splashing over onto his trousers. He rubbed it into the fabric with the thumb of his free hand. Seemed not to mind. One more stain on a suit of boozer's motley.

'O' course, I can't say I'm surprised. I mean, is there anyone half sane who really believes Charlie was innocent? I don't care how many times the government set some pillock on his hind legs in the Commons to clear his name. Charlie was one of *them* – Burgess, Maclean, Leigh-Hunt. It all fits. If the government didn't know our Charlie was a spy, then they're the last ones who didn't.'

Troy had been the first to know. 1956. While the Suez débâcle rumbled on. He had told no one. It was no one else's business. It was between Charlie and him. And how dearly and how often had he wished there had been nothing between Charlie and him. That they should be like children, schoolboys again, when they had had no secrets. He had packed Charlie off to live with his lies one autumn day, one Indian summer's afternoon, seven years ago, knowing they would not meet again. A year later, somehow, MI6 had learnt the truth. Charlie had made too many mistakes, or some recently defected Russian had pointed the finger – Troy neither knew nor cared which – and Charlie had retired from the Secret Service in a flurry of corridor speculation and to a wishy-washy Commons denial, so limp and unconvincing it had fallen not to the Foreign Secretary, but to the most junior of his ministers, a rising starlet of the Conservative Party, Timothy Woodbridge. Woodbridge had exonerated Charlie, gently berated the press for their gossip and cornered his little piece of history as author of what the same press had dubbed 'the Woodbridge Statement'. The last Troy had seen of Charlie was a farewell drink in a pub in St Martin's Lane. He seemed grateful to Troy that Rod had come to his rescue – and Troy had said nothing to this, because Rod had done so without telling him. He had done exactly what he thought Troy required of him without even mentioning it. And for that Troy was grateful. Charlie would not have come to him.

Each time was the last time. A slapdash sequence of partings, each potentially riddled with finality. Now this was the last. Now he really had gone.

'Why now?' said Troy, more to himself than to the two journalists.

For a second he thought Hussein was going to speak, but Alliss stubbed out the remains of his cigar and sounded off.

'Had enough,' he said bluntly. 'If you ask me he never much cared for the job. After all, if he really has ended up in Russia, then it was only a cover, wasn't it? I think he just got tired of it. It's a big territory. You can find yourself in Jerusalem one day and Aden the next. It takes belief. It's the only thing that'll keep you at it. Personally, I never thought Charlie had that belief. More often than not we'd cover for him, wouldn't we, Said? He couldn't be arsed half the time. He was lucky. Without us he'd've gone under. Mind you, he was good company – you get Charlie in the bar with a few drinks inside him. Talk about laugh!'

Troy heard his cue and knew his exit. Arthur Alliss was decidedly not good company. He had heard enough of Alliss's vision of Charlie. If it turned out he really had seen the last of him, then he wanted his vision of Charlie, warts and all, not the spiteful, sentimental vision of a drunken hack who scarcely knew him.

Troy pushed his untouched glass towards Alliss and got to his feet. 'Forgive me, but I'm flagging badly. I really do need to sleep now.'

Alliss bustled and missed the hatred in Troy's eyes. Prised himself from his chair with some loss of breath, stuck out his hand again and said, 'But you'll join us for breakfast? It's not often we . . .'

Perhaps he had read the look in Troy's eyes after all. The sentence dwindled down to nothing.

'Yes,' said Troy. 'Delighted.'

§ 3

He kicked off his shoes, tore off his jacket and tie and lay on the bed beneath the motionless punkah. He decided he'd give it fifteen minutes and then hang out the 'Do Not Disturb' sign. In less than ten there was a gentle tap at the door.

Hussein stood in the corridor, one hand oh-so-casually in his trouser pocket, the other poised to knock again. 'Do you really want to have this conversation now?' he asked.

'If it's the only time you're free of Alliss, yes,' said Troy.

Hussein carefully hung his jacket on the back of an upright chair and sank slowly into a deeply upholstered armchair. He loosened his tie, stuck a fat Turkish cigarette in his mouth, crossed his legs with a fastidious tug at the knee of his trousers and lit up. Troy flopped into the chair opposite, feeling as creased as his clothes.

Hussein could be no more than twenty-two or three, his eyes were bright, his skin shone with health and at the end of a working day he seemed not have a single close cropped hair out of place. The tie at half-mast was a concession to after-hours occasion. He looked like Madison Avenue man launching into a difficult pitch. Compared to him, Troy felt ancient.

'Arthur is colouring the story. You must forgive him. He is an old man. Out of his time.'

The preamble over, what they both knew so succinctly stated, he inhaled deeply and savoured his smoke a moment.

'No one carried Charlie.'

A hand batted the smoke away from his face, the gesture cutting, absolute, to reinforce his words.

'Far from being unsuited to the job, I'd say Charlie was a natural. Arthur got here just after Suez, less than a year before Charlie – just long enough for his nose to be out of joint when your brother hired Charlie. I suspect they were both sent for much the same reason. Suez put us back on the map. Every newspaper on earth increased its Middle East coverage, simply waiting for the next skirmish or the start of Armageddon. I joined them in 1961. My first job when I graduated Yale. I'm the new boy, but being from Jerusalem I'm near enough a native, and I know the lie of the land, and I think I know my job. I've seen enough to know that Charlie loved the job, and rather than letting Arthur carry him, he carried Arthur. After seven years Arthur has only a smattering of Arabic – good French; he'd have been OK here before the war, in his element in the time of the Beiks, but that's another age. I rather think Arthur hasn't acknowl-edged that.'

'England is full of men like Arthur,' said Troy.

'I've never been there,' Hussein replied with an almost impercep-tible shrug. 'But I can quite believe it. He's right when he says you can find yourself in Aden one day and Jerusalem the next. That's the nature of the job. But it was Charlie who made those journeys; it was Charlie who gathered enough information to support his own column and Arthur's news file. Most of the time you can't prise Arthur out of the bar here. We don't live here – even Troy Newspapers can't afford that – but we might just as well. It has its pluses – anyone who's anyone passes through here eventually – and its minuses, in that you can delude yourself that the Saint-Georges Hotel bar is the world. Until very recently Charlie never fell for that. There was always a world elsewhere for Charlie. True, he drank like a fish, I've never met an English reporter that did not, but until last autumn it never interfered with his work.

'Last October he was due three weeks' home leave. He never went home. Charlie's idea of leave was Spain or Morocco – I never heard of him taking home leave to go home to England. Perhaps you will say this is just as well – a man living under a cloud. Perhaps he did pick places where no one gave a damn whether he'd spied for Russia or even whether he still spied for Russia. Last year he chose to go home. He spent his usual ten days in Morocco and then he flew on to England. He visited his mother in Dorset – I gather they had not met in years – and he spent a weekend in London – I think he might have done the round of his old haunts, but the look on your face, Mr Troy, tells me that you did not see him. Whatever, he came back a changed man, dejected, angry, less willing to humour the insufferable Arthur, and his interest in the job vanished. I saw it evaporate like a dish of water put out in the noonday sun for the dog.'

The image seemed a suitably Levantine one on which to pause, inhale deeply from his cigarette, and let the words sink in. He blew a billowing cloud of aromatic smoke at the ceiling and levelled his eyes on Troy.

'And I heard the will to go on snap in him like a rubber band coiled too tight or a bowstring stretched too far. Something in Mr Charlie snapped.'

Troy sat in silent awe of the man's command of a language not his own, startled by his own recognition of this final metaphor. Years ago – in the 1920s – his father had taken him to France to one of those damningly nostalgic cultural get-togethers, organised by the then vast body of Russians in exile – Russians in hope – of Russian arts. Such were their numbers so soon after the Revolution they even ran their own émigré magazine, *Teatr i Zhizh*, and under the auspices of the Teatr crowd the then less than fashionable Le Touquet had staged Chekhov in the original. He had sat in the stalls through *The Cherry Orchard*, aged thirteen or so, enraptured by the play of ideas he soon learnt were wasted on more than half the audience – who surely were those cherry trees? – beautiful, useless. And then as the curtain fell, then rose again for the bows of the cast, his father rose too. 'Where was the breaking string?' he said. Cast and audience stared at him. No one answered. 'Where was the bloody breaking string that comes with the sleep of Feers?' he yelled. 'Chekhov is quite clear: "My life has passed as though I'd never lived. I will lie down now . . . nothing . . . nothing . . ." a distant sound, as though coming from the sky, like the breaking of a string! Where was the breaking string? What do you think the play means without the sound of that string snapping?' Troy had fled up the aisle to escape his father. Even then he was too important to the émigrés to be thrown out. They would have to reason with him, and Troy knew damn well that was nigh impossible. But in the ear of the mind he had heard that string snap even as his father launched full rant on the unfortunate players. He read the play on the train on the way back to from Paris Plage to Calais and finished it on the Channel crossing. He could hear the sound of the breaking string and the life that broke with it. 'Something snapped in Mr Charlie,' Hussein said. Yes, thought Troy, of course it did.

'Why is Alliss so convinced that Charlie has defected? Why can't he just have vanished?'

'He did board a Russian ship. Of that there is no doubt. Charlie was well known. A man from the dockyard did come to us with the story. Charlie boarded that freighter without so much as a briefcase, not even a hat or topcoat. I went to his room. It was as Arthur described it to you, the way I had described it to him. If he was setting out on a journey, he did not know it.'

'Passport,' Troy said. 'Did he take his passport?'

'It wasn't in his desk. I looked. But then not to have a passport on you at all times is a sackable offence in this business. On the other hand, if he really was defecting I doubt it would be an issue. Who asks a defector for a passport? The real issue is this – where was he between eleven in the morning and four o'clock, between his sending of that telegramme – which of course was to you, although Arthur cannot figure that out—'

'Said, please,' said Troy, 'please don't tell him.'

'Of course. It is your secret. The issue remains, where was Charlie between sending that telegramme and his boarding the ship at about four in the afternoon?'

'The telegramme said he didn't have much time.'

'But hours, only hours?'

'No,' said Troy. 'He meant days. He sent for me. He held this room for me for a whole week.'

'Then something changed his mind. And changed it in less than five hours.'

'He knew the game was up or he'd not have written to me. We'd kept our distance. He'd no more seen me these last few years than he'd seen his mother.'

Hussein stubbed out his cigarette, leant across to his jacket, pulled out the packet and lit up another straightaway. He picked a flake of tobacco off his tongue and played with a phrase.

'The game was up. The game was . . . up.'

He smacked his lips over the 'p's. Rendered this lost fragment of Cymbeline as if into a foreign language for Troy. 'How very English.'

Another billow of smoke blown at the punkah, another well-considered phrase.

'Whose game?'

'That rather depends on where he was, don't you think?'

Hussein nodded slowly.

'Can you find out?' said Troy.

'What do you think I've been doing for the last four days?'

Hussein was right. It was an utterly stupid question on Troy's part. The man was a journalist. It was as though someone had read him lesson one of Teach Yourself Detection.

'Sorry,' he said faintly.

'But – it may well take another day, possibly two. Can you stay that long?'

He couldn't, but it looked as though he would have to, or return home without a clue as to Charlie's whereabouts – and to be clueless was, after twenty-seven years a-coppering, the condition he hated most; insomnia or impotence would be preferable.

'A day in Beirut wouldn't hurt,' Hussein was saying. 'You have not been before?'

Troy shook his head.

'There are many ways of passing the time. Beirut is . . .'

Hussein paused for reflection but came up with only a cliché.

'. . . It is the crossroads of the world. The great bazaar. Lemons from Antilyàs out, Citroëns from France in. Everything passes through the port. Everything. Everything from anywhere. It is the city that proves Kipling wrong. East really does meet West in Beirut.'

He rose, stubbed out his cigarette and reached for his jacket.

'If the weather turns, you could drive out to Bayt Miri for lunch – the view will take your breath away – or you could catch a tram into the Suq and buy silk for your wife, or get a pair of sandals made. God knows, everyone does. Or if the weather really cheats the season, you could just stand on your balcony and watch the harbour life. I'll be back tomorrow evening or the morning after.'

§ 4

The weather turned. Troy cheated Alliss of his breakfast à deux and hung out the 'Do Not Disturb' sign until almost noon. When he emerged the clouds had cleared, the wind had dropped and there were the makings of a tolerable day.

He rode a rattling red tram down the Rue Georges Picot. He loved trams. They'd been gone from the streets of London ten years or more. He missed them. The tram stopped at the upraised hand of a gendarme in the Place des Martyrs. Troy got off and walked back up the Georges Picot, a cobblestoned street of tiny shops, open to the street, topped by rusting iron balconies, selling everything, silk and sandals included. Corny though it was, Said Hussein was right, East encountered West in its bit of everything. The sense of a black market, of an illicit trade, hung about the place for all its legality. Not so much Kipling as Masefield, thought Troy. What could be more fitting to the sense of place than that Quinquireme of Nineveh, bound for sunny Palestine in the precise beating metre of Masefield? Ivory, apes and peacocks; sandalwood, cedar and wine. Lemons out, Citroëns in – citron, Citroën. In this bazaar the twain did indeed meet. Young men in sharp suits like Hussein's moved quickly up and down, almost oblivious to the bustle. Troy all but expected one of them to come up to him and offer to sell him what was left of the British Empire. A man in half and half – baggy pants, the frayed jacket of a discarded blue suit, topped off by a traditional kaffiyeh headdress – laboured under the burden of a huge block of melting ice wrapped in sacking and precariously perched upon his back. And a man with no concession to several thousand years of cultural crossing, in full Arab dress, herded sheep between the tramlines.

Troy looked from the shepherd to the shops, gazing, he thought, at the future – symbolised on the wall of a food shop, where a bunch of ripening bananas hung between signs advertising Coca-Cola and

Pepsi. Slurping the world level. Once all the world was wilderness; one day it would all be cola.

He stared a moment too long. A hand pulled him sharply backwards and a donkey saddled with wooden crates of oranges blundered forward and missed him by fractions of an inch. Troy turned to see who had pulled him clear, and found himself facing three women. Mother, daughter and granddaughter, it seemed. The mother wore black from head to foot. All he could see of her were dark eyes above the veil. The daughter, a woman of thirty-something, was dressed conservatively western, rather like a French woman of modest means ten or twelve years ago might have done – a longish skirt, a sleeveless blouse. But the granddaughter wore the uniform of ubiquitous youth, the teenage costume that could be found on the streets of London or New York, or it seemed, Beirut – T-shirt, blue jeans and sneakers. Which had saved him from going under the hoof of a determined donkey? The mother was the nearest. It had, he concluded, been her. He thanked her politely in French.

The granddaughter replied.

'Ce n'est rien, Monsieur. Ma grandmère ne parle pas le français.'

They vanished after the donkey. Walking abreast down the cobbled street, leaving Troy thinking that he had seen colonialism in miniature, history compressed into half a century of a single family.

§ 5

When Troy got back to the Saint-Georges, before he could even ask for his key the concierge told him that a man was waiting to see him. Simultaneously he gestured over Troy's shoulder. Troy turned, expecting to see Hussein, but there sat a man with a face like a walnut, perched nervously on a plush red chair, wearing a multicoloured shirt in the Hawaiian style, sharply pressed black trousers and an expression that told Troy he was deeply unhappy at being there at all. A small man in his late fifties with short grey hair, and a bushy grey moustache hiding most of his top lip. He got up as

Troy approached. He was even shorter standing up, no more than five foot two.

'You are Misterfred?' he said, rolling name and title into one to produce an appropriate near-homonym of 'mystified'. Pretty much what Troy had felt for days now.

'Yes,' said Troy to both.

'Please, sir, could we go to your room?'

They rode up in the lift in silence, and when Troy had closed and locked the door behind them, the man pulled his shirt from his trousers and removed an envelope hidden in the waistband.

'From Mr Charlie,' he said. 'Mr Charlie.'

Troy opened it. The letter was written in biro on the back of a receipt for dry cleaning. Troy turned over from 'T b cllcted Tues 5pm 2 pr gents trsrs 1 drss Shrt' and found, 'Freddie. Stay put. I'll get a message through as soon as I can. Tell nobody. Charlie.'

'Where did you get this?'

'From Mr Charlie, last Tuesday.'

'You saw him the day he left? When?'

'It would be about half past two, sir. In the afternoon. Perhaps a little later.'

'Where?'

The man regarded Troy blankly as though each of a series of rather simple questions must mean more than it appeared to.

'At my place of work.'

'And where do you work?'

The dark eyes lit up. At last it seemed he and Troy were on the same wavelength.

'Oh, sir. Did I not say? I am Abu Wagih. Head doorman at the British Embassy. I am a Druze, sir. All we servants of Her Majesty are Druze.'

He smiled, beamed at his own forgetfulness, and the pleasure of revelation and understanding. All the same, Troy could hardly believe this. Would rather not believe this. It put wheels within wheels.

'Charlie was at the embassy?'

'Oh yes, sir. From just before noon until just after two thirty. Almost three hours. He came for his meeting with Mr Smith. On his way out he wrote this letter and said I was to give it to his good friend Misterfred at the Saint-Georges. My son is bar-waiter in the hotel, sir. Every evening I ask, "Did Misterfred come today?" and every evening he say, "No, Misterfred did not come today. Perhaps he will come tomorrow." Until last night. Last night I came and saw you with the fat English one, and so I went away. Mr Charlie was most anxious that I give you his letter alone.'

'Smith?' said Troy.

'Beg pardon, sir?'

'You say Charlie saw a Mr Smith.'

'Yes sir.'

'An Englishman?'

'I know no Arabs called Mr Smith, sir.'

Touché, thought Troy.

'An Englishman you knew?'

'No sir. Each year a Mr Smith would come to see Mr Charlie. But always a different Mr Smith. The family of Smith is very big I think, sir. Perhaps it is a tribe?'

Big? It was infinite. The nom de plume of the dirty weekend for three generations.

Unsure of the protocol in the matter, Troy rummaged in his pockets and came up with two five-pound notes. Somehow offering a man sterling rather than the local currency made the transaction seem less like a bribe and more like a reward. As though he might frame the notes rather than spend them.

Protocol seemed satisfied. Abu Wagih smiled and trousered the loot.

'Not a word to anyone,' said Troy.

'Indeed, sir. "Mum's the word," as Mr Charlie used to say.'

'I don't suppose', Troy said, pushing his luck, 'that Charlie said what the meeting with Smith had been about?'

'Yes, sir. He did say something about it being "a bollocking waste of time". Then he said, "Goodbye, old chap." Most odd. Usually he would ask after my sons, and after several minutes as I recited who was where and doing what, he'd say, "Don't let the bastards grind you down," and then he would walk away. Always the same, asking after my sons, and in the proper order of their birth, then the same phrase, "Don't let the bastards" . . .'

Abu Wagih stopped. As though he had realised for the first time the full meaning of Charlie's words, that he would not be back, that the bastards had, at long last, ground him down.

31

An hour or so later, the sun was setting. Troy sat on the terrace beneath a vast red parasol, sipped a citron pressé, and watched the sun sink into the Mediterranean. The last hardy hearty roared by on waterskis, rubber-suited against the January day. Small boats and big boats dotted the seascape all the way to the horizon. He knew next to nothing about boats and ships. The little ones, the ones with single masts, he was pretty certain were sloops. The bigger ones sailing into the network of wharves and warehouses on the north side could be anything – he could not tell a bark from a barquentine, a square-rigger from a schooner.

A day without the cutting wind, a day albeit far from his fantasy of floating around in shirtsleeves, had warmed him, literally, to the Mediterranean. He was, he had always thought, 'not a Med person'. He had been dragged uncomplainingly on several grand tours as a child; he had seen towers lean and heard bridges sigh, and gazed unimpressed on the dug-out ruins of a city that bore his own name; but had never seen himself as a man to laze away his days on a Greek island, or become one of those Englishmen in exile, Graham Greene in Antibes, D. H. Lawrence on Sardinia, or Robert Graves on Majorca. He took holidays, when he took them, in England. With his pigs and his long-playing records – though he had yet to get around to the joys of stereophonic sound – and his books.

A waiter coughed politely to drag Troy back to the real world and the present day.

'A package for you, M'sieur. Delivered by hand.'

It was one of those padded envelopes, bulky and heavy. Charlie. It had to be from Charlie.

Troy ripped it open. Inside the package was a second envelope and a short, typed, unsigned message.

'Sorry. Change of venue. Still, you always did want to visit the old place, didn't you?'

In the second envelope was a Soviet Foreign Ministry letter of authorisation in lieu of a visa, stamped and signed and counter-stamped and countersigned, made out in Troy's name, and four airline tickets – Beirut to Athens by Zippo Charters, Athens to Moscow by Aeroflot, Moscow to Zurich by Aeroflot and Zurich to London by BOAC. He checked the itinerary. He had two days in Russia. Two days in Russia. The old country. Land of his father, land of his grandfather and all their fathers before them. It was the last place on earth he wanted to be.

§ 6

Said Hussein found him, checking out of the Saint-Georges in the morning. He looked at the suitcase, he looked at Troy and drew the obvious conclusion.

'You know where he was.'

It was not a question.

'Yes,' said Troy.

'You're not going to tell me.'

'I can't. Believe me, I can't.'

'You're not playing the game, Mr Troy. If I had been the one to find out, I would tell you.'

'What I know you cannot use. If you do, it's Charlie's life on the line. I admit it's not fair on you as a journalist, but that's the way it is. If it's any consolation to you, I'd be happy to talk to the family when I get back. You can have Charlie's job. Dammit, you can have Alliss's too.'

'Which I won't refuse.'

'Glad to hear it.'

'There's a war coming. Israel and the Arabs again. Perhaps two or three years from now, but coming nonetheless. Arthur's not up to a war. He'd have to be replaced sooner or later.'

Hussein paused as he so often did in consideration of his next remark.

'But', he continued, 'don't you think it's a bit ruthless?'

'No,' said Troy. 'No I don't.'

Now he too searched for the considered phrase.

'He's had his day.'

Hussein did not seem to disagree with this.

'There is one thing. I will have to continue to look for Charlie and, worse from your point of view, look into Charlie. My employers will expect that of me. Supposing it turns out that Charlie was a spy?'

'I think that's a foregone conclusion,' said Troy.

'I meant a spy while he was here. Suppose the journalism was merely his cover. What then? Suppose that even now he is a spy. What then?'

'Then you publish what you find. I'm not even going to ask those questions. I don't want to know.'

§ 7

At Athens he changed planes and bought a bottle of ouzo – he'd never tasted the stuff and, besides, it would be a beakerful of the warm south to take into the Russian winter. He also bought the *Sunday Post*. An outrageous price and nearly two days old, but he desperately wanted an English paper.

'Where is Leigh-Hunt?' ran the headline, and underneath it was another version of what Said had told him, bylined to Arthur Alliss, 'our Middle Eastern correspondent'. The piece concluded that Charlie was in Russia. Troy turned to the inside pages. A leader, the work of his brother-in-law Lawrence Stafford, called upon the Foreign Office to clarify the matter – had Leigh-Hunt defected or not? 'Mr Woodbridge was forthright in his denial of rumours alleging that Charles Leigh-Hunt was a Soviet agent some six years ago. It is not for him to remain silent now. Where is Leigh-Hunt? Who is his paymaster?'

Troy thought 'paymaster' a bit histrionic, but then writing about spookery brought out all the clichés.

Under Home News, eclipsed by the Charlie scandal, was an item on the Labour Party leadership. The chief contenders to replace the late Hugh Gaitskell were Harold Wilson and George Brown – both of them politicians swept into the Commons in the great tide of 1945, just like Rod. But Rod's name was nowhere.

§ 8

He had always known Moscow would be cold. Family history, *War and Peace* and School Certificate geography told him that – but this cold? He could scarcely believe thermometers were made that would record temperatures this low. He was wearing every scrap of clothing he had with him, and dearly wished for his Aran sweater or one of those sheepskin things ex-RAF types wore for tearing round the English countryside in little MGs and boring the arse off village pubgoers with their version of the Battle of Britain. At a pinch he'd settle for an extra pair of socks or reinforced Y-fronts. Or a hat, he thought, God send me a hat.

The Russians had not set up one of those flexible tubes that conveyed passengers from plane to immigration like dust up a hoover without ever touching ground, without the literal sense that 'landing' implies and ought to imply. Troy touched ground, or touched tarmac, as near as he would get to the soil of Mother Russia, feeling little or nothing and wondering what it was he should feel. Perhaps wonderment was all and perhaps wonderment was enough? He was the first Troy to return to Russia in fifty-eight years. His father had never set foot east of Berlin, nor had his Uncle Nikolai and neither had ever expressed any desire to. His brother Rod had tried time and time again to wangle his way onto Labour Party or trade union official visits, and failed time and time again. Troy had never wanted to visit the old country. He much preferred it to exist in the fanciful yarns and fables of his grandfather Rodyon Rodyonovitch – or in the precise, near-scientific accounts of his father Alexei Rodyonovitch, which in the end served to foster the mythical status of Russia as surely as his grandfather's highly unreliable tales had done. All in all, Russia, the Russia of his boyhood, the Russia of the nursery, the Russia imbibed at his mother's knee and his father's dinner table, did not exist except as a country of the mind. As he stood on the windblown tarmacadam, beneath an invisible sky, between the Tupelov jet and the vast blankness of the concrete buildings, blinded by arc lights, frozen to his fingertips, surrounded by the sibilant babble of the language of childhood, his sense of wonder amounted to one simple, inadequate question: 'Is this it?'

Troy followed the snaking Russian susurrus into the blockhouse. A lazy silence overlay an intimidated whisper. No jets roared, no propellers thrashed, and the Soviet apparatchiks yawned their way through the routine like men sleepwalking. It seemed too casual, too informal quite to be the Soviet Union. It was Ruritania – anywhere east of the Danube, anywhere they wore outlandish uniforms and looked like chorus boys from the *Student Prince*. He changed that. As soon as he presented his passport and papers the uniformed officer diverted the half-dozen people behind him to a separate table. Troy looked at the uniform. Blue collar flashes with red piping – KGB. He stood several minutes in silence while the officer in front of him looked at every page of his passport, turning it this way and that to see the blurred stamps of countries he had visited, and read the letter from the Foreign Ministry. When the man had finished a second man appeared and he, too, took several minutes to reach the obvious conclusion.

'It's him,' he said to the first.

It occurred to Troy that Charlie would undoubtedly have omitted to tell his Russian masters that he, Troy, spoke Russian. He would probably have told them just as much of the truth as he needed and no more.

The first man looked at Troy. A handsome face. Mediterranean blue eyes, at least the blue of the Mediterranean in January, beneath the low brim of a fur-lined hat. Troy envied him the fur hat. Troy could kill for the fur hat.

'Baggage,' he said simply, and for a second Troy thought it was an insult rather than an instruction. The man gestured upward with his hand and Troy plonked his suitcase on the counter between them. He flicked the catches and turned the case towards the two immigration officers.

They rummaged through, found only the *Sunday Post*, Troy's last clean shirt and his washbag. They felt the lining of the suitcase, tapped the bottom, took apart his razor, gazed oddly at the black-and-white badger-hair shaving brush, sniffed at the styptic pencil that stemmed the flow of blood every time Troy cut himself shaving, and at the end seemed more than slightly incredulous.

'Is this all you've got?'

'I'm wearing everything else,' said Troy.

All the same, the second man patted him down, arms in the air, took his fountain pen from his jacket pocket, unscrewed the top, put it back, and pronounced him 'clean'.

The first man shrugged, the second man responded like an imitative monkey and they got on with the routine.

'Commander Troy. This permits you entry to the Soviet Union for forty-eight hours. It permits you entry only to the city of Moscow and to the airport. You are forbidden to travel outside the city limits. Do not attempt to travel outside the city limits, and be back here in time for your flight the day after tomorrow. If you're not, we'll come looking for you.'

'Of course,' said Troy. 'Thank you.'

The man held out the passport and papers to Troy, and as Troy took them he turned to the second man and said, 'Tell her he is leaving now. And if she loses him she'll spend the rest of her life directing traffic in Novaya Zemlya.'

No – they definitely didn't know he spoke Russian.

He caught up with the tail end of the crowd. A barn-like lobby, drab and makeshift – two styles, as he would soon learn, that the Soviet Union did rather well – and fifty-odd people milling around under the watchful eye of a dozen uniformed militia and God only knew how many out of uniform. The crowd thinned as people made their way out through a wall of swing doors and into the freezing night, and suddenly one door swung inwards with a mighty push and there was Charlie.

'What would you like first,' he boomed, 'The riddle, the mystery or the enigma?'

This was not the man he had known, not the man with whom he had shared the permanence of boyhood and adolescence. Here was a man bloated by booze, elephantine with indulgence. Allowing for the bulk of his heavy fur coat, he was still fat. The chin had quadrupled and was now better referred to in the plural; his nose was a shining red beacon to any stout-hearted fellow boozer in search of a good, miserable time getting to the bottom of another bottle, and as they peeped out from under his fur hat, it seemed to Troy that even his earlobes were fat. How could anyone have fat earlobes?

Charlie crushed him in a bear hug.

'Bugger the enigma,' Troy said. 'I want a coat like yours and I want it now.'

'Trust me,' said Charlie. 'I've thought of everything.'

He usually did.

He stuck his own fur hat on Troy's head. His blond mop had thinned at the crown, his forehead had creased into a hundred furrows, though the blue eyes twinkled still in the falling ruin of what had been a beautiful, heart-shaped face.

'Back of the car,' he said. 'Keeping warm for you.'

Charlie led Troy to his car. A Soviet-built, Soviet-issue, six-seater Zim saloon − defectors for the use of − looking like a poor man's Studebaker from ten or twelve years ago, with a front end like a set of mocking false teeth. An ugly car conforming precisely to the maxim of the late genius of capitalism, Henry Ford, in being available in 'any colour you want so long as it's black.'

Charlie opened the back door, picked up a coat so dense it looked to Troy like a dead mammoth. He wrapped Troy in it as though he were a helpless child, grinning all the time as if they were sharers of some silent, exclusive joke. The grin became a laugh. Troy felt huge arms embrace him once more, the bear's paws clapping him on the back, then pushing him away to arm's length in a gesture that said 'Let me look at you.' He had not changed, he knew. Hardly a grey hair, not an extra pound of weight nor inch of girth since he was twenty-five. They were the same age. They had matched each other step by step throughout their lives until a few years ago, big man and little man, twins of adversity. At forty-one they had parted, divided lives and ideologies. Not that Troy knew for a moment what his own ideology was. It just wasn't Charlie's.

'Can we go,' he said. 'I'm freezing.'

Charlie put the car into gear and lurched off. He was an even worse driver than Troy.

They tore down a tree-lined road, so thick with trees it struck Troy that they had entered some mythical Russian forest, been sucked effortlessly into the plot of *Peter and the Wolf*, not the outer suburbs of a capital city.

'Y'know,' said Charlie, 'I have one hell of job remembering which side of the road the Russkis drive on.'

Troy had noticed this.

'We're being followed, by the way.'

'I keep forgetting you're a detective. Yes, Freddie, of course we're being followed. Give me half a chance and I'll spot the bugger and we can lose him.'

Charlie peered into the rear-view mirror. Troy felt the car meander across the lanes, heard the honks of protest.

'It's not a him, it's a her.'

'How do you know? You've spotted her already?'

'No, I heard them talking about her. Indiscreet because they don't expect foreigners to speak the language. And I don't think we should lose her. They'll find us petty damn quick anyway. Far better a tail you know about than one you don't. Or am I teaching my spymaster to suck eggs?'

'Touché, old chap, touché.'

§ 9

It was a truly dreadful place. A gin house from a Hogarth plate. A joyless hole in which to drink and smoke and smoke and drink. A place with but one purpose, to quench the committed. A brown study of a brown room, a room of worn and peeling paintwork, of years of encrusted dirt, of woodwork shaped and worn with elbows, of floors patterned in spittle, with but a single piece of decoration, a tiny touch of red and gold among the shades of brown – a cobwebbed, foxed portrait of Vladimir Ilyich Lenin on the wall behind the bar. Heroic of posture, caught in a media moment at the Finland Station, making his first speech in many a year on Russian soil. He had to make a speech – how else would he have passed the time in that sealed train except by writing a speech?

'Don't tell me it's a dive, Freddie,' said Charlie, reading his mind. 'It's this or nothing. Or to be precise, it's some other place exactly like this or one of the hard-currency joints in the hotels which are strictly for the tourists. I can't play the tourist. I'm here for life. Begin as you mean to go on, I say.'

Dark eyes under beetle brows occasionally glanced at them as

Charlie forced a way through to the bar. Miserable men, working men, heavily wrapped up against the winter cold, heavily wrapped up against the working life, their heads in clouds of tobacco fug, their feet in puddles on the floor, streaming from their boots. Two toffs, two foreigners, in good clothes, but scarcely meriting enough attention to detract from the serious business of getting seriously drunk.

Charlie got both elbows on the bar and seized the attention of the barman. He was a dead ringer for the late Maxim Gorki, a face consisting largely of open pores, a nose like a ripe strawberry and a moustache the size of a yard brush.

'Now we get to the heart of the matter. Four fucking days in this utter fucking igloo of a country and I still can't muster enough of the lingo to ask this bugger for a drink. I got you here just to order the booze. Tell him I want a whisky, and make damn sure he pours at least three fingers.'

This struck Troy as innocent, but he asked anyway.

'Where do you think you are?' said the barman. 'What do you think this is? Order vodka or piss off the pair of you.'

Troy translated loosely for Charlie.

'It'll have to be vodka. That's all they serve.'

'If your English pal wants whisky he'll have to use his privileges. In this place there are no privileges. We're the scum of the earth. Vodka or vodka. And none of that fancy shit with bison grass or red peppers in it. Take it or leave it.'

'Fine,' said Troy. 'Two large ones.'

'Not so fast,' said Gorki, and pointed over his shoulder to a small blackboard and the chalked entries under the heading 'menu'.

'First you order a meal.'

The kopeck dropped for Troy. It was not a bar; there was no such place as a bar. In a nation of drunks there were only two places to get drunk outside the privacy – or not – of your own home. In the street or in a café. An approximation of which this place seemed to be.

'Charlie – you have a choice. Sausages, fish dumplings or soup.'

'Sausages,' said Charlie. 'Anything as long as the bugger pours me a drink.

Troy ordered for them.

'Nah,' said Gorki. 'Bangers is off.'

'Dumplings then.'

'Nah, dumplings is off too.'

Troy looked around the room at the pack of miserable boozers. Each one of them had in front of him a bowl of yellowish gruel. Not one of them seemed to have touched it.

Another kopeck dropped.

Nobody ate a damn thing in this satanic hole; the pretence of food, the utterly 'off' menu, was just a front to keep a fraction the right side of the law. If a militiaman – the Soviet version of a copper – walked in, doubtless a few elbows would ply a few spoons, but that was it. A bar by any other name in a country where there were no bars was a caff.

Just for the pleasure of the hunt, he said, 'What's the soup?'

'Yeller soup,' said Gorki.

Troy could see that.

'Yellow what?'

'Yeller taters and yeller cabbage, bit o' this, bit o' that.'

'Sort of like saffron?'

'If you like.'

Then a kopeck dropped for him too.

'Bloody good idea.' He turned to a fat man in a greasy apron lounging behind him. 'Andrei, change the menu. From now on its *soupe au saffron.*' He stuck two bowls in front of them and ladled out the yellow mess.

'Good bloody grief,' said Charlie. '*Crambe repetita.* School dinners.'

'You don't have to eat it,' said Troy. 'No one else is.'

'Water?' Gorki was asking. 'You want water?'

'Water,' said Charlie through Troy's interpretation. 'We don't want fucking water.'

'Yes you do,' Gorki said. And he winked hammily at Troy.

'Yes,' Troy replied. 'Two large waters will be fine. Doubles.'

Gorki set two far from spotless tumblers on the bar, splashed vodka generously, but without any sense of measure, into them and shoved them over. He did not ask for money. It looked to be the kind of place that did most of its business on the slate, and Gorki looked to be the kind of man who would never forget your face or what you owed him down to the last kopeck.

Charlie was staring at the disparity in their glasses. Troy swapped his huge one for Charlie's lesser and they touched glass together.

'About bloody time,' said Charlie. 'Cheers.'

He knocked back half the glass in a single swallow. Troy sipped at his.

'Jesus, that's strong. Bloody hell, they certainly mean you to get pissed, don't they?'

'Sole purpose of visit,' said Troy. 'It's probably about 120 degrees proof. You could run a car on the stuff.'

'Good,' said Charlie. 'I can die happy.'

Troy doubted this very much. All the same, he wondered at the shred of truth buried in the statement. That death was the only thing left to look forward to. It did not need to be said that Charlie had no idea what he was getting into, little idea of what kind of a country he had come to. But he felt sure it would be said, and equally sure of its finality. Charlie might live ten or twenty or thirty years, but Russia, the Union of Soviet Socialist Republics, would be home for the rest of his days. And die happy he would not.

Charlie dragged him to a newly vacated table by the window. They sat with two bowls of gruel and two large 'waters' between them. Condensation ran down the glass and the walls to mingle with the sawdust on the floor. He could see nothing out, only the muddied reflection of the room within. As they crossed the room he picked up snatches of the dozen or more conversations taking place within the hubbub.

'So I says to him, I says, you want it doing you can bloody well do it . . .'

'Meat and potater pie? Meat and potater fuckin' pie? I said to 'er. Where's the fuckin' meat? I spend all day in a fuckin' foundry and you serve me meat an' potater fuckin' pie with no fuckin' meat? I clouted the silly mare, didn't I?'

'. . . Commissar or no bloody commissar. If he comes that one with me again I'll do the sod. I don't care if I spend the rest of me life in a fuckin' gulag. It'd be worth it.'

'. . . Women? Women? They're just cunts, aren't they? I never met a one that was anything more than a cunt and that includes the bitch I married.'

A place to drink and a place to curse. It struck Troy that there was not a woman in the room, and that there could not be a conversation taking place – 'the fuckin' wife, the fuckin' boss' – that, with slight variation, could not be heard in the pubs of Liverpool or Newcastle or Glasgow. He hoped Charlie did not mean to stay long, but knew that if he once got a taste for vodka he might stay for ever.

'Where have they put you?' he asked.

'In the Moskva Hotel. The same one Burgess was in. Poor bugger. Nothing permanent. They're being completely coy about that. Not even guaranteeing that I get to serve out my days in Moscow. Bastards. They've had me in a couple of times for debriefing. I think they're as surprised by the speed of all this as I am.'

'Not as surprised as I was.'

'Yes, I'm sorry about that. You slogged it all the way to Beirut for nothing. When I wired you I knew things were getting pretty final. Mr Smith did not usually turn up in January. He came for a summer outing. The linen suit, the panama hat and the chance of getting his knees brown. I sort of had the feeling they were going to pull something out of the hat. When I saw who Mr Smith was, I knew they were going to pull everything.'

'Who?' said Troy. 'Who did they send?'

'As a rule it would be some anonymous bugger from the Secret Service. I think they got to think of it as an office freebie – "Who'll be lucky this year and get a long weekend in sunny Beirut giving old Charlie the once over?" Just reviewing my case, they'd call it. Making me sweat a bit, letting me know I wasn't off the hook yet. Different bloke every time. For all I knew they really could have been called Smith. They were none of them very important, because they were none of them very good at it. I think the point should have been to screw more out of me, at which, to a man, they were useless. This time. This time, they rolled out the big gun. Tim Woodbridge MP, Minister of State. Number two at the Foreign Office. As soon as I saw him I knew I was a busted flush. Good old Tim. Lied through his teeth for me and the honour of the Service in '57. Cleared me in the House when everybody knew I was guilty as sin. Made the *London Globe* print an apology. God, it was rich. I was grinning from ear to ear even as they booted me out. Lies, lies and more lies. But here's the rub – prove it or not, old Timbo knew everything. For them to send him instead of one of the spooks meant trouble. I thought he was going to sit me down and tell me they'd finally got all the evidence they needed. I thought I'd find my life and treasonable times laid out neatly in one of those colour-coded foolscap folders they have depending on the nature and degree of one's treachery – yours was buff as I recall, which means they're pissing in the wind. I should think mine was dick-end purple by now. Not so, not so. Tim and I have a fairly decent lunch for two laid out on one of the upper floors of the embassy, away from prying eyes. No folder, just a fairly simple statement. "Something new has come to light," he says. "What?" I say, and I'd genuinely no idea what he'd come up with. "A body," he says, "we have found a body." At first he was tacking so slowly I thought he was using a metaphor – you know, along the lines of "know where the body's hidden". That sort of thing. But he wasn't. "Whose body?" I said. And then you could have knocked me over with a fan dancer's fanny feather. "Norman Cobb," he says. "We have found the body of Inspector Cobb. We know you killed him."

Troy looked at the two inches of vodka in the bottom of his glass, and took a sip. Bought himself a quick moment of silence and then looked at Charlie.

'Where did you dump the body?'

'Thames marshes, way out somewhere in the middle of nowhere. Out past Purfleet. God knows, I couldn't find the place again if they gave me a map. Jacob's Reach, Esau's Point. Something biblical. I weighted the bugger and watched him sink. And if it took seven years for the fat fool to surface, then I can't have done too bad a job of it. I admired the bluff. They have nothing but circumstantial evidence to show I killed Cobb. Of course, I denied it. And Tim duly called me a liar, and said they knew I'd killed him, and it was the last straw. Something had to be done. I did see that, didn't I? I had to see how far beyond the pale this was. "You can't blow away coppers on the streets of London and expect to get way with it." Then I laughed till I damn near bust. He took hump at that. Well, he would, wouldn't he?'

Troy did not find it funny, but he could see the irony. The last straw. Something must be done. Of all the sins of Charles Leigh-Hunt, and they were many, this was the worst. But he was innocent; he had not killed Norman Cobb. Troy had killed Norman Cobb. Of course, Cobb had been trying to kill him at the time. And had Troy been a slower or a poorer shot, Cobb most certainly would have killed him, and it would now be Troy's bones, picked clean by lugworm, rising up in the Thames marshes. He had not reported the incident. He had given Charlie his chance and with that chance the corpse of Norman Cobb. He had never asked what he had done with the body. He had never even thought about it until now.

'"It's time," said Woodbridge. "You should go now. There are people back in England who would like to see you charged with Cobb's murder." Then he paused, and I think he smiled, and he said, "We can't have that." And then he set out the deal. I was to clear off. He didn't use the word "defect" at any point – odd that, I thought. I'd be exposed back home, spy, traitor, another Cambridge Commie, but the Cobb thing would be kept quiet. In return I was not to give any of those Burgess and Maclean-style press conferences. Once in Russia I was to shut up, be a good boy and keep my nose clean. If I didn't, there'd be recriminations. I could not believe it, Freddie, I tell you, I was gobsmacked.'

Charlie seemed to have reached a natural lull. He shook his head from side to side, looked into his empty glass and seemed to be giggling to himself. Troy pushed his almost untouched vodka across the table to him, and fought his way back to the bar.

'Same again,' he said.

Gorki rubbed finger and thumb together.

'Twenty-five kopecks for the *soupe au saffron*, two roubles fifty for the water.'

It dawned on Troy that he had no Russian currency. He dug into his coat pocket and came up with a one pound note.

'Wossat?' Gorki asked.

'A British pound,' said Troy. 'Sterling.'

Gorki trousered it. Troy had no idea of the rate of exchange but knew from the rate of trousering and way he filled the glasses to the brim that he had just made his day.

'You're English?' Gorki asked with a hint of astonishment.

'Yes.'

'How come you speak Russian with a poncey accent? That's how the last of the toffs spoke when I was a boy. Just before we put 'em up against a wall and shot 'em.'

'Perhaps I come from a long line of ponces,' said Troy.

Gorki roared with laughter and Troy gently wove through the crowd, clutching virtual quarter-pints of vodka.

Charlie sucked down a huge gulp and relished the rush. They stared a while at the soup congealing in the cold. It was, as Charlie had observed, remarkably reminiscent of school dinners, in which a multitude of sins could be disguised with custard – custard from a packet. Perhaps this was were all the British Army Surplus Custard Powder went. Dumped cheap on the Russian market.

Troy wiped a clear circle in the wet glass of the window with his fingertips and looked out. A woman stepped quickly back from the arc of light thrown by a streetlamp. It was the first and far from clear sighting he had had of her, but this must be the unfortunate woman who would be bound for Novaya Zemlya if she lost them. Troy would try to do the decent thing and ensure she kept up with them. The poor woman must be frozen stiff out there.

Charlie set down his glass and picked up his tale.

' "How long have I got?" I asked him. "A day? Two?." "Terribly sorry, Charlie," he says, "it's less than that. They want you gone now." We said goodbye. The bugger even shook my hand. I left the embassy. Slipped old Abu Wagih a fiver to keep an eye out for you, bought a toothbrush at a corner pharmacy and went straight to the docks. You can always count on there being at least one Russian ship in port. I found the captain. Recited him a little speech I'd learnt phonetically for just such an occasion years ago. He calls a Party apparatchik – you can always count on there being one of them too – they get on the shortwave to Moscow. Some poor bugger's turfed out of his berth to make way for me. Three days later I'm met at Piraeus by the spooks and formally put in the diplomatic bag. *Cetera quis nescit?*'

The vodka showed in his face and in his eyes. A slack-jawed, hang-dog, rheum-eyed, tear-brimmed, bloodshot misery. He gazed into Troy's – clear, fleckless black mirrors gazing back at him. It seemed he could not hold his gaze, his eyes flicked around the room and his hand took refuge around the glass once more.

'You know I never noticed before – never could I suppose – they all look like you, Freddie. Little buggers. Shortarses with ebony eyes. About as warm as the outside bog in February. I feel like Gulliver, washed up in Lilliput, out of size and out of place, in a country I'd only dreamt about.'

Troy ignored the dig. If Charlie was this drunk there were more important things to be said before he vanished into incoherence.

'Charlie, if all the British wanted was the guarantee of your silence, why didn't they just have you bumped off?'

Charlie took another huge, corrosive gulp of vodka and thought about it.

'Y'know,' he said at last, 'that's just what I've been asking myself for the past week. It would be so easy, wouldn't it? I could vanish without trace. No body, no culprit. Blame the bloody Arabs if they wanted. Blame who the hell they like. Why didn't they just get it over with? Why didn't the bastards just get it over with? Out to the swamp like Big Lennie. And wham! But – they didn't . . . and here I am looking at the prospect of life in Mtensk . . . or Magneto-Gorsk . . . or Upyer-Bumsk.'

Troy watched Charlie's head begin to loll at the end of his neck like a slackening string puppet. The jowls beneath his jawline, swelling and shrinking, bellows on a concertina, as his head rolled around in a lazy arc, and the palpebral flutter as his eyes fought to keep their focus. It was, he thought, all so implausible. He could understand that the British might not want another trial of a traitor quite so soon after George Blake and John Vassall. Indeed it could be argued, were there a sober opponent to argue with, that a trial would do more damage than a defection any day, particularly to relation-ships with the Americans, who might well be thinking by now that we were a deeply unreliable nation. A trial was dirty linen washed in public. A defection half tucked it away in someone else's laundry basket, concealed as much as it revealed. But a hit? A discreet, untraceable murder? Really, there was no reason at all why Charlie should not have joined Norman Cobb belly-up, face-down, picked white, in the remote marshes at some biblical turning of the Thames.

§ 10

Charlie lay sprawled on his back across the bed, arms and legs spread wide, still in his shirt, socks and underpants, his mouth open, snoring. Troy shook him gently. He did not stir. He shook him harder. His gut wobbled between the gaping shirt buttons and the elastic of his Y-fronts, but he did not wake. It seemed to Troy that he might well sleep off a bellyful of cheap vodka until lunchtime.

He went through Charlie's pockets, pinched a few roubles to get him through the morning, put on the winter wardrobe – the sable hat, the fur coat – and stepped into the Moscow streets. The first time. The first breath of Russian air, the first sight. Last night did not count. Charlie got between him and Moscow. Vodka got between him and Moscow. Again the same question in his mind: 'Is this it?' Whatever he saw – splendour or squalor – 'Is this it?' was the only form response could take in his mind. After so long, after a generation and more: 'Is this really it?'

He found a bookshop on a street corner less than quarter of a mile away and bought a map of the city. The address was imprinted in his memory. Dolgo-Khamovnichesky Street, where Tolstoy used to live, out in the Khamovniki, the old industrial quarter. He could find no such street on the map. Then the obvious dawned on him and he quickly found Lyev Tolstoy Street. For all he knew it had been renamed some forty years or more. All the same, he'd know the house as soon as he saw it. Of that he was certain. The Moscow home of the Troitskys, abandoned by his father in 1905, passed to an uncle in the interim and confiscated by the state in 1922.

He knew as soon as he left the bookshop that she was following him. It confirmed what he had first thought, that he, not Charlie, was the object of suspicion. He would have liked a clear look at her, but the streets offered too few plate-glass windows in which to catch her reflection. He decided it did not matter. She was unlikely to lose him, and sooner or later, he'd have a chance to turn without simply stopping her on the street. He caught a tram out to the southwest. The spook ran and leapt onto the platform at the last minute. If she broke a leg doing it, this woman would not dare lose him.

§ I I

Even the paint was the same colour his father had described to him – a middling, dull shade of green. The house rose straight up from the pavement on Lyev Tolstoy Street, the ground-floor windows too high to see into, the outer doors closed tight against the season. A narrow, gabled house, climbing to five storeys in off-off-white, almost pale brown brick, with copper pipes and gutters dulled by a century and a half of air and rain to a verdigris green brighter than the paintwork. The bars of the gates were folded back, a pattern of blooming lilies, venuses rising from conch-like shells, woven into the ironwork. A splash of yellowy-white amid the greens.

A polished brass plate was fixed to the wall underneath the house number. 'Ministry of Agriculture, Subdivision of Planning & Production, Wheat & Barley'. The house had once belonged to the owner of the perfume distillery next door. His father had told him of the wafting scents that had curled up to his open window all summer long. The ministry had taken both buildings. Not a wisp of summer's scent remained.

There seemed no point in ringing. The doors looked to him as though they opened for no one. Besides, what reason, what excuse could he give for wanting to see inside? The Ministry of Agriculture, Subdivision of Planning & Production, Wheat & Barley could scarcely be accustomed to the sons of the disinherited asking for a quick look round. He crossed the street to look up at the top floors, where the rooms disappeared into the pitch of the roof and reappeared as dormer windows, copper topped and adorned with ironwork so distant they could be fleur-de-lis or budding roses. He could not tell and he could not recall that the old man had ever mentioned them to him. His father's memory was for incident much more than static detail. He described the rooms – the dining room in green, again green, as though it were the colour motif of the building; the main bedroom with its faded wallpaper of vast Monetesque flowers in paintbox colours; the library in red maroon – simply because the boy Troy had nagged him for such detail. Of his own choosing he had told of his own boyhood in the next to attic room that was his nursery, where a German governess had taught him to read and her French successor had let him watch her strip and bathe.

Troy looked slowly down the height of the building, each floor's windows closed and shuttered as though the Ministry of Agriculture, Subdivision of Planning & Production, Wheat & Barley had no need of natural light, and it struck him that the house was blind, that the ministry had put out its eyes, that the house was great and grey and grief-stricken, blind as blind Gloucester. It saddened him. He could recall every room, though he had seen none. The governess's bedroom; beneath that his aunt's; beneath that his grandparents'; beneath that the dining room; next to that the library; beneath that the drawing room; beneath that the scullery. He could have no feeling one way or the other about the use to which the Soviet government put the building. No feeling even about the simple fact of possession. They were welcome to it. But the blindness of the house seemed simple and sad. They should not put out its eyes.

The spook stood at the corner. Awkward and idle. Her back to him as though waiting for anyone but him. She was small, even in the bulk of furs; he thought she could not be much more than five foot four and eight stone.

Troy turned on his heel and set off across the street to the house on the other side, to No. 21, a clay-coloured house with green shutters, looming lime trees beyond a garden fence, and a bigger brass plate reading 'Tolstoy House Museum. Home of Lyev Nikolayevich Tolstoy 1828–1910. Writer.' It could not have been more different as a house. A glorified wooden cottage on a grand scale, grander than the Troitskys' brick house, and found for Count Tolstoy by Troy's grandfather some time in the 1880s.

It reminded him of similar houses he had visited in London. The Soane House in Lincoln's Inn. A house more interesting for itself than any of the junk of antiquity Old Soane had collected and stuffed into it from floor to ceiling. A house that seemed designed for living, inviting one always to sit down. The last thing one was expected to do. So it was here. He felt he wanted to sit in the chair where Tolstoy sat, to have the same view across the desk, to doodle on the same blotter, to look out of the same window as Tolstoy himself, to see a lamp lit in the windows of the Troitsky house. It was all wired off against the invasive backside, just like Sir John Soane's sitting room.

Tolstoy's study was a small, pale green room on the mezzanine. His bicycle was propped outside the door, as though he'd parked it there only yesterday and nipped in for a quick scribble. The pervasive illusion of the preserved home – the big bug-in-amber – that the occupant was merely out for an hour, not long dead. His writing desk was a plain deal table, covered in green baize, at which the old man had worked by the light of a single candle. Just to the left of the desk was a group of framed photographs. Tolstoy in many of the poses made famous in the countless biographies. Young Count Tolstoy in his artillery uniform during the Crimean War. Old Count Tolstoy in peasant garb, the demonically forked beard, the great dome of his forehead. The reluctant husband standing with his dumpy, grumpy wife. The assembled sons of Lyev and Sonya Tolstoy – Sergéi, Ilyá, Lyev Jr, Andréi, Mikháil – sat on a park bench sporting an array of moustaches and beards and winged collars, looking less like the sons of a writer, more like the board of a continental bank posing for the photographer. And shots of the great man and his disciples.

One was a pale print of four people, a little girl, two men – and a boy, stuck between the men, receiving the avuncular touch of Tolstoy's hand upon his shoulder, and looking at the camera over the little girl's head. It was dated 1877 and captioned 'Yasnaya Polyana. Tolstoy with his daughter Marya, Rodyon Rodyonovitch Troitsky and unknown youth.'

Troy stared. His grandfather was just recognisable. A younger version of a man he had known only in extreme old age, a man who must have been over eighty when Troy was born. A tall man, seen here in his late forties, sporting a full, greying beard and looking much like his mentor Tolstoy. The unknown youth standing between the two men he knew at once. He looked to Troy to be no more than fifteen or sixteen, but the look in his eyes was far from young, the eyes of a man already more worldly, more calculating than the two old men he stood between, with their air of Christian innocence, their peasant clothing and their *faux-paysan* surrender to nature. It was his father Alexei Rodyonovitch.

He had never known Alex Troy surrender a damn thing. Never gave up his grip on the solid world and its reality. Left it to his father to idle away time in philosophy and pamphleteering. He had grown up to take responsibility for a family which seemed beyond the practicalities of the Tolstoyan ethic; he had grown up to bale his father out time after time. His perception of a world turning itself inside out, and his ability to keep one twist, one turn ahead of it, had saved the old man, indeed the entire family from a chaos that passed comprehension, the turmoil that was the twentieth century.

The spook had lost her touch. She was standing far too close. She should not have followed him in if she meant to stay hidden. With fewer than a dozen people in the room he was bound to see her. He looked. There were three people between them. A couple so alike they had to be married thirty years – Nikita and Mrs Khrushchev, Charlie and Mrs Chaplin – and a tall, thin man. The man moved quickly away. She seemed not to notice. The couple fell to bickering and drifted off. She should have moved before they did. She had taken off her hat and was pretending to be interested in the photograph of Tolstoy in uniform. Troy could see her in profile. The face of a Russian Jew. Slightly hawkish, a neat curved nose, a mop of thick, shining black curls, bobbing springily on her fur collar. An imp with violet eyes.

''Tis women's hair makes Moscow fair,' Troy said softly.

She did not pretend she had not heard. She looked straight at him startled. Her violet eyes wide.

'They told me you were English,' she said, scarcely louder than a whisper.

'I am.'

'No Englishman would know such a phrase.'

True, it was a dreadful phrase, a corny old Moscow aphorism he had dredged up from a childhood memory, a phrase of his grandfather's, for just this effect.

'What else did they tell you?'

'Not here.'

Her eyes darted from side to side. A passable impression of a scared rabbit.

'Better here than in the street. Who else will be listening? I'm the one being followed, not you. And even if you were, they'd have enough sense to stay outside.'

'Are you going to tell?'

Troy walked on and left her to stew.

§ 12

He did not care to be a tourist in a mythical town. It was the wrong way to see Moscow. The right way – the only right way – was in the stories and dreams of the old generation. The glinting, golden splendour of St Basil's added nothing to his mother's infrequently aired memories of a girlhood in the city; the monumental blocks of Lenin's tomb, its strutting, green-clad, goose-stepping guards, added nothing to the endless, convoluted narrative of his father's youth. You could, he thought, take a copy of *Ulysses*, a street map of Dublin and have a good, if long, if pissed, day out in Dublin. You could take the Russia of family legend, any map of Moscow, and never find it in the stone and mortar of the Soviet Union. He should not have come.

All in all he was searching for a metaphor. If Beirut was what? What had he called it? The Britain of the black market? Then Moscow, Moscow . . . was Britain in the drab age, Britain in the late 1940s, when rationing had gone on far too long, when the nation was heartily sick of it, when the humour, and the glamour if ever there had been any, had gone out of spivvery, and the country was locked into its first, its only five-year plan. Moscow, Moscow was the result of endless, serial five-year plans, of well-intentioned drabness piled upon orderly, dreary, gut-shrinking austerity; the heartless devotion of serial monogamy. It was a monumental city of vast spaces, of stone plains and cobbled prairie, of width and breadth and vista, shaped to the division and the column and the battalion. And its people skulked at the edges, refusing the open space, huddled in the shadows, buried in the bottle, born to narrow lanes and dark alleys, born not to Red Square or any square, born to Lyápin House and Protótchny Lane, born to life within the iron hand. No line of Kipling or Masefield, no skylining metaphor of light or air, would ever so transpose, would ever touch these depths. It was Blok, Aleksandr Blok, who had it right: 'Russia . . . her strength compressed and useless in an iron fist.'

§ 13

It was dark when he got back to the Moskva. It had been dark since three thirty in the afternoon. Somewhere in the darkness, the violet-eyed imp traipsed after him.

Charlie was up. Up, in the bathroom, naked to the waist, braces dangling around his knees, chest hair grey bleaching out to white, pectorals as big as breasts, the sad, defeated slant of his nipples, spreading out like frying eggs. Up, and shaving, and singing to himself. Badly.

'I got plenty o' nuttin' and worraworraglub plenty for me . . . got no slooshwhooshworra château-bottled claret, down to me last Savile Row trousers worraglubsloosh an' bugger all's plenty fo' me.'

He glanced over his shoulder. Grinned at Troy through the mask of shaving foam and went scat.

'Zabdabzabaddyboopshoop, boopshoop plenty fo' me.'

The hot water suddenly ran cold. A pipe in the system heaved and groaned. Large beast in pain. Charlie stared at the ceiling as though asking heaven for an explanation. All Troy could see was the fresh plasterwork where microphones had been set to record their every syllable. He wished the spooks well with Charlie's scat singing, and hoped they were familiar with the work of Ella Fitzgerald. Plenty of nothing could scarcely be more appropriate.

'Do you think all of Russia is going to turn out to be like a seaside boarding-house?' Charlie asked.

'Don't ask me. I've never been here before.'

'Skegness . . . Llandudno . . .'

'You chose it. I didn't.'

'No hot water, baths by prior appointment, no spitting, no loose women in your room . . .'

They seemed to Troy to be having two conversations where there should have been one.

'Should I be grateful for small mercies? The crap hotel has got to be marginally better than the state apartment. You know Guy's in a crummy two-room flat in the suburbs with one of his boyfriends?'

'You've heard from Burgess?'

'Phoned me up two days ago. Pissed out of his brain. Rambling on about how much he missed England . . . . You know what I'll miss about England?'

All of it, thought Troy. 'No,' he said.

'Marmite sandwiches. Who wouldn't? But after Marmite butties I'll miss the women – or rather the lovers – men and women. From the first to the last. Do you know who my first was?'

Of course Troy knew. They'd told each other everything.

'Neville Pym. Blew me when I was twelve. In his study, when I should have been in the nets hitting sixes. The first time I came inside another human being and it was Neville Pym's mouth. I can still remember how his teeth nipped. I thought I'd come for ever.'

On cue, the hot tap added a short spurt of water to the greying scum in the basin. Charlie scraped away at his stubble, the rolls of fat around his midriff quivering at every movement of his arm.

'And then that wet summer of '29, when your sisters had me in the summerhouse, down by the river, in the middle of a downpour.'

As a teenager Charlie had boasted of this to Troy. Ever since, he'd mostly managed enough tact not to allude to it. Troy's sisters never mentioned it. He knew why they'd done it. At fourteen going on fifteen, Charlie had looked divine. At nineteen, Sasha and Masha had been amoral vixens delighting in the seduction of a willing boy.

'Sasha was bloody marvellous.'

And now, thought Troy, she was probably mad. Strung out just shy of alcoholism. Grim, bitter, miserable or ironically, insanely funny. Troy had had little time for an elder sister in his youth. At best Sasha had been a beautiful, inane nuisance. Now she turned up on him uninvited and propped up bars with him rather like a man, wanting for the first time to be a friend rather than a sister. Her husband had hanged himself two years ago and let her out of a loveless marriage. But she could no more play the widow than the wife.

'And the last?' Troy asked to steer the topic to its end.

Charlie pulled the plug.

'Whore in Soho,' he said sadly. 'Knew I was home for the last time. Never done it. Odd that. All the times I could have had a Soho tart and I never had. So I did. Must have looked like classic punter, one of 'em leant out of a window and pinged me with a peashooter.

There I was, wondering, "How do you approach a whore? Do you haggle over the price?" Needn't have worried. Like falling off a log.'

'And?'

'Awful,' Charlie said. 'Absolutely fucking awful. Imagine. I paid to be despised. I should be able to get that for free almost anywhere from now on, I should think. And you're wrong, by the way.'

'About what?'

'I didn't choose Russia. All my life I've heard people saying things like, "If you don't like it here go and live in Russia." Fatuous remark. It was England I was trying to change. Russia was doing very nicely without me. I was committed to an idea – a way of thinking, doing and being – not a country. What's a country? A few arbitrary lines on a map.'

There was nothing, Troy thought, quite like a few days in Beirut – a long weekend with Mr Sykes and Monsieur Picot – to teach one the arbitrariness of lines on a map.

Charlie pulled his shirt on. From beneath its folds Troy heard, 'What d'ye reckon to Russian women? Most of 'em look like Widow Twanky to me.'

'Dunno,' said Troy. 'The one following us is a looker.'

'Is she still following us? Close enough to see her face? Good bloody grief. I must be losing my touch.'

Wrong tense, Charlie.

§ 14

They stepped off the street and into the moist heat of another caff.

'Oh shit,' said Charlie. 'Here we go again. Pure hell with lino.'

'No,' said Troy. 'Look. Listen. It's not the same sort of place at all.'

There was a large party seated at a refectory-length table. Half of them were women. They'd dressed up. There were candles and laughter and the smell of halfway decent cooking. Good God, there were tablecloths.

'I think we might just have stumbled on a real restaurant.'

'But they will serve booze, won't they?'

Enough people were drinking it. One or two of the women even appeared to be drinking wine.

Troy half expected the waiter to tell him one needed to book six months in advance and show the Party card – but he didn't. He showed them to a table by the window, plonked down a menu in front of them and left them to read it.

Troy peered out through the glass. The spook was there again, on the opposite side of the street.

'Do you think it's going to be edible?' Charlie asked.

'It may well be good. If you ask me the other lot at the long table are a birthday or engagement party or something very like.'

Charlie stared at them. 'D'ye know, I think this is the first time I've heard Russians laugh.'

Troy knew this was not true. Gorki had laughed at the pair of them last night. But he knew what Charlie meant. This was fun, not scorn.

Troy ordered for both of them. Beef stew. It would probably be stewed shin, but what the hell. He ordered vodka for Charlie, and Moldavian red, 'claret style', wine for himself.

Faced with his first glass of the day, Charlie was suddenly wistful. Troy had expected him to knock back the first in a single gulp. For a moment he just stared into it.

'The Russkis have given me a shortwave tranny,' he said. 'Want me to keep in touch with the goings-on back in Blighty. I turned on the BBC World Service while you were out. It's official – I'm a defector. It was on the news. Woodbridge made another statement to the Commons. Woodbridge Statement Mark II.'

'With much regret . . . sorely deceived . . . Her Majesty's Government was no more aware of this than Mrs Buggins' cat . . . ?'

'Something like that. Fuck 'im, say I. Cheers.'

He picked up his vodka and belted it back in one.

Troy could guess how Charlie felt. Damned.

He looked out at the spook again. She was stamping her feet like a London cabbie. He got up, opened the door and went across the street to her. She had her hands deep in her pockets, her face all but buried in her hat. She stared at him, motionless, her expression saying, 'This isn't happening – he isn't doing this to me.'

'You must be freezing,' he said.

The spook looked to either side and told him to go away. Troy took her by the arm, so sharply she was almost knocked off her feet, and led her back to the restaurant. She pulled and struggled, but he won.

He asked the waiter to bring food for a third and sat her down at the spare chair between Charlie and himself.

'Didn't realise we had guests,' said Charlie through his third vodka.

'I don't think she speaks English.'

'I don't care if she does. Doesn't matter a damn. But you're right. She's a looker.'

The spook tried to rise from the chair. Troy pressed her back down, spoke quietly to her, persuaded her take off her hat and coat.

'The harm's done. If they've seen us, they've seen us,' he said. 'You might at least get a hot meal before you go back to the street.'

She said nothing. Troy poured Moldavian claret for the two of them. Against all expectation, it was first rate.

Confronted with the meal, Charlie said, 'What's the brown porridge?'

'Buckwheat kasha. Try before you moan.'

Charlie smiled after his first mouthful. 'I suppose I could get used to it.'

The spook had an appetite. She ate in silence. Looking all the time from Troy to Charlie and back again, as Troy recounted for Charlie what Said Hussein had told him – how last autumn 'something snapped in Mr Charlie'.

'Good old Said. Sharp as a bloody razor. Of course, he's right. It was a bad time. But it was *the* time, if you see what I mean. I'd far rather have seen it for myself than read about it in papers two days old.'

'I don't get it,' said Troy. 'Seen what?'

'Oh God, did it really make so little impact on you Freddie? Could you not see the seams coming unstuck last autumn? I could. Poor bloody Vassall. Stupid, vain, greedy, innocent little prick. Set up, picked up and strung out to dry.'

Troy could not agree with this. Vassall, like Charlie, was a paid Soviet agent. As Assistant Private Secretary to the Civil Lord of the Admiralty, he had passed on documents to the Russians for several years. He had been arrested and tried last autumn. He was now serving eighteen years in prison.

'He was guilty of treason, Charlie.'

'He was set up. Trapped into it. Blackmailed because he was queer!'

'Quite, said Troy. 'By your side. Not the British.'

'You still don't get it, do you, Freddie? He was a nobody. Putting the poor little bugger on trial was . . . was . . . like tearing the wings off a butterfly. If who was rogering who wasn't of such godalmighty concern to the English, the Russians would never have been able to blackmail him in the first—'

'It's illegal here, too, Charlie.'

'I know!' he said in a breathy tone of utter exasperation, head shaking from side to side, looking at the floor – and Troy knew damn well that he didn't. 'But . . . but that's not the point is it?'

Troy did not know what the point was. Charlie did not seem to be getting any closer to it.

'Oh fuck it, Freddie. What the British did to him was awful. He had access to nothing that mattered a damn – and they came down on him like a ton of bricks and then . . . and then . . . we went mad. We had a national fit. I can't think of any better way to put it.'

Nor could Troy. At last they agreed on something. It had indeed been a national fit. The papers had had a field day of unsupportable allegation and innuendo. To take them seriously would have been to believe that the Civil and Secret Services were riddled with queers, every one of whom was being blackmailed or readily open to blackmail.

'It shocked me. I am accustomed to thinking I cannot be shocked. First we crucify a man of no importance and then we cry wolf louder than ever. We explode in a fury of national breast-beating. And when the press, and I think I have to say "we", I've been a hack these six years now, are called to account, it happens all over again. They won't name their sources, so two poor sods go to jail for the freedom of the press. What freedom? The freedom to make it up as you go along? It pinpointed a moment for me. It pinpointed something about the country and about myself. Don't expect me to say it shattered my belief. It didn't. But it showed it up in all its ambiguities. We break Vassall, a butterfly upon a wheel. Meanwhile the big fish, people like me, are untouchable. I'm not the stuff of jailbirds; I'm the subject of an annual negotiation, the Beirut Tea Party. On the social calendar somewhere between Ascot and the Henley Regatta. The press went barmy. I'll swear they made up half the stuff they printed about Vassall. And as a hack I'm disgusted with my profession. Then the government wreaks unholy vengeance on the press, and then my sympathies are back the other way. It was madness, Freddie. National madness. All I did was sit in my mother's living room and read the papers, listen to it unravel on the Home Service and earwig a few tap-room conversations in the West End pubs, but it seemed to me that I was at the heart of it. Of course something snapped in Mr Charlie. Weird, isn't it?'

Troy had no idea where this was leading. It seemed almost unbelievable that it was simply the spy's sentimentality over the lost certainties of his uncertain trade. It was, he too thought, a strange moment in the nation's history. A battle over truth and freedom, when there was nothing but lies, but the personal way Charlie seemed to take this he could not grasp.

Charlie rubbed his cheeks and eyes vigorously with both hands as though trying to jerk himself into a finer stage of wakeful coherence. 'Tell me,' he said. 'What is the glue that holds a generation together?'

'Dunno,' said Troy.

'Shared values?' said Charlie.

'Partly. Though I think you'll find they cross generations, or a nation would constantly be at war with itself.'

Charlie blinked at this as though Troy had just given him enough ammo for another day's debate, then he waved it aside with his hand and picked up the thread.

'One generation, then, just one.'

'The shared experiences, the common experiences of any stretch of shared time.'

'Good. For a moment there you sounded just like your father. Now, narrow it down to our generation. What binds us together? What's the glue?'

This required no thought.

'The war.'

'The war,' Charlie echoed.

'Yes,' said Troy. 'The war.'

'Boom,' said Charlie, so softly Troy could scarce make out the word. 'Boom. Boom. Boom!'

Charlie stretched out a hand across the table. His fingertips just touching Troy's. His head on one side, resting on the table in a pool of spilt booze. The voice hoarse and low, croaking and slobbering out of him.

'England will go boom. England is going to go boom. And when it does it will be unrecognisable. The England you and I knew will dissolve into dust. And when it does that's what will go, the common values wrought out of shared experience. The war was the glue, and the glue no longer holds. We're going to come unstuck. Boom!'

Troy had to think about this. He knew exactly what Charlie meant, and whatever his motives, whatever his deceptions, Charlie, like brother Rod and countless hundreds of thousands others, had done his bit in the Second World War. Troy had not. He had spent it entirely as a copper. He had not fought, he had not volunteered, he had readily accepted being in a reserved occupation. Nonetheless, he understood Charlie's point. It was the glue that bound them together. That was undeniable, and its effect was also undeniable. The war, as a phenomenon of memory and culture, persisted long beyond its historical end. The British still lived the war; in their hearts and minds they still fought it. It should not be odd that in the body of a traitor there still beat the heart of an old soldier, and Troy strived laterally to see it as Charlie saw it, to see what snapped, to see what boomed.

'And you think this is tragic, do you? Like Lawrence said after the first war, ours is a tragic age, we just refuse to take it tragically?'

Charlie reared up off the table, vodka dripping from his hair and cheek, a look of pure astonishment in the bloodshot eyes.

'Tragic? Tragic? Bollocks! I'm mad as hell I won't be there to see it! It's everything I've worked for all my life. It's the end of everything I've ever hated about the bloody place. What was it Winston said? It is not the end, arf warf grumff, it is not even the beginning of the end, or some rubbish like that . . . but it is perhaps the end of the beginning. That's it, that's what I saw last autumn, the end of the beginning! Boom, Freddie, boom! England will go boom, the end of the beginning. It'll burst at the seams; they'll be kicking the stuffing out of the old girl; there'll be horsehair and calico all over the shop and where will I be? Where the fucking hell will I be? Freezing me bloody balls off in bloody Moscow, that's where! I'd give anything to be in England. Anything. After all I've done to bring it about, don't you think I'd kill to be in England when the lid finally comes off? London is the place to be right now. London, Freddie, London. Not Omsk not Tomsk not Tosspot-on-Don!'

He swept the bottle and the glasses to the floor with a mighty blow from his outstretched arm, then he followed them down and lay sprawled, motionless, on the cracked linoleum among the broken glass and vodka. The room gave them the full five seconds of attention they thought worthy of a good drunk and went back to having a good time, or as near to a good a time as the Soviet Union permitted.

Troy turned. The spook was looking at the two of them, wide eyed and worried.

'Don't just sit there,' said Troy. 'Give me a hand with him.'

§ 15

They laid him out on the bed, a dead weight, too heavy by far even for the two of them. Troy managed to get his shoes and trousers off, but they could not turn him, so he lay snoring and twitching, tangled up in his fur coat, with a grubby pair of worn underpants gaping at his loins. Troy pulled an eiderdown over him and left him.

He assumed the woman would vanish as mysteriously as she appeared. They stood a moment in the corridor. She looked both ways like a diligent child practising her kerb drill. He said goodnight and thanked her for her help. She returned his words with a silent, wide-eyed stare. He turned the key in his own door and went in. She followed, put a hand out to his arm.

'Are you going to tell?' she asked again.

'I don't know. How do you feel about directing traffic in Novaya Zemlya?'

He meant it as a joke. She did not smile. It wasn't funny.

'Why don't you sit down? Take off your coat.'

She did not move. He walked round her and closed the door behind them.

'OK. Then start with the hat. Work up to the coat.'

She pulled off her cap and sat down, still clutching the cap.

'I'm Troy,' he said, almost as though talking to a child.

'I know. Commander Troy. Royal British Navy.'

'No,' he said. 'I'm not. I'm a policeman.'

'Commander is a naval rank, is it not?'

'Except at Scotland Yard, where it's a police rank. I'm a detective. You are KGB?'

'No. I'm in the militia,' she said. 'Not the KGB. I too am a police officer.'

'Well, we have something in common after all. Shall we drink to our common cause?'

He turned his back on her while he rooted around for the bottle of ouzo he had bought at Athens airport. It would make a change from vodka, and he'd bet she'd never tasted the stuff in her life. He heard the swish as her coat slid off and the double thump as her shoes hit the floor. The moan of the springs as she settled back in the chair.

'What's your name?'

He turned around. She was sitting curled up with her toes under her backside, just like his wife used to do, one hand toying with her hair, her head on one side, the small heart-shaped face looking up at him, eyes as big as millwheels in the dimness of the room.

'Valentina Vassilievna Asimova – but you can call me Vivi.'

§ 16

In the morning Troy dressed and packed, and when he could wait no longer for Charlie, shook him awake.

'What time is it?'

'Past noon. I have to leave in a couple of hours.'

'Where am I?'

'Monte Carlo.'

Charlie laughed till he coughed. He eased himself off the mattress. Propped himself up on one elbow. Looked around.

'We should complain to the management. I asked for the Duke of Windsor's room.'

He laughed again, muttered, 'Russia, fucking Russia, what did I ever do to deserve you?' and staggered into the bathroom to cough fitfully for several minutes.

When he had stopped Troy knocked gently on the door.

'Charlie – we haven't a lot of time.'

'It's not locked.'

Troy pushed, in some trepidation. Charlie was seated on the loo, red-faced and straining. It was a habit born of schooldays, where none of the stalls in the boys' bogs had locks and half of them no doors. Defecation was communal. Troy had hated it.

'I've just discovered a real disadvantage to Russian nosh,' said Charlie. 'It constipates you. I cannot shit for love or money. Shit, shit, shit, I cannot.'

'Why did you get me here?' Troy asked

'Loose ends. The Russkis seemed surprisingly understanding about it, but then they'd want me to cut off any potential problems, wouldn't they?'

'And?'

'And it's chiefly the old dear. My mother. In fact it's entirely my mother. She has a pittance of a pension. It will not keep her in the manner to which and blahdey blah. I've got money in England. Not as much as I had, and nowhere near as much as you'd think. But the old fart won't touch it. Thinks it's tainted. I cannot convince her otherwise. I've about twelve grand tucked away in Mullins Kelleher. I'll write you a cheque. You take the money, and see she's all right. Tell her whatever fib you think'll work.'

'OK,' said Troy.

'Old dear' was just Charlie's figure of speech. Mrs Leigh-Hunt was nobody's old dear. She had been a child bride, eighteen when Charlie was born – and she had been born to raise hell. On the few occasions Troy had seen her in recent years she had been living modestly in a village in Hampshire or Sussex or somewhere, and hating it as much as Charlie now hated Russia. He was a little surprised to learn that she was quite so principled about money. Twelve grand could turn her life around.

'We never did have money, you know.'

This was an Englishman speaking. A Communist, a traitor, and, finally, a defector, but an Englishman through and through. Only an Englishman brought up as well as Charlie would ever speak of his circumstances thus. No money meant not enough money. Not enough after the public school fees and the house in the country. In English terms this was tantamount to poverty, and that clearly was how Charlie regarded it. One rung above the workhouse. It was rubbish, but Troy had no heart for the argument. He passed Charlie his jacket, Charlie fumbled in the pockets for his chequebook, Troy lent him his fountain pen and he scribbled out a cheque for twelve thousand pounds, the wage of the British working man for the best part of twenty years. Troy had no way of calculating how far such a sum would go towards the wage of the Russian working man. A lifetime, he thought, or perhaps two.

'I always envied you, you know. Not the money. The security. At least I think that's the word I mean. After my old man buggered off we seemed to move every couple of years. I'd get home for the hols – it seemed like every couple of terms there'd be new house and a new bloke to call "uncle". I could never hang on to anything. My stuff was forever going in or out of packing cases. Lost me teddy bear before I was seven. I used to envy you, and what I envied was the security of the home. You and your mother and your loony sisters and your big brother – I'd love to have had a big brother – and the house. The sheer solidity of it all. The junk of solidity. All that . . . all that sort of Troyness rolling back in time. I felt more at home in your dad's house than I did in any one of the places I cannot dignify with the word home.'

This made some sense. Judy Leigh-Hunt had been cursed with good looks and a string of feckless men, usually purporting to be heroes of the First World War. On open days at school there was no knowing with which man she'd turn up, and Charlie withstood a lot of ribbing on the subject of his 'uncles' – and in the holidays he would find himself dragged from one watering hole to the next. The cheapskates took him to Scarborough, the spendthrifts to Biarritz. The out-and-out bounders would ditch him entirely, suggesting that perhaps Charlie would prefer to 'spend the hols with a pal' – which pal would inevitably be Troy. But in part it was nonsense.

'Charlie, has it ever occurred to you that most of that junk of solidity was fake?'

'Whaddya mean, fake?'

'It didn't roll back centuries. It didn't even roll back to the start of this one. The old man left Russia with next to nothing. Most of the junk that you refer to he bought at one time or another – the solidity of time-treasured possessions, history as furniture, which I think is what you mean, was left behind. Most of it is probably locked away in the cellars and attics of the old house on Dolgo-Khamovnichesky Street.'

'Ye gods, I'd hate to have to pronounce that when I'm pissed. However, what's your point?'

'That it was his creation. What you saw was the world as he made it. Not as he found it.'

'A lesson for us all, eh?'

A short sentence shot through with silent sighs.

'If you like.'

'I can make my own solidity, my own junk, my own world?'

Troy said nothing.

'Out of Russia? I can make my world out of Russia!'

Charlie was shrilly incredulous. Troy said nothing. He had said quite enough for the half-dozen microphones buried in the plasterwork of the walls and ceiling already. He had been speaking of the past, of lost possibilities. There was no world to make now. It was, as Charlie insisted, a time of unmaking. All Charlie had made was his bed and he had to lie in it, and if that bed was the Union of Soviet Socialist Republics, so be it. He closed the loo door on a ranting Charlie and as he did so heard him sigh, 'Ah, bliss,' and, knowing what it presaged, stuffed his fingers in his ears.

§ 17

Troy waited until they stood on the tarmac at the airport once more.

'I've something to ask of you,' he said.

'Okey doh.'

'Can they hear us?'

'In this wind? This far from a building? Doubt it. If there's a listening device that can cope at this distance in the open air, I don't know of it. In a room, no problem. Train a mike on the vibrations in the window, acts like the ear drum and you can pick up a conversation from a quarter of a mile or more. Out here, the most they could manage is a bugger with binoculars who can lipread. If you really want to tell me a secret, just button up your collar.'

Troy did so.

'A favour, Charlie. Years ago a Pole working for your lot told me my father was a Soviet agent. I want to know the truth.'

'Hmm,' said Charlie.

'Can you find out?'

'Do you really want to know?'

'I've just said so.'

'A riddle wrapped in a mystery inside an enigma.'

'I know, you told me. The day before yesterday.'

'Winston meant Russia. But he might just as well have been describing your old man. I say again, do you really want to know?'

Troy said nothing. Stared at him till he cracked.

'It'll take a while. I'll need to get my knees under the table. I'd have to trade a few secrets. But I've plenty of those. The real problem would be how could I tell you? We'd need a code.'

Troy felt momentarily helpless. This was not his world, not his vocabulary.

'Mind,' Charlie went on. 'I'll think of something. Bound to think of something.'

§ 18

It was still winter when Troy returned home. England under snow. A flying, white visit to Charlie's mother in Dorset. A small, white, utterly implausible lie about the money. A small mountain of work at the Yard. A small row with Rod.

'Where've you been?'

What was the point? The pain he would give Rod if he said he'd been to Russia. The boredom he would let himself in for if he admitted it and Rod banged on with a thousand questions.

'I can't tell you.'

'More lies, Freddie?'

'No. Silence.'

'There's such a thing as lies of silence, you know.'

'If you like, but I still can't tell you.'

'Sod you then!'

Rod could not hold a grudge. Partly because he knew that he might wait till kingdom come only to find Troy still silent before him. Partly because decency, that spurious Anglo-Saxon virtue, ran through him deeper than the word Brighton through the eponymous stick of rock. Within a week they were speaking once more. By the end of February affably so, and early one Friday evening, a couple of weeks before Easter, only days, it seemed, after the last evaporation of the most interminably lingering winter, Rod could be found almost horizontal on the sofa in Troy's sitting room in Goodwin's Court feeling very fridayish, a cup of tea balanced on his chest, rising and falling with his breathing like a small vessel at sea, red tie at half-mast, beetlecrusher shoes off, odd socks on, lamenting the lot of a member of Her Majesty's Loyal Opposition, lamenting in particular the small peculiarities of breeding and character that defined the leadership of Her Majesty's Loyal Opposition.

'They're bastards. The pair of 'em. Bloody Brown. Bloody Wilson. Bastards.'

Troy had known Brown for several years – a young light from the trades union movement, outspoken, emotional, and impossible when pissed. He had met Wilson just the once, at a dinner party Rod had thrown for the Labour nobs — a former Oxford don, a professional Yorkshireman, whom Troy had thought about as fascinating as congealing custard, unredeemed by wit or wickedness or the prospect of a good indiscretion when drunk; a 'man of the people' who chomped on a pipe in public for the sake of the image and in private puffed away at cigars, and who habitually wore a hideous fawn macintosh, spun out of some new synthetic fabric, in an effort to make himself appear more 'ordinary'. He always succeeded in this — effortlessly. Troy had on occasion wondered which of the Labour Party wags — Rod? Or the equally waggish Tom Driberg? — had told him he needed to be more 'ordinary', and why Wilson had not recognised that he was being sent up.

Of the two Troy preferred Brown, and this in no way took account of his politics within the internal, infernal machinations of the wretched party. Brown's tactless unreliability at least smacked of honesty, not a word one would ever think of in the same sentence as the word Wilson. Wilson, it was, some old Socialist had dubbed 'the desiccated calculating machine'. Rod was content with calling him 'Mittiavelli', a poor man's Machiavelli. He had reduced himself and Troy to hysterics a while ago by asking, 'What do you get if you cross Walter Mitty with Machiavelli?' The answer — Harold Wilson. And he'd been Mittiavelli ever since. But if Rod was going to sit here and ruin Friday evening with a whinge about the pair of them, there was an obvious question lurking in the wings.

'You made them a gift of the leadership. Why didn't you stand?'

'Why not?' Rod said. 'Perfectly good reason when it came down to it. Do you remember what Jack Kennedy said in his inaugural?'

'Yep, he said watch out, commies, we're a-gonna blast yer.'

'Jesus Christ,' Rod said softly. 'Do you have to be quite so cynical? He said no such thing.'

'Yes he did. Meet any challenge, fight any foe, zap any country, look out world. He's a cold warrior, Rod. It was a speech of warmongering patriotic hokum.'

'Freddie, I've met the man, you haven't. He is not a—'

'Yes I have.'

'Have what?'

'Met him.'

'When?'

Rod looked at Troy in utter disbelief.

'Just before the war. When his dad was the ambassador. You were busy doing your stint as the *Post*'s man in Berlin. The old man invited the Kennedys out to Mimram. Jack was this tall skinny thing, he'd be about twenty or twenty-one I suppose. I was not much older. The old man stuck us together on the assumption common age might yield common interest. Fat chance.'

'Oh? What did you talk about?'

'We stood on the verandah. Nice sort of evening, sort of balmy, the kind of summer evenings we don't get any more. He said, "Sho this is the English countryshide?" Not exactly a conversation piece − all you can say is "yes". "Sho," he said, "what doesh a man have to do to get laid in the English countryshide?"'

'You're making this up.'

'No, honestly—'

'You know, cynicism will be the death of you.'

'It's true, all of it. I fixed him up with Ted Driffield's daughter.'

Rod's voice rose to parliamentary peak, the polite bludgeoning of the House of Commons. How to shout down an opponent without getting slung out by the Speaker.

'Cynicism and *lies* will be the death of you! The President of the United States does not come to rural Hertfordshire simply to get laid, and it's got nothing to do with the point I was trying to make!'

He ground to a halt. Lost for words.

'What was I saying?'

'Inaugrual speech,' Troy prompted.

'Right. What he said was something about let the word go forth, et cetera et cetera, the torch − that's it − the torch has been passed to a new generation.'

'So that's why you wouldn't stand? The torch has been passed to Harold Wilson? He's the "new generation"? You're mad.'

'It was too late for me and I knew it. The party wasn't looking for a man for the next couple of years, it was looking for a leader to take them into the seventies. By 1970 I'll be sixty-two.'

'So?'

'Too old. I knew it in my bones. Time to pass on the torch.'

'Maybe − but younger men? Wilson and Brown!'

'They're ten years younger than me.'

'So? Wilson's a bore and George is a liability. For God's sake, Rod, Harold Wilson was born middle-aged!'

'As a matter of fact, they're both younger than you.'

Troy shrugged a silent 'so what?'

'Don't you ever get the feeling that it's time to pass on the torch, that your generation has had its chance?'

'No.'

'You will. Take my word for it.'

Rod lapsed into silence, giving Troy time to digest this. Troy silently spat it out. The phone rang. And rang. And rang.

'You going to answer that?' Rod said at last.

Troy picked up the telephone and heard Anna's voice for the first time in several weeks.

'Troy. So glad I caught you. Look, are you free this evening?'

'Depends,' said Troy.

'Don't be so damn cagey. I was only trying to ask you out.'

Anna was an ex-girlfriend – a word that caused Troy on occasion to wonder how pertinent it could be when applied to a married woman of forty-three or four. She was also Troy's doctor, and one of the few women to penetrate the male domain of Harley Street. It was her habit to call from time to time with just such lines as she was using now.

'There's a quartet playing in Notting Hill tonight. Paddy Fitz is putting together a bit of a crowd. We thought you might like to join us.'

Notting Hill was hardly a tantalising qualification to the offer. It was a rough, largely black area of London north and west of the park. For ten years now it had been the rising ghetto of Britain's Caribbean immigrants, a run-down neighbourhood of large houses split into tiny flats and ruthlessly exploited by slum landlords. To call it 'notorious' would not have been overstating the case. But then, Anna thought like a doctor and Troy like a policeman.

'Calypso isn't really my cup of tea,' he said.

''T'isn't calypso. It's jazz. Or I wouldn't be asking. You think I don't know you by now?'

'Putting together a bit of a crowd' brought out suspicion in Troy – a quality, if such it be, never far from the surface at the best of times – but the truth was, the invitation appealed. To go home to Mimram with Rod in this mood would clearly be to subject himself to a couple of days' political whingeing. And whilst he could not rely on Anna's opinion in music, Fitz was known for his discrimination. Fitz, put simply, had taste. He put a hand across the mouthpiece.

'Can you drive yourself tonight?'

'Don't see why not. Your car, I assume?'

Rod drove one of the new mini cars that had swept Britain, and most other countries, over the last couple of years. Fashionable as hell in British racing green – the same deep green as Stirling Moss's Vanwall – but tiny. Rod was a stout six footer and fitted into Troy's 1952 five-litre Bentley Continental much more comfortably than he did into his everyman's Mini Minor. Owning the symbol of Britain's new classlessness, he took every opportunity to borrow Troy's symbol of the old wealth.

'OK. But I must have it back Sunday night.'

'Done,' said Rod.

'Anna. When and where?'

'I'll pick you up around eight.'

§ 19

It was a beautiful evening. A warmish day, a darkening sky patterned with blown clouds and the hint of rain poised in the air. Troy washed, changed his shirt, propped open the front door, sat awhile in the spring breeze that wafted in from the courtyard, and thought of Paddy Fitz. Patrick Fitzpatrick was the senior partner in Anna's practice. He was a good-looking, if epicene, man of fifty or so, tall, affable, cultured to the extremes – eclectic or catholic – and outlandishly well read and well spoken. He would talk of anything and everything in what Troy could only think of as an upper-class English drawl. He was single. And he was also, far and away, the most rumoured-about man Troy knew.

He had begun life as plain Patrick Alan Smith. This, Troy knew to be true. He had changed his name by deed poll to the Fordian symmetry of Patrick Alleyn Fitzpatrick, and had acquired his accent by a mysterious process of practice and attrition – intoning into the mirror while one shaved and cocking a keen ear to the strains those class confrères around one will buff all but the most immovable of accents. Professor Higgins had little on Fitz. He was a grammar school boy from Cheshire. No public school. No Oxbridge. School certificate and a medical degree at a redbrick university. But you would never know it to listen to him. If asked – confronted was hardly the word – he would deny nothing, would even reminisce, in tones of irony, about a childhood in the 'arse-end of nowhere' and joke about wearing clogs and learning the alphabet on a slate. But if not asked, the line between the man he was and the man he had made was seamless. Paddy Fitz was a wordspinner, an inventor, a weaver of dreams. And he spun words by the million, wove who knew what dreams, and invented nothing better, no one finer, than himself. Where his powers of invention stopped, the power of rumour took over. He was single . . . ergo he was queer . . . ergo a roué . . . ergo he swung both ways. He was more than well off from his practice – a patient list dotted with duchesses and ambassadors and cabinet ministers – ergo . . . he could not have come by his money honestly – when he so transparently had if one but looked at his bills – ergo . . . he had fiddles . . . things going on on the side . . . performed abortions . . . sold dope.

All in all, Fitz adored rumours. Troy had long ago concluded that he spread most of them himself and took a wicked delight in seeing how long they took to come full circle. Nonetheless the power of such rumour caused problems. Problems, to say the least, of protocol. Fitz might cultivate a friendship with Troy. Troy did not and could not cultivate one with him. He was thinking just this, to the point of cold feet, when Anna tapped gently on the door.

'Are you ready, you silly old sod?'

Troy could not remember when they had last met. Christmas? New Year? They had ditched one another as lovers years before, in the mid-1950s, and apart from an initially rocky period had managed a passably loyal friendship ever since. Much like the one they had had during the war, the one they should never have surrendered to the futility of sex, when Anna had worked as Kolankiewicz's assistant at the Metropolitan Police Laboratory in Hendon, and their talk had consisted of little else but death.

'You are coming, aren't you?' The eyes wide, the rising tone of hope frustrated in her voice. 'Troy?'

'Yes,' he said. 'I suppose I am.'

She zipped them along Oxford Street, across the top of Hyde Park, in the direction of Notting Hill Gate, in her little Triumph Herald Vitesse. It was a sturdier, more stylish car than Rod's Mini. Strong, square lines, rather than the blown soap bubble of the Mini. But sitting inside it was womb-like, dark beneath the soft top, the first drops of evening rain beginning to patter on the roof. The Triumph Herald would make a great summer car, Troy thought, if we ever had a summer again.

Anna swung the car right at the Gate, left into Portobello Road and brought it to a halt in St Aubyn Street, outside a garishly painted house – the blues and reds of the Cool in the Shade Club, number 98 St Aubyn Street, or as it preferred to put it, 98.6. 'Come in and cool your blood' the sign seemed to imply, rather like the famous hippopotamus in mud, mud, glorious mud.

Down a narrow staircase. Out into a wide basement, far far bigger than the outside proportions would ever have led him to guess. A small stage at one end, a scattering of tiny tables in the centre, and a U-shaped row of booths around the edges. It took a minute for his eyes to get accustomed to the light – or rather the lack of light. It was dimly lit and the dimness augmented by a hefty layer of smoke, a certain something in the air, and by deep blue walls, deep blue ceilings, scattered with myriad stars. To achieve the effect, the club's proprietors had painted over everything – no line had ever given the paintbrush cause to pause – light fittings, doors, windows, the lot, were all the same rich, dark blue.

Troy saw a hand waving at them from a centre booth. Paddy Fitz rose. Kissed Anna – the token tap on her cheek – shook hands with Troy and proffered the introductions.

'Troy. You and Tommy know each other, don't you?'

A tall, fat, balding, smiley man plucked himself from Anna's embrace.

'Of course,' said Tommy Athelnay. 'Long time no see, o' man.'

This was their way. Troy was not his 'old man'. Never had been. He and Lord Athelnay were at best nodding acquaintances. Old Tommy had had far more to do with Troy's brother and sisters than he ever had with Troy himself.

'And', Fitz went on, 'the twins, Tara and Caro Ffitch. Frederick Troy.'

Tommy Athelnay resumed his seat. Whichever of the two blonde women less than half his age it was that had taken up with him for the evening slipped her arm through his, smiled sweetly up at Troy and kissed the old man softly on the ear.

He blushed. Troy could have sworn he blushed. The merest reddening of the ear and cheek, but a blush by any other name.

The other one of these women-like-bookends said hello to Troy and made no response whatsoever as Fitz stretched both arms out along the back of the booth and let his fingers rest lightly on her shoulder. Troy and Anna squeezed in. He found himself facing Tommy Athelnay and one of the Ffitch girls. It was, he concluded instantly, a slumming night. A few Mayfair toffs deciding it would be radically chic to spend an evening in a black club just beyond the boundaries of their known civilisation.

Fitz could be no more than fifty or fifty-one, he thought, but Tommy was in his sixties. He doubted these women were much more than girls, twenty or twenty-one, looking, with their dyed blonde hair, their deep red fingernails and their expensive little cocktail dresses, like sex in a packet. Just add water − well, to be precise, just add man over forty. The women were gorgeous. And whilst they clearly had the desired − or could it be undesired? Who in their right mind would want to be seen sexually aroused, sexually provoked in public? − effect on Tommy, Fitz was as 'cool' as the club they sat in. His arm shot up. A waiter ambled over, casual enough to be 'cool', and took Fitz's order for more champagne.

'You're going to like this, Freddie,' Fitz said, stuffing a cigarette into the end of a short black holder. 'In fact you're going to love it. I thought of you the minute I first heard these chaps play. Reminded me of you.'

Troy had no idea what to say to this, indeed could not remember when Fitz had heard him play. So often he played to and for himself.

They moved and spoke for Troy as though in a bubble. He was there and not there. Fitz flowed on with a languid, witty line of small talk and sat as though holding court, name-dropping, name-gathering and slandering half London in the process. Dozens, it seemed, came up and said hello, and each time Fitz introduced Troy to, invariably, total strangers with a 'You know Troy, don't you?' – just as he'd done with Tommy Athelnay. At no point did he add to this. Troy was not an old friend of Anna's, was not a policeman, was not Scotland's Yard's chief detective. He was anonymous but for the uninformative label that was his name. He was glad of this. The job was a show-stopper and he had no wish to stop the show. At the same time he could not help the feeling that it was all on the level of a private joke, that he knew and Fitz knew, but the endless stream of slumming toffs, cockney wide boys and loudly dressed blacks did not. A feeling began to grow in him that he was somehow Fitz's trophy.

All the time a private conversation was taking place in the corner as Tommy reduced his escort to giggles with inaudible nothings, and the movement of her arm told Troy that beneath the table her hand was almost certainly caressing his cock. They were remarkably beautiful and physically identical, but they were not twins. He'd lived all his life with twins. His sisters moved as one, more often than not thought as one. This pair did not. The sameness of face was not matched by sameness of posture, of gesture, the small, almost uncontrollable, unconscious actions of the body. Even the look in their eyes was different. The one with Fitz radiated self-assurance to Troy; the one with Tommy did not. He could see why everyone else at this table was fooled by their twins line, but he was not.

The band were brilliant, far better than Troy had even dared to hope. A tight, four-piece unit of bass, drums, trumpet and a tenor sax who occasionally played baritone too. He could hear hints of Roy Eldridge and Miles Davis in the trumpeter; he could hear the milder, earlier Coltrane in the sax player, and the rumbling, grumbling influence of Gerry Mulligan when he switched to baritone.

At the end of the first set they took a break. Fitz beckoned and the sax player came over. A tall, thin black man – skin of black hue that looked almost blue. He pulled up a chair. Fitz called for another glass. The man introduced himself as Philly. Troy had made the immediate assumption, entering a club in Notting Hill, that a black band would be Caribbean, but Philly's accent and name told him otherwise.

'Are you all Americans?' he asked.

'Well . . . I am. And I ain't from Philly. I'm from Weehawken, New Jersey. Lou there . . .' Philly squirmed in his seat, pointing to the trumpeter. 'He's Harlem born and raised. Up on Lenox Avenue. Played with Ellington and Basie in his time. Errol on bass is from Barbados and Cliff on drums is English – citizen of Shepherd's Bush.'

'Quite a mixture,' said Troy, failing miserably at the small talk. 'You stir it well.'

Philly accepted the compliment with a silent smile.

'Gets kinda hard to keep it together sometimes.'

'Musical differences?' Troy asked.

'Work permits,' Philly said succinctly. 'Way things are goin', Cliff be drummin' on his own.'

Troy looked at Fitz. He was never certain where Fitz was concerned what his motives might be. It crossed his mind that Fitz might just have got him here in the hope he would drop a word in Rod's ear. But then Fitz said, 'Troy is the chap I was telling you about. Damn fine pianist.'

Philly nodded. 'You wanna sit in on the second set, man? Blow the dust off the ivories?'

This was the last thing Troy had expected. It was embarrassing – it was flattering – to play with a man who played with Ellington. It was corrupting.

'I . . . er . . . why not?' he said, and Philly led the way back to the small stage and threw the dustcover off the upright piano.

Troy riffled through a quick couple of scales. It was tuned.

'Just tell us what you want, man.'

'Rodgers and Hart. Do you know "My Funny Valentine"? The version by Gerry Mulligan and Chet Baker?'

'The '53 or the '57?'

'The '53.'

'Ain't no piano on the '53, man.'

'I know,' said Troy. 'It leaves me a bit of room.'

'You wanna lead?'

'No, I'll follow. Just give me the nod when you're ready.'

The trumpet opened, passed the lead to Philly and from Philly to Troy, who managed not, he thought, to mess it up.

It was one of the most haunting tunes in the repertoire of standards, Troy had long thought. It ranked with Kern and

Harbach's 'Smoke Gets in Your Eyes' and rare, less sentimental renditions of Arlen and Harburg's 'Over the Rainbow'. The audience clearly loved it, and as he rose to go back to the table he felt Philly's hand pressing him back onto the piano stool.

'Just one more, man. Just one more. You got any other tricks up your sleeve?'

It did occur to him to suggest Gershwin's 'I Got Plenty O' Nuttin', from *Porgy and Bess*. Charlie seemed to have lodged the tune perpetually in his mind – but it wasn't 'cool'; in fact it was downright perky. Instead he turned to the band and said, 'How about "My Man's Gone Now"?'

He had been tinkering for weeks with Grainger's piano arrangement, his 'fantasy', deciphering the way the madman had spread *Porgy and Bess* across two pianos and four hands and crammed it into twenty minutes, wondering how much of it he in turn could cram into his own two hands. But it suited the mood, that air of melancholy, almost outweighed by the heat haze of languor that hung about the tune.

They said nothing. Put their heads together. Then Philly turned to him and said, 'OK. Lou will pick up from you.'

This surprised and pleased Troy – a rare pleasure for a front-parlour pianist to alternate with a trumpet. He wove his cautious improvisation around the left hand and saw Lou stick in the mute. He gave it two minutes, gently nodded and Lou picked up the melody with a lost-in-the-distance whine, a steam-train-somewhere-in-the-next-state, canyon-over-the-mountain whine, that almost made his blood run cold. It was good, good enough to make the parlour pianist in him want to give up and listen for the rest of his life. The man blew like the Angel Gabriel. By the time he passed back to Troy seven minutes later, he had the room on its feet stomping and whistling and clapping.

It pays to know when to quit. Troy rounded up the tune like a dutiful sheepdog, brought in the sax, and drew the song to a neat conclusion.

Lou leant in to Troy beneath the applause.

'Not bad. Not bad at all.'

'I know,' said Troy. 'This is where you tell me not give up my day job.'

'Well. Mebbe go fifty-fifty on it. Say, what is your day job?'

'If I told you, you wouldn't believe me.'

'Why? You ain't the heat are you?'

'Hot as hell,' said Troy, and the band laughed like drains. He headed for the lavatory and let them take a bow without him.

In the lavatory the aroma that had troubled him all evening finally showed its source. Two West Indians stood chatting and passing a reefer back and forth between them. Even the presence of a middle-aged white man gave them no cause to do anything much more than glance up as he came in. They huddled against the wall, unsmilingly serious about the business, sucking in their cheeks to squeeze the last hit out of a tiny stub, croaking in strangulated whispers as they attempted to hold in the smoke and talk at the same time. It was all too familiar.

He sat in a cubicle biding his time and giving them five minutes to go away. If they were still there when he came out, he thought, he'd arrest them. Well, he'd probably arrest them. By the fifth minute 'probably' had dwindled to 'might', to an earnest wish that they would just bugger off. They did, and he emerged from the bog to that unmistakable heady, herby smell of pot and a firm resolution that he and Anna were leaving, whether she liked it or not.

When he got back to their booth Fitz was on his feet helping Anna into her coat.

'You don't mind do you, Troy? I'm just . . . well sort of pooped.'

§ 20

He leant well back in the seat. Closed his eyes and replayed Lou's solo in the mind's ear.

'Well,' Anna said.

'Well what?'

'What did you think of it?'

'Band were good . . .'

'I can hear a "but" bubbling to the surface.'

'But . . . whatever the company of young women like those does for Fitz, it makes me feel old.'

'You?! Old?! What the bloody hell do you think it does for me? You haven't got tits heading for the equator faster than Blue Streak. You haven't got dimples in your thighs the size of lunar craters. You don't put on half a stone if you just look at cream cake.'

'Sorry I spoke,' said Troy.

§ 21

It was a week before they spoke again. Anna called him at the Yard, on the eve of the long weekend.

'You have got the weekend off, haven't you? You see, Tommy Athelnay's invited us all down to Uphill for the holiday. You know, one of those pre-war long weekends. Turn up for tea on Saturday, set off home same time Monday, back in London before bedtime.'

'Us?' Troy said simply. 'All?'

'Well you and me, and the Ffitch girls, and a couple of Fitz's friends. Chap called Tony, someone he calls Marty, and a girl called Clover. I know her – she's part of that odd harem Fitz has at the mews house. Funny little thing. Never met Tony or Marty, or at least I don't think I have. Tommy doesn't go a lot on surnames – but it'll be about a dozen in all I should think.'

Troy said nothing, so she prattled on to coax him.

'I say Tommy's asked us, but we'd stay with Fitz of course. He rents the south lodge off Tommy. Tommy's lived in the north lodge ever since Uphill Park got bombed in the war.'

'You think the prospect of prolonged exposure to Tommy would put me off, do you?'

'I never know with you, Troy. The slightest thing can put you off. Tommy can be a bit of a bore, but you're one of the most awkward buggers I know.'

'And what about Fitz?'

'What about Fitz? You're not saying you've anything against Fitz?'

Troy knew Anna. He could imagine her clearly now, spluttering with incredulity. He chose his words carefully.

'He pricks me.'

'What do you mean?'

'I think I mean he flirts with me. It's a kind of flirtation. He flirts with the law.'

'Can't say as I've noticed.'

'You wouldn't.'

'I mean, you're not saying you think Fitz is a wrong 'un are you? He's a rogue, but hardly a wrong 'un.'

'No. I'm saying that he thinks he is. In his own mind he thinks he's outside the law. The flirtation is in wanting also to be above the law.'

'Now you have lost me.'

'Why are most criminals caught?'

'In my limited experience because they leave their fingerprints all over the shop. The average criminal seems not to be able to afford the price of a pair of gloves. Perhaps that's what drives them to crime in the first place? And they don't reckon with Kolankiewicz and his bag of forensic tricks. And then, they don't much reckon with you I suppose. The relentless plod who never stops. You know "neither rain, nor snow, nor something something shall stop . . .", and all that.'

'I think you'll find it's the New York Post Office who never stop. No. Most criminals are caught because they want to be caught. Greater by far than the profit motive is the wish to be able to fling the defiant act in the face of authority.'

'And you think that's what Fitz is doing to you?'

'Yes.'

'But he's not a criminal.'

'No. He's not.'

'Then I still don't get it.'

'You think inviting me to sit in a cellar that reeks of pot-smoking, where men roll up reefers in the lavatory, isn't flirtation, the flirtation I've just described?'

'Did it reek of pot? I can't say I noticed. I mean you expect the odd whiff. It wouldn't be jazz and it wouldn't be jazz in Notting Hill if there weren't a dash of that sort of thing. I mean. Negroes do that sort of thing, don't they? One sort of expects it of them, doesn't one?'

'I don't.'

'Yes – but you're a policeman . . . oh bugger. This is rather where we came in, isn't it?'

'Quite. And I think by now you ought to be able to see that he associates with such people because it gives him sin by association, vicarious pleasure without the guilt, and then, to crown it all he wants me to see it. He wants me, relentless plod as you put it, to see how untouchable he is in the middle of all this vicarious pleasure, this second-hand guilt. The eyes of Nero and the hands of Pontius Pilate. That's Paddy Fitz.'

'He doesn't mean any harm, you know.' There was a bottomless sadness in her voice.

'Convince me,' said Troy.

§ 22

Troy let Anna drive. She was thrilled to be behind the wheel of a seventeen-foot Bentley, and she was a better driver than Troy. Most people were.

He did not go often to Sussex. For all its proximity to London, it was not a part of England he knew well. He thought, as Anna drove him south, that it undulated in that classic way of rolling English countryside. He'd seen it in all those pre-war films, he'd seen it from time to time from train windows on his way to Brighton. He had never been sure of the etymology of the word 'Downs'. Clearly, they were 'Ups', two chains of hills that wended their way from somewhere in the middle of southern England – Troy had no idea where – eastward to the coast. The North Downs sort of fizzled out in Canterbury, and the South Downs leapt to their death near Beachy Head, and between the two lay a curved plain that took up much of East Sussex and Kent. To cross them was a delight, revelation after revelation, a peeling away of horizon from horizon.

In its day, Uphill Park had been famous. It had been built by Inigo Jones for some ancestor of Tommy Athelnay's, with later additions by various hands and, later still, gardens by Humphry Repton. It had peaked about 1860, gone slowly downhill, in every sense but the nominal and literal, throughout the previous century, and had been in very poor condition, though still inhabited, when a stray doodlebug chugged out sixty-odd miles short of its target and finally saw it off in the summer of 1944. Queen Elizabeth may never have 'slept here', but Queen Anne had, and so had Mr Gladstone, William IV, Gilbert White and Admiral Nelson – to say nothing of Lady Hamilton.

All that remained were the walls, and the north and south lodges. But the lodges were on the grand scale and occupied one of the best vantage points in the county, a sharply rising, flat-topped hill that had long, long ago been an island in the tidal inrush of the channel until centuries of silt had embedded it firmly in the surrounding mainland, above which it now rose as sharply as a sandcastle. The lodges had been built as follies by the mid-Victorian umpteenth Viscount Athelnay. From the road, and from the surrounding countryside, they appeared to be the craggy ruins of mediaeval castles, utterly at odds with the big house in Jones's English wet-weather-adapted Palladian style. From the park side, they were houses, far from ordinary houses, bent into colossal horseshoe shapes for the benefit of the illusion, but houses all the same. In between the two lodges lay the ruins of Uphill itself, the neglected Repton gardens, and enough grassy space – lawn it was not – to accommodate a couple of cricket pitches and several tennis courts should anyone desire them. What had been desired was a croquet pitch. All a croquet pitch required was a level surface, a lawnmower, a roller and the banging of a few hoops into the ground. As Anna pulled the Bentley up the hill and around the south lodge, Tommy Athelnay was lining up a shot, his great, overstuffed frame bent at the knees, the mallet swinging smoothly between his legs to whack the wooden ball effortlessly through the hoop.

He was playing the Ffitch sisters, and partnered by a third young woman, whom he brought over to the car as Troy and Anna stretched their legs.

'Jolly good,' he said in his over-hearty tone. 'Jolly good, you're the first. Just in time. We can all have one more bash and then set up tea on the terrace. Now have you met Clover? You haven't met Clover have you? Mind you, the sky's pretty clear. Perhaps we could play another hour and go in for tea, get a nice log fire roaring and . . . er, have you met Clover? Or did I ask you that already? Anyway it's a fine afternoon why don't we . . . er . . .'

Troy wished Anna would say something, do something other than smile, or Tommy might prattle for ever. The girl took the initiative.

'Clover Browne,' she said, and stuck out her right hand at Troy. 'Browne with an "e".'

Troy shook. He didn't know how Tommy did it and he was not at all sure he wanted to know, but this girl was younger and better looking even than the Ffitch girls. She was not their leggy five foot ten, but her hair was long and blonde, natural blonde, and her eyes a piercing shade of blue. It was a face to turn heads. The accent did not match. Her 'with' was a 'wiv'. The Ffitch girls spoke the received pronunciation of a southern girls' public school. They were Roedean or Cheltenham or Bedales. Clover was undisguised cockney – Parson's Green Elementary or Shepherd's Bush High – and no 'e' on the end of her Brown would ever disguise it. It was Brown as in 'knees up'. If she'd added the 'e' herself, thought Troy, she'd wasted her time.

'I'd love to play,' said Anna. 'Just what I need after two hours behind the wheel. I'm a bit rusty, though.'

'No matter, no matter,' said Tommy, hugging her with one huge arm, while the other dangled his mallet. 'It's like riding a bike. You can have the pleasure of falling off all over again. And you, Troy?'

Troy was miles away. Staring at Clover Browne. Tommy had said his name again before he realised he had been staring, and realised the more that the child had not looked away, but had steadily returned his gaze, frowning all the while. Child. Yes, he thought, child. She could hardly be more than eighteen or nineteen.

'No thanks, Tommy. Not for me. I'll get the bags in.'

'Fine, fine,' said Tommy, and Troy surmised that little would ever displease or unsettle such an amiable buffoon.

''Ere, you 'ave mine,' Clover said and thrust her mallet at Anna. 'I've 'ad enough for now.'

Clover walked ahead of Troy up the steps of wide flagstones, their cracks dotted with flowering thyme and creeping mint, past the remains of Repton's terraced garden, to the back door of the lodge, propped open with a weathered stone head at the centre of the horseshoe. She gave him a good view of her backside, so neat in its navy-blue slacks, the sort of slacks that slipped a loop under the foot and stretched themselves to the leg and the backside with every stride. She turned on the top step, watching him, lumbered with all the bags he wished Anna had not brought and his own solitary overnight case. She looked neat standing there. He could think of no other word to describe her – neat in her stretch slacks, neat in the sleeveless white cotton blouse, buttoned high at the throat, leaving her arms bare and tanned. Neat with no wind to ruffle her hair, now nestling lightly over one eye to give her a modern version of the peekaboo. Neat in her stylish way – stylish, he thought, like Veronica Lake. The archetypal short, blonde beauty of the 1940s. But she was staring at him far more intently than he at her.

'Why are you staring at me?' he asked.

'I was just thinking – bet you was a looker when you was young.'

Thanks, thought Troy. And the girl turned on her heel and vanished into the house.

'I know what you're thinking,' said a voice behind him.

Troy looked over his shoulder. Paddy Fitz stood in a bed of miniature roses, in grubby corduroy trousers and a smudged RAF blue shirt, shorn of its collar, pulling off a pair of gardening gloves.

'You were thinking, "I bet she's under age."'

'Not quite,' said Troy. 'But almost certainly under voting age.'

'How tactfully you put it, Freddie. But try to think a bit less like a policeman. She's seventeen. I may have a certain reputation, but not with minors. If she were under age, believe me, she would not be here.'

Fitz threw his gloves on the ground, reached out and took two of Anna's bags from Troy.

'Let's have a drink, shall we? I've been pulling up fucking weeds all afternoon.'

Troy followed Fitz into the house – dark and cool, wooden panelling, heavy furniture and the smell of beeswax polish. Repton's 'red book' stood in the hall, propped open on a lectern. Uphill Park, for all Fitz's efforts, might never look that way again. On into a thoroughly modern kitchen, all stainless steel and yards of that new stuff that had so completely displaced oilcloth and had a name like 'Formica' – and gadgets, gadgets galore, that sliced and chopped and mixed. Troy cooked when the mood took him. He wasn't bad at it, but he'd never win prizes for it. He was simply not the slave to the laziness of living alone, or the dependence on women, that most men of his age were. But this was the kitchen of a man who took his cooking seriously, and equipped it with a vast *batterie de cuisine* – an arsenal. A full set of imported French enamelled iron cooking pots hung from hooks embedded in the beams. A murderous-looking row of Sabatier knives clung to a magnetic strip on the wall as though merely waiting the appearance of the knife thrower and the girl in the tasselled swimsuit. And the dusty harvest of last year's crops dangled from the rafters, great swathes of tarragon and rosemary, and strings of onions, shallots and garlic. The centrepiece was a vast deal table, which bore every conceivable stain and scar of its years of use: the black spots of fag ends carelessly stubbed out, the red rings of wine glasses, the faded brown of coffee cups, the washed-out greens of pounded herbs and the serratic scars of endless slicings and choppings across this maid of all work.

The air was rich and warm with the smell of yeast. Troy had to hand it to Fitz. He didn't know another man in the whole of England who would pass a lazy Saturday afternoon baking his own bread.

'Dump your stuff anywhere,' said Fitz, and Troy did.

Fitz opened a cupboard and reached down a couple of glasses.

'You know, I'm really very glad you decided to come. Anna needs the break. And I'm not all sure she'd have come without you.'

Troy was not all sure what he meant by this. He'd half formed the opinion that he was her escort in a very broad sense of the meaning – convenience, in that he played man to her woman on the social stage; protection, in that while he did this none of Fitz's male friends were likely to regard her as a bit of spare and leap on her. If there was another meaning, he'd rather hear it from Anna than Fitz.

Troy said nothing, and yawned.

'Tiring drive?' Fitz asked.

'Didn't drive. Let Anna do it all,' Troy replied through another yawn. 'I just haven't been sleeping too well lately.'

He could almost hear the click in Fitz's brain as the professional mode cut in.

'Prolonged, is it? Or intermittent bouts of insomnia?'

'Fitz, could you try to think less like a doctor?'

'Touché, old boy, touché. Now, shall we get to the best bit of gardening as a hobby, where one stands amid the roses and the hollyhocks and sips the gutsiest vodka martini known to man?'

'Yes,' said Troy eagerly. 'Stirred not shaken.'

'Quite. Bugger the Bond films. Stirred it is. The only way.'

He mixed up two lethal martinis, and the two of them stood halfway down the giant steps of the terraced garden, with the hoots and shrieks of a croquet battle ringing in the distance, looking at his budding roses, and a host of unspecified green shoots rising spear-like from the earth.

'Tell me,' Fitz began. 'Do you know how many varieties of flowering garlic there are?'

There were many who doubtless thought this the opening gambit of a colossal bore. Troy was not one of them.

§ 23

He took a nap before dinner and woke to the distant sound of a television. He found Clover in one of the smaller rooms, seated on the floor, arms around her knees, watching a programme he knew to be called *Juke Box Jury*. A 'review' of the week's pop record releases. Hits received a ding from a bell, misses were klaxoned into oblivion. He rather thought it was the klaxon that woke him.

He stood behind her, watching. What struck him most was firstly how out of touch he was with the new wave, and secondly that most of the 'judges' on this 'jury' were over thirty. He wondered if they knew or appreciated it any more than he did himself.

When it finished, Clover stood and said, 'It's hottin' up. Things are really hottin' up.'

And then she disappeared upstairs once more.

In an hour or so Fitz's dinner guests began to arrive. He introduced Troy to a seventy-year-old woman in a paint-spattered shirt whose surname appeared to be a sequence of Hungarian polysyllables.

'You know Magda,' he said, as he always said, regardless of whether one did or not. 'Surely you've seen her work in the Tate – *Red and Blue No. 4*?'

Troy could not have put a name to her, but he knew her work. She painted nudes pretty much in the manner of Lucian Freud. But she painted men – fat men, hairy men, bald men, men with scrawny slack muscles and bloodshot eyes, men with limp dicks and grey hairs on their balls. *Red and Blue No. 4* was, for want of no other word occurring to him, grotesque. Too real for comfort.

Fitz introduced him to a young man. Not a face he knew, but a name he did: David Cocket, not much over thirty, a barrister of some renown and a hot tip to take silk before he was much older.

And the last face he did know. Martin Pritch-Kemp, professor of English at London University, probably about Troy's age, a man who pitched his work squarely at the whybrow market – academic tomes made accessible, made into bestsellers by an inherent grasp of the commercial possibilities of the lay market. Helped, of course, by his having been the star turn a couple of years ago at the Trial of Lady Chatterley, which was how the case of Regina *v*. Penguin Books – over the matter of the pornography or not, obscenity or not, of the D.H. Lawrence novel – had come to be known. He had inescapably become known as, if not the face, then certainly the voice of liberated England. Pritch-Kemp was one of those men who thought to drag England screaming and kicking, although whining and cowering was far more accurate, into the twentieth century before it actually turned into the twenty-first.

The women, that is the younger women, dressed for dinner. The men did not – Fitz's concession to an occasion of his own making was a clean shirt, and the painter woman stuck with her artist's motley as though it were a uniform. It had been a while since Troy had seen quite so many little black dresses. Tara and Caro Ffitch did not dress identically. Tara's dress was strapless, and probably required whalebone engineering to keep it up. Caro had opted for shoulder straps, one of which she seemed to have to hoik back into place every five minutes. And Clover appeared transformed. Had Troy not known she was seventeen he would have revised his guesses to twenty-two or three. She had achieved a startling, diagonal asymmetry with an off-one-shoulder dress, and her hair piled high above the opposite ear. His one, if silent, complaint was that she favoured too much black eyeliner.

Anna was wearing a frock he'd seen her in a dozen times.

'Well,' she said, smiling nervously, shoulders back, tits out, teasing a lock of hair into place.

'Well what?'

'Pig,' she said.

Fitz served an exquisite rack of lamb. All through the meal there was a place set and a seat unoccupied next to him. He complained lightly over the carving that 'one can never rely on Tony to be on time' and after two or three glasses of wine, was asking first one sister and then the other, 'Well, where is the bugger? You told Tony seven thirty for eight, didn't you?'

Fitz had split up couples. Even the pretend couples. Troy had found himself seated between the painter woman, whom he quickly decided was barking mad – she said next to nothing, hummed to herself through most of the meal and interjected only when she was absolutely sure of a cast-iron *non sequitur* – and Tara Ffitch. Tara he took to. She sat opposite her sister, and although the resemblance was striking, he still could not understand why anyone fell for their 'twins' line. They were so different in character. Tara was wittily cynical, cutting acidly into conversation and expert at the poker face. Once or twice in the evening she caused Tommy Athelnay to double or triple take at the things she said. Only when Caro corpsed and gave in to a fit of giggles did he get the gag. Caro reacted much more than she initiated. She was an unrepentant giggler. The twin thing, he concluded, was their game.

Clover played a game of her own. No longer the surly brat who had left him on the doorstep. Now she was charming, now she was coy, now she cracked a joke with the men, reduced Caro to more giggles – and a moment later was looking at Troy with an intensity that bored into his skull.

She was the first to cut and run.

'Well, I gotta go. You old farts will bore the knickers off me and Lennon's calling. See you all at breakfast.'

Troy did not think this was funny. Tommy Athelnay thought it the funniest thing he had ever heard and laughed till he choked. Fitz simply said, 'Can't you two teach her any manners?'

'No,' said Tara. 'Your department, I believe. I do make-up. I don't do manners.'

'Who's Lennon?' asked Troy in all innocence.

'Who's Lennon? Who's Lennon?' said Cocket. 'Troy, where have you been? You sound like one of those old buggers I get stuck with in court. Last year I had a judge pull me up because I'd mentioned Marilyn Monroe. "Who is Marilyn Monroe?" "An actress, m'lud" – and I knew in my bones he'd not known the name of any actress since Ellen Terry or Mrs Patrick Campbell! Really, Troy, you must get out more.'

'I keep telling him that,' said Anna. 'John Lennon's one of the Beatles, Troy. You must be the only person who hasn't heard.'

Tommy Athelnay moved to the piano, began singing dirty lyrics – the sort most associated with rugby players and all-male communal baths – to melodies more appropriate to the metre of Tennyson or Lear. It was an old trick. Edward Lear had provoked Tennyson to rage at London soirées ninety years ago by taking the 'tune' of Tennyson and setting to it his own 'nonsense' lyrics. Tennyson had failed to see it as homage, much as Tommy's audience failed to appreciate 'Four and Twenty Virgins' rearranged as 'The Owl and the Pussycat'. It sounded like heresy.

'Oh, for Christ's sake – somebody stop him!' Fitz was yelling.

Tommy rose up from the piano stool, pissed and wobbly on his feet. 'Never let it be said that Tommy Athelnay exploited a captive audience. I yield, sir. I yield.'

'Troy, be a love and take over before remorse wears thin. He'll be at it again in five minutes if you don't.'

Troy slipped onto the piano stool, slipped into a lazy version of 'The Lady is a Tramp', slowly jerking the melody around, pulling it away at the tangents. Quite the opposite of Tommy's style.

The stool was long enough for two. He looked out of the corner of his eye to see Tara Ffitch seat herself next to him.

'Is this your coded judgement on us, Troy?'

'No. Nothing of the sort. Just listen to the lyrics.'

'You're not singing them.'

'Not my forte. Just run them through the mind's ear for a moment and you'll see what I mean.'

Tara watched his hands for a few seconds.

'Well,' he said. 'Do you get too hungry for dinner at eight?'

'I've usually demolished the bread rolls before the waiter gets to the table.'

'Are you late for the theatre?'

'Punctual to a fault, that's me.'

'And do you bother with people you hate?'

'Not any more. Not since the day I left school. The first freedom is the freedom not to bother with those you hate.'

'That', said Troy, 'is why the lady is not a tramp.'

'No, Troy – *is* a tramp.'

'The irony is there in letters six foot high, and still you miss it.'

'Then play something less subtle.'

He blended the Rodgers and Hart tune into Cole Porter's 'Love for Sale'.

Clearly Tara knew the words to that too. She got up and left.

Troy pootled through the tune, thinking all the while of what to play next. 'Smoke Gets in Your Eyes' won the silent, inner debate – the languid, devious arrangement Thelonious Monk had laid down some ten or so years before. It brought home to him, as it usually did, why he liked the piano as an instrument and, the obverse side, why he felt less than good at it. The piano was, he had read somewhere, three instruments in one – melodic, harmonic, percussive. A good pianist could exploit all three. Art Tatum, and no one matched Tatum in Troy's estimate, could exploit them all at the same time; 'A Foggy Day in London Town' spun under his fingers like a Catherine wheel. But then Tatum had six hands, which was what Troy had thought the first time he had heard him. Monk had only two, but where they would wander next was anybody's guess.

He watched the dinner party fragment into lesser parties. Fitz and Anna adored bridge and coaxed Pritch-Kemp and the painter woman into playing. He heard the clump of Clover's feet overhead, and the bass of her Dansette through the beams and boards as a pop record rumbled on. Tommy and Cocket stayed at the table drinking and flirting with Caro. Tara slumped in front of the fire with a magazine. Troy could not be certain whether this was petulance or not.

He played 'Night and Day' – slowly, far more slowly than Tatum would ever have played it; strictly for his own amusement, if that were the word for the memories it evoked, for a tune he could not separate from the dark nights of the war, a slow foxtrot in the face of death; strictly for himself – he doubted that anyone else was listening.

JOHN LAWTON

He helped himself to another glass of claret, slumped in an armchair, made the most of the flickering fire. Tara glanced up at him once, said, 'Bridge is such a bloody bore,' and turned over a page in her magazine. From the far room he could hear the cries that seemed to be turning bridge into happy families, heard Tommy Athelnay laughing like a jackass. He closed his eyes.

When he opened them he was not sure whether he had nodded off or not, but a tall man stood before the fire sloughing off a drizzle-spattered raincoat, and Tara had vanished.

Troy could scarcely believe his eyes, but he knew Anton Tereshkov at once. He had not seen him since 1956 – had met him only once, at an interminably dull reception given for Khrushchev at the Soviet Embassy, where he had been, as he put it, 'Comrade Khrushchev's man here' – but he was unmistakable. He looked, Troy now thought, rather like that new actor that was wowing women in the cinema aisles, the Scottish bloke, Connery, who played Ian Fleming's upper-crust, public school spy James Bond – and at that played him with an Edinburgh accent, full of deliciously wet and sibilant sounds. Connery was a former body-builder. Tereshkov could only have been in his mid- to late twenties seven years ago, but at thirty-three or so he had filled out in that same muscular way – all the weight not only above the waist, but high on the chest and shoulders, so that the rest of the body seemed to taper. And the eyebrows – Troy had been fascinated by Sean Connery's eyebrows, which seemed to trail away to infinity either side of his head and still not to vanish at all, very like Tereshkov's, one of which was now raised at Troy in quizzical greeting.

Before either of them could speak Tara returned clutching a bottle of brandy and a glass, and Fitz interrupted his bridge to pay a fleeting visit.

'Tony, you'll be late for your own funeral!'

So this was the Tony who'd upset the host so much by his absence?

'Still, no harm done, there's plenty left. Cold of course, you'll just have to help yourself.'

Fitz went back to his game. Tara kissed Tereshkov on the ear, poured him a brandy and whispered to him. Then she too left, kicking off her shoes and running for the stairs. Tereshkov took the empty chair.

'It's been a long time, Commander.'

'Quite,' said Troy. 'You've been at the embassy all this time?'

'No,' said Tereshkov. 'I've been home twice. This is my third tour of duty. I am getting rather fond of London.'

Troy found it easy to believe. He'd seen Moscow. Anywhere was better than Moscow.

Tereshkov swirled his brandy around, seeming to think, looking at Troy from under those remarkable eyebrows, and read his mind to the letter.

'I do hope you enjoyed Moscow. Comrade Khrushchev regrets deeply that he was not able to see you.'

The evening, so mixed in its pleasures until now, took a clear turn for the worse. Of course, the Russians knew, knew everything . . . but . . .

'I find it hard to believe he cares at all,' Troy said. 'Tell me, do you think the British know I was there?'

'No. I doubt they know a thing.'

'But you,' said Troy cautiously. 'You know everything?'

'Me? Oh yes. Everything.'

Tereshkov leant back from their confidential huddle, stretched and smiled, his eyes fixed on Troy's.

'Everything. And wasn't Vivi simply marvellous?'

Troy said nothing.

He sloped off to Fitz's study, found a book he'd always meant to read and retreated to the safety of the bedroom. Whatever game Fitz was playing, it wasn't bridge and it most certainly wasn't cricket.

§ 24

He sat up in bed reading Lawrence's *Seven Pillars of Wisdom* by the dim light of the bedside lamp, reading of El Aurens leading the Yahoo life. Trust Fitz to have a numbered first edition. Every couple of pages he flipped back to the opening line, wondering how much effort, how many revisions had gone into an opener that once read could never be forgotten – 'Some of the evil of my tale may have been inherent in our circumstances.'

His father had given him a copy for his eleventh birthday. A precious gift, a private edition. He had got scarcely further than the first page – a prose so difficult, a mind so extraordinary, beyond the grasp of a child – and had protested to his father, 'Not another book about the war, Dad?' 'No,' said his father, 'it is so much else besides.' The English had gone on reliving the war, much as they now did with the one after. He had never forgotten the line, and he had long pondered, through the numbing ritual of chapel at his school, the idea of an 'indifferent heaven', but he had never finished the book. He was forty-seven, forty-eight in August; perhaps he was ready for it now. He had lived half a lifetime under that same 'indifferent heaven'.

The door opened softly and Anna crept in. She pushed the door to with her backside and leant on it. He heard the click of the latch, the sharp intake of breath and counted the seconds until she spoke.

'I don't suppose you fancy a fuck, do you, Troy?'

He didn't. He wanted to read. He looked at her across the top of his book. She had her back pressed to the door, as though fearing someone might come in. Or that he might leave. One palm spread across the wood panel, one fist bunched in the candlewick fabric of her dressing-gown, pulling it closed over her bosom. They hadn't made love in years. Even then it had been a mistake.

'OK,' he said.

She let the dressing-gown fall behind her. Her nightie was hideous. A synthetic fabric in a floral pattern meant to put you off flowers, a horticultural contraceptive meant to put you off sex.

'It's practical,' Anna said. 'Warm. Besides you haven't seen me out of it yet.'

She reached for the hem and paused with it bunched at her thighs like a spent hula-hoop.

'Are you going to put the light out?'

'No.'

'On your own head be it.'

Her face disappeared into the nightie, accompanied by a vicious crackle of static.

'See! Big bum! Fat legs! Don't say I didn't warn you!'

Of course she had changed. In all the ways she was saying she had.

But he could not understand the fuss she was making. She dived beneath the sheets as though picked out by the glare of limelight not the forty watts of Troy's reading lamp. All he could see was the top of her head.

'Put it out!' said a voice muffled by the sheets.

He lay T.E. Lawrence face down on the bedside table and switched the lamp off. A quick yank of the curtain and they had traded electricity for moonlight. Anna surfaced. She had a beautiful face. Small and dark, with big black eyes not unlike his own. An un-English face. Looking up at him from her rabbit hole.

'It's been an age.'

'Where's Angus?' he asked.

'Are you trying to piss on it, Troy?'

Angus was Anna's husband. A colossal, red-headed drunk, former hero of the Battle of Britain, one-legged escapee from Colditz. Daring, decorated, drunk – he'd been in a tailspin for years.

'No. I just—'

'He can't get it up any more. The bastard's wasted the best years of my life. I'm forty-three. No kids, a marriage that comes and goes like the sun in Wimbledon week, a husband who's pissed every night – Oh God, Troy. I don't don't don't want to talk about Angus!'

She pulled the sheets over her head and vanished. From beneath them he heard her say, 'Gone walkabout again. Weeks ago.'

'Sorry.'

'If you're so concerned about the sod, go down the Streeb and Spigot and look for him in the sawdust—'

'Sorry, sorry, sorry.'

Her head popped up again.

'Oh fuck, Troy. Just touch me, will you?'

He ran his fingers through her hair and brought them to rest on one ear.

'Nooooot theeeeeere yooooou fooool!'

He had no idea four syllables could be stretched to such length.

A cold coming they had of it. He couldn't come. He was glad there wasn't a clock in the room, because it felt like hours of pounding meat and if it were he'd rather not know. He thought Anna might have come. He rather hoped she had. He hated to think that she was finding it the butchery that he was.

'I say, Troy. You couldn't . . . well . . . you couldn't just sort of well . . . come. Could you? It's just that I'm getting a bit . . . well . . . you know . . .'

Anna squirmed under him. Feeling cramp in one leg, she slipped it over his shoulder and stretched out the muscles in her thigh and calf. Just as Valentina Vassilievna Asimova had done. The last time he had fucked. Valentina Vassilievna Asimova. A freezing night in Moscow. Call me Vivi. A violet-eyed imp with maroon nipples, curled beneath him. Legs in the air. Hands roaming blindly across his face. And thinking of Valentina Vassilievna Asimova, he slipped Anna's other leg across his shoulder.

'Ooh,' she said.

And thinking of Valentina Vassilievna Asimova, he came.

Later, much later, Anna spoke. Her hand resting on his stomach, below the rise of his ribcage. Her fingers tracing circles in the sparse column of hair that stretched from balls to belly button.

'You're getting awfully thin, you know.'

'Nonsense.'

'How much do you weigh?'

''Bout nine and a half stone. Average for a bloke my size, I should think.'

'Have you weighed yourself lately?'

'Don't have to. Been the same weight since I was twenty or so.'

'I doubt it.'

'Eh?'

'Troy. You're more like eight and a half stone or maybe even less. Look.'

She pulled at the skin of his belly.

'There's nothing here. No adipose tissue. It's tight as a drum.'

'Quite. As it should be.'

'Troy. We're at the age when we put weight on, not lose it. Feel!'

She took his hand, tucked it into the roll of her spare tyre. It was like prodding marshmallow. After all her complaints about dimples, big bum and fat thighs, it didn't seem necessary. After a night of flesh-slapping intimacy, it didn't seem necessary.

'That's fat. It's normal at my age. Your age. I wish to God it weren't. Troy, you're a bag of bones.'

'Can we go to sleep now?'

'Are you sleeping OK?'

Fitz had asked much the same question. He did not much care to answer. He had one arm around her. He slipped it down her back to her waist. Pulled her in closer, and with the other hand made show of pulling the sheets and blankets higher and tighter. The infinitesimally small nest of intimacy. The bounded frontier of conjugality, far short of the ridge where the west commences, never gazed at the moon never lost their senses. The illusive voice that cried, 'Do, by all means, fence me in.'

He could not kid himself she'd fallen for it – but she had fallen asleep. He prised himself free of her, slipped on his dressing-gown and went in search of food. The main staircase led down to the hall. Further along, the back stairs led directly to the kitchen, in the west wing. The corridor was dark, only a shaft of light from one of the bedroom doors gave him anything to aim for. As he got nearer, the door swung on its hinges and the shaft became a flood. He stopped, scarcely believing what he saw. Tereshkov stood with his back to him. Not for him the coyness of lights out. Every light in the room burned as he fucked Tara Ffitch from behind. She knelt on the bed; he stood with his back straight and his knees bent, thrusting at her – and standing on the bed, legs astride her sister, head up, back arched, eyes closed, Caro shoved her cunt in his face and played her lips across his. This was believable.

What was not was the casual, the relaxed figure of Fitz, in an armchair, by a reading lamp, a cigar and a hefty glass of brandy on the go, watching – just watching. Head nodding gently, knees crossed, all but tapping his foot to the human rhythm as though the groans and moans of coitus – for real or for fake – were more a concert on the Third Programme than a Home Servicing.

Suddenly he turned and was speaking to Troy. Mouthing words silently that Troy could not make out. Logically he should be saying 'sod off', but he wasn't. He was beckoning. Troy entered, bent down to Fitz to hear what he was saying.

'Pull up a chair, old boy. Make yourself comfortable. Tara's in fine voice tonight.'

Troy fled.

§ 25

The *non sequitur* seemed to be an essential part of Fitz's *modus operandi*. They had circumnavigated Uphill Park straight after breakfast, down into Rye, wound their way through Peasmarsh, a drink at a country pub, and back up the steep flank of Uphill. It was a fair walk and Troy found himself acutely conscious as they came up the hill of the number of times Fitz had had to slacken off his pace or simply stop and wait for him. It was worth it. I may be out of shape, Troy thought, but it's worth it. To see England roll away to nothing beneath them and the English Channel glisten in the light of noon.

Breakfast had been just the two of them. Fitz not only baked his own bread, he had found time last autumn to make his own bitter orange marmalade. Anna slept; there was no sign of Tereshkov or the Ffitch twins; Cocket, Pritch-Kemp and the mad painter woman had gone and the thump thump of the Dansette told Troy where Clover was and what she was doing. He and Fitz had rehashed his garden, his garlic obsession, his miniature roses, and Troy had told him of the delights of keeping pigs. Each man in his own private world striving for the vocabulary that might make it less private. The more Troy saw of Fitz the more versatile the man seemed to be and the more he liked him. He was banging on about his Old English roses, 'so much nicer than the modern varieties, don't you think, the looseness, the spread of them, rather than that artificial, almost plastic density of the modern thingies?' Then, suddenly, as they crested the hill and as he was wont, Fitz tacked off.

'Of course,' he said, 'you know Tommy's trouble? No money.'

'How does he live?'

'He puts in a lot of time in the Lords, which gets him his daily allowance, and there's a couple of firms have him as a director just for the sake of having a title on the headed notepaper. But the reality is he's usually broke. I pay him rent of course. But it's bugger all. The place was little more than a ruin when he let me have it. I spend a damn sight more maintaining it than he can ever ask in rent.'

'How long has it been?'

'Eleven years. Near enough. I took the lease in the July of '52. I suppose you think it's a pretty rum set-up?'

Troy didn't know what he thought. He had found Fitz better company than he thought he might – far from flirting, he seemed oblivious to Troy's peculiar way of making his living, and he doubted very much whether he had bothered to tell anyone else. And Troy had skimmed across the surface of an encounter with Tereshkov without fall, though not without surprise. And in the last hour Fitz had had enough tact not mention their own brief encounter in the small hours of the morning. All in all it was turning out to be a pleasant break – Anna notwithstanding. He did not want to be made to comment on the 'rumness' of it all. So he said nothing.

They had reached the croquet pitch. It no longer was a croquet pitch. Troy had a good view of Tommy Athelnay's upturned backside, shod in heavy corduroy, as he serviced the contraptions that launched clay pigeons.

'Bugger,' said Fitz. 'He's got mad keen on this the last few weeks. He found all the clobber for it in a shed no one had looked in since before the war.'

'Not your sport?' Troy asked.

'I've no idea what my sport is. But it's the guns that I object to, the guns and the racket. I can't abide guns. I'd even diagnose myself and say I'm phobic about them.'

'How did you get through the war? I thought you were an ex-serviceman.'

'Oh, I did my bit. Didn't we all? North Africa, then France, with the Royal Army Medical Corps. But I never picked up a gun. They said it was obligatory for an officer to bear a side arm and know how to use it. If only to shoot our own side when they mutiny. "So court-martial me," I said. Of course, they didn't. You know what they did? They carved me one out of wood. I went right through the war carrying a wooden gun. The Army was like all authority. One colossal bluff. Taught me a valuable lesson. The best way to deal with the crassness of authority is simply to stand firm.'

Troy wondered how long he would have to go on listening to other people's 'war'. Everyone seemed to have it in them, though he was grateful to Fitz for the brevity and novelty of his narrative.

They came close. Anna was looking at an old shotgun as though to identify the object correctly were a parlour game – and Troy had had the feeling for the best part of two days that this whole venture was a form of parlour game. Tommy was loading clays, and a man in a white shirt, billowing in the breeze, impervious to the weather, stood in profile, pushing shells into a rather expensive-looking Purdey over-and-under.

It was a famous profile. The filmstar looks, the tall, elegant shape of Her Majesty's Minister of State at the Foreign Office, Conservative MP for Somewhere-or-Other, Tim Woodbridge.

Tommy saw them.

'You don't fancy a go do you, Freddie? I've a spare gun. Woodbridge brought his own.'

Troy looked at Fitz.

'Go ahead,' Fitz said. 'I'll go back to the lodge and get on with lunch. Come up in about half an hour.'

He left them to it.

Anna made the introductions, adding, 'You have something in common. You're both patients of mine.'

Troy would not have been surprised to find that that was all they had in common. If there had been a mental list of 'people I least expected/wanted to meet here/there/in any circumstances', Woodbridge would have been high on it.

He smiled a good, white-teeth smile and shook Troy's hand. 'I've crossed swords with your brother a few times in the House,' he said, aiming at non-partisan affability.

Such vanity, thought Troy. Rod always wiped the floor with the arrogant bugger.

Anna had never shot clays before. She missed four in a row. Troy put down his gun and proceeded to teach her.

'No,' said Troy. 'Lean into it. There's almost no recoil, so don't anticipate it. Put your weight on your leading foot.'

Anna shifted her balance, steadied the gun and called. A clay soared up from the left. She followed it, fired and missed.

'What did I do wrong?'

'Don't follow. Pick your window, wait for the clay to enter it.'

'What? Let it come to me?'

'Sort of. If you pick your window, you'll find you don't swing the barrel wildly. In fact you'll find you only need to put the gun to your shoulder to aim.'

The obvious example was at hand.

'Just watch Woodbridge for a minute.'

Woodbridge never missed. Every time he yelled 'pull' two clays took to the air and he blew both to smithereens without even seeming to aim. He'd be chatting amiably to Tommy, weight on his left hip, gun at waist level, and would still be talking as he casually shifted to the right foot, put the gun to his shoulder and fired both barrels seamlessly. It was like watching Fred Astaire in one of his old films, whacking away at golf balls in the middle of a dance routine, a rhythm so perfect he never missed, an aim so true he must have been the envy of half the golfers on earth.

Troy talked Anna through it. It struck him as pitifully simple. He had been the world's worst shot, and had paid for it with the loss of half a kidney to an assassin's bullet twenty years ago. Only a lucky shot had saved his life. Recovering – long, still summer days of immobility and pain, the distant hum of traffic, the puttering sound the V1 flying bombs and deadly, ear-splitting explosion of the V2 – he had determined that he would never again rely on luck where guns were concerned, and a few lessons had long since taught him how to hit the bull's-eye. As a copper he still disliked guns, and rarely felt the professional need of one, but he took a refresher course every year just the same.

Woodbridge was beginning to irritate him. After a couple of dozen more clays Anna had got the hang of it, and was hitting two in three. Woodbridge had not missed once. Woodbridge had pissed him off no end. Somehow Anna seemed to know this.

'He's rather flash, isn't he?'

'Just a bit,' said Troy. 'But he's using a far better gun than you.'

'Why do I have the feeling you're being kind to me? Why do I have the feeling the quality of his gun matters less than his skill or my lack of it?'

'Well fuck 'im,' muttered Troy, and picked up his gun.

Anna stepped back. Woodbridge was still blathering with Tommy.

'Load three,' said Troy.

A silence followed.

'Eh?' said Tommy.

'Three,' said Troy.

He had Woodbridge's attention now.

'There's only two barrels, Troy.' Anna whispered the obvious.

'Just stand over there and load up. When I throw you my gun, you throw me yours.'

Tommy synchronised the two traps and nodded to Troy.

'Pull!'

He took out the first two effortlessly, threw the gun to Anna, caught hers, shouldered it and caught the third clay far and low and heading for the treetops. He knew from the way it spun that he had only nicked the rim with the shot, but it broke, it shattered and it counted.

'Bugger me!' said Tommy Athelnay.

'Good Lord!' said Anna.

'Well done,' said Woodbridge. 'Fine shooting, but I'll wager twenty quid you can't do it again.'

Troy looked at him. He'd half expected him to try to top whatever he had done with a meretricious display of his own. He was smiling – smiling, but quite serious.

'Twenty quid?' said Troy a little peevishly.

'If you hit all three.'

'No,' said Troy.

'No?' said Woodbridge.

'A hundred,' said Troy.

'Bugger me,' said Tommy Athelnay again.

Woodbridge looked to Tommy, who shrugged a 'don't ask me', then he looked at Troy, grinned broadly and said, 'You're on.'

Troy and Anna swapped guns like jugglers trading Indian clubs in mid-air, but the third clay had flown wild and low. By the time Troy had it in his sights it was below the treetops and the barrel of his shotgun was nearing the horizontal. He took his finger from the trigger and lowered the gun, heard the distant crack as the clay hit the trees.

Woodbridge was behind him, standing where he could follow the clay from Troy's point of view.

'You know,' he said, and Troy turned to him, 'you could've hit that.'

'It was too low,' said Troy.

'No, honestly you could have hit it. You're really very good.'

'Too low,' said Troy. 'Well into the woods. Could be people

there for all we know. Aim too low and you never know who you might hit.'

He put a hand to his eyes, stared off into the woods for a moment. Nothing moved.

'I owe you a hundred.'

'Cheque'll do,' Woodbridge said in a 'don't mention it old chap' tone of voice and before Troy could say anything Tommy Athelnay chipped in with, 'I don't know about you lot, but I'm starving. Why don't we all toddle off and see what Fitz has rustled up?'

Woodbridge broke his Purdey, stuck it in the crook of one arm and held out the other to Anna.

'Mrs Pakenham?' he said, investing two words with several buckets of practised charm, and she took his arm and they strolled off towards the south lodge. After a dozen paces she turned to stick her tongue out at Troy.

'You know,' Tommy said, as he and Troy pulled the covers across the traps, 'he's not at all bad when you get to know him.'

'*When*,' said Troy emphasising his disbelief with an inflection lost on Tommy.

'Terribly sad man. Terribly sad. Never got over his wife's death.'

This was common knowledge. Sarah Woodbridge had died in a car crash along with their six-year-old daughter four years before. Woodbridge had been driving – the family's annual holiday in Italy. A twisting road south of Naples, a reckless lorry driver and the car had plunged off the road and down the hillside. Somehow Woodbridge had walked away from it. Much of the time it seemed as though he wished he hadn't. His grief had been public. The heart of the nation – an organ in which Troy found it hard to believe – had gone out to him. He had been the rising star of the Conservative Party, a man with, as the curriculum vitae demanded, a 'good war' behind him – he had roared across Europe to Lüneberg Heath in command of a tank battalion and picked up more medals, even, than Rod Troy – a safe Commons seat since the election of 1950; a wife heralded as an asset, the brightest, prettiest young wife of the man-in-the-making. Woodbridge was a future prime minister many said, certainly a future foreign secretary. He had been number two at the Foreign Office. But he had resigned at once. And no blandishments of Macmillan would make him reconsider. Last summer Macmillan had sacked half his cabinet in an effort to revive the standing of a flagging government and, if rumour were to be believed, had offered Woodbridge the post of Foreign Secretary. Woodbridge had declined, and at this juncture it might have seemed that it was all over for him – one can be a rising star for only so long before there comes a point at which one has either risen or one has not. And the role of bright young thing is best played by the young and, if at all possible in politics, the bright. It was all but impossible nearing fifty – and Woodbridge, Troy knew, was much the same age he was himself.

Then at Christmas he had suddenly relented. He had taken his old job back, Minister of State at the Foreign Office, number two to Lord Home – a man Troy thought not long for this politic world once Mac had sharpened his next case of knives – and since Alec Home sat in the Lords, Woodbridge was to all intents and purposes the Foreign Secretary for the Commons. It was a shrewd move. It gained him all the press attention, all the House attention he needed to renew his chances, but kept him out of the firing line. Anyone calling for heads to roll was unlikely to name him as the man who must go. The safe job was 'Number Two' – and it was in this capacity that he had turned up on Charlie in Beirut. Troy wondered in what capacity had he turned up on Tommy Athelnay and Paddy Fitz?

Right now this 'terribly sad man' was reducing Anna to hysterics. Troy and Tommy Athelnay walked to the lodge some thirty yards behind Woodbrige and Anna. Troy could not hear a word of what he was saying to her, all he could hear were her giggles. And then the gesture. The affectionate arm slipped from his to wrap itself around his waist, as his came around her shoulder. Last night Troy had humped her sore and not seen such affection from her. Only the rawness of her own need.

§ 26

He could not deny that Woodbridge was a charmer. He and Charlie were two of a kind – were it not for Charlie's decline into booze they'd even look alike – but by the end of the evening Troy had concluded that Woodbridge and Charlie deserved each other. Even a good-natured rogue could be a little wearing. He was glad when Woodbridge slipped an arm around the helplessly squiffy Tommy and ushered him home in an ostentatious chorus of 'goodnight ladies'. Glad to be able to call an end to the round of bonhomie and fall into bed. Preferably alone. There had been tense moments, moments when he could have sworn Woodbridge bit his tongue and did not say what he had it in mind to say – perhaps even moments when he might have unsaid what he had said. No matter, not a single one of the man's asinine sentences had stuck in Troy's memory. All in all, he concluded, it must have put a bit of a damper on the evening to find himself at Fitz's table with someone quite so closely associated with the Opposition as Troy. He watched the waving torch as the two of them picked their way across Uphill Park at midnight, and said goodnight to whoever remained. There was no sign of the women – Anna had gone up an hour before and he'd no idea what had become of the others. There was only Fitz, still at the dining table, a little the worse for drink, humming softly to himself. Troy left him to it.

He had drunk too much. A scraping dryness at the back of his throat kept him awake an hour or more. He slipped on his shirt and trousers – to bump into Anna in his dressing-gown seemed too much the invitation – and set off for the kitchen. Again he passed the Ffitch girls' bedroom door in the west wing. It was closed. But the same sighs and whispers of sexual intercourse crept through every crack in the panelling. It froze him mid-stride, foot hardly daring to press down upon a potentially groaning floorboard. He hesitated too long. The door opened, he had the merest glimpse of a man's plunging buttocks and the uplifted legs of a woman, her ankles crossed behind his back, and Caro Ffitch emerged, bare-arsed, a sheet clutched to her front, and dashed across the landing to the bathroom. She put a finger to her lips – a silent hush – but Troy wasn't saying anything. Was she hushing his thoughts?

Then she whispered, 'Can't watch tonight. Tim thinks that's a bit too kinky,' pecked him on the cheek and vanished into the loo.

It embarrassed him to think that she thought he was queuing at her bedroom door. Embarrassed him to think that she'd noticed him the night before. He'd rather hoped she hadn't. He should never have stood so much as a split second with Paddy Fitz watching their antics. It was too kinky for him too.

He found Fitz where he had left him, in the dining room, centre-table amid the debris, the thin man's Henry VIII, finishing the last of the wine − two and seven-eighths sheets to the wind.

'Going to get pissed. Care to join me?'

Wrong tense, Fitz.

He wandered the length of the table and gathered the bottles in a half-moon around him, sampling and mixing almost regardless of grape or vintage. It seemed to Troy that it was a sorry drunkenness he was aiming at − a sorry-for-himself piss-up.

'Woodbridge isn't playing the game,' he said miserably, seemingly à propos of nothing, as though he and Troy were picking up the threads of a ragged conversation.

'What', said Troy seizing the moment, 'is the game?'

'Peekaboo.'

'Peekaboo?'

'I peek and nobody says boo. Tell me, Freddie, are you familiar with the work of the Victorian pornographer known to posterity as "Walter"?'

Troy doubted he was familiar with the work of any pornographer. Was D. H. Lawrence a pornographer? Was Henry Miller?

'No.'

'Among other things − well to be honest among many things, the man wrote at inordinate length − he once asked of his readers, "Who among you, offered the chance to watch two people fuck, would not look?" The answer, as I'm sure you grasped, was implicit in the question. Who indeed would not look at a fucking couple given half a chance?'

Troy said nothing.

'It is . . . my pleasure, my pleasure above all others to watch people fuck. Twos or threes. I have no puritan principle about the sanctity of the couple. I have other pleasures, of course. Booze, my garden, music, booze and more booze. On occasion I too will fuck . . . but to watch . . . to watch is my particular delight.'

Fitz lingered over the 'ck' of fuck, the 'ic' of particular and slurred down to silence at the end of his sentence. Troy thought he might have ground to a drunken halt. Wistfully lost in contemplation of his perversion.

'And?' he prompted.

'Perfectly simple. House rules. We all watch. If we want to.'

Troy began to realise he'd had a lucky escape. Thank God Anna had begun by asking for separate rooms. Thank God for her indecision, her lack of foresight, her impulsive actions. If Fitz had thought they had . . . God knows?

'But . . . Woodbridge isn't playing the game. Bastard.'

'Has he ever?'

'Oh yes.'

Troy trod carefully through the next sentence.

'Perhaps . . . perhaps it's me?'

'Oh good Lord. Are we back to you being a copper already?'

'Looks like it. Look at it his way. Would you want the brother of an Opposition MP hanging about? Would you want a Scotland Yard detective watching you fuck? Would you want him knowing you fucked women half your age – and in pairs?'

This scarcely required thought, yet Fitz seemed to think about it.

'It's not illegal, is it?'

Good God, was the man really so naive?

'I mean . . . as you say . . . looking at it from his point of view . . . I think I'd be more bothered by a reporter than a copper.'

'If I were Woodbridge, I'd be bit more careful. If I were you, I'd be a bit more careful.'

Suddenly Fitz managed if not a sober moment – that was impossible – then a clear one. He leant in and spoke sharply to Troy.

'Am I to take this as a warning, Commander?'

'I wouldn't put it that way.'

'Am I to take it that your interest is professional?'

'Knock it off, Fitz. You know damn well what I meant.'

Yet, clearly, the man didn't.

'It's not illegal,' he said again. 'I'm doing nothin' illegal.'

'In your house, under your roof, as your guests, one of Her Majesty's foreign ministers shares mistresses with Khrushchev's embassy representative. A KGB colonel for crying out loud! Can you imagine how that would look?'

A dreadful question formed itself in Troy's mind.

'They do know about each other? Don't they?'

'Of course. They've been here together half a dozen times. Never in the same bed, but then they're both conservatives – if you see what I mean.'

'Did they know I'd be here?'

'Mmm . . . Tony did. Seemed quite pleased at the prospect of seeing you again. Tim didn't, but that's his fault. Never tells anyone when he's coming. Sort of turns up on Tommy – and he is, after all, Tommy's guest not mine – at the last minute. He must take us as he finds us. I rather think he thinks you think he went home when old Tommy did. But then, a good pussy always gets the better part of his discretion. A touch or a taste and the man's senses all but desert him. He'll probably slope off before dawn and assume you never knew. Silly sod.'

Fitz picked up three or four wine bottles and plonked them down like a studious chess player until he found one half empty – or, as he most certainly saw it, half full. A plain white label reading, 'Le Chambertin 1952'. He paused to drink more and when he had drunk returned to the ragged ends of conversation and picked up a different thread.

'You know, what you said about being bothered by reporters—'

'I didn't say that. You did.'

'Did I? Anyway, there has been one.'

'One what?'

'Reporter.'

'From which paper?'

'*Post.*'

'Did you get me here to tell me that?'

'No, of course not.'

'Do you know his name?'

It seemed as though Fitz might never speak. He downed another glass and sat staring at the empty vessel in his hand.

At last he said, no more than a surly, self-pitying mutter, the single word 'Troy'.

And Troy was quietly furious with him.

'So I'm not here because I'm a copper?'

'Whoever said you were?'

'I'm here because I'm a Troy.'

'Right now, o' man, I find myself wondering why we're either of us here. But as I recall Anna wanted your company and I'm rather partial to your way with the piano.'

He swayed drunkenly and braced himself, elbows on the table.
'Alex. Alex Troy. Cousin perhaps?'

It crossed Troy's mind not to answer and let him stew.

'Nephew. My brother Rod's son.'

'Whatever . . .' Fitz's arm swept the table dismissively and sent
two wine bottles spinning to the floor, '. . . whatever . . . he's been
. . . sniffing. Asking questions in London . . . and in the village.
Y'see, Woodbridge's constitunency − ye gods, that's a stinker to
pronounce when you're pissed − anyway the damn thing is in the
next county, in Kent, less than twenty miles away. It would have
been no problem for this nephew of yours to have followed him
here. Common knowledge he's a friend of Tommy's, and he's a
patient of Anna's, which ain't common knowledge, but I suppose he
has to work a few things out for himself.'

'And he knows about Woodbridge and the Ffitch girls?'

'Dunno.'

'Does he know about Tereshkov?'

Fitz seemed suddenly reluctant to part with the information.

'Does he?'

Still Fitz said nothing.

'And I suppose you'd like me to have a bit of a chat with Alex?
Convince him we're all chaps in a chaps' world and that some things
might be better left unsaid − or, should I say, unwritten?'

Fitz got to his feet, the pathetic beginnings of a drunken rage
visible in his reddening cheeks, but he'd drunk too much to pull it
off. Where there should have been temper there was only tantrum,
where he should have roared he could only squeak.

'Look, Troy. I don't need your help. I don't need your
protection. I did not get you here on false pretences. Any friend of
Anna . . . oh bugger . . . oh bugger . . . got to piss—'

He staggered off in the wrong direction, to the door of the sitting
room.

'Don't need *your* protection. Ace in the fucking hole. D'ye hear
me? Ace in the fffff . . . fffff . . . fffff . . .'

Troy followed and watched Fitz get as far as the large Knole sofa
and pass out. He nudged him and called his name, but the man was
already snoring. He went back through the dining room to the
kitchen, in search of the cold drink that had got him up in the first
place.

Clover Browne stood in the open fridge door, swigging from a coke bottle.

'Help yourself,' she said and handed him the bottle.

She was bizarrely dressed for two in the morning – fur coat and wellington boots. Either she had not bothered to take off her make-up for the night or she'd just put it back on.

'Love the dressing-gown,' said Troy.

'It's not a dressing-gown. I'm off out.'

'Out?'

'Just a walk over the park. Wanna come?'

Troy looked through the open doorway, past the table, into the sitting room. All he could see were Fitz's feet sticking out.

'I wouldn't worry about Fitz if I were you. Worst that'll happen is he'll wet 'imself. You gonna come or what?'

'Why not?' said Troy, and the part of his mind that thought came up with a dozen reasons why not, and the part of his mind that worked his legs and his groin did not hear them.

Crossing the open space of the croquet lawn a bird shrieked. Clover grabbed his arm with both hands.

'Wossat?' she said.

'A little owl,' said Troy. 'Several little owls in fact. They'll be out hunting this time of night.'

'How little's little? Like a sparrer?'

'No. More like a pigeon. A fat pigeon.'

'That's what I hate about the bleedin' countryside. All those things in the night that you can never see, and all those creepy crawlies that you can. I been comin' 'ere since last summer and I still can't get used to it.'

'City girl are you?'

'Leave it out,' she said.

They entered the ruins of Uphill House. Inigo Jones favoured high ceilings at the best of times, and with most of the upper floors missing, the view up two floors to the sky was like stepping into a cathedral. The chimney stacks towered over them – stars motionless in heaven, a cloudless, clear night sky.

She led Troy to the far side of the ruin, treading across the broken shards of what Troy was sure had once been Jones's high-pitched roof. They came within sight of the north lodge. Lights glowed upstairs and down. Someone on the first floor facing was fond of fresh air and had left a window wide open to the night.

Clover whipped off her coat. She was naked but for knickers.

'Hang that up for me.'

A large rusty nail protruded from the wall. He looped the coat over it and turned back to her. She braced herself with one hand on his shoulder and kicked off her wellies. The knickers followed. A thumb in the elastic to ease them off her hips, then she stepped neatly out of them.

Naked.

He stared.

Her flesh came up in goose pimples.

Stiff little nipples.

Blonde bush like whore frost.

'You was wonderin' weren't you?'

'Was I?'

'"Is she a real blonde?"'

'Never crossed my mind.'

'Well — I am. Not like the twins, they're not blondes. Out of a bleedin' bottle.'

'They're not twins either.'

'Come again?'

'I've been around twins all my life. I grew up with twin sisters. I'd say there's the best part of a year between Tara and Caro.'

'Lyin' tarts. Now — me coat pockets. Hand me the shoes and the mask.'

Troy rooted in the pockets of the fur coat, and found a pair of high heels and an operetta mask. The mask covered her cheeks and her nose, framed the mouth, buried the eyes in emphatic darkness, gave wings to her ears.

'Right. Gotta dash or the old sod'll be wonderin' where I got to. Tap tap at the bleedin' window — "'Eathcliff it's me" — silly old sod.'

'Lucky Tommy,' he said.

'Tommy?' she said, and the inflexion baffled him, question or statement? 'I should cocoa. Right, give us a kiss for luck.'

This embarrassed him more than her nakedness. The thought that he had to move; even the mere stoop and turn of the head the gesture required held up a mirror to his foolish face. He felt he must be the colour of beetroot. He pecked her on the cheek as dutifully as he could.

'Nah. Not like that.'

She slipped her arms around his neck, slapped her lips on his, pressed her hips into his groin and snogged him – an overlong, overly wet juvenile kiss in best back-row-of-the-cinema tradition. He came up instantly. The worst, the hardest of unbidden erections. It was impossible she would not notice. She pulled back, one hand reached down and squeezed his cock.

'Now, now,' she said. 'Plenty of time for that later.'

Troy felt as though he had been scalded. He felt as he thought those fat, seedy, middle-aged men must feel in Soho strip joints, he felt as Charlie must have felt with his last whore, ashamedly grubby, foolish to the point of stupidity, feeling the chasm that yawned between intelligence and cupidity. He ran all the way back. With any luck he'd never see that woman again.

§ 27

Anna was in his bed. Her back to him, the lights out. Asleep, he hoped. By the time he had slipped silently between the sheets she had turned. Her hand slid across his chest, brushed one nipple and came to rest on the flat of his belly. Had she felt his heartbeat, the unwilling suspension of his breathing? The hand slid on, wrapped around his cock. It came instantly to life. She rose up without a word, slid onto it, braced her hands upon his shoulders and began to prise herself on him, off him, on him.

She was smiling sweetly. To herself, not at him. Her eyes were closed. He put a hand out to her breasts. She slapped it back, her eyes flashed once and closed again. Then, unbidden as all his responses, the image of Clover Browne darted into his mind and he came.

Anna stopped. Waited while the gush spent itself inside her. Her eyes opened. He thought she'd be annoyed, but she was smiling still.

She leant forward, nipples touching his chest, hands buried in the pillow either side of his head, one finger tracing the outline of his ear.

'Good Lord. What's got into you?'

The nature of guilt eluded him. At the best or worst of times he felt so little of it that its occasional descent to his unwilling shoulders took him by surprise. He had fucked Anna twice, come twice, whilst thinking of other women. The unfamiliar pattern of guilt flickered across his mind – a magic lantern light thrown upon a crumpled scrim, the shifting shadow of the demon faint as Nosferatu – and disturbed his sleep. He did not know what to make of it. When he awoke it had gone, gone as though it had never been.

§ 28

Scotland Yard was a complex structure. A complex structure rendered *complicated* by the legacy of recently retired Commissioner of the Metropolitan Police Sir Stanley Onions, KCMG, OBE. Onions had been Troy's champion. Against the odds, and scarcely without wavering, but Troy's champion all the same.

In 1944 Troy had blotted his copybook – been caught in possession of an illegal weapon, still working on a case Onions had told him to drop, and damn near killed in what Onions had called 'a shoot-out at the OK corral.' He had delayed Troy's promotion by the best part of a year. In 1956 he had accepted an undated letter of resignation from Troy and simply sat on it. It covered Onions for things Troy had done that he had thought it better not to know about. All he heard were rumours and Troy doubted very much whether Onions ever believed Troy was connected with the disappearance of Inspector Cobb – but if Stan had really had an inkling Troy had killed Cobb, nothing on earth would have saved his skin. But rumour persisted without ever seeming to gel. And Onions' reaction to uncongealed rumour had been to promote Troy. As the cliché had it, he put his money where his mouth was.

He promoted and he promoted and he promoted. By the summer of
1961 Troy had risen to Commander of Criminal Investigation, in all
but name Scotland Yard's chief detective. Under him were all the
arms of the CID responsible for investigation of crime. And there
they came unstuck.

'What are you up to in Soho?' Stan had asked one day late in
1961.

'I need coppers. I can't afford to waste them on the trivial.'

'Trivial?'

'Crimes without victims.'

'Oh aye?'

'Do you know how many men we waste chasing whores around
Soho?'

'According to Superintendent Wiggins, not enough.'

'Ah. He's been to see you?'

'Did you expect him to take it lying down? You've stripped his
squad by three-quarters.'

'I've a crime wave on my hands. Burglaries are up twenty per cent
on last year and there's an organised gang wreaking havoc in sub-
post offices all across the south of England. I need every man I can
get. The whores aren't walking the streets any more, and nobody
whistles, "Psst, wanna buy a dirty postcard?" It's all indoors now.
Things have changed. The Wolfenden Report changed everything.
I'm not going to waste coppers policing what consenting adults do
behind closed doors.'

'Jesus Christ! You're not serious?'

'Anyone who wants a French model on the third floor in Meard
Street can just walk up. I don't care.'

'Freddie, for Christ's sake – the job of the Vice Squad is to stamp
out vice!'

'Fine. Are we going to nick schoolboys for wanking? The notion
you can stamp out vice is fatuous; you cannot police the
unpoliceable. I've left Wiggins enough men to cope with the pimps
and the wide boys and with the girls if they get so bold as to solicit
on the street. Beyond that I propose better uses for the lazy buggers
he calls his Vice Squad. They can try detecting real crime for a
change, instead of sitting on their backsides in the coffee bars leafing
through tit-and-bum magazines and taking backhanders off ponces!'

Onions had taken the squad away from him. Troy was glad. Vice was a pain in the arse.

It was a simple matter of reorganisation. Onions ran the Met. Under him was a deputy commissioner; under him a bevy of assistant commissioners, each responsible for a section of the Met: A, the uniformed coppers; B, transport; D, a hotchpotch of recruiting, training and communication, and C, crime. C section was what the average man in the street thought of as Scotland Yard. The Criminal Investigation Department. Traditionally C had three branches: the Metropolitan Police Laboratory under its Director, Ladislaw Kolan-kiewicz, MD, MSc, ARCSc, DIC, FRIC, MBE, a mad Pole of remarkably, foully fractured English; Special Branch under Deputy Commander Graham Tattershall MM, CBE; and everything else, all the way from fingerprints, via robbery and murder, to liaison with the metropolitan divisions, under Commander Frederick Troy, a man without title and likely to remain that way. Neither the Branch nor the labs answered to Troy, but directly to C section's Assistant Commissioner, Albert Scudamore. To Scudamore's direct responsi-bilities Onions had added Vice, under its own deputy commander. This division of labour had stayed in place when Onions and Scudamore had retired in the autumn of 1962. Troy did not want Vice back and did not ask for it.

In the long-awaited spring of 1963, the Commissioner was Sir Wilfrid Coyn, KCMG, the Assistant Commisioner for C, Daniel Quint – and between the two the vacant post of Deputy Commissioner. Coyn was a rustic, recently Chief Constable of Wiltshire and regarded by all and sundry as a stop-gap, a chair-filler aged sixty-three, warming the seat until the powers that be made up their minds who should really run the Yard. Rank deceived no one. Quint had been brought in at the same time as Coyn – a tough big-city copper, fresh out of Birmingham – to offer the toughness which Coyn, for all his administrative expertise, might be held to lack. No one much valued the role or rank of the various assistant commissioners of A, B or D. Anyone could direct traffic or order spare parts for wirelesses. When Coyn retired in eighteen months, the race was between Troy and Quint.

It did not make for a happy Yard. It did not make for happy coppers.

Troy missed Onions dearly. He had come to loathe meetings with

Quint, to tolerate those with Coyn and if at all possible to avoid meetings with both of them at once. He had his own team, officers who were 'his' as he had been Onions'. Superintendent Jack Wildeve, who ran the Murder Squad in C9, as Troy had done in his day. And Troy's two assistants: Det. Sgt Edwin Clark, a man who had refused promotion on the grounds that it might take him from behind his desk and might just force him to take a little exercise; a man who spoke five languages; a man who could finish *The Times* crossword in twenty minutes; a man from whom Scotland Yard had no secrets – Swift Eddie was the perfect rogue, the perfect spy, Troy's eyes and ears – sooner or later every memo in the Yard passed by his gaze. And Det. Sgt Mary McDiarmuid, pretty much the opposite of Clark, a cynical, straightforward Scotswoman who spoke only one language, but spoke it to perfection – pragmatism.

On the Tuesday after Easter at Uphill Troy emerged from a meeting with Quint and Coyn feeling bloody.

'Your doctor's been calling you,' said Mary McDiarmuid.

Clark had never called Troy anything but 'sir'. Off duty, behind closed doors, it made no difference, Clark invariably called him 'sir'. Mary McDiarmuid was scrupulous about rank in front of Troy's superiors, but in their absence frequently called him nothing – and on off duty did what Anna did and called him 'Troy'. It was Anna trying to reach him now. What could the woman want that she didn't want at six thirty yesterday evening when he had dropped her off at the conjugal hell in Bassington Street, Marylebone, that was her marital home with Angus, and inevitably dubbed by him 'Unbearable Bassington Street'?

'She didn't say. Just wanted you to call her.'

'At the surgery?'

'Yep.'

Troy called.

'Are you through for the day?' Anna asked.

'Just about. Why?'

'You couldn't pop in, could you? I'd like you to come in.'

'What?'

'Just for a check-up.'

'There's nothing wrong with me.'

'What about your cough?'

'What cough?'

'You were coughing half the night on Sunday. You were coughing all through the evening we spent in Notting Hill.

'No . . . I wasn't.

'Honestly, Troy, you were. Look, just come in. A routine check-up. Let me take a professional look at you.'

'Routine?'

'Of course. It's probably nothing, but we should make sure. Just a few tests.'

Afterwards, looking back, he could not see what had possessed him to believe her. So often as a young detective he had invited people to the Yard on a matter that was 'just routine' and held onto them all the way to the dock in the Old Bailey. Only Anna, he kept telling himself, would ever have got him to do it.

§ 29

Troy found himself confusing the categories. Something he presumed Anna did not do. A necessary, simple trick of the mind – and, he flattered himself, she did not fuck all her patients. All the same, he wondered. What was she discovering about his body in the course of these few minutes with the cold end of her stethoscope and the tap tap tapping of her fingertips across his ribs that she had not learnt in the best part of fourteen hours in the sack together?

'Don't put your shirt back on. I'd quite like a second opinion.'

'What?'

'Fitz. I'd just like Fitz to take a look at you.'

They were partners. All the same, she'd never asked Fitz to examine him before. In the odd narratives of her working life she'd not once mentioned asking Fitz to look at one of her patients. Anna simply did not do this.

Fitz came in, in his full Harley Street private practice outfit. Black jacket, striped trousers, fancy waistcoat. His fingers were cool, and unnaturally long. A fine manicure had left his almond-shaped fingernails with just a hint of an edge. Their touch brought Troy up in goose pimples. He could not find that simple trick of the mind that would enable him to separate the doctor – the good doctor, Fitz was clearly that – from the sensualist, the extraordinary sensualist, he knew him to be. They did not feel like a man's hands, and he found himself wondering – what sexual use, what precise sexual use – he could guess the general area – did such long fingernails have on the male of the species? And it had to be sexual, didn't it? It wasn't just affectation or decoration, was it? The little fingernail of his left hand was longer than all the others, like a tiny barb, pressing its moonsliver mark onto his skin.

Fitz listened to Troy's inner grumblings at half a dozen points on his chest and back with a stethoscope, put him through the same routine of deep breathing that Anna had, and finally said, 'We'll need an X-ray. You don't mind an X-ray, do you, Freddie? Clear things up once and for all.'

'I have a job to do, Fitz. I really must get back to the Yard.'

'We can do it right here. We're state of the art. Can't develop, of course, but if you call back in a couple of days . . . honestly, Freddie, it won't take long.'

Troy gave in. Afterwards, finally allowed to dress, he could feel her eyes on him.

'I suppose you got me down to Uphill just so he could look me over,' Troy joked, and from the averting of her eyes, the faint reddening of her cheeks, knew it was not a joke, that the two of them had set him up.

§ 30

Two days later Troy was returning to London from an overnight stay at his Hertfordshire home. He had turned the Bentley off Shaftesbury Avenue, down Monmouth Street and was rounding Seven Dials into the lower reach of Monmouth Street, the short stretch before it blends seamlessly into Upper St Martin's Lane. He felt dizzy, his vision blurred almost to blindness, and only the sheer familiarity of the manoeuvre enabled him to pull out of the circle and leave Seven Dials for Monmouth Street. Then he knew he could not see at all, and his fingers tingled and his breath failed and his hands left the wheel. He awoke with blood streaming from a cut on his forehead to find the car half buried in a shopfront. His windscreen scattered in his lap like diamonds. Leathery incunabula strewn across the bonnet like dead bats. He had demolished the premises of a second-hand bookseller.

In the Charing Cross hospital they X-rayed his skull, pronounced him sound, stuck an Elastoplast on his forehead and sent for his physician.

She did not say, 'I told you so.'

She said, 'There's no time to lose. We have the X-rays of your chest. I'd like you to see a specialist tomorrow.'

'What's wrong?' Troy asked.

'You weigh eight stone, you black out and crash your car. That's what's wrong.'

'I meant – what is the nature and name of my ailment?'

'Just see the specialist will you, Troy. Do it for me. My surgery, ten o'clock tomorrow morning.'

§ 31

A good-looking young woman. Taciturn, dark – thick black hair piled high on her head in an out-of-the-way-for-work, no-nonsense fashion. She asked him his full name, as though she did not have such information from Anna, and wrote down what he told her on a form of many dashes and lines. She listened to his heart and chest through a stethoscope. Then she showed him the examination table, told him to strip off and pulled the screen around him.

It was thorough handwork – they flew over him, fluttering like birdwings, kneading him like catspaws, pinching at him like the mandibles of insects. Compared to hers, Anna and Fitz's once-over seemed almost perfunctory. Her hands read his body like braille.

JOHN LAWTON

'That was quite a war you had, Mr Troy.'

She touched the raised seam of the scar on his right thigh. One that had never seen a physician. The shallow tear of a .22 bullet. Hand-stitched from a sewing kit in a hotel bedroom. Ragged like a torn hem. Detective Inspector Cobb's parting shot in 1956.

'I wasn't in the war.'

She raised an eyebrow at this. She knew bullet wounds when she saw them. The tiny ridge above the hairline, left by a Browning 9mm. Detective Inspector Cobb, again. The Webley .38 scar on his right arm. A captain of His Majesty's Household Cavalry, 1940. The punctured slash in his side where they had dug a Colt .45 slug from his left kidney and cut out half the kidney with it. Diana Brack, 1944.

'I mean I wasn't in the forces. I'm a policeman. Have been for nearly thirty years.'

The hands moved to his side, pressing into him, above the appendix he had lost at seventeen, the one on top of the other.

'So you're quite high up then?' she said, and he could not be at all certain how idle a question it was.

'Inspector?' she mused. 'Chief Inspector?'

'Commander,' he said.

It meant nothing to her. There were so few commanders.

'Have you considered some other line of work, Commander Troy? This one looks like the death of a thousand cuts. I've seen the odd body as battered as yours, but their owners had survived the Burma Railway or the Battle of the Bulge.'

Troy said nothing.

'OK. You can get dressed now.'

He emerged from behind the screen, tying the knot in his tie. Something he had never managed to do without thinking about it. She was hunched over one of her forms, filling it in at the speed of light, talking to him without looking at him.

'How old are you, Commander Troy?'

The drawn-out vowels of a careless routine.

'Forty-seven, I'll be forty-eight in August.'

'Are you a married man?'

Troy knew where this was leading.

'Just get to the point, doctor.'

She looked up. 'I'm sorry?'

'Forget your form. The statistics don't matter a damn. I have no dependants, and plenty of money. Just spit it out.'

She put down her ballpoint pen. The slightest pause for breath, then she did exactly what he asked, and it still shocked him.

'You have tuberculosis, Commander Troy.'

Troy said nothing.

He was furious. She must have known. Anna must have known that day she phoned him at the Yard and asked him to 'pop' in. Everything since had been check and double-check, but she had to have known. He'd give her hell for doing this to him.

The doctor misread his blankness, his manic self-absorption, for disbelief.

'I can show you on the X-ray if you like.'

'No,' he said. 'There's no need for that. How long?'

'How long have you got? Mr Troy, it needn't be fatal. These days it hardly ever is—'

'I meant. How long have I had it?'

'Hard to say. Tuberculosis can lie dormant for ages. I've known some strains to appear fifteen years after the presumed infection. I doubt that's the case here. You've a specific and readily identifiable strain. Quite rare. There've been very few cases in Britain, but in Eastern Europe they call it Khrushchev Flu. Of course it isn't flu — nothing to do with flu. I'd say you've been incubating it for about six months or so, perhaps less, eight at the most.'

Moscow. Fuckit Moscow. He'd caught the damn thing in Moscow. Fuck Moscow. Fuck Charlie. Fuck Anna.

'Six months?'

'Give or take, yes.'

'So it's early days?'

She fumbled.

'I . . . er . . .'

'I mean. I don't have it bad.'

'Oh dear. I'm so sorry. No. It's not early days. I'm rather afraid you do have rather a bad case. Mr Troy, you're going to have to prepare yourself. You're going to be off work for a long time.'

'How long? A month?'

She said nothing.

'Six weeks?'
She said nothing.
'Three months?'
She shook her head vigorously enough for all three questions at once.
'We can't play this game. A year, maybe more, but at least a year.'
Troy said nothing.

§ 32

Anna drove. All the way home. Troy did not speak to her.

§ 33

'We'll find you the right place. I mean, some of them can be very good. And of course we'll get you the best that money can buy.'
'You don't get it, do you?'
'Get what?'
'You can't stick me in some private sanatorium up a Swiss mountain – this isn't Thomas Mann – you can't stick me anywhere outside the National Health system. It's an election year. How do you think it's going to look for Rod if I buy private medicine and jump the queue?'
'Bugger, hadn't thought of that.'
'We're looking at a public ward in some dreadful public sanatorium in the home fucking counties!'
'Some of *them* can be very good too.'
'There is another way.'
'What?'

'I take every bit of leave I have due to me, then you sign me off sick with the flu or something, I hole up here, take the damn drugs or whatever, and get back to work as soon as I'm over the worst of it.'

'Troy, it's an infectious disease. They put you in a sanatorium for the good of the rest of us, not just your own. It's a notifiable disease. I have to tell the Yard what you have. Surely you understand? I'm your physician. It's my duty. If there's a second case it would be criminal to have deceived them.'

'You don't have to send that form in.'

'I do, really I do.'

'If you do that I'll be off work for a year! By the time I get back, if I get back—'

'You just don't get it, do you, Troy?'

'Get what?'

'I've already done it. I had to do it.'

§ 34

Troy had never heard of Dedham, nor of the wide valley of the Stour in which it sat, the boundary river of two English counties, Essex and Suffolk. Then one of his sisters muttered something about Constable, and Gainsborough, and Munnings, and he knew what it meant. That stretch, one of those stretches of England associated with whichever painter or writer had stuck it down on canvas or paper. It was 'Constable Country'; it was, Troy thought, a deplorable notion, as unspeakable as 'Wessex'. It was where Anna found an agreeable National Health sanatorium for the tubercular – The Glebe, Dedham.

Rod drove him down the following Wednesday, at the wheel of Troy's Bentley – a new windscreen, radiator, bumper and right headlamp. Troy stared silently out of the window at the dull Essex countryside, wondering if there'd ever be a glimpse of a hill. There was one, just the one, and that in the last half-mile before Rod swung the Bentley off the road and into the gravelled drive of a small Regency mansion, creamy brick and broad bow windows, just south of the village. The house sat on the side of the hill – at least he'd have a bit of a view, quite possibly the only one for miles.

Rod turned off the ignition. Looked at Troy.

'OK?' he said.

'Let's get it over with,' said Troy, and it struck him at once how stupid a remark it was. He'd no idea when it would be over. It could take for ever.

By the time Rod had played big brother and opened the passenger door for him, a blue-and-white uniformed nurse had appeared on the doorstep. Rod set down Troy's case on the threshold and before Troy could reach for it she picked it up. Between the two of them they were determined to make him feel like a cripple.

'Don't come in,' said Troy.

'I wasn't going to.'

And Troy remembered how much Rod disliked hospitals, and how often he had visited them – every time Troy got into a scrape and needed bailing out. And a sanatorium was just another word for a hospital, wasn't it? He'd put Rod through a lot in his time.

'Ready?' said Nurse.

She led. He followed. He felt a bit like a dog.

'It's Frederick?' she asked.

And he dearly wished there were any other answer to that question but the 'yes' he now uttered. Why, with all the lexicon of Russian and English names to choose from, had they made him a 'Frederick'?

Across a large hallway, an elaborately tiled floor, an elegant staircase, the lines ruined by fire doors in reinforced steel-mesh glass, cutting the smooth, rounded trajectory of Regency into the sharp angles of modernity. Through the fire doors into what she called 'our day room'.

Three men sat around a rickety green-baize card table. The furrowed brows and forced smiles of the serious pontoon player.

The woman stood, almost to attention, and coughed. It was obviously meant as politesse. In a sanatorium, thought Troy, it must be the most common background noise. It was. They ignored it. She harrumphed at them in the most hammy style.

'Nasty cough you got there, Nursie,' said one of the men without even glancing up.

'We have a new face on the ward. This is Frederick,' she said.

They stopped the hand and all turned to look at him.

'We're all Christian names here,' she said and ran through their names like the naming of parts.

'This is our Alfie.'

Thin – but weren't we all? – tall, blond and curly – the wicked smile of a natural wide boy.

'This our Geoffrey.'

Less thin, almost chubby of cheek – nearer his discharge than the rest? – receding hairline, five o'clock shadow, about the same age as Troy.

'And this our Eric.'

Gaunt – at death's door, surely? – but the man was upright, and judging from the pile of sixpences and threepenny bits in front of him ahead in the game of pontoon if not in the game of life.

'Now,' said Nurse, 'where's our general?'

Troy winced inwardly at the maternal possessives, weighed the contradiction between 'we're all Christian names here' and the prospect of a man called 'general'.

'Up in the ward,' the one called Alfie volunteered, 'with 'is ear'ole glued to the radio.'

Nurse took Troy's suitcase and led off up the broad, curving staircase to the ward in one of the larger first-floor bedrooms, blathering at him without ever turning to see if he was listening. He wasn't. Phrases such as 'walks of life', as in 'we have people from all walks of life here', which she had just used, usually sent him off into anger's oblivion. He hated the phrase. It was the sort of phrase men from his background used if they'd just been stuck at signals for half an hour on the slow train from Frisby-on-the-Wreke, been forced by impecunity – passed off in anecdote as a democratic impulse – to share a third-class compartment with a pig farmer from a Leicestershire village – perhaps his pig too – and a uniformed RAF mechanic on his way back to base – smoking Park Drive – and found, wonder of wonders, that they both spoke English. Delivery of the tale necessitated the use of said phrase, implying, as it did, that this was the great leap forward for democracy, furthered by his private decision that the incident had, at a stroke, abolished the residues of the English class system. They all had different tasks in life – 'allotted' here was optional – but they were all the same underneath, even if some of them earned less than a fifth of one's own income, and even if one wouldn't actually want to encounter any of them at the dinner table. Great Unwashed to Salt of the Earth within the short span of but a single cliché. Or was it three clichés?

An old man lay in a reclining chair, his ear, if not glued, then certainly very close to the loudspeaker of an old wooden-case wireless. To call it a radio offered it no dignity; it hummed on valves rather than crackled with transistors. He was bald but for two tufts of white hair, roughly pinpointing each cerebellum, and matched by the symmetrical tufts of a white moustache. His eyes were closed, his face a mask of absorption in whatever he was listening to. It sounded to Troy like a public event of some sort – respectful, hushed Dimblebyish tones dimbledoodling out across the airwaves, the echoes of a church.

'General,' Nurse said rather too loudly.

The old man opened his eyes, lifted his head.

'We have a new boy.'

Troy was rapidly growing to hate the woman.

'This is Frederick, from London.'

He felt like a contestant on *Take Your Pick* or *Double Your Money*. He definitely hated this hag.

The old man stood, a newspaper slipped from his knees to the floor in a smooth glissando. He seemed to Troy to wipe a tear from his eye.

'Do forgive me. I always get like this at weddings. Sentimental old fool.'

Troy looked blankly at him.

'Princess Alexandra and whatsisname . . . Angus Ogilvy.'

'Oh,' said Troy.

'On the wireless. So much nicer than the television, don't you think?'

He stuck out his hand. 'Catesby, Arthur Catesby.'

'Troy,' said Troy, hoping the tag would stick and free him from his Frederick.

'Well,' said Nurse. 'You two seem to be getting along swimmingly. I must be getting back to work. You're the bed by the window, Frederick.'

She strode off, sensible shoes squeaking across the linoleum.

'Infuriating woman,' Catesby said. 'You don't mind if I . . .'

'Not at all,' said Troy, who, left to his own devices, would not have disturbed him in the first place. He'd no idea it was Princess Alexandra's wedding day – which showed how utterly consuming his ill-health had become in a single week – but he well remembered her mother's wedding, but for whom there would not be an entire generation of English women christened Marina. And if Troy had this man's measure aright, the sentimental tears were not for this generation of royal weddings but the last.

He set his suitcase down on the bed. Sat next to it. Looked around. It was not an unpleasant room. It still smacked of the private house it had once been. Elaborate cornices still intact around the ceiling. A grey, silver-and-rust-iron-rippled marble fireplace, crudely battened over with pegboard. Elm floorboards a foot and a half across. Almost homely. A ward with only five beds was privacy compared to some of the London hospitals. All the same he hated Nurse, and he was going to hate this too. He knew it.

§ 35

Troy took his first bath, before the unnaturally early bedtime. The sky had scarcely darkened, the moon peeped between the hurrying clouds, and the room was a vast echoing chamber, almost as high as it was long, and his knees stuck up like white-bone mountains in the lagoon of cooling bathwater. He climbed out and stood dripping onto an inch-thick cork mat. Stood clutching the towel, facing a full-length mirror bolted to the wall. Then it hit him. Everything he had not seen or had refused to see came home to him. He saw himself with Anna's eyes. And he did not recognise himself. He was not tall – under height in fact for the job of copper, and only enlisted by a waiving of the rules – but even so, eight stones in weight made him look little short of Belsen-like, half-starved and half-dead. He let the towel fall. He could count every rib in his chest. His stomach was not just flat, it was concave. His thighs looked like sticks, his cock, exaggerated by the contrast, made him seem almost priapic – the Errol Flynn of the Eastern Counties. Why did one not lose weight in proportion; why did one not lose it everywhere; why not a thin cock; why not thin toes? He looked at his toes – they were thin. He stepped on the scales. Seven stone nine pounds.

He revised the image. Swapped Germany for Russia. Tuberculosis – the Victorian word had been consumption, the preferred disease of so many novelists. Who was it in what Dostoevsky novel who died slowly of consumption, and made such a song and dance about it? *The Idiot*, it was some . . . dammit . . . some idiot in *The Idiot*. Troy would not make a song and dance. But he would waste away just the same.

§ 36

He sank towards a bottomless silence. Days passed in a waking dream of idleness and exhaustion. He got to know the others, even as he ceased to know himself.

He knew the Alfies of this world. For that matter he knew the Geoffs too, pompous men – little men, his sisters would have said, dripping scorn – born to be local councillors, aldermen, justices of the peace, and to run, as Geoff did in Brentwood – a briar patch of which he seemed inordinately proud – a car showroom. Not for him the tat of the second-hand trade, but plate-glass windows and shiny new Wolseleys and Rileys and a turntable on which to revolve them. Geoff was a bore and best avoided. Alfie was a bore too, but a bore of the type that at least held professional interest for Troy. Alfie was the sort of young man – twenty-five or six years old – who had gone from job to job for the last ten years, ever since getting out of secondary modern school, working his little fiddles. Man on the make, but with so little imagination of just how much one could make. He wasn't a villain – and Troy doubted very much whether the application of the term would strike him as anything but insult –

but he was a rogue. The sort of rogue who could do no job without 'somefink on the side, knowotahmean?' And it ran, as a rule, to nothing bolder or smarter than one hand in the till. The ever-cheerful, ever-chattering, smirking cockney wide boy. Troy knew Alfie. He'd seen Alfie all his working life.

He took to the conservatory on the southern side of the house. It was warm in the mornings, and since he could not sleep, it suited him well enough to sit there before breakfast and through the morning that crawled towards noon. If it overheated, he could simply throw open the doors, with a view across the rhododendrons – Himalayan weeds his mother had always called them, and would not have them in her garden at Mimram – out over the meadow and its leisurely herd of milk cows. He could watch the dazzling play of dragonflies across the pond in the late westerly sun. And when the sun had set a small army of grumbling toads would emerge from the shrubbery, toad-strutting like miniature bulldogs, to share the pond and debate the night with their elegant, long-legged, vociferous cousins, the frogs. All the while a short-eared owl would watch from the lower branches of a birch, wondering which was which and which was edible.

Few others seemed to care for the place. Catesby would occasionally come in and chat, or if Troy was particularly uncommunicative he would read, unbidden and aloud, from the national newspapers, as though Troy were in some way part of his duty. Alfie would pass through, but like the best of bores would always move on in minutes in search of new audiences, and the nurses soon tired of asking Troy how he was. He did not answer. He had fallen down a glass well.

§ 37

The lid came off Britain exactly as Charlie said it would, and Troy saw it like watching the world through a blown bubble. Finer than glass, streaked like a rainbow, shape-shifting, distorting, bursting to the touch only to find another blown, floating down around him, a renewable, permanent membrane between him and the world.

§ 38

The first he knew of it was Catesby reading to him. But for this, it often struck him later, he would not have known for days – weeks, even. How little of it would have broken through the bubble?

'What do you suppose this means? Here, in the Henry Esmond column on the back page.'

The old man was holding a copy of the *Sunday Post* folded over a couple of times to make it manageable.

'"What larks I hear at Uphill Park. As the black Zim roars out of one entrance, the black Humber growls in another." Now what on earth is that about?'

Troy knew. 'Henry Esmond' was the *Post*'s William Hickey. Gossip, unattributable gossip, and anyone with a story he wouldn't dare put his name to was free to use it. This was undoubtedly the work of Troy's nephew Alex, staying just the right side of the libel laws by not naming the individuals frequenting Uphill. Only the makes of car. But, cabinet ministers drove Humbers, and few, if any, outside the Soviet Embassy staff drove Zims . . . just the odd British defector in Moscow.

It was an old technique. It might just work. Flush out your bird by daring the other newspapers to run with what they have. Let the competition beat for you. Then run with the whole damn shooting match and claim prior publication as your defence.

Sure enough, the following day Catesby appeared with the London *Argus*, still trying to make two and two make four.

'Blowed if I understand it. Like a damned crossword puzzle. "Dr Patrick Fitzpatrick's weekend parties at Uphill Park have of late been graced by guests of some distinction. Indeed it is reported that East has met West, and that Dr Fitzpatrick's flatmates, the former fashion models Tara and Caroline Ffitch, are among the most obliging of hostesses to be found along the prime meridian. Oh lucky man who passes a weekend at country matters in this delightful Sussex retreat, long home to Viscount Athelnay." D'ye think it's in code?'

Troy did not as a rule read gossip columns and for a moment he wondered why Catesby did, then he realised that he read everything in the paper – cover to cover. It was his way of getting by. This was crude. 'Country matters' was the crudest of Shakespearian puns – too crude to need explanation, he thought. And if it did, he would not offer it.

Three days later the tabloids all ran with photographs of the Ffitch girls. None of them mentioned Tereshkov or Woodbridge. Oh, lucky Woodbridge. At the weekend, the *Sunday Times* ran a profile of 'Harley Street socialite – Patrick Fitzpatrick'. The *Observer* interviewed him on the subject of his garlic beds. He must, Troy thought, have been drunk or desperate. Or perhaps this was Fitz's way of containing the damage – give them a photo-opportunity and an interview on something absolutely harmless? But nothing Fitz could say now was harmless. They'd got him in their sights, and he was a fool not to see it.

Then, after ten days of unsubtle innuendo, Alex took his finger from the dyke and let the flood burst.

Catesby read it to Troy. He felt like a bad actor making far too much use of the man in the prompt box.

'"Passing Dreyfus Mews the other day who should I find popping out from number 21 but that man-about-the-corridors-of-power Tim W★★dbr★dge MP, Minister of State at the F★r★ign Office. Stopping to tie my shoelace I saw his red Mini Minor leave the mews at the northern end, and deciding that public safety necessitated I retie the other lace, I found myself still there when a dark blue Morgan rolled in the south end and that man-about-the-KGB Anton Tereshkov rang on the bell to be greeted with hugs and kisses by the delightful Ffitch sisters, the house guests of that man-about-everywhere Patrick Fitzpatrick. I sincerely hope the ladies do not catch cold, for it seemed to me that they were somewhat scantily clad for the time of year."'

Catesby did not, for the first time, ask what it meant. It was all too obvious.

'There'll be questions,' he said. 'At least there'd better be.'

'Could I see?' said Troy.

Alex had swapped the symbolic vehicles for the real ones. Woodbridge did drive an outrageously red Mini, and Tereshkov had parked his expensive, un-Soviet, British-built Morgan next to Troy's Bentley at Uphill. All the same, the precision of the encounter – in one end of the mews and out the other – seemed just that, symbolic, as it had in the first snippet, and it left Troy wondering about the extent of the real evidence. He wondered at the blanking out of five vowels. It did not keep the *Post* the right side of libel and he doubted that they expected it to do so. It was a red rag to a bull. It showed exactly the direction they expected to take issue – it would not be Fitz or the sisters, and if it were Tereshkov it would be the first time in history that an agent of a foreign power had issued a writ for libel.

'D'ye suppose he'll sue?' Catesby asked.

'He'll have no choice. They want him to.'

'They want him to sue!'

'They've got proof. Cast-iron proof, I should think. They clearly have much more than they're saying. They've blanked his name to make him think they're being coy for safety's sake. In reality they want him to step outside the Commons and enter a realm where he has no immunity. If he sues he's a fool. The most he can hope for is that it doesn't get raised in the Commons. And I don't think he stands a cat in hell's chance of not being asked about it. Then the best he can do is say he does not have the time or the inclination to answer every piece of scurrilous gossip and whichever honourable member has raised it ought to have better uses for his time and so on.'

'I see. What do you think he'll do?'

'I think he'll deny it. And if he does, protocol demands he sue – last refuge of honour after all – and then the *Post* will produce God knows what, photographs, letters, and they've got him.'

'It wasn't like this when I was young.'

'Yes it was,' said Troy. 'You just didn't know it.'

It took less than a day. That evening, Jack Dorking, Woodbridge's opposite number on the Labour benches, rose to ask if he would deny an affair with the mistress of a Soviet agent. It was more subtly put – one of those 'Is the House aware?' openers, when all of Britain was aware – and addressed not to Woodbridge but to the Home Secretary, Nicholas Travis, in his capacity as the man who should investigate should the gossip prove unfounded and a slur upon 'a member of this House'. It defied logic, but it worked. Woodbridge got together with half a dozen cronies and denied it to the House the following day.

Just before lunch on the day after that, Troy and Catesby met as usual. Catesby shuffled into the conservatory, the morning papers under his arm and read out the 'Woodbridge Statement Mark III'.

"'I wish to deny any rumour or allegation of any impropriety between myself and Miss Tara Ffitch or her sister Caroline. I have met the misses Ffitch, they are house guests of Dr Fitzpatrick of Harley Street. Dr Fitzpatrick maintains a weekend cottage on the estate of Lord Athelnay. Lord Athelnay and I are old friends – we have known one another since the war – indeed there are many in this House who would claim such friendship with Lord Athelnay. I have been a frequent recipient of his hospitality at Uphill, and I have met the misses Ffitch both at Lord Athelnay's lodge and at the cottage of Dr Fitzpatrick. I can only recall two meetings with Mr Tereshkov. The first at a reception given by the Soviet Embassy for the visit of Mr Khrushchev in 1956, and the second at a reception given by the Prime Minister some eighteen months ago for the Russian cosmonaut Major Gagarin. I have accordingly instructed my solicitor to begin proceedings against the *Sunday Post* for libel.'

'Well?' said Catesby.

'He's damned,' said Troy. 'Damned for a tart.'

§ 39

The last person he wanted to see usually turned out to be whoever came to see him – a moveable feast. The *real* last person he wanted to see finally arrived. Anna, less than a week after Woodbridge's statement.

Troy stood. He had the memory of her power over him, her life sentence. To sit seemed to give away too much. He let her kiss him and ask after his health like a friend and pronounce on his health like a physician.

JOHN LAWTON

'You're looking better. That's a very good sign. Bit of colour in your cheeks.'

This to Troy sounded as medically precise as reading the weather in seaweed and bunions. He had no idea whether he was better or not − a regime that froze him with fresh air and stabbed him with hypodermics left him little sense of his own wellbeing. He stood in the conservatory window. Half looking at her, half not.

'And you,' he said, not caring what she said as long as she did not talk about him. 'What about you?'

She slipped one hand into the other, twisted the rings on her fingers like changing the combination on a safe.

'I hardly know where to begin. There's been so much happened. Tommy Athelnay died, you know.'

'No. I didn't know.'

Catesby read obituaries, he was sure, but never out loud, never to him. Some things there were that never crossed the generations.

'Heart. Died last Thursday. Poor old Tommy. I think this whole damn thing finally did for him. And then there's Fitz, of course. They're hounding him, you know.'

'The press, well . . . he's asked for that. He should never have agreed to talk to them in the first place.'

'No. Not the press. The police.'

'Which police. The Yard?'

'Chap called Blood. A chief inspector. In the Vice Squad.'

'I know Blood. He's in Special Branch, not Vice.'

'He told me Vice.'

'You?'

'He's been talking to most of Fitz's friends. Harassing them would be a better word. He came to see me in Harley Street. He asked me about Fitz and Tony. I said I was not at liberty to discuss the relationship between my partner and one of his patients. I was well aware that appealing to the conventions of confidentiality was wasted on him, so I said something that perhaps I shouldn't. I said, "On the other hand Tim Woodbridge is a patient of mine and so's Commander Troy − perhaps you'd care to discuss their medical histories instead." Did the trick though − shut 'im up. He'd nothing more to say after that. I didn't hear from him again. He pestered a lot of Fitz's patients, and I'm not at all sure how he worked out that they were Fitz's patients. But he left mine alone and he left me alone. I'm sorry, I used your name to scare him off.'

'Doesn't matter.'

'But he won't be scared off. He's wrecking Fitz's practice just trying to get something on him. He'd talked to old Tommy. Tommy might be alive now if he hadn't.'

She came up behind Troy. One hand upon his shoulder. Trying to break the illusion of indifference he tried so fiercely to maintain.

'Look, I've never asked this before, and I wouldn't be asking now if it weren't such a bloody mess. Fitz has done nothing wrong. You told me so yourself. Couldn't you get that through to this Blood chap? He's looking for a scapegoat. Couldn't you tell him not to?'

'I don't run the Branch. It's wholly separate.'

'He's Vice. Really he told me he was Vice.'

'I don't run that either.'

'I thought Vice was C section?'

'It is, but Onions took it away from me not long before he retired. It's had its own deputy commander for quite a while.'

'But you could have a word, all the same.'

'No I couldn't.'

'Troy, they're persecuting Fitz!'

'If he's done nothing wrong, he's nothing to fear.'

'How many times have you told me the opposite? That the law is an ass, that justice isn't blind, it's blind drunk?'

'There is nothing I can do.'

'I mean it's not as if—'

'I know what you mean and I cannot do it. I'm on sick leave. I am stripped of all responsibility. Those bastards at the Yard are cockahoop, because they think I'll never make it back. I'm on sick leave, I'm out of it. I'm not at the Yard, I'm here, waiting for death. I'm here where you put me. I have no more power! It's all used up! I'm on the sick list where you put me!'

'Couldn't you just—'

Troy took her face between his hands, his fingers spread to the temple, the palms flat across her cheeks.

'Do you know what you've done to me? Do you know?'

He squeezed. She did not move. He knew he was hurting her and he held her in his grip, and as the tears rippled silently down her cheeks, he said again, 'Do you know what you've done to me? Do you know?'

She was looking straight into his eyes, hers dark and glistening, his black and cold. She did not move, did not flinch, did not try to escape.

Her tears were hot beneath his hands, and still he held and still she cried. He let her go, wondering if he had not crushed the spirit out of her, and might she not fall at his feet, but she rubbed one eye with her knuckles, picked up her handbag and left without looking back.

§ 40

At five that afternoon Catesby summoned him to the wireless and the BBC news. Woodbridge had written to the Prime Minister, owned up to everything he had not long since denied, apologised and resigned.

In the morning the *Herald* led with Tereshkov's return home – 'WHERE IS TERESHKOV?' asked the headline, and then answered itself with the Soviet Embassy's statement that they would not say where he was, except that he was no longer in England – whisked away under notion of the diplomatic bag.

'D'ye suppose they really put them in bags?' asked Catesby.

'Nothing would surprise me, bags, boxes or posted home airmail,' Troy replied.

He'd no idea what the Russians had done with him, welcomed him back as a hero who'd embarrassed the British or as a candidate for the salt mines who'd embarrassed them – all he was certain of was that he'd seen the last of Tereshkov.

For days afterwards – or was it weeks, surely it was weeks? – the same half-dozen photographs of the Ffitch girls were to be found in a hundred newspapers, hawked like dirty postcards, again and again and again: Caro caught leaving her hairdresser's; a little black dress flash photo of the two of them accompanied by Hooray Henries reprinted from an old *Tatler*; a blurry grey snapshot of Tara topless on a Greek island ('topless' was a new world neologism – inseparable in Troy's mind from the idea of dismemberment). He could not make out whether they were regarded as national heroines or national villains. All he was certain of was the adjective: national, national whatever they were, the women now – indisputably – public property.

§ 41

Without the precision of the phrase the national obsession, at least the national press obsession, became one of 'who fucks who'. Such precision as there was was habitually blurred by being disguised as moral enquiry. And where it was not so disguised it became a round robin . . . the bishop fucked the duchess; the duchess blew the cabinet minister; the cabinet minister licked the tart; the tart shagged the spy; the spy swung both ways and in his turn rogered the bishop, while the dog in his wisdom slept with his backside to the wall – and only the poor duke got none. If this did not spur the nation to outrage, the moral enquiry did. Scarcely a Sunday passed without one of the newspapers running with an enquiry into the morals of 'our young people' – sex and kicks, the degeneracy of popular music, the excesses of teenage fashion – the sin of short skirts, tight trousers and winkle-pickers . . . and so on *ad infinitum*.

On occasion Catesby would read such a piece to Troy, more for its comic value than its pretence of sociological analysis. Catesby was rueful, disbelieving. Geoff was the one to rise to outrage – he seemed endlessly fuelled by it. One such piece, entitled 'Do you know where your daughter is tonight?', appeared the day Geoff was due to be discharged. They had all gathered in the conservatory to see him off, the invalids in their dressing-gowns, Geoff, predictably, in the uniform of post-war man, the blue, shiny-buttoned blazer with military crest. Catesby read the piece out as they waited for Geoff's wife to turn up. He smiled, his eyes twinkled, and when he was through said simply, 'Piffle.'

Alfie leant over and looked at the photo the paper offered of a young lady of the night – some actress paid to pose as a teenage whore.

'I quite fancy her meself,' he said.

Geoff steamed.

'Kids,' he was saying. 'Kids. What does she think she looks like? Painted hussy.'

More than most aspects of the world they watched from their confinement, the deeds and mores of teenagers provoked Geoff to a rage Troy could only see as proprietorial. It was his world, at least it had been until they'd stuck him in The Glebe, and it would be again once he got out and got to grips with the world he did not know and turned it back to the one he did. Blinkers would be useful. So would a bit of bluster.

'I should think she looks like what she wants to look like,' said Alfie.

'She should know better. Where was she brought up?'

Troy thought Alfie might laugh in his face. He hoped he wouldn't. Geoff would go from red to purple – it could not be good for him.

'Wotsit matter where she was brought up?'

'If you're brought up in a good home, by decent people—'

'Bollocks,' said Alfie, as he was wont.

'There's no talking to you, there's no talking to you. "Bollocks", that's your answer to everything.'

'If she was brought up in a good home – by which, Geoff, you mean a posh one – she'd be learnin' to do wot the bleedin' 'ell she likes. 'Cos that's what the toffs do. You think Woodbridge gave a toss, you think this Fitzpatrick Lloke gives a monkey's bum what you think of 'im? You think all them lucky sods in all them orgies at Uphill give a toss?'

Geoff stopped at the puce phase of coloration unto rage, and tried for a calm sentence. 'That's got nothing to do with it.'

'It's got everything to do with it. Wot's sauce for the goose—'

'Alfie, there's no comparison. You cannot compare the actions of a cabinet minister and a feckless teenager!'

'Wot about a feckless cabinet minister then?'

Geoff sighed with exasperation. He had spent his life being led by the Woodbridges, voting for the Woodbridges. He had marched behind the Woodbridges of England into battle and ballot.

Catesby filled the silence. 'Alfie has a point you know. One does look to the Woodbridges of this world to set an example. Woodbridge has let us all down as badly as any tearaway — worse if you think what his responsibilities were.'

Out in the driveway Mrs Geoff honked on the horn and cut short the argument.

Geoff shook a manly hand with them all. Told Troy that if ever he wanted a new Riley he knew where to come. Then he picked up his bag and stepped away from his brush with death, and his brief encounter with the social melting pot — back to his own 'walk of life', as Nurse might have put it.

'Would you adamaneve it,' Alfie said. 'A born bleedin' NCO. He'll be a fool till the day he dies. Do you know he was on the brink of tellin' me he fought in two world wars for the likes of that young tart?'

This was exaggeration. Geoff was far too young for this, no more than fifty, but it was a cliché of the times.

Catesby, however, *had* fought in two world wars.

'How so?' he said.

Troy dropped out of the debate. He had never really joined in, listened with half an ear. They argued across him as though he wasn't there. Indeed he wasn't. Man down glass well, blown in a bubble. Invisible.

'When I was in the army,' Catesby was saying, his most frequent opening gambit, 'it was understood, as so many things were, that one could not do certain things. Rank had its responsibilities. It still does. Noblesse oblige and—'

'Knob what?' said Alfie.

'Noblesse oblige.'

'What like French? Like foreign?'

'Do let me finish, Alfie, then you might understand what I'm saying. It was expected of us. It was our duty. We could not do what our men could not do. Even more, we could not do what they did do. Avenues of behaviour open to the common man were not open to officers.'

'S'at wot you fink I am, the common man?'

'I did not say that.'

'S'wot you fink, though, innit?'

'Alfie, the social standing of you or I is hardly germane to the argument.'

'Yes it bleedin' well is!'

And Troy could hear Alfie momentarily suspend his wide-boy act long enough to strike home, and he had not asked what the old man meant by germane.

'All you're saying is Woodbridge was a toff, and it's up to the toffs to set an example to the 'oi polloi. Well, what I say is, speakin' for yer actual 'oi polloi, is who the bleedin' 'ell needs it?'

'The nation needs it,' Catesby said calmly, seriously, with a creeping hint of exasperation in his voice to tell Alfie that it was not a trifling matter, it was on a par with love of country and loyalty to the crown. 'It is up to some of us to set an example to the rest. And when I was a soldier it was understood that the example one set ran the length of one's chain of command. An officer cannot ask of the man what he cannot give, cannot do, himself.'

'Wot's *not* sauce for the goose, eh?'

'If you like,' said Catesby, much as Troy might have done himself.

'I don't like,' said Alfie. 'Bollocks to it.'

'Well – if this is the level the argument has sunk to—'

'And levels ain't got nuffink to do wiv it neither. Wot I say is this. We don't need your bleedin' example. That went out years ago. Tell it to Mrs Noah. From hereon in it's every man for himself. If Woodbridge wants a bit of fanny, best of British luck to 'im. It's got nothing to do with chains of command, it's got nothing to do with the likes of you setting a good example to the likes of me. And you know why? 'Cos if I had to wait on the likes of you for the likes of me to get a bit of fanny, I'd be waiting till doomsday, and me right 'and'd be worn to the bone. The world ain't what it was when you was young, general. Fings 'ave changed, fings ain't never gonna be the way they was again, not ever—'

'Don't tell me,' Catesby said softly, invoking a West End musical hit of recent years. 'Fings ain't wot they used to be?'

Troy would not have thought the man had the wit in him.

'Too bloody right they ain't,' Alfie replied. 'And a bloody good thing too!'

Troy thought Woodbridge an unworthy subject of a national division. But clearly he was. He exercised the national conscience, put on, scratched and tore off the national hair shirt upon a daily basis.

'What do you suppose he takes me for?' said Catesby, when Alfie had gone.

Troy said nothing. To say anything at all might be to compound an insult. Better by far to let the old man answer his own question.

'A fogy, d'ye think?'

'I should think to a man of Alfie's age we're both fogies.'

'How old would you say he was?'

'Twenty-five.'

'Too young for the war?' Catesby asked pointlessly.

'War baby. Born before it. Brought up in the worst of it. An evacuee, I shouldn't wonder.'

'And we're fogies?'

Catesby seemed to kick this one around a while, then said, 'He's wrong, y'know. I'm out of touch, but then, I'm sixty-five, and not as out of touch as some. He's a right to dismiss us. A right to his rebellion. I made mine in my day.'

And he led off along a line of thought Troy had not expected.

'When I was sixteen the First War started. I lied about my age. Volunteered for the Public Schools Battalion, the Sixteenth Middlesex, Kitchener's New Army, when the posters went up. Kitchener needed me – but not half as much as I needed him. Got me out of everything. Home, school, the prospect of university in a year's time. It looked . . . it looked like blessed relief. And I wasn't completely green, I wasn't one of the ones who though it would all be over by Christmas. And I hope I wasn't one of those who prayed it wouldn't end before I saw action. I saw action. One day of it. July 1st, 1916.'

Troy knew the date. Every schoolboy of his generation did. He was less than a year old then. He'd learnt it in school and before school. The Somme.

'I was Second Lieutenant Catesby. Seventeen pretending to be twenty. Took a couple of rounds from a German machine gun in my thigh two minutes after I went over the top. No time to be a hero. Shattered the bone in three places. Couple of our blokes got me back into the trench. One of them said, "It's a blighty wound, sir. You'll be going home." Then he stuck his head up too far and got it shot to pieces. I spent over a year recovering. Learning how to walk again. Transferred to the regular Army. I couldn't face the thought of the old regiment. None of them – at least none I knew – had survived. By the time I got back to the front it was 1917. The

Americans joined us and the next year we began pushing the Boche back. Did me time. Picked up me gongs. Counted up the dead friends and saw most of my illusions vanish. But it served its purpose, my personal, my selfish purpose. Got me away from all that bound me. Created new ties that I thought would bind me for ever.

'I was out by the summer of 1919. Married in 1923. First child in '24. Very odd time. Very awkward time. Perhaps you remember it? You must have been a nipper yourself. Perhaps you remember blokes like me. I couldn't settle to anything. Couldn't settle to anything sedentary. I was a fool. Took my inheritance, what there was of it, went into chicken farming and went broke. Time was you talked to any chap with an accent like mine and a threadbare suit doing the rounds, looking for work, and he'd tried chicken farming. But I'd another string to my bow. I'd been on the reserve list since 1919. So, in 1931, at the age of thirty-three, I applied to rejoin the army. I'd've signed on as a private just to be able to earn a wage. I was lucky. My old regiment took me back at my old rank – captain. Old pals' act? Who knows? Perhaps someone saw the day coming when we'd need an army again. Perhaps they didn't? Things moved so slowly. The thirties raced by. Every year seemed to throw up a new crisis – the Rhineland, Austria, Munich, Czechoslovakia. But Britain seemed to crawl along – wallowed in its own misery, filled up with refugees, and failed to listen to what they were saying. I was only a major when the Second War broke out in 1939. I was a brigadier when it finished. I'd seen Dunkirk, El Alamein, Salerno, D-Day and Germany. I picked up another lot of gongs, and this time I came through without a mark on me. At least no physical mark.

'In the winter of '43 I spent a few weeks training in Egypt – on a base not far from Alexandria – and I saw for myself the work of the Army Bureau of Current Affairs. Now, I knew our blokes had guts. This might have been the first time I knew they had brains. I'd seen them fight and perhaps I finally learnt what they were fighting for. It wasn't enough to invoke simple patriotism. The British working man was fighting for a better Britain. And this time he wasn't going to be conned the way my generation had been with piffle about homes fit for heroes. The Bureau held a mock election. Every other party but Labour was annihilated. I knew then what would happen in '45 – or whenever the war ended. I'd always been a Liberal myself. But I voted Labour that day, and I have voted Labour in every election since. And I've done so because I believe in the right of the individual to have his share in the nation's wealth. The wealth he has created. And to share in it without going through what I went through. What they went through. We shouldn't have to prove our courage in battle, we prove it every day. Every day we get up and go to work and try to put food in our children's mouths and a roof over their heads. That's heroism enough. Chicken farming was heroism enough. Half my generation died on the battlefields of Flanders, and the rest seemed to go under in the crises of the twenties and thirties. That was heroism enough. I suppose young Alfie would find that hard to grasp.'

There was silence while Catesby found a way to round off his tale, fought his way back along the ribbon of his narrative.

'I was promoted again in '48. Major-general. Retired with that rank in '57. People call me general. Only natural after fifteen years I should answer to it. I am "general". Hugely symbolic to Alfie, I shouldn't wonder. I'll answer to general. I'll be blowed if I'll answer to fogey.'

He got up. Put down his newspaper on the chair. He seemed to Troy to be succumbing to memory, to the emotionalism of the sentimental man, much as he had been at the moment they had met. He had set his memory in motion like clockwork and for all Troy knew was reliving things he would rather not relive.

'Excuse me a moment, won't you.'

He shuffled off. Troy had taken to the old man. But he'd never in a thousand years understand such emotions.

§ 42

He found he could not bear television. The inmates, he could think of them no other way, clustered round a ten-inch television watching Britain unravel with every passing news bulletin, crowded the common room, where the one-eyed beast sat, on Saturdays to watch late-night satire in the form of *That Was The Week That Was* –

which Troy had watched in unblinking silence. The man with the silly haircut and the Uriah Heep voice seemed to be the funniest man alive. As far as Troy was concerned he might just as well have been talking Martian.

It was the nature of the complaint. The nature of consumption to consume, to waste mind as well as muscle. And in part it was the nature of the man, as child is father to the man, as the boy Troy had succumbed to one damned illness after another in the teens and twenties of the century, each had taken him this way. Each had lost him to the world. Each world had had to be slowly rediscovered.

He stuck with newspapers, began reading for himself, followed Alex's trail through what was now firmly dubbed the 'Tereshkov Affair' – Woodbridge had been lucky again, it could so easily have been the 'Woodbridge Affair' – and stuck with the wireless, tuning into the Home Service and the Third, and making occasional forays to the Light Programme. And on occasion the bubble would burst and he could see clearly, only to form again its milky sheen. So often he felt apathetic. More often just pathetic. Anger focused him wonderfully, but then it always had. Anger pulled him back from the brink. He could have gone so quietly into goodnight had it not been for the high tide of his own anger, and few things roused more anger than his visitors. Few visitors roused more anger than Rod. Rod turned up just in time to let Troy grasp at the lifeline. Another day, one more morning down the well, one more afternoon in the bubble and he might have been lost for ever.

Complacent in victory, pulling at the ragged sleeve of government, Rod crowed.

'So Woodbridge lied,' Troy said. 'Big deal.'

'One does not lie to the House of Commons, Freddie. It is a matter of principle. I cannot tell you how strongly that principle is regarded in the House.'

'Don't be so bloody preposterous. Woodbridge lied to the Commons in '57 when he cleared Charlie. Most of the voting public might have believed him. But the House didn't. Did you?'

'That's . . . that's different.'

'How so? Because no one called him a liar? Because he lied by common – or do I mean Commons – consent? Or is it all OK as long as he didn't get caught?'

'It's different. Believe me it's different.'

'What is this? "Trust me, I'm a politician"? Rod, you gave Charlie a job on *American Week* knowing damn well he was a spy.'

'He had been cleared by a government minister.'

'That's your excuse? Your "get out of jail free card"? A government minister says something you know to be untrue, and that sanctions you to endorse the untruth publicly? Woodbridge lied, blatantly, and no one gave a damn because it suited them not to give a damn. I do not see how a profession that lies for a living can be so concerned about one more lie.'

'It is perhaps a lie too far.'

'And they should have better things to do than debate the sex lives of their own people! Who fucks who is none of their damn business.'

'It's not the sex. Well not just the sex. There's the security issue.'

'Look me in the eye and tell me you really believe Tim Woodbridge whispered state secrets to the Ffitch girls, one of whom was probably gagging on his cock, the other probably sitting on his face. Into what organ did he whisper? Then tell me the Ffitches rogered Anton Tereshkov, and in between blowing him, fucking him, and I know not what, found the time to mutter the same secret somethings to him!'

'My God, Freddie, you can be crude when you want to.'

'Rod. Look me in the eye and tell me you really believe there was a security risk!'

Troy leant in and fixed him, an eye wide. Rod squared off, big brother to little brother. Bickering adolescents once more. And he could not say it. The posture was ridiculous. Troy began to corpse. He could feel himself cracking up with an uncontrollable fit of giggling.

At last Rod spoke, and Troy knew from the tone that he'd won.

'Tell me,' he began, tacking away from the storm. 'Have you heard the latest one about Harold Wilson that's doing the rounds?'

Troy shook his head. There was a playful, wicked flicker around Rod's lips.

'How can you tell when he's lying?'

'Dunno,' said Troy.

'His lips move.'

Rod grinned. Troy cracked. Rod laughed till he cried.

§ 43

His visitors now came if not in droves then in serial caravan as though The Glebe stood like some Arabian oasis between the wadis. Troy could scarcely believe the effort and the frequency with which denizens of the metropolis sought him out. He decided that he was probably the basis of a good day out. Motor down to Suffolk, spot of lunch on the way, look in on poor old Freddie.

Two days after Rod he could scarce believe the visitor at all. A mirage at the oasis. Catesby leant into the conservatory and yelled with his customary bonhomie, 'Another one for you, old chap,' and Troy turned from his copy of the *Herald* to see Woodbridge standing awkwardly in the old window between the house and the conservatory, clutching a couple of books and a pineapple. It was one of the miracles of the modern age, mass communication – television, the rise of easy-to-read tabloid newspapers full of pictures, all but devoid of text – and yet, it seemed, Catesby and the nurse who had ushered Woodbridge in still failed to recognise the man.

He waited till they'd gone, then said, 'I hope you don't mind my dropping in?'

'Not at all,' said Troy. 'Bored out of my brain. But let's ditch the pretence. One doesn't just drop in to this neck of the woods, one seeks it out.'

Woodbridge turned around a wicker armchair to face Troy, and sat in it. Set the pineapple to sit between them on the low table, uneasily, like an unexploded, oversized hand grenade.

'It's bloody murder. You know I would never have imagined it could be so bad. A lifetime in politics and I thought I was ready for the worst. I suppose some naive node in my brain actually thought the gentlemen of the press needed sleep occasionally. Couldn't be more wrong. They've camped on my doorstep, and I do mean literally – thermos flasks, sleeping bags, like the queue for the first day of Harrods' sale – camped there day and night for weeks now. Only the police will move them, and since I stepped down I might as well be a fugitive Nazi as far as the local coppers are concerned.

This morning seemed to double their numbers, but then every new twist in the tale does. I suppose you've seen the papers?'

Troy held up the *Herald*. 'FITZPATRICK ARRESTED AND CHARGED. IMMORAL EARNINGS AND PROCUREMENT' screamed a banner headline.

'God knows what they expect me to say. But they were out in force when it emerged that Fitz had finally been charged. I really needed a break from it all. I felt I'd go mad if I had to say "no comment" one more time. I drove like a lunatic across London, and found myself on the North Circular road, looked in the rear-view mirror and I couldn't believe it. I'd lost them. There I was heading towards Whipps Cross and not a Fleet Street hack in sight. I hadn't a clue what I was doing. I was elated I'd lost them. I'd actually shaken the buggers off. No idea where I was going, then I saw a signpost saying A12, and I thought "A12? Doesn't that lead out towards Suffolk?" And then I thought of you. I do hope you don't mind. If you think about it, it's the last place the bastards'll ever look for me.'

'I've already said I don't. All the same, how did you know I was here?'

'Anna,' Woodbridge said simply, and it was quite enough for Troy.

'I stopped off at a bookshop in Chelmsford. Wasn't a lot of choice. But there's a new Marge Allingham and a Graham Greene I didn't know was in paperback. I don't know whether you like Greene?'

'None better,' said Troy. He'd read *Our Man in Havana*, but he'd enjoy reading it again. He'd not read the Allingham, but then he never read detective stories – not since he was young, before he became a copper – but Rod read them, as he put it, as a "parliamentary relaxation", and Rod rated Allingham. It was thoughtful of Woodbridge and Troy hoped he wasn't about to pay their price in an afternoon bearing witness to his self-pity.

Woodbridge picked up the *Herald*. Looked at the headline. Tossed the paper back on the coffee table.

'I don't even know what "procurement" means. I'd never heard of it.'

'It means introducing a woman under the age of twenty-one to a man over the age of twenty-one for the purposes of sexual intercourse.'

'Parliament must have been mad to pass a law like that!'

'Most of the time you are.'

'I mean – how is a chap to know when he introduces Miss X to Mister Y that they're going to do it? Half the chaps I know would be in jail if that were illegal.'

'What do you mean "if"? It is illegal.'

'But the twins are twenty-four or five!'

'They're not twins. So, they're lying about the age of one them regardless. And how old is Clover?'

'I didn't have sex with Clover.'

'Really?'

'Believe me, Troy. Not only did I not fuck young Clover, Fitz did not introduce me to the Ffitch girls. I met them at his house, true, but the mood he was in he offered no introduction. I chatted to Tara and asked her if she'd have dinner with me some time. She said, "We do everything together." I said, "Everything?" "Yes," she said, "so if you think that'll cramp your style I wouldn't ask any further." She short-circuited all the chat-up lines I knew. We all three of us had dinner in the West End a couple of times and then we all three of us went to bed together. Fitz had no part of it. I shouldn't think he knew till we started going down to Uphill on a regular basis.'

'And now, according to the *Sunday Post*, Major Ffitch is threatening to horsewhip you.'

'Worse. Young Clover's grandfather has threatened to thrash me in public if he finds out I had his granddaughter.'

'I didn't see that.'

'No. It's not in the papers, it's just gossip, but these days what few friends I have left seem to think it essential to tell me every whisper that reaches their ears.'

'Who is this old fool?'

'Dunno. Sir Somebody Something. Nobody seemed to have a name. Just some old bugger with a knighthood.'

'Good Lord – did Clover strike you as a recent descendant of anyone with a title?'

'I give up on accents these days – I thought she was a cockney sparrow, but it could have been an affectation. The number of people you meet nowadays affecting Scouse, I'm surprised she didn't sound like John Lennon.'

'Classlessness ain't what it used to be.'

Woodbridge laughed at this. It diverted them both, but as the laughter died Woodbridge reached a new level – a frankness Troy could not see as wholly devoid of self-pity and the self-centredness which seemed an inescapable part of the man's charm.

'You know, I did nothing wrong.'

'Try telling my brother that.'

'I'm a widower. I'm not a married man. I'm not an adulterer. I took the view that who I slept with was no concern of my colleagues in the House, nor of anyone else. If people think three in a bed is kinky, I can't help that. I did not do it in the street. I did not frighten the horses. It's not illegal. I didn't choose it, but between you and me I'd recommend it to any man past his prime as a way of taking ten years off the clock.'

'I'll bear that in mind,' said Troy flatly. 'However your pleasure is no more important than your guilt. The point is Fitz.'

Woodbridge got up, walked to the window and stared out. A plump Jersey cow ambling into view. Coming summer in an English meadow, the dappling light of trees in leaf, the vast parasols of oak and sweet chestnut nibbled level by countless cattle. He sighed and he dragged it all out, but Troy would not prompt him. This was a man hoisted on the hook of his own naivety, and he saw no reason to let him off it. Men like Woodbridge and Fitz lived by unwritten codes and Troy could not understand why they bleated like lambs when an unwritten code turned out to be a code like any other for all that it was unwritten. They protested as loudly as Rod when he caught Troy cheating at Monopoly. But they were the ones cheating, and they were the ones protesting, 'It's not illegal!' – as though that meant a damn thing.

A pair of iridescent blue damselflies had flitted in through the window. They hovered, as though suspended in the spell of Woodbridge's silence.

'There's nothing I can do for Fitz,' Woodbridge said at last. 'I'm out of it. I'm nobody now.'

The spell broke. The flies circled one another and flew away.

He probably was 'out of it'. Troy doubted very much whether the prosecution would dare call Woodbridge as a witness. It would be to unzip Her Majesty's Government like a ripe banana. It would also seem that Woodbridge was not volunteering for the defence, and for reasons Troy could only guess, Woodbridge also seemed to think they were not going to call on him either. But it baffled Troy how anyone like Woodbridge, anyone who had done what he'd done, been who he'd been, and had half the hacks in Fleet Street camped on his doorstep, could ever assume such counter-arrogance as to believe he was 'nobody'. Whatever happened in the Old Bailey, when or if the state managed to get Fitz in the dock and begin Regina *v.* Fitzpatrick, Woodbridge would be the ghost, the nobody in the machine. And if he didn't know that, he was not just naive, he was stupid too.

Troy heard tapping. Someone trying to attract his attention on the glass door. Woodbridge turned before he could and he knew from the utter transformation in his demeanour, the sudden brake put on his self-pity, the synchromeshed shift into oversmile, that his visitor was a woman. He was at an awkward angle, his neck ached as he squirmed in his chair, and then he saw Foxx.

She set down her packages by his chair, pushed him back into it as he tried to get up.

'Gosh, you look startled,' she said.

'I . . . just wasn't expecting you.'

She kissed him on both cheeks, her hair falling into his face as she stooped, a lingering scent swept over him – hours later he could smell it still.

'I've not come at a bad time, have I? I meant to surprise you. I thought it would be so easy to surprise you. But it wasn't. It's taken me four hours of trains and buses to get here from London. I've got to set off back soon. As my mum used to say, "I won't tek me coat off, I'm not stopping." '

'I'm going back to town,' said a voice from behind Troy. 'I could give you a lift.'

Troy realised that Woodbridge was waiting for an introduction, waiting for an entry – his voice that languorous baritone that Troy had long presumed men meant to sound seductive.

'Shirley Foxx, Tim Woodbridge,' he said reluctantly. 'I'm sure you've seen Tim's face in the papers.'

Foxx ignored the sarcasm.

'A lift? That'd be marvellous.'

Troy glowered at him. Woodbridge threw in a glance-at-your-watch gesture and said, 'Look, you two don't have long together. I'll pop out for a while. Just come and find me in the car park when you're ready to leave.'

He disappeared through the glass doors into the house.

'I didn't know you knew Woodbridge,' Foxx said.

'I'm not sure I knew it myself.'

'I thought you might be bored so I brought you something to while away the hours.'

She pulled her two packages over, set the smaller of them in Troy's lap and sat down opposite him. It was a stack of long-playing records and the larger package was a Dansette record player – the sort that looked like a small leatherette case with a plastic handle.

'That's very kind. It's just what I needed. I find I can't read much. Something to listen to besides the wireless will be great.'

He looked at Foxx, seeing her and wondering how she saw him. He'd known her since she was twenty-two – the best part of seven years. They had lapsed as lovers. Lapsed and retrieved, at his count, no less than six times in seven years. Until his present wasting ailment, he would have said that she had changed more than he. The edges smoothed off her Derbyshire accent. Her habitual look of the American teenager – blue jeans and baseball boots – had long since given way to a dazzling wardrobe of whatever was stylish and fashionable – today a vaguely Mary Quant look, a neat suit with huge pockets and big buttons, her hair shorter than usual, curling in at the chin to wrap her face in a blonde oval. She had grown sophisticated, just as his own sophistication had ground to a halt. He'd known for years now that he'd end up like his father, drunk on words, lost in the power of language, never out of his dressing-gown whatever the time of day. Foxx's new-found sophistication, plus the natural attributes of blonde hair and bottle-green eyes, added up to Woodbridge woman, the green-eyed version of Tara and Caro. He was not surprised Woodbridge had turned on the charm – Foxx had pushed his buttons simply by being Foxx – what surprised him was that so many fell for his particularly vacuous brand of charm. But she wouldn't. He was sure she wouldn't.

Every so often the jeans would reappear. She would, especially in summertime, turn up on his doorstep looking exactly as she used to – the faded blue of denim, the bright white of T-shirt and the scuffed and fraying canvas boots. She had made blue jeans her business. A small shop in Kingley Street in the West End of London, selling imported American teen clobber. She rang the changes. She had taste. He had never been entirely sure that he had.

'When do you get out?'

'Wish I knew.'

'Whenever it is – I want you to come and see me in the new place.'

'New place?'

'I'm moving the shop. Not far. Only about fifty yards. Into Carnaby Street.'

Carnaby Street? He knew Carnaby Street. He did not like it. Bad memories. England's first jazz club – the Club Eleven – had opened there a few years after the war. He had been to the club several times to hear the British version of be-bop – and had been lucky enough not to be there the night the Vice Squad had chosen for a raid. He never was very good at noticing things – like who was smoking dope – he was too busy watching the sax players. He'd never allowed himself to go there again. To be caught in a raid would be . . . embarrassing, unforgivable. Objectively, Carnaby Street was narrow and poky, the wrong end of Soho and hardly the height of fashion. Hardly the place for a clothes shop. Scarcely better than Kingley Street. And Kingley Street was an alley. It was not so much frying pan to fire, as frying pan to frying pan.

'Bit risky, isn't it?'

'Good God, Troy. You sound like my bank manager. Of course it's a risk. What isn't a risk? If I wasn't into risk I'd've slammed the door on you years ago.'

He looked at the Dansette. Her eyes followed his. It was remarkably like the pink suitcase he'd been clutching when he had turned up on her Derbyshire doorstep at breakfast all those years ago.

'Take me away from all this,' he said.

'Eh?'

'That, more or less, is what you said to me at the time. Just when you should have slammed the door.'

'If you say so. I've no regrets.'

'I wish I were saying it now.'

'Just get better, Troy. Look, I've got to dash. I have an architect coming in at seven. Kiss and run.'

Over his shoulder he caught a glimpse of Woodbridge, biding a little of his endless time beyond the glass doors. He had been buttonholed by Alfie. Troy could read his lips but he did not need to. He could have written the script blindfold.

'You know what you are Woodbridge? You're a bleedin' 'ero, that's what you are!'

'Are you really going to accept a lift from Woodbridge?' he said.

'Why not? You don't think he'll leap on me between here and London do you?'

'He's a wide boy.'

She glanced at the two men, grinning at each other, laughing. God knows what gag Alfie had seen to fit to split with him. Two peas in a sleazy pod, thought Troy. Class rendered into classlessness – sex the leveller. He who fucks and fucks around is equal to he who also fucks and fucks around. As the song had it, it's a man's, man's, man's world. Troy did not feel like a man. He felt like a wraith.

'Wrong class, surely, Troy?'

'Maybe, but a common characteristic. He thinks the world was created for his pleasure. It revolves round the end of his dick.'

'You know, Troy, I don't think I've ever met a man who didn't think that.'

He wondered if she meant him. It was pretty damn clear she did.

'I've got to dash. Really I have. Enjoy the music, and do come to the new shop when you get out. I've so much to show you.'

She pecked him on the cheek. Squeezed his hand in hers. He felt cheated.

Later that evening he plugged in the Dansette and looked through the pile of records Foxx had brought him. Miles Davis, from the mid-fifties, when Coltrane had played sax for him on 'Steamin', Cookin' and Relaxin''. They were American records, imports, expensive – she must have searched everywhere. The fourth LP was new. Four hairy blokes leaned over a staircase and grinned at him – The Beatles. 'PLEASE, PLEASE ME, with Love Me Do and 12 other songs'. There'd been a lot of fuss about this lot. The papers were full of them. They cropped up every so often on the Light Programme of the BBC. At best they'd been background to him, but then so much else had – out beyond the bubble.

He stuck it on. He knew it at once. It was the record Clover Browne had played over and over again that long weekend at Uphill. He found she had, by repetition, lodged every tune in his mind, as unconscious melodies and rhythms. He knew them. He just didn't know he knew them. There was a Broadway cover, an old song from *The Music Man*; there were two or three cover versions of what he knew to be black American songs – but what pleased him was what he knew to be original. He found a piano in the upstairs sitting room, blew the dust off the keys and tried picking out the tune of the title track. It didn't lend itself to the piano at all. It seemed to be conceived wholly for the primitive set-up of the beat group: three guitars, drum kit and a dubbed-on mouth organ. He was not at all sure he could ever come to terms with it. It was remarkable, as startling to his ears as when he had first heard Little Richard a few years ago, or Thelonious Monk – and that was fifteen years ago now – but it did not invite him in. He played the record a couple more times, until they told him to put a sock in it. Then he stuck it in his bedside locker and thought little more about it.

A day or two later Alfie appeared in his tartan dressing-gown, hands deep in the pockets, a twinkle Troy could never be sure lacked malevolence in his eye, and said, 'Why not put on yer Beatles record, Fred.'

It was not a question. Troy had no objection. Besides, to give in was the line of least trouble with Alfie – to argue was to risk being talked to death.

The Beatles tore into 'I Saw Her Standing There'. Alfie sat on the edge of Troy's bed. Jigged up and down without ever taking his hands from his pockets.

'They got summink, though. Entthey? Don't you think they got summink, Fred?'

He did not understand Alfie. A man in his mid-twenties, or thereabouts, articulate in the restricted mode, confident in who he was, wholly devoid of self-knowledge, worldly, innocent – the perfect wide boy. A man of the moment, living, it seemed, for that moment. A man whose memories of the war were a child's memories . . . and in so thinking, for he said nothing by way of reply, and Alfie did not seem bothered enough even to repeat the question, just jigged and smiled the more, Troy realised the truth of Charlie's last rant. The glue that held them together would not hold once their generation passed – well, not passed exactly, but lost its grip. Catesby's had loosened long ago – for all he'd said, Troy still doubted whether he had entirely grasped the Second World War. He had fought in both but was so very, very much a man of the

First, of a generation made and unmade by it. Now Troy's, the generation of the Second War, the coalition held in place by the 'glue' that was that war, was facing the children of the war, the war babies, as Troy now faced them – that new generation – in the shape of Alfie. Alfie, in all his struggle for meaning; Alfie, in all his terrifying banality.

'Alfie?'

'Yers?'

'Did you do National Service?'

''O' course. RAF, 1955 to 1957. Hated every bleedin' minute of it.'

'Aircraftman?'

'Leading Aircraftman. A difference of about seventeen an' sixpence a week. Why do you ask?'

Troy asked because it was the obvious question to put to a man of his age. National Service – a euphemism that did nothing to disguise the true nature of peacetime military conscription – was the war's bequest to its war babies. It was gone now. After eighteen years. The last reluctant tommies, the cockleshell antiheroes, were tearing off their blues and khakis at that very moment to return to civvy street, only to find that their Teddy Boy suits hung on their spare military frames like sacks, and that no one wore winkle-picker shoes any more. Peacetime conscription had been unique, pointless, undemocratic and decidedly un-English – but Troy did not doubt this last tendril of the war marked and bound Alfie in some way.

'I was wondering,' he said, 'whether you and old Catesby might not have more in common than you think. I mean, I wasn't in the forces.'

'Then you was lucky. I 'ated it. National Service – bullshit, that's what it was, Fred. Bullshit. Screamin' an' shoutin' at yer from the minute you dropped off the back of the lorry till the minute you climbed back on two years later. And a total waste of bleedin' time. Do you know what they had us doing in summer? We was in Nissen 'uts. Hoops of corrugated iron, about as friendly as yer average igloo. Heated by a cast-iron tortoise stove. Used to burn coke. In summer they was out. Never lit 'em from May till October. So in summer I had to blacklead the stove. Inside and out. I ask you. Inside! Blackleading the bits no bugger ever saw. Then, I used to whitewash the coke. Can you think of anything more futile than wastin' a bloke's time whitewashing a pile o' coke? When I could be earnin' a good wage back in civvy street, they 'ad me whitewashin' coke! Can you think of a bigger example of bullshit? 'Cos I can't. Then it dawned on me what the British Empire was. It was a bunch of poor sods like me, scattered to the four corners of the world to whitewash coke. The red bits on the map aren't red, they're pink – and all because of buggers with buckets o' bleedin' whitewash whitewashin' everythin' in sight. I whitewashed the flight lieutenant's jeep once. Got three weeks in the glass'ouse for that. But I learnt me lesson. I learnt that it was every man for 'imself and I've stuck to it ever since. Now, I know what you're thinkin, that I'm gonna say it was blokes like Catesby told me to whitewash coke. It wasn't. It was corporals and sergeants, species somewhere between a whelk and a winkle on the food chain; but it was blokes like the general they answered to, and to this day I 'alf suspect there's officers who'll say they didn't know what was going on. But it did go on. And it was bullshit. And there's no excuses. I lost earnin' time, an' I lost drinkin' time, an' I lost totty time. So from 'ereon in it's every man for 'imself.'

'Quite,' said Troy.

'Quite,' said Alfie exactly as Troy had said it. The perfect piss-take. 'You kill me sometimes, Fred. You really do.'

'I was saying – you may be right.'

'I know bloody well I am.'

'But we won't shove it down old Catesby's throat, will we?'

Alfie's feet shuffled on the lino. His shoulders shrugged. It hardly needed a deal of thought.

'Nah,' he said. 'What'd be the point? He's a decent old cove is old Bludnok.'

A little, just a little, he began to understand Alfie and to wonder about the Ffitch girls and Clover Browne. Charlie was right. The lid was coming off. He would listen for the 'boom'.

§ 44

Each day he took three doses of medicine. Each morning he took an intramuscular injection straight in the backside. The prevalent side-effect was skin ulcers. Sooner or later the nurses ran out of unpunctured bumskin and would have to shoot the drug into an old wound. You could spot the longer-serving patients. They tended to stand for an hour or two each morning. Troy was lucky. He healed fast. His skin closed and repaired itself with the mechanical ease of a zip fastener, and he began to realise that whatever the ebb of his spirits, his body was mending. He was thin and he was weak, but compared to, say, a man of Catesby's age, he had good recuperative powers. Four months after Rod dropped him off at the door, they told him he could leave. 'You'll feel tired,' they said. 'And you must rest and not work, but you can leave.'

§ 45

His sister Sasha had telephoned. 'We'll come and get you,' she'd said. We. Somehow Troy had expected Rod. Rod driving Troy's Bentley. He was late.

Troy sat in the open windows of the conservatory, case packed, coat on, like a soldier awaiting demob, watching the empty drive, the dancing butterflies of August, half-hearing the meaningless mutterings of General Catesby behind him, the low murmur of the Home Service on the wireless. Then the slow crescendo of a very familiar noise, that mixture of roar, putter and purr, preceded first sight of his carriage home. Not a brother, not a Bentley. It was a motorbike. A motorbike with sidecar. A motorbike without snowplough. A motorbike with sidecar and without snowplough driven by an extremely fat man in a leather helmet and an old Second World War London County Council Heavy Rescue Squad navy-blue leather-elbowed battledress, unbuttoned to the summer breeze, its belt tail flapping and its pockets billowing.

The Fat Man scrunched to a halt in the gravel, pushed up his goggles and said, as he always did, 'Wotcher cock.'

'Do you expect me to ride in that?' said Troy. 'I'll catch my death of cold.'

'Nah. You'll be fine. That good-lookin' young woman as is your quack told me you needed fresh air, lots of it.'

'Fresh air! It'll be like riding in a hurricane!'

'Trust me, old cock. I got the 'orse blanket to wrap you in—'

'I'm not wearing anything previously worn by a horse!'

'Just a figure o' speech. Keep yer 'air on. 'Orse blanket.'

The Fat Man reached into the sidecar and held up a grubby old blanket.

'Thermos flask.'

The Fat Man pointed to a flask mounted on the nose of the sidecar's fuselage, with a little leather strap, where the snowplough used to be.

''Ip flask. With a nice drop of Armagnac, as I knows yer partial to it.'

The Fat Man pointed to a half-bottle of brandy mounted after the same fashion.

It was like the obligatory armourer's scene in a James Bond film. Where the exploding talcum powder? Where the 9 millimetre Walther automatic? And the fifty quid in old sovereigns?

'And at the back 'ere. Yer Fortnum's 'amper. Plus all the Sunday papers. We s'll 'ave a nice little picnic, and be 'ome to the family before dinner. They'll all be there. They can't wait to see yer. The pig's been pining.'

Troy was not at all certain that pigs pined. But he believed the rest of the Fat Man's tale. *They* would most certainly be waiting. He could do without that. Without *they*.

They cut a path across the northern corner of Essex, via back lanes and villages. Every so often the Fat Man would bring the bike to a halt on some picturesque village green, pink-painted cottages, black mansard barns, windmills for the tilting, some corner on the English quilt, and say, 'Do you a fancy a bite to eat?' and Troy would say, 'No.'

Two hours and more later they were within fifteen miles of home, the hamper still unopened. They pulled onto the green in Datchworth and Troy heard him say, 'Sod yer, I'm not wasting it.'

The Fat Man got off, unstrapped the hamper and began to lay out the picnic.

'We're only twenty-five minutes from home,' Troy protested.

'I don't care if we're two furlongs from the back door. A picnic I brought and a picnic we shall 'ave. You be as miserable as you like, I'm going to tuck in.'

Troy said nothing, accepted defeat, and climbed out of the sidecar.

'There you are,' said the Fat Man. 'Baguliar caviar.'

'Beluga.'

'Same to you.'

'No – I mean it's pronounced Beluga.'

'Beluga, begorrah – I don't care – so long as it's the best.'

'It is,' said Troy. 'And it's kind of you, but I really can't stand caviar. Sorry. It's like a cross between tapioca and fishpaste to me.'

'No apology necessary, old cock. It's yer brother you should thank. He slipped me a pony, said I was to go down Fortnum's and fill a namper o' the best. Besides I'm very partial to a spot o' caviar. Go down a treat that will. Or did you think I was a fish an' chips man?'

'No,' said Troy. 'I thought you were a ham-sandwich man. If I've seen you eat one of a Saturday morning, I've seen you eat a hundred.'

'True enough. But after bein' a nam guzzler, I'm most definitely a caviar guzzler. But on top of yer Baguliar, we got quails' eggs, smoked salmon, and a jar of that dill sauce, a quarter moon of ripe camembert, half a duck, a jar of pears in port . . .'

Troy felt sick just listening to him.

'Smoked salmon,' he said, clutching at something that sounded safe.

'Pâté de fois gras, a tin o' snails in jelly, truffles . . . a bottle of Mouton Rothschild '53 . . .'

'Any bread?'

JOHN LAWTON

'Yes, cock – one o' them there French sticks.'

'Just a little bread and salmon then.'

'Comin' up.'

Troy nibbled. The Fat Man started on the caviar with a dessert spoon and in two gulps it was gone. Then he tore into the duck like Henry VIII just coming off an enforced diet. He ate the quails' eggs, shells and all, and managed to find room for half a loaf and a quarter pound of fois gras. The camembert seemed not to appeal, or perhaps he was saving it for later. Troy felt like an invalid.

A young woman of thirty or so came into view, wheeling a large black pram, and took the bench next to them. Troy looked at her face, wonderful blue-grey eyes. The Fat Man looked at the infant set down from the pram to crawl its infant crawl upon the grass. It was a small child, Troy thought, six or seven months at most.

'Oochie coochie coo,' said the Fat Man to the child, and began to prattle meaninglessly, and Troy wondered whether the man was any better with children than he was himself. They were aliens. Creatures from some other universe. He looked again at the woman, beaming with evident pride and pleasure in her offspring, and the thought occurred to him that this was everything he had missed in life, everything he had avoided, rejected – wife, child, family – locked away in the attic of the mind. But he did have a wife, somewhere – a brown-eyed, short-arsed American – somewhere. She smiled at him. He knew he wasn't smiling. Wrapped up in the horse blanket like a forgotten parcel. And he knew her smile said 'poor sod' and he hated her for it.

Time to go.

'What's 'is name?' the Fat Man was saying to the blue-eyed blonde.

'Samantha,' she replied.

'Wot? Like the Kenny Ball song?'

The Fat Man hummed a few bars of some inane hit of couple of years ago. The thankfully short-lived 'Trad' Jazz boom. It was the sort of music that drove Troy demented and brought him to the brink of smashing wireless sets.

The woman's expression showed she had taken umbrage at this suggestion of topicality in the naming of children. And it dawned on Troy that the Fat Man had probably expected a boy, and had addressed the child thinking it was a boy. He could not see the Fat Man as a ladies' fat man. He had utterly failed to charm this local beauty. Nor could he see himself as a ladies' man. The last thing he wanted was women. And the house would be full of them.

'Can we go?' he said. 'I'm suddenly very tired.'

The Fat Man chugged slowly up the third of a mile from the gate to the house, letting Troy take it all in. It had scarcely been spring when he had seen it last and now it was the dry end of summer, August winding down into September – a month that in the British Isles could be summer or autumn depending on the fickleness of the weather. Troy did not know the place. As often happened, it rose up before him as though he had seen it only in some distant dream.

They stood on the steps, waiting to meet him. His twin sisters Sasha and Masha, his sister-in-law Lucinda, Rod, their son Alex, their daughters – the second set of twins – Eugénie and Nastasia, his brother-in-law Lawrence, his Uncle Nikolai and so *ad infinitum*. Troy stumbled from the sidecar, shed the horse blanket, and nobody moved. For a moment he felt like Haig inspecting the troops. Then they fell upon him – wolves upon the fold. An enveloping curtain of women, a solid wall of clashing scents, a buffeting bolster of soft arms and smothering breasts. He would gladly have murdered the lot of them. It was like being eight years old again, the youngest again, and the last thing he could say was what he had said when he was eight – a brutally simple 'Get off!'

By the time he had extricated himself he became aware that Rod and the Fat Man had bunked off. The women bundled him onto the porch steps and he heard Masha saying, 'Half a mo'. We've got a surprise for you.' They were not words he much wished to hear.

Then they turned him around like the victim of blind man's buff and the surprise surprised him.

There, standing between Rod and the Fat Man, was his prize Old Spot sow, Cissie. Cissie, wearing a lead, and upon the lead her runner-up's rosette from last year's Hertfordshire show.

'Schnuck,' said the pig – in Troy's experience pigs said little else.

''Ere,' said the Fat Man. 'Look who's come to see yer.'

He was delighted to see the pig again. Clearly the pig did not know him. But then one of the things Troy had always liked about pigs was their wilful contempt for humanity. They were like tortoises, and he'd kept plenty of those when he was a boy. They moved through your world, took what you had to offer, but didn't want a great deal to do with you. Their evolution oddly followed mankind's: they were closer companions than even the trusty dog; they had emerged from the forests when we had; they ate what we ate – anything and everything – but as far as they were concerned we were all yahoos, and ours was the yahoo life.

§ 46

Wondering how he would get through dinner, he found the voice of self-censorship muttering at him.

'Miserable bastard,' it said.

So he dutifully took his place at the head of the table. Why not? he thought. It was his house and probably his money blown on a banquet for which he had little physical appetite.

He found he had Rod's wife Lucinda on one side and his sister Masha on the other. He did not mind, but that Nikolai, the one person he would have relished as company, was at the opposite end, beyond the reach of any normal conversation. But what was normal conversation? He seemed now to Troy to be ancient, well into his eighties, to be frailer by far than he was himself even in the pit of his infirmity. He was getting deaf and his retreat from deafness was to and talk less and so have to listen less. He passed whole meals now eating little and merely nodding in answer to questions put to him. It was a small miracle he had come out at all – most of the time he was holed up in his flat at the back of the Albert Hall working, Troy had long assumed, on his magnum opus of applied physics, the book he had always put off writing to write some other book – on the molecular structure of custard, the magnetic properties of raindrops, the aerodynamic possibilities of porcine aviation.

The Fat Man carved. A flourish of steel upon the blade and he sliced a rare roast beef so thin one could not but admire the artistry. He had always told Troy that he earned his living as gentleman's gentleman – an anachronism to be anybody's Jeeves in this day and age, and he had never so much as hinted for whom he performed such services. Besides he was old, far too old, to be anything but retired. It was, Troy thought, the one advantage to baldness: you never went grey and people spent for ever guessing how old you were. As he served up, Troy realised he had just seen the first clear evidence of the man's trade. He really did do it like a pro. Better by far than the cack-handed hacking of Rod.

Softened by booze, the family dissolved into a dozen conversations. Troy said little and listened and the drunker they became the more he heard a dozen topics resolve into the component parts of one, and then fuse to the single subject. All tongues led to Woodbridge and Tereshkov. There was only one topic beneath all the others.

'There's an absolute hoot doing the rounds at Westminster,' he heard Rod say. 'Apparently someone told Macmillan that six high court judges had been caught at an orgy. Mac thought about this for a minute and then said, "Two high court judges I could believe, possibly three, but six!!!" – as though the numbers lent any credibility to the story.'

And then he topped his own anecdote, waited for the laughter to die and fired his best shot.

'Jack Kennedy phoned me up from the White House in June. Said if ever the Ffitch twins were in the USA would I give them his address. "Fire away," I said, "I've got a pencil and paper right here." He laughed fit to bust and hung up!'

By the last course one voice held forth – Rod's eldest, Alex, all too frequently known to the family and to Fleet Street as 'young Alex' to distinguish him from his grandfather, a man dead these twenty years.

'The bugger of it is we were watching him like hawks,' he was saying to all and sundry, 'and he completely gave us the slip. We chased him as far as Tottenham and then we lost him. By the time I realised where he'd headed he could have been anywhere in the whole of eastern England. Made me wonder – has he got a woman out there too? God he was fast. Stirling Moss doesn't have a thing on Woodbridge.'

Life is a series of circles, thought Troy, circles that touch but never quite connect, that seem to pass invisibly and impossibly through one another like the prestidigitation of some Chinese conjurer.

Sasha got to her feet, whacked the table with an empty bottle and called for a toast.

'We are gathered here this summer eve to welcome our little brother back from the jaws of death.'

Troy distinctly heard the other twin, his sister Masha, seated next to him, mutter, 'Oh bloody hell.'

'I am sure I speak for us all – and if I don't, sod you – when I say that I thought the grim reaper had finally got you. You are, Freddie, a man with seemingly scant regard for life and death, but most especially your own. More knocks and scrapes and scars than one could ever hope to count. But you've cheated death yet again. So, the toast is "Fate – bollocks to 'im!"'

Just for the moment Troy wondered if his family would balk at the proposal, but then to a man, and moreover to a woman, they lifted their glasses to him and in unison echoed Sasha's toast.

'Fate – bollocks to 'im!'

Troy looked at Nikolai, toasting the cheating of death when it stood impatiently at his own shoulder. Then Masha whispered softly, 'I love my sister dearly, but there are times I wonder if she isn't completely mad.'

It confirmed what he had been thinking for a couple of years, that the indivisibility of the twins had ceased, that they had gone their separate ways and were no longer, as he had been wont to put it, one dreadful woman with two bodies. Masha was still married – happily, Troy assumed, for all her infidelities – to Lawrence, editor of the *Sunday Post*. While Sasha and the late Hugh had begun their family before the war within a year of their marriage – her daughters were now in their twenties, married themselves, scattered and absent – Masha had married during the war and almost of necessity had begun her family only when it was over. Even now her boys were only in their early teens. Sasha had a freedom denied her sister, and it would be in character for her to go wild with it. Masha was rooted, he could think of no better word, but then as the twins changed their alignment so they changed in alignment with him, formed a new constellation, and he knew that he now had more in common with Sasha than he did with Masha. He was not rooted, nowhere near as rooted as he thought and the last thing he wanted was Sasha adopting him.

Suddenly a figure was at his side. His nephew Alex.

'Sorry, must dash. Just thought I'd say welcome back, old thing.'

He clenched a fist, tapped Troy gently on the upper arm – a hammily chappish gesture – and left.

Troy found himself exchanging looks with the young man's mother, Lucinda. 'There are times', she said, 'when I think he's got a banger up his arse.'

It was unlike her to be quite so Troyish in her speech, but her dissatisfaction with her son was so evident.

'He won't sit still for anything. I told him this was special and that if he was going to do his usual cut and run, then he shouldn't come in the first place.'

Looking down the length of the table at the extended, the vast tribe of Troy, drunken, garrulous, foul of mouth and mind, Troy could not much see that one more or less mattered.

'It doesn't matter,' he said to his sister-in-law.

'Yes it does,' she said. 'It's the Tereshkov affair. It's made a Fleet Street hero of him. It's made him a bighead. One way or another I think the whole sorry business will make fools of us all before the year's out.'

And she looked at her husband as she said it.

§ 47

Bliss. He had slept. Not the night through, but he had slept. Had not seen dawn. It was almost eight o'clock. He felt he could safely nod off and sleep until ten. If he could sleep properly again, he might just get through this mortal mess.

At eight thirty a boom-boom-boom like rolling thunder woke him. It was not overhead. It was closer. It was inside his head. He yanked back the curtain. A large Bedford tipper truck was backed up to the kitchen garden, dumping a mountain of bricks. Rod was yelling and directing the driver. Troy would get up, get dressed, and then he'd kill him.

'You're up with the lark,' Rod said by way of greeting. 'You must be feeling better.'

'What are you doing?' Troy asked.

Rod was bizarrely dressed in undersized overalls that hovered about his shins, flashing half a yard of socks – as ever, they did not match – and he was wearing a tatty straw hat. If memory served, Troy thought, it had belonged to one of his sisters some time between the wars. He was mixing mortar, bending over a pile of sand and cement and stirring it with the end of his shovel. Whatever the purpose there seemed to be as much delight in making pretty patterns in powder grey and dull yellow as there was in achieving the mixture.

'Building a brick wall,' Rod said.

'Do we need a brick wall?'

'Yes. We most definitely need a brick wall.'

'Well then, do we need it now?'

'Yes. Been saving it for years, saving it for just such a moment as this.'

'Since when?'

'It was the summer of . . . oh bugger, when was it the summer of? '29? '30? Hang on '30, yes definitely '30. I'd be twenty-three. Winston was out of office. Start of that long phase that kept him in the political wilderness until Chamberlain asked him back to the Admiralty. Now when was that?'

'Doesn't matter. Get on with it.'

'Eh?'

'Doesn't matter when it ended. You were talking about the start.'

'Was I? So I was. Anyway. That summer Winston asks the old man and our mother down to Chartwell for the weekend. And the old dear won't go. Winston irritates her. Clementine bores her. So the old man asks me to go instead. Wonder where you were? It was just the sort of jaunt he'd ordinarily ask you on.'

'If it was 1930 I'd be fourteen. Hardly likely to gee up the dinner-table chat with the Greatest Living Englishman. He'd never have asked me.'

Troy knew exactly where he'd been. It was the summer he turned fifteen. Biarritz. With Charlie, his mother and one of the better 'uncles'. After surrendering his own virginity to Troy's sisters the previous summer, Charlie was determined to get Troy laid. Troy was determined that he should not, and when Charlie succeeded in pulling the chambermaid – 'pour mon ami, le petit Russe', as he had told her – Troy had left him to it. Hours later he returned from a 'bracing' walk to find Charlie still in bed. 'Mireille was marvellous' Freddie, bloody marvellous. You don't know what you're missing.'

'Quite,' said Rod. 'He wasn't the GLE in those days, but I suppose you're right. Anyway. Winston is whiling away the time thinking up books. He has it in mind to do a "State of Europe" book, and he's asking the old man to give him the gen on Russia. The old man succeeds in talking him out of it. "Don't even try," he says. "It's a riddle wrapped in a mystery inside an enigma."'

Troy raised an eyebrow at this. It would be typical of Alexei Troy to have pinched one of Churchill's better lines and claimed it for his own. Equally it would be typical of Churchill to have picked up a throwaway line of Alex Troy's and made poetry of it. It also reminded him that he had recently glimpsed the enigma (or was it the mystery?) and he wasn't about to tell Rod this.

'Winston accepts this, and as I recall they fell to arguing about Germany. "How long do you give Hitler?" Winston asks. "About two years, perhaps two and a half," the old man replies, meaning about thirty months until the Nazis come to power. Should have had a tenner on it. He was absolutely right. "How long before the war starts?" Winston asks. And the old man spins him some line about there being no need for war but on the other hand it could come any time, and they start to argue and they go on arguing, and they went on arguing for the next ten years. Which, come to think of it, is why, when I got interned in 1940, the old man would not ask any favours from Winston. Even to get me out of jail.'

'Rod,' Troy said softly, 'is this leading anywhere?'

'Quite. I digress. On the Sunday morning, before they started rowing, I took a stroll. I came across old Winston down by the kitchen garden. He had a couple of tons of red bricks, a load of cement, a pair of overalls, a straw hat and a trowel. He said he was going to build a wall the length of his vegetable beds – massive, absolutely bloody massive – said it would balance his life nicely, and if he was out of office for any length of time would relax him

purposefully. He invited me to roll up me sleeves and I laid two rows
with him. I suppose I have been storing up the memory of that for
these thirty-odd years. I have even, as you have doubtless observed,
been saving the overalls and the straw hat. And now I find I have
need of purposeful relaxation, I've ordered a ton of bricks and I too
am going to build a wall for the kitchen garden. It will do for me
what it did for Winston, pass the time and stop me from going mad
with impatience. And I bet I'm as good at it as he was – after all, his
rows wobbled more than a bit. He was well suited to the Admiralty,
being, as he was, well acquainted with wavy lines.'

'Impatient for what?' said Troy.

'We are a year away from an election. At the most. But it could
happen any time. In the meantime, we are in for a period of what I
shall call pre-electoral madness. I shall show patience and discipline.
Better by far to lay bricks than drop them, say I.'

§ 48

But for Rod and Sasha they all went home. In the course of the day
Sasha looked in on Troy more times than he could count, and he
realised that she did indeed mean to adopt him. To nurse him,
insofar as she knew anything about nursing beyond plumping pillows
and saying, 'Do you fancy a little drinkie?' She appeared in his
father's study amid the dust and junk with her mid-morning coffee.
And again at lunchtime. He walked around the garden to escape her,
felt tired and retreated to his bedroom, and she called on him again.
And just before seven in the evening she swanned in for 'a natter'.

She was, he thought, on her third gin of the evening.

'Do you think there were people like us fifty years ago?' she said, à
propos of nothing.

Troy had no idea what she was talking about.

'Or even twenty or ten. Except of course for us – I mean. Were
there people like us?'

Troy said nothing.

'Didn't you grow up – didn't we both – feeling, well, different, sort of?'

'Sort of? How sort of?'

'Remember that bit in *Jude* the thingumajig?'

'*Obscure.*'

'Quite. *Jude the Obscure*. He's married, well, come to think of it he hasn't married, this silly tart who says something like, "We weren't meant to be, we were born before our time, too sensitive for the age we live in." Bit of a moan really. Silly tart. Never liked her, but you turn it around and it just about makes sense. We were ahead of our time. We did not, and I could not – dunno about you – behave as others did or as others expected of me. But we were not too sensitive. Far from it.'

What was the damn woman blathering on about?

'Tell me, how many women have you had?'

'Dunno,' Troy lied. He knew exactly. There had not been many.

'Do you know there are some women who've only ever slept with their husbands? Most women in fact have only ever known one man.'

She was pissed, definitely pissed.

'I'm fifty-three years old. In my prime I had most of the men I knew. Fucked all your friends.'

Troy knew this. Charlie had simply been the first.

'I cuckolded Hugh at the reception. Had one of his ushers in your bedroom.'

Troy didn't want to hear this. And he'd still no idea where she was heading. Then she threw down the newspaper she'd been clutching. More sleazy headlines from the Summer of the Sleazy. Troy gave it the merest glance. 'Britain's Raunchiest Bishop. The Duchess speaks out!' It was the composite headline. Next Sunday they'd simply transpose the nouns. Somewhere in the bowels of Fleet Street a subeditor on night shift flicked through a thesaurus for synonyms of 'raunchy'.

'We lived rather fast, I think. I don't think we let our morals be decided for us.'

'Rod did,' said Troy, and it sounded like a miserable bleat even to him.

'Oh yes, Rod did. But I didn't and you didn't and Masha didn't. But don't you think the world is catching up with us?'

'Are you saying you're the new moral standard?'

'No. I'm not.'

'Then what are you saying?'

'Not sure.'

'The cakes of custom cracking open?'

'Dunno. Why does custom come in cakes? Why not tins or packets?'

This was a classic twins remark, either one of them could have uttered it. Troy wished she'd just go away. He was not at all sure how long he could refrain from saying it.

'I think I'm saying that things are breaking up. And the more the world becomes more like the one in which I have lived all my life, the less I like it.'

The woman could drive him mad.

'Because it inverts, it becomes the new moral imperative. Decided from outside, by popular acclaim. If you see what I mean?'

'People expect loose morals?'

'Sort of. And it won't work. It's a false freedom. It's prurience, and prurience does not do what it wants, it does what outrages. One eye always over the shoulder looking back at the moral code, seeking permission in defiance. It won't work because it only works in dissent. If it becomes, as it were, "permissive", if we are now entering upon a permissive society—'

'A what?'

'A permissive society.'

'What's that? What the hell is a "permissive society"?'

'I rather think I just made it up. But it does describe pretty well the society we are becoming, but if we are "permissive" – can you hear the inverted commas, Freddie? – then are we not forced to ask "whose permission?" I never needed anyone's permission. I did what I did because it was what I wanted to do. Not because it outraged the bourgeoisie. Fuck 'em, I say.'

It was the most complicated statement he had ever heard the wretched woman make. She who lacked all self-awareness, a born anarchist, who did first and thought about doing, if at all, much much later, had come up with something that passed for analysis. A statement of her 'position'. 'She didn't need 'em.' And Troy did not need Sasha.

'Sasha. Could you just fuck off?'

She stood up, little legs ramrod straight, the lips a letterbox line. Picked up her drink and her newspaper and stared at him.

'You know, Freddie. When you were young you were very pretty. A complete shit but a very pretty boy. One forgave you everything. Now you're an emaciated wreck, you're going to have to be a lot more careful about playing the complete shit!'

She slammed the door on the way out. He knew now. He'd have to go to London or they'd all drive him totally mad.

§ 49

Salvation was at hand. Two days later he woke late after another bad night and heard the sound of someone playing his piano. Badly. A deep and truly awful voice drifted up from below.

'You look sweet, talk abaht a treat, you look dapper from yer napper to yer feet . . .'

Troy swung his feet to the floor and reached for his dressing-gown.

'Dressed in style, wiv yer brand new tile, yer farver's old green tie on, buuuuuuut ah wunt give yer tuppence for yer old watch chain, old iron, old iron!'

Descending the stairs, something told him this was not an unannounced visit from Lennon and McCartney.

'Any old iron, any old iron, any any any old iron . . .'

The Fat Man sat at the piano, a brace of dead pheasants on the piano lid. He was in black jacket and stripes, a bowler hat the size of one of the lesser planets plonked down next to the pheasants. His gentleman's gentleman outfit. Troy had never seen him in it before.

'I was in this neck o' the woods,' he said. 'The guv'nor fancied a fresh bird, what with the glorious twelfth just passed. So I got on me bike and bagged a couple o' yours. You wasn't up. So I was just passing the time at the old joanna. They don't write 'em like that any more do they?'

No, thank God.

'You're going up to town?'

'All the way to the 'Dilly, old cock.'

'Any chance of a lift?'

''Allo, 'allo,' said the Fat Man. ''Ere we go again.'

§ 50

Once he had settled into Goodwin's Court it seemed a good idea to call Anna. So he did. She drove over at once, clutching her doctor's bag, wearing a flowery cotton dress, poppy-like flowers on a black background, flat shoes without stockings. It was still summer. Her arms were bare and tanned. She had lost weight. Probably the same half stone he had gained. She looked the better for it – he remembered vividly the slim young woman he had met in the 1940s. But there was a mask across her face, a flat unemotionality in her voice, that he had put there.

'I really should have come and seen you as soon as you were discharged.'

He said nothing. She seemed hesitant, confused.

'Of course . . . that would have meant me coming out to Mimram . . .'

Of course, he had not asked her to Mimram.

'But here we are,' he said and so evaded whatever it was she might have meant, as such phrases are intended to.

Anna took his pulse, his blood pressure, listened intently at his chest and insisted he got down the bathroom scales so she could weigh him. He had indeed gained half a stone, nine pounds exactly.

'You've been very lucky,' she said. 'You're mending well. You're still giving yourself the jabs?'

Intramuscular injections, self-administered to the backside with the aid of a mirror. To say nothing of a large handful of pills each day.

'Yes. I was wondering how long?'

'Oh, weeks yet.'

'If I'm recovering well, how soon can I—'

'Work? Oh God, Troy. Don't press me on this please. Months, honestly months.'

She stuffed the stethoscope back in her bag, smoothed down the front of her skirt, and looked grimly at him. She had not smiled once.

'Now, is there anything else?'

'I'm still not sleeping. I feel as though I've heard every dawn chorus for ages.'

'Well, I can easily do something about that.'

She sat down, took a prescription pad from her bag, scribbled quickly and then tore up the top sheet.

'What's up?'

'Oh, nothing. Damn near killed you with the wrong dose, that's all. I've been so distracted lately.'

'Distracted?'

'You know. Angus.'

'You've heard from Angus?'

'Don't be daft, Troy. Of course I haven't heard from Angus. I doubt whether I or you will ever hear from Angus again. It's been nine months. He's never vanished for that long before. And Fitz. You know.'

He didn't know.

'Fitz?'

'Today's been particularly bad. The trial started today.'

In the pit of self-obsession he'd missed the matter entirely. Anna handed him the prescription.

'They're called Mandrax. They're strong, Troy. Promise me this. You'll never take more than two at once, and never, never with alcohol.'

Sleep became bliss. Physical heaven. It took him a while to get going again in the morning, but sleep washed over him like waves, a giant, sensuous hand gently pressing him down into the bedding.

§ 51

The cab dropped him twenty yards from the side entrance of the Old Bailey's Court No. 1, near the corner of Newgate Street. He had not anticipated the crowd. At best the Public Gallery held twenty-five people. Here were eighty or ninety at least. On the corner, trying to keep an eye on both entrances, were a bevy of press photographers, shooting randomly. Anybody might be somebody. One came running, and Troy found himself blinded by the flash as the bulb popped in his face. He pinched the bridge of his nose and closed his eyes, and before he had opened them felt the heavy hand upon his shoulder.

'Move along there!'

The hand shoved him forward. He opened his eyes to see exactly what he had expected to see. A large constable hell-bent on doing his duty. Troy's eyes were level with the top button of his tunic. The man stared down at him a second, hand raised to push him along and then it saluted him sharply.

'Sorry, sir. Didn't recognise you there.'

'That's OK. I'm off duty. I was just hoping to see a bit of the trial.'

'What? From the gallery? You'll be lucky. I'd be risking a riot if I shoved you in ahead of the queue, sir. It's day two. Some of this lot have been camping out since the night before last. The pecking order's all worked out. You just come with me, sir.'

He chaperoned Troy to the front entrance. They caught up with the happy hack who had snapped Troy.

'Oi you! I'll have that last plate or you'll feel my boot up yer backside!'

To Troy's amazement the man did not argue, just muttered 'shit' and tore the strip of film from the back of the camera. Troy had not, he realised, been out with the boys in blue in a very long time.

'Now, sir. Up the steps, into the court. City benches on your right, just behind counsel. Privileged seats, just tell 'em all to move up and flash your warrant card.'

There were hundreds of people outside the court. Troy felt almost abandoned as the man left him and resumed his duties. He felt acutely conscious of his stature – was everyone in the world bigger than he? – and his frailty. He had not found himself in the midst of a crowd since . . . since he did not know when.

The interior was hardly less busy, a mêlée of journalists, lawyers and policemen. All in motion like the scattering of the reds on a snooker table. The courtroom, by contrast, was quietly sepulchral. He soon realised that the copper had done him a favour. The view from the privileged planks of the City Lands Committee benches was a good one. He found himself sharing the back row with a dozen women in daft hats. They were, it struck him, dressed for church – a little too florid, a little too much powder, a discreet smidgeon of lipstick. He had forgotten the space a good trial occupied in the social calendar, somewhere between the Church of England and a West End play. He had not attended as a spectator since his first year on the force, when it had been part of his education to know the workings of the law at this level. For most of the last thirty years he had faced these benches from the opposite side, from the witness box, occasionally glancing at women such as these and wondering at their fascination with crime.

The woman in lilac next to him smiled and inched along the bench to make room for him without a murmur. Perhaps he looked like an invalid; perhaps his very pallor said 'poorly'? The woman on the other side of her, so obviously her mother, looked all of eighty, head bent over her knitting, humming softly to herself, the skin of her hands liver-spotted, her cheeks chalk-white beneath the dusting of powder.

Fitz, on the other hand, put up in the dock, looked the picture of health – out on bail, spared the sunlessness of prison, the perils of perpetually boiled meals. His head turned, moments before the court rose for the judge, and for a second he looked straight into Troy's eyes. Troy could read nothing. Not reproach, not guilt – then Fitz smiled. And the smile was the mereness of recognition.

Troy found he had encountered all the major players at one time or another. He had given evidence before Sir Ranulph Mirkeyn on half a dozen occasions. He was not one of his favourites, a former member of the Plymouth Brethren, a man and a mind deeply rooted in the Old Testament. He had answered the questions of Prosecuting

Counsel Henry Furbelow twice, as he recalled, and he had met Defending Counsel David Cocket at Uphill. The choice of Cocket worried him. Charged with anything more than drunk and disorderly, Troy would opt for the best lawyer money could buy, not a friend – well, not necessarily a friend – and certainly not a friend who conceded, at Troy's estimate, twenty years' experience to the prosecution, and who had yet to take silk. He had liked Cocket, he was sharp, he was witty, but could he hold his own against a warhorse as experienced as Henry Furbelow QC?

The first goal was an own goal.

Furbelow rose.

'My Lord, the prosecution wishes to withdraw the charge of procurement.'

Good bloody grief. Mirkeyn would eat him alive for this. It could mean only one thing. They had taken a chance the day before on drumming up evidence they had failed to find. They were conceding defeat now – a day too late for the good temper of any judge.

To Troy's amazement Mirkeyn simply accepted this. The court hissed with whispers. Mirkeyn called for silence and when the whispers had stopped Cocket was smiling and Furbelow not. The first victory – however large or small. It bothered Troy, bothered him professionally. A prosecution as sloppy as this had just appeared to be meant sloppy police work. If it had fallen to him to refer a charge for prosecution he would never have let it get this far without the proof. Nobody came out of such chaos looking good. Troy knew exactly what had happened – somewhere along the line they had lost a witness.

§ 52

It was gone four o'clock. Everyone was flagging. The day had been a non-event, a bogging-down in procedure, aptly summed up by the stage whisper of the old *tricoteuse*, who turned to her daughter and said: 'Have the tarts been on yet, dear? Have I missed the tarts?'

Half the court, it seemed, had heard her. Cocket turned round, involuntarily perhaps, tried not to grin. Fitz looked over from his seat in the vast emptiness of the dock and smiled again. The same smile he had smiled at Troy. It wasn't recognition, Troy now realised. It was not an outward motion at all. It was something in Fitz. Some absolute resolution not to be unnerved by it all. As though the man had induced a state of calm, by power of will alone or, more likely, by surrender of will. A beatific, a Buddhist serenity, Troy could not but see it as a dangerous condition. He who isn't fearful in the dock does not know the power of an English court. He who isn't at least cautious in any seat in the Old Bailey, from counsel to public gallery, does not know the law of contempt, the absolute power of a judge to imprison without trial.

Mirkeyn's demonstration of his power was brief. He hammered his gavel and adjourned until the following morning.

When Troy had made his way slowly out from the City benches – letting the women in hats stream out ahead of him – he found a tall, dark, handsome young man waiting for him. His nephew, Alex.

'You're just about the last person I expected to see.'

'Call it a hobby,' said Troy. 'It may well be all that's left of my job. However, you're not the last person I was expecting. In fact I would like a word with you.'

'I have to file, Freddie. I should be running hell for leather for Fleet Street right now.'

'Then get me a cab. We can share a cab as far as the *Post*.'

'Quicker if I walk at this time of day, but I'll happily find you a cab.'

Troy stood on the pavement, while Alex waved his arm at indifferent cabbies and elbowed the competition aside.

'I merely wanted to ask you why they've dropped the procurement charge.'

But Alex had bagged a cab and bundled Troy into it.

'Freddie, why don't you call me? I'll be happy to give you all the dope some other time.'

Alex banged the door shut. The passing thought 'they grow up so quickly' passed through Troy's mind, but he consigned it to the ragbag of poor thinking almost at once. He'd been brushed off and that was all there was to it.

He was about to tell the cabbie they should go, when the door opened again. He assumed it was Alex, thinking better of his haste. But it was an old, familiar face. That of Percy Blood, Chief Inspector at Scotland Yard. An ugly, old-school copper. The old school that favoured black boots and grubby brown mackintoshes. They went nicely with the greasy strands of hide-the-bald-spot hair combed in furrows left to right across his dome, and nicely too with the bitten, nicotined fingernails. He was fifty-five or thereabouts. Long since passed over, he would see out his days as a chief inspector, and this had lent to his naturally unpleasant disposition an edge of bitter resentment. He was a plodder. If he were in Troy's section Troy would have put him out to an early pension.

'Mr Blood. Can I offer you a lift to the Yard?'

'No thank you, sir. I've a squad car waiting.'

'Then how can I help you?'

'I saw you. In the court.'

'Yes?'

'I was wondering. If your interest in the case was professional like. The Yard said nowt to me.'

'I'm on sick leave, Mr Blood. As I'm sure you know. I'm simply passing the time. Call it academic interest.'

He looked blankly back at Troy as though the phrase meant nothing to him.

'So – you're not . . . you're not . . . like . . .'

'No. I'm not. But since you're here I do have a question.'

Again the blank look as though they spun words from a different yarn in Manchester and twenty years in London had not taught him the lingo.

'When did you transfer from Special Branch to the Vice Squad?'

Blood pretended to think about this, pretended to come up with nothing.

'A while back,' he said, and closed the door.

Stupid, thought Troy, it was a simple question, and the answer simply found if he just called Records. He'd been brushed off again, but it didn't much matter.

§ 53

The following day, Troy sat waiting to see who would be called next. Tara? Caro? But it was a name he'd never heard. The cry went down the court for one 'Moira Twelvetrees.'

It was a face he'd never seen – but a face he'd seen a thousand times. The pathetic 'want-a-good-time-dearie?' face of a London streetwalker.

He remembered vividly the burning embarrassment the first time a Soho whore had put the question to him. Want a good time, dearie? He had had two reactions: firstly that she probably wouldn't know a good time if it fell on her, and secondly that it marked him. He was only twenty-seven, but one of the *rites de passages* of middle age had to be the moment when a Soho whore first takes you for a fare.

The whore was young, pretty but utterly lacking style. She had no idea how to dress or to apply make-up or, more likely, had an idea which was wholly parodic and therefore wholly wrong. Would Fitz, Troy thought to himself, have left anyone so untutored? The Ffitches were sophisticates; Clover, her way with eye make-up notwithstanding, even Clover had style. This woman had none.

He listened as Furbelow drew from her the story of Fitz accosting her near Paddington station and taking her back to Dreyfus Mews for, as Furbelow so emphatically intoned, 'sexual intercourse', a phrase with which the woman had some little difficulty, calling it as she did 'sectional intercourse'. Troy yearned for the legitimacies of plain English, the unambiguity of fuck and swive. At the end of their sectional intercourse Fitz, the court was asked to believe, had offered to find her more clients and let her use his bedroom, in return for half the take. She had agreed and fucked a dozen or more of Fitz's contacts over a period of weeks earlier in the year. Prostitution, pimping, cut and dried.

Cocket rose for the cross. He ignored the singular coitus between Fitz and Moira Twelvetrees and chose instead to ask her for detail upon detail. A wealth of small questions.

Troy could see her lips move silently as Cocket put his questions. It seemed to him that she had been tutored after all – but not by Fitz – and before Cocket could even finish the question she was mutely rehearsing her answer, drawing not upon memory but on the rote-learning someone had dunned into her. The front door was yellow, there was a big Chinese vase on the left as you went in. On the right or on the left? Oh, the left, definitely the left. Fitz's bedroom was on the first floor at the back, the lavatory was – shock upon shock – black, to match the washbasin. From this the jury was left in no doubt that she knew Fitz's house very well; the details were, for want of a less loaded word, intimate.

And then Cocket jumped in at the deep end.

'You are saying, are you not, Miss Twelvetrees, that you had sex with a variety of men over a period of twelve weeks from December last year until March of this year in the Dreyfus Mews house of the defendant?'

'Er . . . yeah.'

'And you know these men only as Bill or Nicky or David?'

'They didn't tell me surnames. None of 'em.'

'And you didn't recognize any of them?'

'Recognise?'

'We heard in the prosecution's opening address that the defendant was acquainted with the rich and famous. I was merely wondering if any of his rich and famous friends might have been among those clients you claim to have serviced.'

'My Lord . . .' Furbelow rose, did not finish his sentence.

'Mr Cocket,' said Mirkeyn, and Cocket in the face of two half-sentences graciously withdrew the question. Had Troy believed for a moment that the lovely Moira had serviced the toffs of London town he might well have listened out for the velvet swish as the establishment ranks closed over her.

'Did you ever practise the sexual act in the missionary position?'

'The what?'

'On your back. Did you lie on your back with a man on top of you?'

'Well . . . o' course . . .'

'How often?'

'You what?'

'Did you assume this position for every client?'

'No.'

'No? Why not?'

'Well some of 'em . . .' and her voice dropped to a crimson whisper, 'some of 'em wanted to play doggies.'

From the colour of her face Troy felt that the woman knew no other phrase for the act and wished she did.

'So,' said Cocket, 'some of your clients played doggy?'

Go on, thought Troy, be the perfect English judge and ask her what she means. But Mirkeyn did not.

'Did most of them play doggy?'

'No.'

'So . . . I can safely say most of them had you on your back?'

'S'pose so.'

'Tell me, Miss Twelvetrees, have you ever feigned an orgasm?'

'Come again?'

Furbelow rose.

'My Lord, is this relevant?'

Mirkeyn passed the question.

'Well, Mr Cocket, is it?'

'Yes, my Lord, I believe it is.'

'Continue, Mr Cocket. Continue with care.'

'Miss Twelvetrees?'

She muttered, redder than ever.

'I'm sorry, I didn't quite catch that?'

'Do you mean, like, come? Like faking coming?'

'Yes.'

'Then . . . yes.'

'Yes, some of the time? Or yes, all of the time?'

'Yes all of the time.'

So much for British manhood, and with Mirkeyn glaring at the gallery, none dared gasp and none dared giggle.

'And while you were ah . . .' (hammy pause from barrister) '. . . faking it . . . what did you do?'

'I make like . . . noises.'

'You make noises? What sort of noises?'

'Sort of . . . ooh ooh ooh.'

'Ooh ooh ooh?'

'Yeah. And after a while I just sort of stare at the ceiling.'

The shift in tone and gear was startling to hear in Cocket.

'Miss Twelvetrees, what colour is the ceiling in Dr Fitzpatrick's bedroom?'

It was, Troy realised, very far from being the titillating waste of time he had taken it for – it was a superb stringing out of a witness to an unwitting conclusion.

'I . . . I . . . dunno.'

'Come, come, Miss Twelvetrees. You went to Dreyfus Mews countless times – and you have told us many details of the interior. You had a dozen regular clients, most of them on your back, with whom you faked orgasm and stared at the ceiling. What colour was the ceiling?'

'White,' she blurted out.

Cocket reached for an envelope and removed a 10 × 8 colour photograph, which the usher passed to Moira.

'I took this myself, on the day the defendant was charged. It is the ceiling of the defendant's bedroom. What colour would you say it was?'

'It's blue,' she said.

'Blue,' said Cocket. 'Blue and what?'

'Blue with little silver stars. An' little silver moons.'

It put Troy in mind of Yeats's Wandering Aengus – 'little silver apples of the moon'. Chief Inspector Blood had been betrayed by his copper's nose – too close to the ground. He had been looking in the gutter when he should have been staring at the stars.

'My Lord, I submit this photograph as defence exhibit A. It is witnessed on the back by my clerk of chambers. I ask that it be so marked. Now, Miss Twelvetrees, have you ever been inside the defendant's house?'

'Yes.'

'But that was only on the one occasion, when you had sex with the defendant, was it not?'

She was looking about her, her eyes seeking help.

'That's not true. It was lotsa times. Lotsa times!'

And try as he might Cocket could not get her to admit that she had made up every other aspect of her story. But it would be an odd jury indeed who could not see the truth in her for all that she kept on lying. It would be an odd juror who thought a blue and star-spangled ceiling less memorable than a Chinese vase. Moira looked cornered, she looked like a liar and the fact that she went on lying only served to convince Troy that someone had put the fear of God in her.

Cocket sat down. Troy wondered how much the lost admission mattered. If she had told the truth ... it would amount to a Prosecution cock-up, and the defence could ask for a dismissal. He might not get it, but he could ask.

Mirkeyn looked at his watch, slipped it back into his waistcoat pocket, and adjourned.

An old woman was waiting for Troy as he slipped from the row. She was staring intently at him – huge, heavy-lidded, dark eyes, almost as dark as his own.

'You don't remember me, do you?'

He did not, but he had noticed her. She sat each day in the press box, scribbling furiously, deftly shuffling two pairs of spectacles as she looked from her notebook to the witness box and back again. She must be about seventy, he thought, and she spoke the received pronunciation of a lost Edwardian age – almost, not quite, a female Mr Macmillan in her tones – a squeaky voice, wet on the 's's. If she had known him, it might well have been in his childhood. He found too often these days that he had a poor memory for all those grown-up faces that had graced his father's dining table. It was hard to think that the old man's heyday had been more than thirty years ago, but it had. How much could she have changed in thirty years?

'You're Frederick, the youngest, aren't you?' she said. 'I used to write for your father.'

So many had.

'I'm Rebecca West.'

Troy stuck out his hand. Dame Rebecca held it lightly and performed the almost touchless old lady's handshake. The coldness of her fingertips upon his palm.

'I'm so sorry. Of course. I'm afraid I didn't recognise you at first.'

'Nor do you now. Have I changed so much?'

Indeed she had. She had been one of 'the beauties', one of those ageless, beautiful women that had seemed so abundant, so unattainable in the days of his long adolescence. Ageless – she had probably been in her mid-thirties then, younger by far than his parents, older by far than him. He had the embarrassing memory of a schoolboy crush, that overly polite term for unuttered, unutterable lust.

'Do you have time for a drink and a chat?' she asked, and a

schoolboy dream came true, thirty-five years too late, but impossible to refuse nonetheless. 'We'll find a caff somewhere shall we?'

'Caff' was not a word he would expect to hear on the lips of a woman of her generation, but she was smiling as she said it and he recalled that she could be one of the most unpredictable – hence, one of the prickliest – of people when she wanted. She was relishing the word.

He found just such an establishment in Carter Lane. No other word would do. Soho it was not. No Gaggia machine, no 'froffee coffee', just tea, dark brown, pungent, milky, scummy tea served in half-pint cups at refectory tables of scrubbed, cracked and fag-end-burnt Formica. Nor were there the denizens of Soho – no would-be Bohemians in sloppy-joe sweaters, clutching copies of the *New Statesman* and boring on the subject of Dave Brubeck or John Coltrane – no flash bastards in tight trousers, winkle-picker shoes and greasy quiffs. It was a working man's caff – pie an' mash at lunchtime, packed in twelve to a table – or it would be if any of them had looked as though they had jobs. Most of them didn't; most of them looked down and out, eking out three penn'orth of tea and a Woodbine as long as they could.

'There's so much I would want to ask you,' she had said as they crossed Ludgate Hill. The tense had baffled him – she had made it conditionally and temporally impossible. And to prove it she said nothing more until he set her cup of tea in front of her, and one ringed finger had picked up a teaspoon to stir.

'But I won't,' she said as though there had been no interval between one sentence and the next.

He filled in the blank, half a dozen connections forming themselves simultaneously in his mind. She had been very attached to his father – possibly too attached; Troy had seen a few blazing rows between them – but she had vanished from his, Troy's, life when he had joined the police and spent less and less time at Mimram. And after his father's death she had not, he was certain, been asked back to Mimram. But who had? His mother's regime had been so different from that of his father. 'Les Anglais' bored her, as she symbolically made clear in most conversations. She spoke Russian or French to her children. Their father, almost invariably English. Rebecca had written lengthy pieces in the press at the time of the first rumours about Charlie, six or seven years ago – her endless, seemingly endless, speculations upon the meaning of treason, as though it needed meaning. She had busied herself in the lives of Burgess and Maclean, and before that such as William Joyce. If, now Charlie's cover was blown, she was expecting a few snippets from Troy, she could whistle for them. She was the most vociferous of anti-Communists, as was Troy's Uncle Nikolai. She was also rumoured to be writing a novel about the Russian revolutions, one of which his father had participated in, the other two – there were another two, weren't there? – had never ceased to be the subject of his commentary. And . . . and there was the hidden link of Diana Brack, H. G. Wells's mistress in the thirties – as Rebecca had been in the teens and twenties of the century – and Troy's in the forties. 'How much did the old woman know?' he wondered – and wondered without wanting resolution. Whatever she said next, let it not be a question about Diana Brack.

'You know Fitzpatrick, don't you?' she said.

'Yes. How do you know that I know?'

'He looks your way from time to time. When he bothers to look at anything, that is. I don't suppose you can see what he does from where you're sitting, but he's blasé beyond belief. One would think he was not listening at all. He passes the time drawing caricatures, wicked, pornographic caricatures of the court. He's sketched Mirkeyn in the nude three times already. And he somehow manages to draw Furbelow with three buttocks and make it seem anatomically accurate. But . . . when he looks at you and when you look back it is clear – you know one another.'

'A friend of a friend,' Troy said for simplicity's sake.

'And so your interest is not professional?'

'I'm off duty. In fact I'm off sick. But any Scotland Yard case brought to trial is inevitably a professional interest.'

'Do you think he's guilty?'

'I've hardly heard the evidence yet.'

'Try to think a bit less like a policeman.'

These had been Fitz's own words to him not so long ago. In another lifetime.

'I doubt it,' he conceded. 'Didn't need the money. He loves risk, but I cannot see the fun in the risk of poncing. Sex is fun, money is fun. Put them together and suddenly they're not. That's about as fundamental as the square of the hypotenuse is equal to the sum of the squares on the other two sides in a right-angled triangle.'

'Aha. Do you think he's a spy?'

'A spy!'

'There has been much privileged speculation on the point.'

Privileged meant one thing – what those slander-immune buggers in the Commons said.

'What sort of speculation?'

'Oh, you know how they do things in the House. Your brother's one of them, after all. "So-and-so may not be a Communist," you say, thereby implying that equally well he may be.'

'No,' said Troy. 'I doubt that too. A dupe perhaps, a spy . . . highly unlikely. I've never thought Fitz capable of keeping a secret. Primary qualification for the job I should think. If those clots in the Commons think he's a spook, they're mistaking the bond between Fitz and Tereshkov. It wasn't politics; it was sex.'

'How quickly we arrive at the heart of the matter,' Rebecca said.

'Sex?'

'Sex.'

'Sex?'

'Power.'

It felt like moves in an invisible chess game, and she'd just put him in check in half a dozen swift manoeuvres.

'Power?'

'The power men have over women.'

'Old as history,' said Troy, quickly switching rook for king, knowing this added nothing to the point she was making, but then he had no idea quite what point she was making.

'We're on the verge of a new age, you know. I keep hearing that.'

'So do I,' said Troy, 'I've been listening out for England going "boom". Not sure I've heard it yet.'

'I doubt you will. Have things changed at all since I was young? I was one of the New Women – it's a label that's made me highly sceptical of the use of "new" ever since. I see nothing new in Fitzpatrick's relationship with these girls.'

'The oldest profession?' said Troy.

'No. I didn't mean prostitution at all. In fact I thought we'd just agreed he wasn't guilty of that. But he's betrayed those girls as surely as if he'd put them on the streets. He has made them commodities.

He's packaged them. Whatever it was in them that was "new", that was of this "new" age, he has put into the same old packet.'

Troy remembered his first reactions, the first time he had seen the Ffitches. His own unspoken phrase had lodged in his mind. They had looked, as he thought it, like 'sex in a packet'. As instant as coffee. But she could hardly mean anything so . . . so . . . so slight as appearance. They looked – surely? – the way they wanted to. What woman ever dressed for a man? Except to attract one – but then perhaps that was what Dame Rebecca meant. The commodity must appeal to the purchaser.

'Well,' he said, 'Fitz is not on trial for that.'

'Is he on trial at all? It is England on trial. The old one trying this nebulous new one – or the new one trying the old. I cannot work out which. The court we sit in isn't the only court in operation and may well not be the one that matters in the long run. There is so much more to this than meets the eye and so much much more to it than the sexual mores and dubious income of Paddy Fitz.'

'He's not a villain, you know.'

'Oh? So he's a good man is he?'

'Hardly that either. He and Woodbridge are two of a kind. Now, I don't know Woodbridge at all well, but they are both men presumptuous enough to think they are above, not the law, but perhaps the rules that govern us.'

'Laws nonetheless,' she said.

'If you like,' said Troy, using his father's phrase and seeing her smile warm at the familiarity of it. 'But that doesn't make them criminals. And the common cry of them both is, "I've done nothing illegal," by which they mean nothing wrong, as though the only rights and wrongs were the rights and wrongs of law.'

She was nodding her assent now. He was, he felt, talking her language.

'What separates them is merely class and power.'

This, in English terms, was pretty much the same as saying that what separated them was infinity itself, but she let it pass.

'They aren't villains . . .' he went on.

And racked his brains for what they were.

'They are sybarites. And if there is an abiding characteristic to the sybarite, a sybarite's code if you like, it is that what's good for him is good for the rest of us. Denying him his pleasure does him no good, if us no harm. Granting it does him good and his good is our good. Thereby we all benefit. The only sin is denial.'

'I'm sure you're right. In fact you're probably right about both of them – Fitzpatrick and Woodbridge – both of them every *other* inch the gentleman . . .'

She smiled as she said it. It was very funny, and so true. Both of them gentlemen for the odd inches only, and rogues for all the evens.

'But,' she picked up, 'but, it isn't the fate of the men that concerns me. It's the women. Have you been round the back yet and seen what happens when the witnesses leave? The Ffitch girls have been booed, hissed and yesterday I saw a lone lunatic pelt them with rotten fruit as though they were in the pillory. Indeed, they are – in the pillory of national opinion. Tarts, as that old dear so rightly put it yesterday. Our national tarts. And do you know, they don't deserve it?'

Troy wondered about the nature of her sympathies. She was quite possibly one of the most infamous unmarried mothers of the century. Sexually liberated in the last days of whalebone and bloomers, just before the First World War. The mistress of H. G. Wells at twenty-one, the mother of his child at twenty-two. He had in his youth wondered if, sexual liberation notwithstanding, she considered herself abused by Wells – she certainly saw the Ffitch sisters as abused by men. And he recalled now that his father, that most expansive, eclectic of hosts, a man who delighted in the absurd juxtapositions of people, had never invited H. G. Wells and Rebecca West at the same time. Come to think of it, he had never invited her to his Hampstead house, the house in Church Row he had bought from Wells, the one Rod now occupied. But, then, it was not absurd, perhaps merely embarrassing, as though for Wells and West to meet would offend, not the other guests, but Wells and West themselves; as though a public secret could still not be paraded in public. For Wells and West to meet might be the fusion of matter and anti-matter, followed by social annihilation at molecular level. God knows why his father had done this. Perhaps he had felt the sense of injustice in her. Plenty of others had been happy enough to entertain the two together.

'Do you think they've given up the search for the third girl?' Dame Rebecca asked.

Whatever he said now might well be to give a hostage to fortune. She was, after all, a working hack – and for all he knew at work on a book too. Better by far to tell her nothing, to throw the question back at her as disingenuously as possible.

'Were they looking?'

He hoped he sounded innocent.

'Oh Lord, yes. Of course they were looking. The police and the press. If the police don't know she's called Clover Browne then they should ask the gentlemen of Fleet Street. But no one's found her. With any luck they'll never find her. Browne with an "e" is merely Smith into Smythe. I'm sure you remember what Groucho Marx had to say about that. Browne can hardly be her real name, now can it? In fact I hear rumours of some influence in the family.'

'Sir Somebody Something,' Troy muttered.

'Eh?'

'That's what Woodbridge called him. Sir Somebody Something.'

'Well, if we knew who Sir Somebody Something was we'd know who Clover Browne was. Tell me, who do you think this old buffer is? Some retired general from the shires?'

Troy thought of Catesby, just for the exemplar, and could not conceive that he, or anyone remotely like him, could possibly be related to Clover.

'Dunno,' he said lackadaisically. 'Haven't a clue.'

It did not concern him. Really it didn't.

§ 54

'I call Tara Ffitch,' Furbelow declaimed.

Troy had last seen Tara at Uphill, naked under the thrusting buttocks of Tim Woodbridge. She made her way to the witness box, the whisper of anticipation circling the room and dying away in a slow diminuendo as she did so. The star had just descended the golden staircase, the house lights were down and the spot upon her.

She had chosen a deliberately muted look, hair up, no hat and a black two-piece. The flat shoes looked to Troy to be against her nature, but then she was, he thought, trying hard to make herself

JOHN LAWTON

acceptable in the eyes of little men, and in heels she must have touched six foot or more – a metaphor too far. She gazed around the courtroom – unashamed – a stern look at Furbelow, the making of a smile for Cocket and was that an eyebrow raised at Troy himself or merely his own wishful thinking? She did not look at the dock.

Furbelow set out to establish Tara's sexual history. Cocket objected at once and Mirkeyn overruled him. It was what the crowd had bayed for. The tale of a good girl from a good home in the shires who had kicked over the traces in the wake of the unfortunate early death of her mother and embarked on a life of promiscuity. It would have been unremarkable in the extreme if narrated by a man. It wasn't Troy's life, but it was the life of many men he knew. It was Charlie's and it bore a more than passing resemblance to the life of Troy's old colleague Superintendent Wildeve, a handsome young copper when they had met during the war, courting every Wren in sight, and now a handsome copper untrapped by marriage in early middle-age and still as promiscuous as ever. And no one thought the worse of him for it.

It seemed to Troy that, laboured though it was, Furbelow was trying to establish the link between promiscuity and prostitution. He was taking his time. Cocket raised no further objections, sat quietly and seemed to Troy to take no notes while the entire press box scribbled furiously. All the same, they had adjourned for lunch and reconvened before Furbelow found his target, and along the way he'd made damn sure that every newspaper in the land had got its headlines for the following morning.

By early afternoon Furbelow had coaxed this narrative – breathless in its courtroom hush to the extent that Tara's exasperation could be heard in exhalation by all – almost to the present day, to the cohabitation of Tara and Caro and Fitz at Dreyfus Mews.

'What was the basis of your presence at the Dreyfus Mews house?'
'I'm sorry, I don't understand.'
'Were you lovers?'
'No. We were friends.'
'You and your younger sister and Dr Fitzpatrick shared a common abode merely as friends?'
'Yes.'
'Who owned the property?'
'As far as I know Fitz . . . Dr Fitzpatrick owned the house.'

'And you and your sister were his guests?'

'Yes.'

'How long did you live at Dreyfus Mews?'

'Almost four years.'

'As guests? Wouldn't the word lodger be more apt than guest?'

'If you like.'

'And as lodgers did you pay rent?'

'Not as such, no.'

Troy could hear the changes in the tone and pace of Tara's answers. She had narrated her tearaway teens and twenties with a sense of boredom with her own life. She looked for all the world like a reluctant celebrity cornered by Eamonn Andrews for *This Is Your Life*, going through the motions for the sake of family and friends, listening patiently as significance she did not share was attached to incidents she had long since dismissed. Now she was, he thought, cautious. An invisible boundary had been crossed. For the first time since taking the stand she had looked directly at Fitz. Troy knew the look. He was a poor copper if he didn't. It said two things. It said, 'Sorry' and it said, 'Lies'. Whatever she said from now on he knew to take with a pinch of salt.

'If not as such,' Furbelow said, 'then as what?'

'We – that is my sister and I – gave him money on an occasional basis.'

'And what were these occasions?'

'Usually occasions when we had money.'

'And when did you have money? You have, I need hardly remind you, already stated that you have had no paid work since 1960.'

'We had money when we were given money.'

'And who gave you money?'

'Men,' said Tara. 'Men gave us money.'

Mirkeyn silenced the courtroom buzz with his gavel and glared at the gallery.

'Why would men give you money?'

Tara kept her eyes on Furbelow, as though burning a hole in the man's face.

'Men gave us money, because they wanted to.'

'Men gave you money out of the goodness of their hearts?'

'Not exactly. Men gave us money because we pleased them.'

'Pleased them sexually?'

'Yes.'

'And where did this sexual pleasing take place?'

'There was no one place. Lots of places.'

'But since you lived at Dreyfus Mews can the court not safely conclude that you pleased men at that address?'

'Yes. We had men at home.'

'Men who then paid you for your services?'

'Yes.'

'One man in particular?'

'Yes.'

'And who might this one man be?'

'The Professor.'

'And you and your sister had sex with the Professor at Dreyfus Mews for money?'

Cocket rose to speak for the first time in what seemed like hours.

'Objection.'

'Your grounds, Mr Cocket, your grounds,' Mirkeyn replied.

'M'lud. It is perfectly obvious to the court that both the witness and my learned friend know the name of the Professor, in which case he should be named. And if I am wrong, and they do not know the name of the man so referred to, then the evidence amounts to no more than hearsay and as such I would suggest is inadmissible.'

This caused Mirkeyn no great deal of thought.

'From the first reporting of this case, and I mean by that many weeks before it was brought before me in this court, the names of individuals have been dragged through the mud in what I can only call a frenzy of innuendo. I will not further that process. There will be no mud-slinging in my court. Overruled. Pray proceed, Mr Furbelow.'

Troy found this astounding. Mirkeyn was admitting evidence concerning a material witness whom the prosecution were being allowed to keep anonymous.

'Now, Miss Ffitch. The Professor paid you for sex, did he not?'

'Yes.'

'How often? Every time you had sex?'

'Yes. More or less.'

'And how much.'

'It varied. Sometimes he'd leave fifty, sometimes a hundred.'

The court gasped. Troy saw two men in the jury turn to each

other and exchange whispers. He did not need to hear them. There could be only one line: 'They must be a bloody good screw to be worth a hundred quid!'

'And how much of this money did you subsequently give to the defendant?'

'That varied too.'

'Well – would you say half?'

'No – less than that.'

'A third then?'

'Perhaps. Yes, about a third.'

'Miss Ffitch. How long did you and your sister continue this relationship whereby the Professor gave you money for sexual intercourse at Dreyfus Mews and you in turn paid a significant proportion of that money to the defendant in lieu of rent?'

'About three years.'

Well, it may have taken all day but Furbelow had done it. He'd laid before the court clear evidence that Fitz had lived off the immoral earnings of Tara and Caro. It was just that Troy did not believe a word of it. And all this without a single mention of the name 'Woodbridge'.

It was almost four o'clock. Mirkeyn wound up for the day.

Troy sat and let the rush go by. Which of them would accost him today? There was no sign of Blood, Alex dashed past him and shot him a 'Not now' look, and he found himself watching Dame Rebecca slowly approach. She stopped, smiled at him, turned to smile at someone out of sight on his right, whispered 'later' and walked on. He could feel the presence, almost the shadow cast over him, and twisted in his seat to see at whom she had smiled. It was Onions. Sir Stanley Onions, former Commissioner of the Met, his old boss, mentor and what-have-you. He should be on his allotment in Acton digging up spuds, or sitting on an upturned orange box smoking a Woodbine – any of the pleasures of retirement. What was he doing here?

'We should have a bit of a chat,' he said.

Troy hated Onions's bits of chat. They weren't bitty and they weren't chatty.

It was a walking-stick day for Stan. There were days when he needed his walking stick and there were days when he didn't. There were days when he carried one, and days when he didn't – and the two categories did not necessarily coincide. He led off north towards Smithfield at a cracking pace, Troy bursting his frail lungs to keep up with him, the stick crashing down like a bolt from heaven, fit to crack paving stones.

He led Troy to a caff. Much the same as the one he had shared with Rebecca West, but catering to the market porters, and at four in the afternoon all but empty and anxious to close.

Onions ordered two teas.

'We shut in fifteen minutes,' said the bloke in the greasy apron.

'Bring 'em over,' Onions said, sounding every inch the copper he used to be. Why, thought Troy, can I never sound like a copper?

Onions hooked his stick across the back of the chair and sat down.

'I've been wanting a word,' he said.

'Oh,' said Troy. 'How did you know I'd be at the Bailey?'

'I didn't. I'd've been round to see you straight after. I came to get a look at the bugger for meself.'

'Oh, I see. Professional curiosity.'

'Professional poppycock. It's our Jackie I want to see you about.'

'Our Jackie' – the habitual Lancastrian possessive – 'Our Jackie' was his granddaughter, only child of Onions's only child.

'Jackie?' asked Troy with a breathless innocence he would come to see as plain stupid.

'The lass's gone off the rails. More'n a year now. Always a bit wayward, but this is too far by half. You know 'er. You know what she's like.'

Troy didn't. He could not remember when he'd last seen little Jackie.

'I might've known she'd be the one to fall in with a fast set.'

Troy had not heard the word 'fast' used in quite that way for more than thirty years. It was a bit Noël Coward. And he'd no idea what Stan was on about.

'Fast?' he echoed.

'Parties. Wild parties. Reefer smokers. You know.'

'I see,' said Troy, not seeing.

'That's why I had to see the bugger for meself. See what kind of a man he is.'

'You mean Fitz? I don't follow. What has Fitz to do with Jackie?'

'Everything. He's the Svengali in the whole bloody mess!'

'And Jackie's Trilby?'

'No. Our Jackie's "Clover". Leastways that's what she calls herself. Clover Browne.'

Troy's heart sank. It was a dreadful thought, Sir Somebody Something . . . Sir Stanley Onions? He had never thought of Onions as Sir Anybody Anything. He was Stan. The title went with the job. You became Commissioner of the Met and they bunged you a knighthood. No one had ever turned it down; Troy did not even know if one could turn it down. And if he became Commissioner – all sins, if not forgiven, then safely buried – he would be Sir Frederick Troy. It didn't bear thinking about. Not for a moment had it occurred to him that Stan was Sir Somebody Something and that Jackie Clover – good God, the name alone should have told him – was Clover Browne.

'You mean Jackie is the third woman the press have been looking for? She's one of Fitz's—'

He thought he might have said 'harem' or 'set' next, but 'set', as Stan had demonstrated, was a noun that went only with 'fast', and he never got the chance.

'One of his tarts?' Onions bellowed. 'Of course she wasn't one of his tarts! She's a virgin! For Christ's sake she's only sixteen!'

'Seventeen,' Troy blurted out.

'Eh?' said Stan. 'What makes you say that?'

Mental arithmetic was not Troy's strong point. Right now he felt as though his life depended on it. He tried to see the figures in his mind and the only figure he could see was Jackie's, stepping out of her knickers in the ruins of Uphill House, and the memory of that unabashed teenage kiss. A mental image for which, for all he knew, Onions might well thrash him in the street. He thrashed around with the subtraction and came up as if by magic with the words '1946. She was born in 1946, wasn't she?'

'Aye, she was.'

The glare of suspicion Troy had seen in his eyes began to fade.

'Surprised you remember. But it was September. She's not seventeen till this month.'

Damn Fitz. Damn Fitz and his lies. If what the girl had told Troy was true, that she'd been knocking around with Fitz since the previous summer, then she had been under age. The question was, who had been knocking her?

'I've had a word with her mother.'

Jackie's mother was Valerie – 'our Valerie' as Stan would call her. Valerie Clover, née Onions, was, Troy thought, an hysteric. But then that was pretty much what her father thought too. One of Stan's jobs in recent years had simply been to try to keep her sober. Years ago – in the last summer before the Second World War, when they were both single – Val and Troy had been an item. What he hoped Stan never knew was that they had been an item once more in the early fifties, when Valerie's husband Ken had been away at the Korean War. When Ken had been killed in the skirmish over Cyprus in 1956 Stan had brought Val back from Manchester to live in London. Troy had avoided her ever since. All the same, they managed to end up in the same room once a year or so. He had come to dread such meetings, to dread even the mention of her name. Few people gave him more hell than our Valerie.

'How is Val?' he asked, dutifully going through the motions.

'Dryin' out. She'll be out and about in a couple of weeks. Like I said, I've had a word with her. We've decided. Something's got to be done about Jackie.'

Troy could not agree more.

'She's got to be . . .'

Stan searched for the right words and came up with the ambiguous '. . . taken off the streets. Right now, I'd put her in a nunnery if they'd take 'er.'

The phrase 'never darken my door again' came unbidden to Troy's mind.

'But I can't. So we've got to stick her somewhere.'

'Quite,' said Troy, for the sake of saying something.

'We've agreed. We want you to have her.'

'What?'

'You're on sick leave, aren't you?'

'Yes, but—'

'You could take her in. Just for a few days. Till the trial's over. Till the press lose interest. After all, it's the last place the bastards'll ever look for her.'

Troy dearly wanted to say no. He found the word would not form on his lips. It was a preposterous suggestion. It was a bag with too many cats in.

'Stan . . . I . . . I . . .'

'It'll not be for long. Just let the dust settle. It's open and shut.

Jury'll not be out ten minutes. The bugger goes down, and two days later he's yesterday's news and they wrap fish 'n' chips with his headlines.'

'Stan, it's not that simple. It's not going to be that simple—'

But Stan's grasp of the trial and mistrial of Patrick Fitzpatrick was nothing next to his absolute conviction that Troy should have Jackie Clover at Goodwin's Court.

'Whatever!' Stan dismissed any argument. 'It's good of you, Freddie. I'll bring the minx round tonight. 'Bout half past seven.'

Stan got to his feet, unhooked his walking stick from the back of the chair. Troy still hadn't said 'yes' and if he did he doubted Stan would hear. He had railroaded Troy, but then he'd always had that talent, and if at any point in their long relationship Troy had ever kidded himself it was rank not talent, he knew now. He watched the table shake as the beast rose, watched Onions's tea slop around in his saucer, watched the bull hobble off to some other china shop, whispered goodbye and wondered how he had ever got himself into such a pickle.

§ 55

Troy opened the door. Stan stood in the courtyard towering over his granddaughter, one hand holding her suitcase, the other in the small of her back, shoving her forward like a recalcitrant truant. Jackie looked like the schoolgirl she should have been. Stan had 'cleaned up her act'. Clover had become Jackie. Little Jackie, with her mop of blonde hair in a ponytail, held in place with a plain brown rubber band. A grey skirt, a blue jacket, a white blouse and what could only be described as 'sensible' shoes. She looked as though she could willingly murder Stan. The girl wore not a scrap of make-up: her fingernails were unpainted; her eyes stripped of the strong black lines she usually favoured. Troy could imagine the scene which had preceded this.

'Get that muck off yer face, girl! You're going nowhere looking like that!'

Jackie would have said 'no'. Knowing Stan, he would simply have belted her one, taken her to the kitchen sink and scrubbed the make-up from her face. God knows how he'd got rid of the nail varnish. A blow lamp?

'Come in,' said Troy, trying to sound pleased to see them.

Stan prodded the girl into the house, set down the suitcase. Jackie stood sullenly regarding Troy, both hands gripping the shoulder strap of a white PVC handbag. Troy hoped she'd keep up the dumb act. He dreaded whatever it was she might have to say.

'You remember your Uncle Freddie, don't you?' Stan prompted.

'Of course,' the lying tart said. 'You took me into Manchester the day before me dad's funeral. Bought me an Alice band and a pair of socks.'

Troy could not have said he'd remembered this till she said it, but yes, he had driven a silent child of ten into the city to get her out of her mother's way. The smile on Jackie's face had become a smirk. Jackie said the words but it was Clover who looked at him now and silently took the piss. She'd known him from the first at Uphill, and she knew now that the last thing Troy wanted was any mention that they had ever met at Uphill, and she was playing this for all its silent worth.

Troy stuck out his hand for her to shake, but she stepped forward past the hand and kissed his cheek.

'I've missed you, Uncle Freddie,' she hissed into his ear, and since he could do very little about her, Troy determined to get Onions out of the house as soon as possible.

But Onions showed no inclination to stay. He didn't take his coat off and he didn't suggest putting the kettle on. 'I'll be off then,' was all he said, as though he'd done his bit by delivering the human parcel.

'Fine,' said Troy, since in a situation where nothing was even tolerable, let alone fine, this was the nearest to it, that Stan should leave before the small scene in a small room blew up in their faces.

'I'll phone. Don't worry, I'll phone. And as soon as this mess is cleared up I'll come for her. But I'll phone.'

'Fine,' said Troy.

'There is one thing,' Stan said, looking at Jackie. 'Open your handbag.'

'Wot? . . . Nah.'

'Open that handbag, my girl or . . .'

Stan raised his hand. Jackie did not flinch. Stan dropped the fist, snatched the bag from her, and half turned his back so she could not stop him opening it.

He held up the prize. A small black lump of cannabis resin about as big as an Oxo cube, and much the same colour.

'See! Did you think I didn't know about your stash?'

The girl sneered. A curling lip Elvis would have envied.

'Did you think I didn't know the jargon after forty years a copper? D'ye think I don't know about pot an' reefers?'

'They're called joints, Grandad.'

Onions hit her so hard with the flat of his hand that his palm print rose upon her cheek in brightest red.

'It's not just the illegality. God knows that's bad enough. It's the contempt you have for me. Other blokes' kids can smoke dope and they can turn their back on it. I'm a copper, girl! Doesn't that mean a damn thing to you?'

'You're not my dad!'

'Jesus Christ, girl. Who do you think I am? I've been father *and* mother to you these last ten years!'

He stuffed the dope in his coat pocket. Headed for the door. Turned as he reached it. Finger upraised, golden with sixty years of nicotine.

'Behave yourself. Do what yer Uncle Freddie says. D'ye hear me?'

On the doorstep, with the door half closed, barely masking their conversation, Onions said, 'I'm sorry, Freddie. She'll be better with you, really she will. It's her mother, and it's me – we seem to provoke her. You won't, I know that. But if you catch her with this filth again, then as far as I'm concerned you can charge her. I'm sorry, really I am. I'll phone every day. I will.'

And with that he was gone.

The door swung creakily on its hinge and Troy stood in the open doorway, half in, half out. Listening to Stan's boots resounding down the courtyard, looking at Jackie.

'He can't make me cry,' she said. 'I won't. I won't. I don't care what he does, I won't cry.'

Troy believed her. This woman-child was carved in granite.

He resorted to the English truce – a nice cup of tea. There was, as the English told him far too often, nothing like a nice cup of tea.

Jackie Clover kicked off the sensible shoes, took the band from her hair and shook it back to the peekaboo look he had first seen at Uphill. When Troy sat down by the fireplace, she took the hint and sat opposite him, legs dangling over the edge of the chair.

'Wossis? Time for a bit of a chat, Uncle Freddie?'

'Yes. House rules. We'd better have them clear from the start, Jackie.'

'The name's Clover!'

'And my name's not Uncle.'

'What do I call you?'

'Troy.'

She smiled. 'Fair enough.'

'Now – you don't really want to be here.'

'Too right.'

'And I don't want you here.'

'Shall I go now?'

'Hear me out. For Christ's sake, hear me out.'

'OK. Shall I be mother?'

She picked up the teapot and began to pour. If the worst she had to offer was to take the piss at every turn, then it might not be so bad after all.

'We're stuck with each other, Clover.'

'Are we?'

'You know that as well as I. You know the mess we're in. Or else you'd have ratted on me to your grandfather.'

'Couldn't see the point. He thinks Uphill was some sort of brothel. No point in telling him it wasn't. No point in telling him you were there too. Only make things worse for both of us. Like you said, we're in it together.'

Troy did not care for her sense of conspiracy, but she was right.

'Quite. He's not alone in that view. Most of the nation thinks it was a brothel.'

'Not true, though. Is it?'

'No, it's not. But it's because the nation, or to be precise, our much respected free press, thinks it was, that you're here. I've no intention of acting as your jailer. You can come and go as you please. But take my advice. The press do not know who you are. They're looking for you. They'd love to put a name to you, but they don't know. And you should keep your head down until the trial's over and the dust has settled. A few days indoors won't kill you. There's a gramophone—'

'What?'

'Record player to you. And there are plenty of books. Just lie low. You might even like it.'

'Why? There's a bob or two to be made. Caro and Tara have been offered hundreds to write their stories for the Sunday papers.'

'And they've neither of them taken it. If they had we'd have seen something of what they had to say by now. Neither of the girls want to see him stitched up. If the press find you, you'll make a few hundred, but they'll use you to beat down Fitz and so will the prosecution. Clover, I've been to Fitz's trial. Do Fitz a favour, do yourself a favour, stay in until it's all over. What did Fitz ever do to you?'

'Fitz,' she said, rolling his name around. 'Fitz? He rescued me from miserable bloody Acton, miserable drunken Mum. Took me to the clubs with 'im, taught me 'ow to cook, 'ow to mix 'im a Martini, 'ow to drive, 'ow to play bleedin' croquet. Fitz? He taught me 'ow to have fun after ten dreary years at Tablecloth Terrace watchin' me mealtime manners with an old man who 'asn't noticed the ark 'as landed yet and a sozzled baggage who thinks the world ended some time in the 1950s when she last got laid. I was just a kid when we met. What did Fitz do to me? He taught me 'ow to grow up. That's what he did to me.'

It was an impressive little speech. He was not sure he entirely believed her, but it leavened her ostensible selfishness. Though he questioned silently how grown up she could be or would want to be at sixteen – or was it seventeen? His father had taught him, younger by far, at twelve or thirteen, as he had put it all those years ago, 'how to be'. It was a beginning. That's all one can ever ask. And in the years that followed he became, with each passing day, more aware of the omissions in his education into being.

'I'm glad to know you appreciate him. If they find you you'll make plenty of fairweather friends on the newspapers, but you'll lose Fitz and you'll make one enemy you cannot afford to make.'

'Who?'

'Your grandfather. And whatever you think of him, he was telling you the truth. He may not be able to teach you how to mix a Martini but he has been father and mother to you since your father died. Believe me. I know your mother.'

'So do I. She hates you. Absolutely hates you.'

'Then why has she sent you here?'

'Simple – we all do what the old man says, don't we? Isn't that why you're having me here?'

It was too true to answer. Troy dearly wished she were in any other house but his, but he could not argue with Stan.

'And don't let me catch you smoking pot.'

'You won't. He took me stash. Funny to think of my grandad walking round London with half an ounce of shit in his pocket. Hope he doesn't get nicked. But it'd be bloody funny if he did.'

She giggled. Put down her teacup and rocked with laughter. It wasn't funny. She reminded him of nothing quite so much as his selfish sisters in demented mood. Really, it wasn't funny.

§ 56

In the morning he found he had overslept. Deliciously fogged by sleep. And when the fog cleared he found that Clover hogged the bathroom. A wafting air of talc and scented soap. The sound of her singing. A song from her Beatles record. The one about there being a place to go when she's down, inside her own head. He tried patience, but soon ran out. All the same he could not bring himself to hammer on the door, stop her singing – tuneful singing, 'playayayace', 'miyiyiyind' – and tell her to get a move on. He skipped shaving, pissed in the sink, made a mental note to buy a second toothbrush to keep in the kitchen cabinet, and set off for the Old Bailey. He arrived in time to see Tara step down and the court adjourn for lunch. He had missed Cocket cross-examining her.

He took lunch with Dame Rebecca. The same walk to Carter Lane. The same caff. He bought two portions of pie and mash, while she read quickly from one of those large yellow pads made for the legal profession in America.

'You can talk while I write. You don't mind, do you? I must get this in.'

She took out a sheet of white foolscap and began turning her yellow jottings into publishable prose.

'Dame Rebecca . . . ' he began, meaning to ask her to elaborate on what she had said two days ago about the Ffitch sisters, only this time to see how it fitted Clover, now that he was stuck with Clover.

'Call me Cissie,' the old woman said. 'Your father always did. It is so nice to be reminded of him again. Your nephew looks just like him, of course, but then he doesn't seem to have time for anybody.'

Troy hesitated. He could not call her, or any woman, 'Cissie'. It was his pig's name. The dilemma so confused him he completely forgot what it was he wanted to ask her.

'Did I miss much?' he asked at last.

'This morning? No. Young Cocket could not budge Miss Ffitch. Odd, when you come to think about it. When have you ever seen a young woman quite so willing to brand herself with the scarlet letter?'

§ 57

He arrived home to find the dining table set for two, the heat and smell of cooking drifting out from the kitchen.

He found Clover at the gas stove, hair up, wearing a man's shirt and grey cotton trousers. A large pan of oily water coming to the boil, a small pan of deep-red sauce, a bundle of pasta wrapped in floury paper.

'Spaghetti,' she said to him, rubbing at her nose with the back of her hand.

He looked at the cookery book she had splayed on the kitchen table. *The Kitchen in the Corner* by Katharine Whitehorn. He turned

to the title page. There, in Paddy Fitz's best doctor scrawl, was
'Clover – new girls begin here. All my love, Fitz XXX.'

'Wot you lookin' at?'

'Oh . . . nothing.'

'Nothin' my arse. When I said spaghetti you thought I meant out
of a tin, din't yer?'

'Yes, I suppose I did.'

'I told you, Troy. Fitz taught me everything. I know a lot more
than how to cook in a bedsit. The pasta's fresh from Brewer Street,
so's the parmesan, an' it's yer reggiano, not the common stuff and it
doesn't come in a plastic shaker. And the sauce is bacon and tomato.
Only I add a bit of red wine, which she don't mention in the book
because she's trying to keep the cost down.'

Clover's bit of red, from the look of the bottle, had been a whole
glass of '55 Fronsac. This was *cuisine au coin* with a bottomless wallet.

'Found it under the sink,' she said.

'That's fine,' said Troy. 'It's there to be drunk. Where did you
find the clothes?'

'Wardrobe in the spare room. Not the one you put me in. The
other. You don't mind, do you?'

No, he didn't mind. It was curiously nostalgic to see her in his old
trousers, one of his cast-off collarless shirts from the days before
mass-production decided to save five minutes in the working day of
the average man by sewing the collars in. Tosca had dressed this way,
had worn these same clothes. That was why they were still in the
wardrobe. Exactly where she had left them and where he had
forgotten them. Clover was only an inch or so taller than Troy.
They fitted her far better than they had ever fitted Tosca.

'Keep them,' he said. 'They were my wife's. She nicked them off
me. You might as well have them.'

'You're married?!'

'I think so.'

'Eh?'

'We're separated. I haven't seen her since 1960.'

Clover did not know how to react to this. It was not, he knew,
the awkwardness of the fact of separation, it was discovering that
there were things her mother had not told her.

'Wot's 'er name?'

'Tosca.'

'Tosca?'

'That's her surname. She's called Larissa, but hardly ever uses it.'

Troy decided to kill this subject or they'd be into 'When did you meet?', 'Why did you split up?' He reached into the cupboard and set out two wine glasses. Poured.

'How long?' he asked.

'As long as it takes to cook the pasta. No more than ten minutes. If you clear out the way, that is.'

He retreated to the sitting room, still clutching the cookery book, and decided to read quietly for the while. It purported to be a survival handbook for life in a bedsitter. He'd never lived in one, never had to. He was surprised to find the author moving readily between food and sex. She was establishing the sexual semaphore that is food and drink. Tosca had once told him that the American for sex was 'coffee'.

'I don't get it,' he had said. 'Doesn't everyone get very confused at breakfast?'

'No, at breakfast coffee means coffee. At night, say eleven going on midnight, if you say to a woman, or a woman says to you, "Youwannacuppacawffee?" then it means sex.'

'What does "Youwannacuppatea?" mean?'

'That means orgy. Two men and a woman, two women and a man, three women, two men and a German Shepherd. All the peas in the goddam pod. Whatever. Why do you think most of us don't drink tea?'

'Memories of Boston?'

'Nah. The whole issue's too darn risky! You nod to a cup of Earl Grey and the next thing you're in bed with half of Yankee Stadium!'

If only, he thought, there had been such a book as this in 1935 when he was twenty. How differently life might have flowed. His life did not flow. It flooded and it froze, but flow it did not.

A mouthful of what smelt delicious had scarcely touched his lips before Clover asked, 'What do you think? Is it all right?'

'Don't ask.'

'Bad as that?'

'No – I mean, "Don't ask" appears to be one of the rules.'

He picked up the cookery book from where it lay splayed next to his plate.

'It's one of her rules for social success. Here we are. "Elementary

JOHN LAWTON

Rules', subsection entitled 'Cooking for Men'. Never ask if it's OK and never apologise.'

'Is she right?'

'Of course.'

'OK. So Fitz didn't teach me everything.'

'I'm sure he tried.'

'But . . . it is OK, isn't it?'

'It's super. You really can cook.'

Head down, she was smiling. He wasn't at all sure that she wasn't also blushing a little at the over-solicited compliment.

Afterwards she sat at the table and perused her book while he made coffee. Damn it, let caffeine and Mandrax fight it out in his bloodstream.

And when he set the cup in front of her she spooned in sugar and stirred. He could see the operation of thought as the spoon switched from clockwise to anticlockwise, and he knew, more or less, what was coming.

'I wonder if I should be there.'

'Why?'

'Why? To help him of course!'

'In what way do you think you could help him?'

'I could give evidence.'

'Indeed you could. After all, the prosecution were only too keen to be able to call you. However they can't find you and without you they've had to drop a charge. You're helping by not being there. If you were there I doubt there's a thing you could do for Fitz.'

'I could speak for the defence.'

'There'd still be a cross-examination.'

'Such as?'

'Well, let's begin with the obvious. Did you have sexual intercourse before you were sixteen?'

'Of course I did. Didn't you? I mean it's not illegal, is it?'

'Yes it is. Did Fitz sleep with you?'

'Yeah, but that's different.'

'How so? You were over sixteen?'

'No . . . I wasn't. But it was different. Me and him. Different.'

Troy thought better of asking what she meant. He did not wish to hear the mitigation of the 'special' – she surely meant special when she said different? He preferred not know. Sixteen was a line, a legal line, an arbitrary line, below which the law stated that there was no basis of personal responsibility. It was arbitrary whilst trying to be accurate – there were plenty of women knowing and responsible below it and plenty above it who would never be either – but it was a wilfully stupid man who ignored that line.

'Did Fitz ever introduce you to men with whom you subsequently had sexual intercourse.'

'What? You mean deliberately?'

'Doesn't matter. Fitz doesn't even need to know you slept with them. The question is did he effect the introduction?'

'Nah. Fitz didn't find boyfriends for me. I don't need anyone to find boyfriends for me. You may not have noticed, Troy, but I'm a looker. Men queue up to 'ave me!'

She stopped, let the change in Troy's expression sink in.

'Wossamatter? Have I said something wrong?'

'Not wrong. Awful. Damning. Imagine that it is not me talking to you across the dinner table, but Henry Furbelow, Queen's Counsel and in this instance the prosecuting counsel at the Old Bailey. Imagine the effect of your last remark upon him. Upon a jury of middle-aged men and women. If I were Furbelow, I would have a ready follow-up. Are you now or have you ever been a prostitute?'

'Nah. Leave it out!'

'They don't leave it out. Men like Furbelow leave nothing out. Have you ever accepted a gift in money or goods from a man with whom you have just had sexual intercourse?'

'Yeah. Lots of women do that. If a bloke wants to bung you a few bob for a frock or some make-up it's no different from if he brings you flowers.'

Troy shook his head.

'As things stand Fitz isn't facing a procurement charge. If you get up in court with all your good intentions, they'll revive that charge and add another count of immoral earnings. And if you ever tell anyone you slept with him before you were sixteen they'll lock him up and throw away the key.'

'Tell me what you think, Troy. Is Fitz going to get off?'

'If the case against him unrolls as I have seen it do to date, then it's a shambles, but the judge is old school and cuts the defence no slack. And I've watched the jury. There are no free thinkers there. They may just convict him despite all they've heard. Stay out of it, Clover.'

He gathered up the plates and stacked them in the kitchen. When he returned she was still sitting there.

'What you mean is, don't meddle. Leave well alone. That's what my grandad says.'

She was angry. He had treated her as a child. What had appeared to be a promising evening without hostilities had just taken a turn for the worst. He pleaded tiredness, told no lies, and went early to bed.

§ 58

Clover caught him out again. By the time he was up in the morning she was already in the bathroom. He'd bought a spare toothbrush, so he pissed in the sink once more and dashed off to the Old Bailey.

Caro stepped into the witness box, and Troy saw every head in the room turn to the head next to it in silent, wide-eyed amazement. She was dressed exactly like her sister. Down to the last detail, from the hair pinned above her ears, via the chic black two-piece down to the flat-heeled shoes. And there the awe at identity ended for Troy. Tara had looked boldly around the court, her surrender of a couple of inches in height had been the tall woman's attempt to be unintimidating to short men like Furbelow and Cocket – a calculated move. Caro was simply trying to make herself invisible. Invisible and inseparable, Troy knew. Troy knew most people in the room could not tell one sister from the other. A doubt only relieved when she stated, almost whispered, her full name to the usher.

'Caroline Alexandra Sarah Ffitch.'

And her date of birth.

'September 3rd 1939.'

It was, as an English comedian of the old school had put it at the opening of so many lugubrious monologues, 'the day war broke out . . . ' Caro Ffitch, younger than her sister by fifteen months, was the perfect war baby.

Troy did not think Furbelow would be long about this. He would get her to confirm her sister's evidence and then Caro would face hell from Cocket, as he exploited the weaker sister as he could not the stronger.

Furbelow skipped the family life of Caro, lingered a moment on the gap in their ages that had kept her at home for a year after Tara had escaped, and how Caro had wanted nothing more than to forsake her home and her father to join her sister in the city. Then he moved quickly to her life at Dreyfus Mews.

'Are you acquainted with a man known to your sister as the Professor?'

'Yes,' said Caro softly.

'Am I right in saying that this man regularly gave you money?'

Cocket rose and objected.

'M'lud. My learned friend is leading the witness.'

'Sustained,' said Mirkeyn.

'Miss Ffitch. Did the Professor ever give you money?'

'Yes, from time to time.'

'Did you do anything for this money?'

'Did I do anything? I don't understand.'

'Well . . . did you provide a service of any kind?'

Troy distinctly heard the old tricoteuse say, 'Just like *What's My Line*, dear,' to her daughter.

'No,' Caro replied. 'I didn't.'

Furbelow was momentarily nonplussed by her answer. It was not in the script. He ruffled the papers in front of him, adjusted his glasses and came back to the issue.

'Miss Ffitch are you familiar with the phrase sexual services?'

'Yes. I think so.'

'Then let me ask you again. Did you provide any services to the Professor, services of a sexual nature?'

'Do you mean did I sleep with him?'

'Yes, but more than that, did you sleep with him for money?'

'No.'

Furbelow rummaged among his papers again.

'Miss Ffitch, I have here the statement you made to the police at Scotland Yard in June.'

Furbelow held it out to the usher who passed it to Caro.

'That is your signature at the bottom is it not?'

'Yes . . . but . . .'

'There are no buts. It either is or it isn't!'

'But . . .'

Furbelow was well into his best bullying manner now.

'Is it or isn't it?'

Troy could see that Caro was on the verge of tears. She could not answer Furbelow. He should have waited her out, but his own impatience got the better of him.

'In this statement you wrote, quite clearly, that the Professor gave you money after sex.'

Caro fumbled with the sheet of paper, opened her handbag, took an age to take out her handkerchief and blow her nose. When she looked up again tears were rolling silently down her cheeks.

'The Professor did give us money. But not for sex. And not that often.'

'How often?'

'It was irregular. Sometimes he'd just open his wallet and say, "Treat yourself."'

'Was one way of treating yourself to pay money to the defendant?'

'No. Why would I do that?'

'Might you not have done it because he asked you?'

'No, that's not true. Fitz never asked me for money.'

'Miss Ffitch. Would you look again at the statement you have in your hand and tell me, is that your signature?'

'Yes,' Caro said.

'Yet you have just refuted two of the strongest statements to which you signed. Can you explain that?'

Troy thought Furbelow was tacking badly here. If he'd been the prosecuting counsel he'd have passed the matter up to the bench several minutes ago.

Caro looked at the statement, looked around the court as though she was utterly lost. Then she looked at the statement again, her lips opening soundlessly, as though she were making a desperate effort to comprehend what she had written, as though the words were swimming like tadpoles in front of her eyes.

'I . . . I . . . didn't read it.'

The roar from the gallery and the press box felt to Troy like the coming of a hurricane – loud and airy at the same time, belief and disbelief in a single breath.

Mirkeyn pounded his gavel, and at last did what a good judge should have done by now – he addressed himself directly to the witness.

'Miss Ffitch, are you saying you did not write this statement?'

'I didn't write it and I didn't read it. I mean . . .'

Caro held up the piece of paper.

'It's typed,' she said sadly. 'I can't type.'

The gallery exploded into laughter. Mirkeyn banged away once more. All the same, it took a couple of minutes to subside and another minute for him to spell out his power and his willingness to clear the court if needs be. It was more than sad; it was pathetic. She could not type. It was a fundamental skill of many women of Caro's class and age, learnt if only as a means to a husband, and here she was waving a piece of paper and bleating pathetically that she could not type. A woman with no other known skills, save sex.

'Miss Ffitch,' he resumed, 'it is an accepted practice in every police station in the land that a police officer types statements for witnesses based directly on what the witness has said to them. It is for the witness then to read the statement and to ask for emendations accordingly. Once signed your signature is taken as assent that what precedes it is true. Do you understand?'

'Yes . . . but I didn't read it.'

'Why did you not read it?'

'I was . . . I was . . . I was too upset.'

She thrust her hanky to her nose. Her tears now came in floods. Troy wondered how far they'd get with her. All the same, he would not put it past Mirkeyn to remind her of the meaning of perjury, or to threaten her with contempt, when all a good judge needed to do was to adjourn for half an hour.

'Why were you upset?'

It seemed to Troy as though he was now witnessing a private conversation. Mirkeyn looked only at Caro, Caro looked only at him. A ludicrous public intimacy. He was, Troy thought, not a man at ease with women's tears, and she was weeping buckets.

'I'd . . . I'd been there all day . . . not just that day . . . lots of days . . . all on my own . . . all on my own . . . just being asked questions

. . . over and over again. I've lost count. I must have been called to Scotland Yard a dozen times.'

Troy looked across at the press box. Every Biro jiggled. They'd have a field day with this. The Yard would not come well out of it. Blood was an idiot.

'Nonetheless . . . the police would not have typed up what you had not said.'

Careful, Caro. Mirkeyn is inviting you to call the police liars. If you do he will find some excuse to send you down for contempt or, worse, perjury. One must never call a policeman a liar. Even though many of us are.

She wiped a hand over each cheek and the streams of her tears, her sobs still audible in every corner of the courtroom.

'I'm sure they typed what I said, my Lord. It was I who did not know what I was saying. I was confused. I was very mixed up, I don't know what I said . . . may very well have said everything they say I said . . . but it was not what I meant to say . . . I was . . . hysterical.'

The word seemed to clunk down like a brick in front of Mirkeyn. Caro could not have chosen a better word. It was part and parcel of the vocabulary of men like Mirkeyn. Women were hysterical. It was why they were intellectually unreliable. This seemed to tip the scales. Mirkeyn drew back and turned to Furbelow. He would not threaten to imprison Caro. She'd been damn lucky. A man less contemptuous of women might not have been so susceptible to their 'hysteria'.

'Proceed, Mr Furbelow.'

Furbelow was startled. Proceed? Proceed where? He no longer had a witness.

After lunch Cocket, wisely, had only one question for Caro. The same one Troy had put to Clover the night before.

'Are you now or have you ever been . . . ?'

To which she gave a clear and unhysterical 'no.'

§ 59

It was a mess. A farce of a case. It made Troy angry. It offended his professional sensibilities. At the end of the day's session Troy looked around for Blood, but he wasn't there. He had been dismissed. It was unlikely his workload would let him indulge his curiosity hanging around the court. Cocket could recall him in the light of Caro's evidence, but this would be to call the police liars, and no one was going to do that. More would be lost than gained.

Troy decided to visit the Yard on his way home. He would see if he could get five minutes with the Commissioner – and whilst he too would not call the police liars, he could at least air his professional opinion.

He made his way up the stairs, wheezing a little, and came to rest on a landing between floors – only to find Sir Wilfrid Coyn descending the same staircase.

'Freddie. Just paying us a visit? How are you?'

'Fine,' Troy said, still wheezing.

'Popping in to CID?'

'No. I was looking for you, actually.'

'Me? Look, I've a car waiting. I have to go home and change. Dinner at the Mansion House. Why don't you walk down with me and tell me what's on your mind?'

Troy followed him down to the car park, talking to his back all the way.

'I've been passing the time at the Old Bailey.'

'Oh? Something juicy, I hope.'

'Court number 1.'

Coyn looked quickly over his shoulder at Troy.

'The case is falling apart. It's a shambles. We should never have brought the prosecution. Too much of the evidence is being shown up as flimsy.'

They reached the car park. A driver held the car door open for Coyn.

'When this is all over we're going to look like fools. This case will not enhance the reputation of the Yard in any way. We'll end up looking like a bunch of monkeys.'

Coyn stopped with his hands resting on the top of the door. 'You don't think it's for the defence to move for a dismissal?'

'It's not quite at that stage.'

'Then what stage is it at?'

'The stage when it's becoming obvious to everyone that we should not have brought the prosecution in the first place.'

'Freddie,' said Coyn, 'your job's getting well again. I need you fit. The Yard needs you fit. Why not just let us get on with our job in the meantime, eh?'

He patted Troy gently on the upper arm, climbed in the car and drove away. It was as close as men like Coyn came to saying fuck off.

§ 60

He felt worn out by the time he got home. He had lingered too long. It was past dusk. He had walked too many streets, sat on too many park benches and stared too long at nothing in particular. He sloughed off his coat, kicked off his shoes, draped his tie over the doorknob. The house was quiet. There was no sign of Clover but for the faint scraping sound of the gramophone stylus orbiting the final loop of a record. He pulled the arm back and turned off the power. Then he heard her voice. She was in the bathroom on the half-landing at the back. Still in the bathroom? He looked at his watch. He'd been gone the best part of twelve hours. She was hogging the bathroom, again.

He stomped up the stairs, fist clenched ready to hammer on the door. He stopped his hand, laid his palm flat on the wooden panel. Clover was singing to herself again — and not one of her Beatles' songs — her voice filling the bathroom, echoing off tiles, seeping out onto the staircase with wafts of steam, following him up the stairs to his bedroom. He had not thought that she possessed such a voice, a clear, wonderfully controlled contralto. He had not thought she knew any song that was not bang up to date. This was old. The last century at least. He knew it well – it was an Irish folk song called 'She Moved Through The Fair'.

> My young love said to me
> Your Mother won't mind
> And your father won't slight me
> For our lack of kind
> And he stepped away from me
> And this did he say
> It will not be long love, till our wedding day.

He lay down on his bedroom floor, used his jacket for a pillow, closed his eyes and listened to the song push its way through the floorboards.

> He stepped away from me
> And moved through the fair
> And fondly I watched him move here and move there
> And he went his way homeward
> With one star awake
> As the last swan of evening moved over the lake.
>
> The people were saying
> No two were e'er wed
> But one had a sorrow
> That never was said.
> He went away from me with his boots and his gear
> And that was the last that I saw of my dear.

It was a sinister tale. He knew of two or three variants on the theme in English, which probably meant there were at least two or three dozen known to the likes of Cecil Sharpe or Percy Grainger and those fanatical turn-of-the-century collectors of folk music. It was a demon lover song. The lover seduces. Too late the seduced discovers that her lover is a cloven-hoofed demon, or simply dead to begin with. The last verse was a killer. Beautiful, stark and deadly.

> I dreamed it last night
> That my dead love came in
> So softly he came, that his feet made no din
> He laid his hand on me
> And this he did say
> It will not be long love, till our wedding day.

The words stopped. Clover continued the melody in scat. And as the words ceased the tune grew, the volume swelling, to the point where he opened his eyes almost certain of what he would see, her backlit in the doorway, wrapped in a scarlet bath towel, hair pinned up, stripped of make-up.

'You OK?'

'Yes. Just a bit tired I think.'

'Wot you doin' on the floor, then? You might as well stretch out on yer bed.'

He could not think of a lie. Occasionally this happened to him.

'I was listening to your song. This end of the room's right over the bathroom. I could hear you quite clearly. It was beautiful. You have a good voice. Where did you learn that song?'

'My mum taught it to me when I was little.'

'I didn't know Val sang.'

'If you ask me, there's a lot you and my mum didn't bother to find out about each other.'

'Let's not talk about your mum.'

'Fine by me. Look, you ain't 'alf lookin' peeky. Is there anything I can get you? Cup o' char? Is there anything you want?'

She stepped closer, the towel swept the floorboards and brushed against his shirt. She wafted it across his face. Playfully, he thought.

'Well? Wotcher want?'

Was that a smile or a grin? She wafted the edge of the towel across his face once more. Talc. Nothing he could name. Something floral. He grabbed the end. Clover held the towel with both hands clutched at her sternum. Troy pulled the towel gently taut and she let go. The towel floated down, scarlet folds on the boards. Clover caught one corner before it could land – a broad red ribbon leading from him to her. Him in shirt and socks and trousers, her naked as she had been amid the ruins of Uphill Park.

'You gettin' up or am I gettin' down?'

'I haven't the energy to get up.'

'Troy, there'd better not be a two-letter word missing from that sentence.'

Her strength surprised him. His lack of substance surprised him. She took his hands in hers, pulled him to his feet and fell neatly back on the bed, head straight to the pillow, with Troy on top of her. She popped every button on his shirt, slid her hands down his chest, pulled at his zipper and, when both hands were wrapped around his risen cock, whispered in his ear.

'Take your socks off.'

'What?'

'I've never made love to a bloke still wearin' his socks and I don't intend to start now.'

Troy could not tear them off quickly enough. Nor his trousers, nor his underpants, nor his flapping shirt. He found himself standing over her, cockstiff and crazy, gazing at her, dappled with patches of talcum powder – the small breasts, the stiff nipples, the tiny waist, a vertical slit of a belly button. She reached across and took his left hand, placed it between her legs. He slipped in a finger. She put her hand behind his neck, pulled him down and kissed him. Lips, nose, eyelids. Slowly he became aware that she was steering him. His lips drifting southward, across her throat, over one breast, in and out of the belly button – her hands gripping his head, her fingernails nipping his scalp, talcum powder dusting his lips. Yet he could not find the scent of her. The talc was freesia, the soap peach, but she was so fresh from the bath, so well scrubbed, he could not smell Clover. He had reached her thighs, with her fingers still locked in his hair. He took his left hand away and put his lips to her cunt.

He'd no idea what to do. He'd never done this before. No woman he'd ever been with had ever suggested it. He'd never dared to ask.

§ 61

He awoke to find himself flat on his back, Clover half draped across him, the scentless air now scented with the alkaline smell of sex – part cunt, part semen, faintly acrid, impossible to mistake. Why did it always remind him of mangoes?

'Sorry,' he said. 'Must have nodded off.'

'Nodded off. You was snoring.'

'Sorry – shouldn't sleep on my back. Never do as a rule.'

'Don't matter. You want to fuck some more?'

'I couldn't . . . I'm drained.'

'No you're not.'

One hand stroked his cock from tip to balls. He was up already. She had coaxed him to an erection even as he slept. The damn thing had its own life even as his seemed to have slipped from him.

'I couldn't . . .'

'Right you are. It'll 'ave to be girls on top.'

She slid one leg over him, all her weight on her knees, her hands flat on the mattress either side of his head. Less did he enter her than she enveloped him. With his cock inside her, her back arched, her hands flitted lightly over his face, fingertips tracing the line of his cheekbones and lips. Then they came to rest at the back of her neck. She pulled the rubber band off, shook her hair free and smothered him in it. For a while he thought it bliss. Flat on his back, getting fucked silly.

§ 62

The next day was Saturday. He spent it in bed, reading, recovering from the exertions of the day and the more demanding exertions of the night. He spent it in bed avoiding Clover.

It was gone six in the evening before she put her head round his door. She came in and sat on the end of the bed.

'It's Saturday night,' she said.

'I know.'

'Let's go out.'

'Go out?'

'It's Saturday night. People go out of a Saturday night. I been indoors since grandad dumped me on your doorstep.'

'Where would you like to go?'

'Dunno. You say.'

'Ronnie Scott's?'

'Not my scene.'

'The Flamingo?'

She pursed her lips, held one hand level at waist height and twisted it like an aileron – neither up nor down, neither yes nor no.

'How about the Marquee?' she said.

'That's not my scene,' said Troy.

'So we're stuck in. Sittin' in front of the fire like Darby an' bleedin' Joan!'

Darby and Joan. What she really meant was Stan and Valerie.

'A film,' he said. 'Let's go to the pictures.'

'The flicks? Is that the best you can do?'

'It's dark, it's anonymous.'

'What's on?'

'*Lawrence of Arabia.*'

'Not the bloody war again!'

'No – a quite different war.'

'Don't matter. Seen it anyway. Can I pick?'

Troy tossed a copy of yesterday's *Evening Standard* at her.

Five minutes later she had found nothing she liked and let it slip from her fingers, let her lip curl into the petulant beginning of the Elvis-sneer.

Troy took up the paper.

'*Jules et Jim*'s on at the Academy,' he said hopefully.

'What, that place with all the foreign films?'

'Yes.'

'Subtitles?'

'Yes.'

'I'd have to wear me specs.'

'Who's going to see?'

Dressed in Troy's macintosh, buttoned to the chin, collar up, her hair wrapped in a headscarf, he felt Onions himself might not have known her. The spectacles came out as soon as the houselights dimmed. Vanity preserved. He feared her restlessness, her insatiable, lazy boredom, but she sat silently – so silently he soon recognised it for what it was. Rapture.

Emerging into the street once more, close by Oxford Circus, she stopped. Grabbed him by the sleeve.

'You seen it before?'

'Yes. Must have been about a year ago now, perhaps a little longer. When it was new.'

'It's . . . it's fuckin' fabulous!'

'I know.'

He walked on in the hope she'd bend if not break her trance and follow. He didn't want to stand in the bustle of Oxford Street all night. It was one of the most depressing places on earth.

'I mean that's it, isn't it? That's got to be it, hasn't it?'

He'd no idea what she was talking about. But then all he had to do was let her walk and talk.

'To die for each other. I mean. There is no greater love.'

Inadvertently hitting upon a jazz standard as her qualifier, she had also hit upon a colossal fallacy.

'For each other?'

'Yes. To die for each other. To know it's all pointless, to get in that car, to drive off that bridge and die together, for each other.'

'You mean like a suicide pact?'

'Yeah.'

This was startling. Had they seen the same film?

'She murdered him.'

'What?'

'She could not have him. So she murdered him.'

'She loved him!'

'She did, throughout the film, exactly what she wanted. She was the most selfish of heroines, and when Jim comes to his senses and recognises this she kills them both. It was murder.'

'But she was so beautiful. Wotsername was so . . .'

'Jeanne Moreau.'

'So beautiful. I don't mean to look at . . .'

Why not? thought Troy, he'd fallen for Moreau at first celluloid sight.

'But in herself.'

'You're wrong.'

'Damn you, Troy. You just won't see it the way it was. To die for each other. To die for.'

She lapsed into silence. He wondered what she was dredging up.

'Romeo and Juliet,' she said at last. 'There was to die for. They died because they couldn't be together.'

'Indeed they did, but it wasn't suicide. It was the great cock-up.'

He had to think quickly. Romeo and Juliet. Who killed who?

Which one had the knife, which one had the poison? Who licked poison off whose lips? Who ever watched Shakespeare for his plots?

'One of them commits suicide – or maybe both of them – but not together, and then only because one of them thinks the other's dead, when they're not, and thinking they're dead commits suicide, and then the one that wasn't dead but looked to be wakes up and seeing the other one really dead commits suicide too.'

'Eh?'

It was perfectly logical remark on Clover's part. 'Eh?' indeed. He should have known better than to try to summarise a Shakespeare plot in a single sentence.

Pyramus and Thisbe, he thought, that was easier. One of them got eaten by a lion . . . or was it a bear? Oh sod it. She'd probably never read Ovid anyway.

'I can think of only one example of a suicide pact by lovers, and it isn't fiction, it's history,' he said.

'And?'

'Mayerling. About twenty years before the First War. The heir to the Austrian throne, whose name escapes me, and his lover, whose name also escapes me, killed themselves at his hunting lodge.'

'Why?'

'Can't remember.'

'But people do do it, don't they. They do. It's true!'

'Idiots do,' said Troy.

'Can't you see the love in it? Can't you imagine a love so powerful you'd die for it?'

'No,' he said truthfully, 'I can't.'

Troy cut a devious route back home. Along Oxford Street, down Great Chapel Street into Soho. Then the double-back into St Anne's Court. Clover dawdled, idly looking around. The habitual affectation of the bored teenager – at least habitual for as long as there had been teenagers. Troy could not remember that he ever was one. He wondered if she'd even notice his aberrant navigation. He stopped before a glass panel, next to a newsagent's, and feigned reading the posted advertisements. And found he could not feign. He paid so little attention to London's square mile of vice, perched as it was upon his own doorstep, that the advances in subtlety since the law had hustled the whores off the street, begat an inventiveness little short of startling.

'Well padded sofa – pretty in pink.' And then a local telephone number.

He could not for a moment think what this meant. Then he felt Clover's chin descend to his shoulder, her eyes next to his as she leant on him and stabbed at the ad with her finger.

'White woman, good looker, big tits,' she said as though she had read his mind to the letter.

'Really?' escaped him. He would have preferred to have said nothing.

Her finger shot out to 'Double fronted mahogany wardrobe – suit bachelor.'

'Black woman – even bigger tits. Anything else you don't understand?'

In for a penny, he pointed to 'Tired old 3 piece suite? Let Maggie the Upholsterer whip it into shape.'

'Jesus, Troy. Where have you been all your life?'

She walked off and left him. He caught her up at the corner of Wardour Street. She was smiling gently and seemed almost to be laughing to herself. At Meard Street he turned in and she followed.

Meard Street was bolder. Prostitutes risked arrest, stood in their doorways, leant out of windows. Troy had few doubts that most of these women were slipping backhanders to his colleagues on a weekly basis. It was what he hated about vice and Vice – everybody bent to it.

A roguish whore smiled at him. He quickened his pace, only to feel Clover's hand restrain him.

'What do you take me for, Troy? You think I haven't seen all this before? I been coming up West since I was thirteen. I seen all this and so what? So bleedin' what? Is this your morality tale? Are you trying to tell me this is where I'll end up? Poor little Jackie Clover on the stony path to hell, earning her living on her back? Troy – it's not my problem. It's yours. You're the one with this vision of hell, not me. And you're about as wrong as you could be. It's been a wasted lesson. I've learnt only one thing I didn't know.'

OK, he thought, play the game.

'And what's that?' he said, dutifully playing.

''Ow to use a peashooter.'

She pointed down Meard Street towards the narrow end where it bottlenecked into Dean Street to emerge almost opposite Gennaro's restaurant. Good bloody grief, he'd never even noticed. A young whore was leaning out of a first-floor window blowing dried peas at passing men. She had discrimination – only those whose footsteps lingered – and she had aim – Troy watched her ping one right off the back of a bloke's neck. He slapped a hand to his neck and looked around, as though expecting to see an aggressive insect of some sort. His eyes caught the whore's. She waved, fingers in a rolling fan, like an elementary five-finger exercise at the keyboard. The man reddened and walked on.

'See?' said Clover.

She left Troy standing again, turned into Dean Street. Troy followed before the Maid Marian of Whores drew a bead on him. He could not grasp Clover. Equally he could see no reason why he should be able to grasp her, but grasp her he could not. The naive romantic, entranced by his Mayerling tale; the hardened cynic unintimidated by the bare facts of metropolitan prostitution. Perhaps he'd asked for this? Served him right. But then . . . when he'd been thirteen he was still making models of balsawood aeroplanes.

§ 63

It was raining before they reached home. Cold enough for the gas fire. He lit it and lay back in the chair. It was the time of day he flagged badly. Past that time. He'd pushed it by a couple of hours. Not been out this late in an age. Closed his eyes.

Clover kicked off her shoes and whacked them carelessly into a corner. He felt her hand on the top of his head, fingers playing with a strand of hair.

'Are you coming up?'

The proprietorial nature – good fucking grief, the middle-aged nature – of the remark. It went with slippers and cardigans, rollers and the permanent wave, and milky drinks before bedtime. It reached into his blood, colder than a Moscow night.

'Up?' he whispered, incredulous.

'You know . . .'

'I can't.'

He was not at all sure why he had chosen the word 'can't' in preference to 'won't' or 'couldn't'. The prospect of sex with Clover rooted him to the spot. He who knew no guilt, rigid in a recliner while a woman of sixteen or seventeen propositioned him in the vocabulary of a tired housewife.

'All right then. We'll do it here.'

'I can't,' he said. 'I couldn't.'

She was quickly undoing the buttons of her blouse, fingers dancing down the line from neck to belly button. Then it was off, and she stood in her bra and slacks. The slacks zipped at the hip. The beguiling twist of the torso, the thrust of the hip sideways as she pulled the zip.

'Why not?' she said bending to push her slacks off her feet. 'What's a fuck between friends?'

What's a fuck between friends? Was this the philosophy of the incoming age? What's a fuck? Only the most complex action he knew. Lives bent around the act; new lives came into being because of it. And she made it sound like a handshake.

'And we are friends. Aren't we?'

Leaning over him. One hand on each of his knees, bracing herself.

'I can't.'

Then he did.

§ 64

He awoke on the hearth rug. Gas fire hissing soporifically. Clover looking at him in the pink light of the flame.

'You din't take your pill.'

'Forgot.'

'Forgot?'

'Maybe I'll sleep without it tonight. Make a change.'

'Can I have it if you don't want it?'

'Not a matter of "it". There's plenty. If you can't sleep, take one.'

She dashed to the bathroom, returned with a glass of water and a jar of his pills. She sat cross-legged, naked, on the rug, and tipped a couple of dozen into her hand.

'One's enough,' he said.

'You got hundreds.'

'Not hundreds. *A* hundred. Fifty in that jar, fifty in the other.'

'She wrote you a 'script for a hundred!'

She palmed two, tipped the rest back, capped the jar and handed one to him. He swallowed it with a gulp of water. Watched her do the same. Watched her grin at him.

'What's the joke?'

'You don't know about Mandies do you?'

'Mandies?'

'Mandrax. The pill you just took.'

'It's a pill. A sleeping pill. That's all.'

'Yeah, well . . . but if you don't go to sleep.'

'The point, the whole point, is to sleep.'

'Just you wait, Fred. Put it off, stifle the yawns, prop up your eyelids and stay awake for another half-hour.'

'I find they tend to work in about half that time.'

'Trust me.'

She went upstairs when he complained of the cold, pulled the eiderdown off his bed. Wrapped them in it. A cocoon for two. The bounded frontier. Him helpless. A ridiculous desire to grin. Then it hit him. A wave of erotic arousal that forced the grin. Into laughter. Almost a giggle.

'Told yer,' she said.

Then he saw the same stupid grin reflected on her face, felt the same wave from her, and felt it wrap around them deeper than the eiderdown, warmer and wetter than the night.

It was like playing wigwam. The containing game of childhood. Refugees, orphans of storm — bigger storms by far than the celestial tantrum which danced outside the window now. It buttressed what she felt — or what he thought she felt, had to feel, didn't she? — abandoned by her father's death, neglected by her mother's life. Buttressed what he felt, certainly — the conventional coital conceit that the rest of the world had ceased — buttressed by the madness of idleness that was TB and its cure.

JOHN LAWTON

§ 65

Clover emerged from the bathroom as Troy was buttoning up his overcoat – the childhood ritual of keeping well wrapped up when poorly. It went with string vests and Vick rubs. By contrast she wore only the towel, clutched to her front.

'Troy. Lend us a few quid, will you?'

'What for?'

'There's things I need. Grandad bundled me up so fast I scarcely had time to pack.'

'What sort of things?'

'God, you're suspicious. Thing things. Woman things.'

Troy said nothing.

'All right, you asked for it. Knickers. I'm right out of clean knickers. And Tampax. I've got no Tampax at all.'

Troy unbuttoned his coat and jacket, reached for his wallet and took out a five-pound note.

'Make it a tenner,' Clover said.

'A tenner!'

He should have put his wallet away instead of standing with it folded open. She pulled another fiver from it and ignored his protest. Then she flipped the wallet shut and shoved it back inside his pocket. She had to let go of the towel. It fell to the floor. She locked her arms around his neck – the familiar wrestling hold of a woman wanting something – a five-pound note in each hand. He could hear them crackle past his ears. She pressed her chest onto his, and he felt her nipples pushing through the fabric of his shirt.

She kissed him. One ear. Then the lips.

'Ta. You're a sweetie, really you are.'

And he knew he'd never see his ten quid again.

At the Bailey Troy wondered whether Cocket would put Fitz on the stand. If he were Cocket he would not – there was too much in the life of Paddy Fitz which Furbelow could exploit to advantage. But if not Fitz, who?

Cocket rose. 'I call Professor Martin Pritch–Kemp.'

226

The court buzzed softly. Mirkeyn asked counsel to see him in chambers, and when they returned the call went out for Pritch-Kemp. Troy could guess what had been said. Mirkeyn reiterated that he had not allowed the Professor to be named, because he had been told quite clearly that the prosecution would not call him. Cocket would have replied that he had never said he would not call Pritch-Kemp, had no obligation to disclose such information and what the prosecution chose to do or not do was not his domain. Cocket would also have said that the court could not prevent Pritch-Kemp from giving evidence if he volunteered. And he surely had volunteered? God knows what Furbelow had said. Nothing, would have been the wisest course. If the prosecution had gambled on Pritch-Kemp wanting to avoid scandal, then they did not know the man. Or perhaps it had never occurred to them that the Professor could be Pritch-Kemp?

'Are you the man known to Tara and Caroline Ffitch as the Professor?'

'Yes.'

'What was your relationship with Tara and Caroline Ffitch?'

'We were lovers.'

'All three of you?'

'Yes,' said Pritch-Kemp. 'Can't have one without the other.'

Mirkeyn stared out at the court, simply daring anyone to snigger at the unconscious rendition of a line from a popular song.

'Where did the three of you have sex?'

'At their home.'

'Dreyfus Mews?'

'Yes. At my home, in Little Venice. At various hotels. We visited Paris and Amsterdam. At Dr Fitzpatrick's cottage at Uphill . . .'

Pritch-Kemp trailed off and Cocket let him. It would not help for Pritch-Kemp to add to the list. They'd probably fucked in half the London parks and the backs of taxis, and Pritch-Kemp was just the sort of bloke to tell you so.

'Were you charged by any of these establishments?'

'Of course. Hotels are not free.'

'But you paid no money at Dreyfus Mews or Uphill?'

'Paid for what?'

'For the use of a bed . . . or for services rendered.'

'The answer's no to both questions. Fitz didn't rent me a bed, and I've never paid the Ffitch girls for sex.'

'But did you ever give them money?'

'Yes. I gave them presents and I gave them money so they could buy their own presents.'

'Why?'

'Why not? I'm a wealthy man. I was born rich; I've a good job and my books are bestsellers. Why should I not share my good fortune with my friends and lovers?'

'And this . . . these gifts were not associated with sex?'

'Not directly. But there was a time when, more often than not, if the three of us met we had sex. Hence if I decided to treat them it would, more often than not, be on an occasion when we had also had sex. But that is no more than coincidence.'

'Did Dr Fitzpatrick know you had sex with the Misses Ffitch in his home?'

'Of course.'

Don't say he watched you do it, thought Troy, just don't say it.

'And do you know if either of the Misses Ffitch passed on the money you gave them to Dr Fitzpatrick?'

'I do. He used to complain, jokingly, that they were eating him out of house and home, that they contributed nothing to his household.'

'Jokingly?' Cocket queried.

'Just a tone of voice. A way of getting his point across. He said it often enough to make me think it rankled with him from time to time.'

'To your knowledge, did Dr Fitzpatrick ever ask either of the sisters for a share of any money you gave them?'

Furbelow rose. 'This is calling for hearsay, m'lud.'

'Sustained.'

'I have only one more question,' Cocket continued. 'Did either of the sisters ever ask you for money in exchange for sex?'

'No,' said Pritch-Kemp.

Cocket sat down.

It had been neatly contained, a thorough refutation of the basis of the prosecution case. Pritch-Kemp was a loose cannon who had not sent grapeshot flying off in every direction. At least not yet. As

Furbelow rose again Troy was sure he saw in Pritch-Kemp's eye the glint of combat.

'Professor Pritch-Kemp,' Furbelow began with relish – if the man was to be named, then he would at least have the pleasure of rolling the name around on his lips. 'Are you in the habit of giving money to women you sleep with?'

'Habit? I'll do it if the mood takes me. Don't you ever give your women a little something?'

This brought the public gallery to hysterics. Furbelow blushed, Troy could have sworn he blushed. The judge hammered his gavel and gave Pritch-Kemp what for.

'Mr Pritch-Kemp. May I remind you that there is such a thing as contempt of court.'

'Indeed you may, m'lud. For I have no contempt of this court. I am merely amazed at the ignorance of m'learned counsel. One would think he had never been with a whore, for he certainly seems not to know the protocol.'

There was an audible communal gasp. Pritch-Kemp had just given a hostage to fortune. In spite of all he'd said for the defence, caught on the cross he'd as good as called the Ffitches whores. Freud moved in mysterious ways.

'I warn you, Mr Pritch-Kemp, choose your next remark carefully. Mr Furbelow, I take it you wish to continue?'

Furbelow would have to be a complete idiot not to want to press on now.

'Thank you, m'lud. Am I to understand, Professor Pritch-Kemp, that you regularly go with prostitutes?'

'Not regularly, no, but enough to know the ropes.'

'Oh?' Furbelow played to the gallery and Troy thought him a fool. 'And what are "the ropes"?' he sneered.

'It's perfectly simple,' said Pritch-Kemp. 'And half the men in London will tell you so. With a whore one agrees terms up front and nine times out of ten one pays up front. One agrees conditions up front—'

'M'lud,' Furbelow chirped, 'the witness is giving me a lecture!'

Laughter from the gallery. More laughter as Cocket intervened.

'M'lud, am I to take it my learned friend is objecting to his own question? The witness was merely answering the question as put to him.'

It pained Sir Ranulph Mirkeyn deeply but he said, almost *sotto voce*, 'Continue, Mr Pritch-Kemp.'

'Thank you, m'lud. One agrees the price with a tart, and one agrees the conditions.'

'Conditions?' said Mirkeyn almost involuntarily.

'You know,' said Pritch-Kemp. 'All her clothes off or just the necessary. Whether it's half an hour or all night; whether it's the full works or a hand shandy.'

'A hand shandy!?' Mirkeyn exclaimed with more vowels than Edith Evans could have inserted into three words. And then he had to hammer with his gavel for nearly two minutes to achieve enough quiet for the trial to continue.

'And', Pritch-Kemp went on to the dismay of the prosecution, 'there's a world of difference between agreeing a few quid up front, and I do mean a few quid, and deciding that your lover would look nice in a new hat or a new frock the next time you see her and leaving her fifty quid to treat herself. I defy the married men of England to say they do not treat their wives. I defy the unmarried men of England to say they do not so treat their lovers.'

Furbelow looked pole-axed. He had foreseen an easy victory over the defence's star witness, and even after a colossally dropped brick, the man had just wiped the floor with him. He ducked out with a wimpish 'no further questions', only to find Cocket asking to return to his witness. Clearly, it was crossing the old sod's mind to refuse but, Troy knew, that would be merely another hostage to fortune, an unexploded shell for the appeal. 'After all,' Mirkeyn was probably thinking, 'the harm's done.'

'Very well, Mr Cocket.' And then the irresistible dig. 'If you cannot prepare your case well enough to ask your questions at the right time and in the right order.'

Cocket did not mind the sarcasm. He knew there was yet more damage he could do.

'Professor Pritch-Kemp, could you define prostitution for the court?'

Furbelow rose. Before he could speak, Cocket headed him off at the pass.

'M'lud, Professor Pritch-Kemp holds the Garrat Chair in English at King's College. Might the court accept that the meaning of words is his profession and hence his testimony be accepted as that of an expert witness?'

If I could read minds, Troy thought, then the words 'Jesus wept' just passed through Mirkeyn's. The judge put one hand over his eyes, quickly withdrew it and uttered a 'yes', scarcely concealing his rage.

'Professor, when is sexual intercourse prostitution?'

'When there is no element in the relationship between the man and the woman except a desire on the part of the woman to make money – when it is separated from any attachment and is indeed just the sale of her body – and no other desire on the man's part but self-gratification.'

'No further questions,' said Cocket.

Troy wondered what this precision had achieved. He had seen the jury's faces. This had not been well received. They were not the kind of people to flirt with the new morality or to find the moral and intellectual flirtatiousness of a man like Pritch-Kemp amusing. It had given the gallery a good laugh; it had made a fool of Furbelow, but it had angered the judge, and this final definition had left him wondering what it said about Fitz. It said plenty about Pritch-Kemp, but if this was the defence's last word in the way of evidence, then it left an emphatic feeling of heartlessness – and he was not at all sure that it had not misfired. In trumpeting that Pritch-Kemp bought flesh, that he knew when he was with a whore and when he wasn't, hadn't the defence put too subtle an argument to the jury? Pritch-Kemp went with whores, *ergo* all women he went with were whores, regardless of his ability to define the terms? It may have worked wonders when the defendant was three hundred pages of paper and the whores fictional. Troy doubted whether it had helped a living, breathing man. They had been, he thought, too clever by half. If he'd been defending, he would have put one last question – 'Do you consider your relationship with the Misses Ffitch to have been prostitution?' – and he'd have told Kemp to keep his answer down to a simple 'no'. He knew what the jury were asking themselves: 'Was she or wasn't she?', when the defence's job was to leave them with no subtlety and in no doubt.

Cocket called no other witnesses. All that remained were the final addresses to the jury and the judge's summing up. Mirkeyn adjourned for an early lunch and told them all to reconvene at one.

It seemed to Troy that this might be it. The court could get through what it had to in what remained of the day. Then, he thought, the jury would probably be banged up in a hotel for the night.

He had no appetite for lunch. He had a cup of tea in a caff in Blackfriars Lane and phoned home. The line was engaged.

As he walked back to the Old Bailey he caught sight of a large red-headed man ahead of him. A man walking with the laboured geometrical swing of a tin leg, kicking out into open space with all the weight of a vast body resting on the other hip. Up, swing, clank, bonk. He'd know that walk anywhere. Angus Pakenham, Anna's wandering Aengus-husband. The red giant rounded the corner. Troy, as much as breath allowed, ran to catch up, but when he turned into Pilgrim Street there was no sign of the pilgrim. Perhaps it hadn't been Angus? Perhaps he had better not report it as a sighting?

§ 66

Judges, in Troy's experience of them, and it was no doubt a peculiarity of the English system, could raise hell if counsel attempted to mislead the jury, but were not above doing it themselves. Mirkeyn was a master of the art.

He had the problem of contradictory evidence to convey to the jury – so contradictory in Troy's opinion that Cocket would have been justified in moving for a dismissal. Pointless: Mirkeyn would not have granted it, but it might just have lodged the possibility in the jury's mind.

'I come now to the evidence of Miss Moira Twelvetrees. She was precise in her evidence as to the facts of her prostitution and the money given by her to the defendant. The counsel for the defence rests his challenge to her sworn testimony on one thing and one thing only – that the witness could not remember the colour of a ceiling. I ask you to consider whether it is reasonable to expect the witness, so clear upon the salient facts, to remember quite so much of the lesser detail as counsel would wish her . . .

Now, I shall consider the evidence of Miss Caroline Ffitch – a self-confessed hysteric – and I would emphasise that the statement she made to the police, in which she stated quite clearly that she had accepted money for sex and had passed on that money to the defendant, was made entirely without coercion. I would ask you to consider which is the more likely, that her behaviour to this court was hysteria, or her statement freely given at Scotland Yard . . .

And the evidence of Professor Pritch-Kemp. I would remind you that it was the word of a man who admits to regular carnal relationships with prostitutes . . .'

Troy watched the jury as Mirkeyn droned on. They'd never struck him as social radicals disguised by cheap hairdos and hideous suits. They were what they appeared to be. Middle England. The drearies. Twelve narrow minds and true. And their expressions told him they did not incline towards notions of Fitz's innocence even after all they had heard in support of the notion. What mattered was what they were hearing now – highly coloured, decidedly prejudicial, and highly selective in its emphases . . . Moira's evidence was 'her sworn testimony', Caro's only her 'behaviour'. If Pritch-Kemp was not to be believed because he *went* with whores, they were, in the turn of a phrase, being asked to believe Moira, who *was* a whore.

He wondered what chance Fitz stood.

Again, Troy sat out the rush to leave. By the time he decided it was time to move, he had the benches to himself. A constable approached.

'Mr Troy, sir. I've a letter for you.'

'A letter? From whom?'

'From the prisoner, sir.'

Troy took the folded piece of paper from him. Less a letter than a note. A note in best Fitz doctor scrawl. 'I'm downstairs. If you can spare a minute I'd like a word before you leave. Fitz.'

The constable was still waiting.

'He wants to see me,' said Troy.

'Follow me, sir.'

He led Troy downstairs, away from the world of panelled walls and into the world of painted bricks and iron bars. He stopped by an open cell door.

'In here, sir.'

Fitz was sitting on a bentwood chair, legs crossed, smoking calmly, but then he'd looked calm from start to finish.

'What are you doing here?' said Troy. 'I thought you were on bail?'

'Don't blow your stack, Troy. It's not what you think. I gather there's an unusually strong gathering of the gentlemen of Fleet Street and the morally outraged waiting outside. The police were kind enough to offer me a cell until the mob disperses. The Old Bailey would not appear to run to a green room. You never know, with any luck they might even make us a pot of tea.'

The constable returned with a chair for Troy.

'Just tell me when you're ready to leave, sir.'

Troy sat down, still wondering what was going on.

'I hope I'm not causing you any problems, being seen with a perv, I mean,' Fitz said.

'Not at all,' said Troy. 'He probably thinks it's police business. I've come to take down your confession.'

Fitz almost choked laughing with a cigarette between his lips.

'Not quite, Troy, not quite. I was wondering. Would you be free for dinner tonight? Marty's been round almost every night during the trial – I can't stand the nights – but he has to go down to Kent tonight. His father's none too well. I thought we might go to Leoni's. You never know, if I do decide to confess, you can take down my statement on the back of the menu.'

'Of course,' said Troy. 'About what time?'

'Early. Shall we say seven thirty?'

§ 67

Troy walked home. Clover was upside down on the floor, her legs on the chaise longue, her feet in the air, as though she had dropped clumsily from heaven and was waiting for mortal man to right her again. She was reading a magazine, held over her head and lit by the reflected glow of the gas fire.

'How can you see to read in this light?'

'That's wot Grandad would say.'

Which ended that conversation. It was marginally less insulting than 'That's what my Mum would say.'

She had not one magazine but half a dozen, ranging from the solidity of *Woman's Realm* to the teen zeens of *Marilyn* and *Romeo*. He wondered how careful she was when she went out. He wondered who she had phoned. He did not ask. He went up to his bedroom and lay down for an hour with the Home Service news on low, listened to the chimes of Big Ben, and mustered enough energy to cope with a Fitz evening.

§ 68

Even as a copper on the beat, Troy had been in the habit of reading the blue LCC 'lived here' plaques on the buildings of London, as a way into other, imagined lives. He'd often gazed a moment or two at the one on the outside of Leoni's restaurant – it read 'Karl Marx lived here' – not considering the doctrine that had overturned the old regime, the old country, simply trying to imagine the life of an academic in late-Victorian London, grinding away at words, living with his wife and daughters in chilly, foggy London, in a flat above this restaurant, unheated save for miserably smoking coal fires. In this flat *A Doll's House* had been given its first English 'performance' for friends and family . . . One of Marx's daughters had played Nora . . . Bernard Shaw had directed. He stopped daydreaming, looked at his watch. Time to go in.

Fitz was there before him. A corner table. Cocktail in hand, smiling to himself. Lost in what seemed to be pleasing thoughts.

'I'm not late, am I?'

'No. I was early. I thought better of going back to the mews and running the gauntlet of the press one more time – your nephew is particularly persistent by the way – so I walked around, cooled my heels, saw myself on screen at the News Cinema at Piccadilly Circus and strolled on here.'

'How on earth did you manage that without being spotted?'

Fitz leant back to the hatstand behind him and rummaged in the pockets of his coat, his back half turned to Troy. When he turned around again he was wearing a cloth cap and a Clark Gable, pencil-line moustache.

Troy laughed out loud. Fitz joined in and by the time the waiter appeared, they were cackling like hyenas.

Fitz peeled off the disguise.

'Theatrical suppliers in Drury Lane, one and ninepence. Works every time. Could have had a Durante schnozzle if I'd wanted. Now, can I get you a cocktail?'

'No thanks, I'm swimming in pills. I'll pass on spirits and go straight to the grape. Just one glass. Something red and rich if they have it.'

The waiter left menus and went for the wine.

'I usually put it on in a gents',' Fitz said. 'First time I looked in a mirror it was a shock. With the cap and the moustache I look the very image of my father. I suppose we all turn into dad in the end. However, you have less to fear in so doing than I.'

With a fresh Margarita in front of him, and glass of claret in Troy's hand, Fitz proposed a toast.

'Freedom in the morning.'

And Troy knew he had a tough time ahead. He could see no value in not telling Fitz the truth, and much damage in letting him continue to kid himself. The sooner he faced up to it the better. He was going to go to prison.

'You're not drinking.'

Troy set down his glass untouched. 'It's not going to be simple as you think, Fitz.'

'Don't let that ruin your evening, Troy. You were bound to talk shop. It's your nature. Now, what are you going to have?'

'Something simple. The soup and a grilled sole?'

Fitz looked at his watch. Beckoned the waiter.

'Fine. You can have till halfway through the fish course. At which point I shall change the subject with a vengeance whether you appear to be listening or not. Now, be a love and drink to my freedom, whether you believe in it or not.'

'Freedom,' said Troy, feeling he had pissed on the chips.

Fitz ordered. Fish for Troy, veal for himself. He was still in the pleasant, smiley frame of mind Troy had found him in. Perhaps he would hear him out, listen to sense after all?

'Tell me,' Fitz said, 'do you not think David Cocket made a good job of my defence?'

'I didn't see the whole trial. I missed whole swathes – Blood in the box, Cocket cross-examining Tara.'

'I'd still value your opinion.'

'Yes. I rather think he did. I was a little worried at first. He is so young. But on the whole I think he served you well. When Moira Twelvetrees blew her testimony it crossed my mind that he should move for a dismissal – but the ceiling was the only point he scored and he could not shift her further so I doubt Mirkeyn would have granted it.'

'Dear Moira. I rolled her on her back, pointed out the stars and moons and described to her the ceilings I had seen in Italy. All she could say was "nice init?" Poor girl. Memory like a sieve.'

Fitz was not smiling. He was grinning.

'You mean she conveniently forgot?'

He grinned the more. 'Do carry on, Troy. We were talking about young Cocket.'

'When Caro went to pieces on the prosecution it was possible to ask for a dismissal again. But by then I had the measure of Mirkeyn. He would never have granted it. I think Caro helped you enormously, but at great risk to herself. She caught Mirkeyn on his weak spot. Even the most appalling old chauvinists can't stand to see a woman cry. But there's your problem. Out of sight is out of mind. Unless you can embarrass him perpetually, the memory of tearful woman will not move him. Only the woman herself. Mirkeyn stitched you up in his last words to the jury.'

'But Cocket told them in his final address that the prosecution had "signally failed to prove their case".'

'And he was right. But juries aren't as bright as you might think. The judge speaks last and they attach most importance to the last thing they hear. Mirkeyn as good as told them to bring in a guilty verdict.'

'I didn't think he had.'

'Believe me, it was as biased a summing up as I've ever heard.'

'Give me your worst.'

'My worst? You are found guilty and the old sod sends you down for three to five.'

'Your best.'

'He's given you a superb set of grounds for appeal. The law lords overturn conviction and sentence and set you free—'

'And I pick up the threads of my practice. Notorious but innocent and my fame spreads far and wide.'

'Not quite – there's something in between.'

'What?'

'You don't get bail. You serve time while the case gets to the Appeal Court.'

'How long?'

'I'd say about twelve to sixteen weeks. That would be no joke.'

'I spent a fortnight on remand, but you're going to tell me prison is different, aren't you?'

'I've seen the inside of a prison less often than you might think. I've interviewed prisoners inside, and as a young copper I had to collect them for trial or appeal. I've hardly ever seen the cells. But, yes it's different. The presumption of innocence is gone.'

'So you can't really tell me what it's like?'

'I can tell you what it's like in terms of the people I've sent there in my time.'

'Not a lot of people like me.'

'Not a lot, no.'

Fitz shrugged. Tucked into his veal while Troy picked at his Dover sole. It was the first silence they had hit.

'But', Fitz said at last, 'you think I will win on appeal?'

'Ordinarily I'd put money on it.'

'But this is . . . I am . . . *extraordinary*?'

'Quite.'

'Well . . . you needn't worry. I'm glad you told me. It's as well to know. And I do value your opinion. But do not worry. It's all taken care of.'

Troy had a vague memory of the pissed Fitz at Uphill telling him he had 'an ace in the fffff . . . fffff . . . fucking hole'. He had no idea now or then what he might mean by this. But it did seem to imbue him with confidence.

'What do you mean, Fitz?'

'I mean I'm not going to go to prison. Arrangements have been made. So I don't want you to worry. More than that, I want you to tell Anna not to worry.'

He watched Troy finish his fish, looked at his watch again.

'Your time's up. I don't want to talk about the trial any more. Let's discuss your health.'

'My health? I'd far rather talk about the trial than my health!'

'I didn't get you here to talk about the trial. I got you here to give you this.'

Fitz dipped into his inside pocket and produced a very creased and battered envelope.

'For me?' said Troy.

'For you. I've been meaning to give it to you for ages. First at the club, then at Easter, and I plain forgot both times.'

Troy tore it open. It was a single sheet of headed notepaper, reading:

One West Seventy-Second Street
Apt # 66
New York
NY 10023

December 15th 1962

Dear Troy,
    Been living here a while now. Come up and see me some time.

Larissa XXX

It was startling. He waited for it to sink in, but it floated on the surface, recognisable but hardly assimilable.

'So that's where she is,' Troy said, more to himself than to Fitz.

'You mean you didn't know? I'm most awfully sorry, I've known for a couple of years. I just presumed you did too.'

Troy folded the note and put it in his jacket pocket.

'We haven't met since 1960. I always knew she was in America. I could guess that, but I suppose I thought she'd avoid New York.'

'Why would she? It's her home town?'

'Exactly,' said Troy. 'Her home town. Have you seen her since?'

'Since December? No.'

'Do you know, I hardly know the first thing about her. I thought she might have divorced me *in absentia.*'

'On the contrary. She calls herself Mrs Troy. Clarissa Troy. Very well known on the art and fart circuit in Manhattan.'

'What does she do there?'

'Not sure. Something bookish. I tend to come across her at the galleries and the book bashes. I bumped into her at the first night of some dreadful Ibsen revival in the summer. She was at a book booze-up just before Christmas. But I couldn't tell you what she does exactly.'

Troy ground to a halt. Fitz was right. He had changed the subject with a vengeance. Troy had come crashing to earth; Fitz was still up there. Nothing Troy said had dented his confidence. He was ordering dessert and Muscat de Beaume de Venise, and prattling pleasantly, as he rightly predicted, whether Troy was listening or not, and he wasn't.

Around ten o'clock, they parted in the street.

Fitz said, 'When it's all over I want you and Anna to come down to Uphill again. We'll forget all this ever happened.'

He couldn't believe that. He could not possibly believe that.

Walking home through Soho, head full of Tosca, a random thought hit him out of nowhere. He finally found the answer to Clover's obsessive question, and wondered why he had not thought of it before. Literature's great joint suicide was in *Rosmersholm*, the Ibsen play whose heroine is called Rebecca West, who leaps with her lover into a millstream somewhere offstage. He wondered why he had not thought of it at once.

§ 69

When he opened the front door, he could see Clover slumped awkwardly in an armchair. Arms too loose, chin too close to her chest. He knew at once this was not the posture of sleep. On the coffee table, in the small circle of light thrown by the lamp, was a brown screwtop jar, lying on its side. Next to it were two envelopes.

The tableau froze part of him, all of him unwilling to believe what he was seeing. He picked up the letters. In her neat, unformed, stick-man hand they were addressed 'Grandad' and 'Troy'. He picked up the jar and shook it. A single pill rolled out.

The Charing Cross Hospital was only yards away. A couple of hundred at the most. Down Bedfordbury, across Chandos Place, almost to the Strand.

He picked her up and ran. He'd no idea where he'd find the energy and once he'd stormed into casualty, dropped Clover onto a chair and yelled 'Overdose!' he'd just enough to answer the question put to him.

'Overdose of what?'

'Mandrax.'

'How many?'

But he couldn't speak now. His breath came in great tearing wheezes, ripping up his throat and larynx as though he'd just inhaled barbed wire.

The young man in the white coat made him sit. Two nurses whisked Clover into a cubicle and swished the curtains closed around her.

'Ten?'

Troy shook his head.

'Fifteen?'

'Nearer thirty,' Troy croaked.

'Oh bloody hell. Look, are you all right?'

'I'll . . . I'll be . . . fine.'

'Sorry, but I don't believe you. You look absolutely awful.'

He summoned another nurse. Taller than Troy and twice as strong, she woman-handled him onto the bed in a cubicle of his own. He lay back gasping. The doctor reappeared. 'Oxygen,' he said simply.

Troy lay a long time breathing in the heady gas of life and felt nearer to death than at any time he could ever recall. Being stabbed was nothing to this; being shot was nothing. Pain galvanised. This was numbing, soporific, the weak and sleepy way to hell. He went under, felt the bliss of temporary oblivion.

When he awoke he wondered for the splitting of a second if he was dead. Then the young doctor came in and told him. It was Clover who was dead.

'I'm terribly sorry. There was so little we could do. And if there had been I could not have assured you of the consequences. A dose that large . . . possible brain damage . . . plays all hell with the liver.'

Troy said nothing.

'Look – you seem to be in the most awful shape. I want to admit you.'

Troy did not argue. It was the first time in his life – and he'd been in half the hospitals in London – that he had been admitted conscious and had not argued.

Around one in the morning a uniformed constable looked in.

'They told me you were awake. I was wondering if you were up to a few questions. We have to ask them in cases like this.'

'Fine,' said Troy.

The bobby parked his helmet on the floor, where it sat like a bizarre species of horned tortoise. Troy had never known what to do with his when he'd been a constable. It was too heavy for a hat peg, and wherever you set it down people would bump into it or fall over it. Daft things, police helmets.

'Sir?'

'Sorry. I was miles way. By all means ask your questions.'

The bobby took his folding notebook and his Biro from a breast pocket and turned to a blank page.

'Your name first, sir.'

'Frederick Troy.'

'Address?'

'Goodwin's Court. WC1.'

'Occupation?'

'I'm head of CID at Scotland Yard.'

Troy watched the Biro veer off at a tangent, a thin blue line trailing across the page and off it to stab the poor bloke in the thigh with the sharp end of his own pen.

'I . . . I . . . er . . .'

'You could try asking me for my warrant card. It's in my jacket on the end of the bed.'

The bobby fished it out. 'I'm sorry, sir,' he said. 'I didn't . . . I wasn't . . .'

'Why don't you just carry on with your questions, constable? You've an unexplained death to investigate.'

'I don't know what to say next.'

'Try asking me who the girl was.'

'Who was she, then, sir?'

'Jacqueline Marjorie Clover.'

This was not the name Troy had given the nurses.

'Aged sixteen or seventeen. I'm not sure. She might have turned seventeen some time this month,' he went on.

'No relation?'

'No.'

The constable thought for a moment, resisted the obvious question, then asked it. 'Could I ask what she was doing at your house, sir?'

'I suppose I was looking after her.'

'Like . . . her guardian?'

Troy had never once let this word reach the level of conscious recognition, but yes that was what he had been. And a bloody awful one at that.

'Daughter of a friend was she, sir?'

'She's the granddaughter of Sir Stanley Onions, the recently retired Commissioner of the Met.'

'Oh, bloody hell. Oh, bloody hell.'

This, clearly, was more than the man could stand. He flustered himself to silence, the blood drained from his cheeks.

'Tell me,' Troy said, 'do you have any doubts that this was a suicide?'

'I don't know.'

'Then you do. And so you should. Why don't you write up the report from what you now know and drop it into Mr Wildeve's office? Tell him you cannot accept the facts at face value and request his department look into it. Quote the only witness – me – as saying I know of no reason why Miss Clover should have taken her own life. Do it before you go off shift. See he gets it first thing in the morning. And I'm sure I don't have to tell you, talk to no one about this.'

The constable seemed relieved to have a plan of action. He thanked Troy, put his warrant card on top of the sheet across his chest and fled.

Habit took over. Troy reached for his jacket to put back the card, and found the two envelopes Clover had left, one addressed to him, the other to Stan. He'd no memory of ever picking them up. Damn. He should have told that young bobby there were notes.

He opened his.

Dear Fred, Lovely Fred,

I'm sorry to do this to you, and I know it's a mess. But it pays to know when it's all pointless. You been great – really you have – but this was always there, always with me, and it was never going to go away. Was it?

I'm really very sorry, really I am.

Love,

C. XXXX.

He'd no idea what she was talking about. He thought about calling Stan. It would destroy him. Better to let him sleep. It might be the last good night's sleep the old man would ever get. He put the letter marked 'Grandad' back into his pocket unopened.

§ 70

He rose around six thirty the next morning, only minutes before the overhead neon lights flickered on with their blinking light and the clanking sound of their metal housings expanding in the heat. He found a coinbox telephone on a trolley in the corridor.

Time to phone Stan.

He'd be up by now. Fire lit, first fag of the day, sitting by the range in his pyjamas and dressing-gown, cursing the cheerlessness of smokeless coal, and thoroughly relishing the onset of autumn.

'What's up?' he said, instantly suspicious. Troy never called at this hour. The Troy Stan had known was hardly ever up at this hour. Only murder got him up at this time of day.

'Where are you?'

'I'm in the Charing Cross Hospital. Stan, Jackie's dead.'

He'd learnt not to mince words about death. Stan had taught him that years ago in his first days at the Yard. 'Forget "Sit down, I've something to tell you" – just spit it out. There's nowt ye can say'll save 'em so much as an ounce of grief.'

All the same Stan's response shocked him.

'Oh, oh, oh, oh, oh, oh!'

And he did not stop. His voice rose, louder and shriller. And he did not stop. 'No, no, no' might have made more sense, but this wasn't denial. It was unstoppable, unplumbable heartbreak. Troy heard the phone fall. Waited minutes, a passing age, before Stan picked it up.

'Which ward?'

'Bevan.'

'I'll be there in an hour.'

§ 71

Stan sat backbone rigid on a hospital chair, his face bloodless – but shaved, shaved and groomed. Troy had never seen him turned out any other way, whatever the crisis, and he could not count the crises in the best part of thirty years. His hair and his mac glistened with early-morning rain, and his shining black boots sat squarely on the lino, as unmistakably police as a helmet.

He heard Troy out in silence. When Troy handed him Jackie's letter, emotion betrayed him for the first time. He stretched out his hand and it seemed that he could not make himself grasp it. The hand withdrew, dived into his pocket. Out came his glasses. Like grandfather like granddaughter – he was rarely caught wearing his glasses in public.

Troy waited till his eyes left the page and his fingers refolded it. He half expected Stan to return the letter, but he didn't. He put it, almost delicately, back into its envelope and slipped it into his pocket with his glasses. It occurred to Troy that few letters so private in intent were ever quite so public as suicide notes. It was evidence.

'If there's anything . . .'

Stan read his mind. Cut him short.

'There isn't. Just asks me to forgive her and to explain to her mother. Explain what, I ask you?'

'Then it can be between you and her. No need for Jack to read it.'

'Jack?'

'Jack Wildeve. He'll be here any minute.'

'You don't believe it was suicide?'

'I don't know what I believe.'

Stan stared right through him for almost a minute, then thrust the chair back with an ear-splitting scrape.

'Her mother. I must see her mother.'

'Stan!' Troy called to his back. But he was up and lurching down the ward. At the doors he ran into Jack. Troy saw Jack put a hand out to Stan's shoulder, heard softly spoken condolences and saw Stan blunder on, speechless in his rage and confusion.

Jack looked as bad as Troy. 'Been up all night,' he said simply. 'Got your message around four o'clock. Saw no reason why we should both lose a night's sleep. You don't suppose there's any chance of a cuppa, do you?'

'They don't do room service. You can drink mine when they bring it.'

Jack rubbed at his eyes with his fists and said, 'Fire away.'

And when Troy had finished – how he spent the evening with Fitz, how he found Clover in a coma, where the damn pills came from – Jack said exactly what Stan had said.

'You don't think it's suicide, do you?'

'Inside pocket of my jacket,' Troy said. 'Just behind you.'

Jack read Clover's letter.

A nurse appeared with Troy's morning tea. Jack slurped at it greedily, sat with the letter in one hand, the teacup in the other and Troy used the distraction to wonder what he really did think.

'Ordinarily,' Jack said, 'I'd say it was pretty conclusive. You're certain it's her handwriting?'

'I've never seen her handwriting. You'll have to check with Stan.'

If Stan chose to show Jack his own note from Clover, so be it, but it seemed beyond the pale to Troy to mention it now.

'I'm sure it's genuine. It's her turn of phrase. And it's clearly the half-formed hand of a teenager. But since you ask, the note notwithstanding, I can't think of any reason why she should kill herself.'

'Cheerful, was she?'

'Cheerful enough. A damn sight more cheerful than me most of the time.'

'And Fitz?'

'Oh, he was fine, cocky – stupidly so.'

Troy had just enough warning of what was coming. Jack had slipped the question in as neatly as he would have done himself.

'Fitz shot himself last night. About an hour and a half after he said goodnight to you at Leoni's. Put the barrel of his revolver to his ear and blew his brains out.'

§ 72

Jack took Troy's keys. A new doctor took his blood pressure and listened to his heart, but then discharged him. He was home by ten o'clock. The front door propped open, morning light streaking down the yard, projecting his shadow towards the inhumanly huge feet of a waiting, uniformed constable.

The man saluted and said, 'Scene of Crime still inside, sir.'

It was as near to barring Troy's way as the man would dare. Troy stuck his head around the door, just in time to hear the pop of a flash bulb. A police photographer was shooting the chair and the coffee table from all angles. A fingerprint man was dusting doorknobs and tut-tutting to himself. Jack sat on an upright chair between the hallstand and the grandfather clock, jotting notes into his little black book.

'Ah, Freddie. Just in time. Prints are asking if you've had many visitors lately?'

'None at all,' said Troy. 'Stan was the last and that was the day he brought Jackie round.'

Was that a glimmer of guilt he saw in Jack's eyes? No one had been to see him. Not a damn soul. Not Swift Eddie, not Crazy Kolankiewicz, not Jack, not anybody.

Jack folded his notebook. 'If you're fit enough to talk we should find somewhere quiet and let this lot do their job.'

'The Salisbury,' Troy suggested. 'Won't be open for another hour. We can bang on the door till Spike opens and have the place to ourselves.'

Spike yelled, 'Bugger off' through the closed door, and, 'Go home, you drunken bastards.'

Jack rattled the door and said, 'Open up! Police!'

What was traditional was also effective. The door inched back. Spike's head appeared. 'Good Lord. Mr Troy, and Mr Wildeve too. It's not often we get the pleasure of both of you at once. In fact, it can mean only one thing. Another dead 'un?'

'Yes,' said Troy. 'Over the road. In the Court.'

Spike ushered them in. 'What, right on your own doorstep?'

'Closer,' said Troy.

'Jesus Christ,' Spike said softly. He stepped behind the bar and shoved two glasses under the optics. 'On the 'ouse,' he said, and left them to it.

The two glasses sat either side of a tiny round table. The smell of the brandy almost brought Troy to retching. Neither of them wanted it.

Jack could not sit. He seemed to Troy to be at that stage of exhaustion where to settle would be to sleep. He pulled back a chair, slung his coat over it, and paced the room, rubbing at his forehead, occasionally screwing his fists into his eyes. His notebook stayed buttoned up in his pocket. Troy rolled up his coat for a pillow and stretched full length on a mock-leather bench beneath the window. He could feel the rumble of the traffic in St Martin's Lane, he could see the fancy plasterwork of the ceiling if he looked straight up, and if he twisted his neck he could hold a conversation with Jack's knees.

They were wooden figures in a Swiss weather house – at opposite poles of activity.

'Let's go over the basics one more time,' Jack began. 'Jackie was Clover Browne?'

'Yes.'

'And Stan knew this, or he just suspected it?'

'He knew.'

'And Clover Browne was the third woman in the Fitz business?'

'Yes.'

'And how many people knew this?'

'Every hack in London I should think. No one ran with it because of the libel laws, and because Vice apparently couldn't find her and hence could not call her as a witness. I doubt any newspaper wanted to be the first to name her. Stan's instincts were right. If he could just keep Jackie from blundering into the press she was probably safe, and the good name of Onions safe with it.'

'It was Percy Blood's investigation, wasn't it?'

'Yes.'

'And Blood never identified Clover as Jackie? Hence the procurement charge was dropped?'

'Without Clover the charge was nonsense. It was a waste of time charging Fitz with something so weak, but then so was so much else of what was produced as evidence. I went to the Old Bailey most days. It was a botched case. I told Coyn as much. I don't think the press know. Rod's son Alex has been making all the running in the papers, and he's never let slip to me that he knew who Clover was. And if he knew he'd have asked. He'd have come to me with a stream of questions.'

'Do you think Fitz knew?'

'Knew what?'

'Knew that he was entertaining the granddaughter of a senior policeman.'

'I've no idea. It would not have bothered him if he did. He collected celebrity and pseudo-celebrity. I mean, it even seemed to amuse him to know me. I cannot work out whether he enjoyed risk or whether he simply had no concept of it. As far as Fitz was concerned, risk was probably stealing or forging or killing – I don't think he recognised a notion of social risk. Rules were for idiots. Rules were not for him. Rules were made to be broken. But then, Fitz's grasp of reality struck me as being as flimsy as the case against him. I could not get him to see that the judge meant to see him go down. He might have got off at appeal, but I really think this morning would have seen Fitz sent down for a couple of years. He'd have done a few months before the appeal, and you know what a meal the hard boys would make of a man like Fitz. Couldn't get that through to him.'

'You don't think he might have thought it through after the two of you parted, and thought the worst of it?'

'It's possible. Of course it's possible. I might have tipped him over the edge. But I know this – he would never have chosen a gun as his ticket to the next world. Anything but a gun. He hated guns. Went right through the war as an officer without even touching one. And why would any doctor have need of a gun to kill himself? Why would a man as fastidious as Fitz leave a mess? He could have opened his doctor's Gladstone bag, swallowed a handful of Nembutal and gone happily to Valhalla.'

'So we agree.'

'Do we?'

'There is no evidence, at least none I've found at this very early stage, to suggest that Fitz was anything but alone at the time of his death. He'd given Pritch-Kemp a key and he's spent the past few nights with Fitz. Company, I suppose. Stopped him thinking. Pritch-Kemp let himself in some time after midnight, as he seems to have done every night this week, and found Fitz dead. An army-issue Webley still in his hand.'

'But?'

'It was murder. I know in my bones Fitz was murdered.'

'And Clover?'

'How much faith do we put in coincidence?'

'It's a pretty cool customer who pumps a young woman full of drugs in Soho and then nips off to Paddington to shoot someone.'

'But . . . as you said in the hospital, you have doubts. No reason to want to kill herself.'

This was a familiar moment, one they used to reach so often in cases. Jack was appealing to Troy to support his instinct. The vagaries of rank, the vicissitudes of ill-health meant nothing. Jack was saying, 'Let's be a team.' And Troy could not respond. He could not tell Jack that he knew in his bones that Jackie Clover was murdered. He knew nothing in his bones. His body talked to him of raging silence.

Jack put his coat back on. Looked at his watch. Troy swung his feet to the ground and found he had but one thought and that idle.

'Two murders,' Troy said. 'And I just happen to be the last person to see both victims alive. Now that is a coincidence.'

'Well, I'll arrest you if you really want me to. But the last people to see Fitz alive were half a dozen ill-assorted hacks from Fleet Street. I doubt Fitz got past his own front door without running the gauntlet. But then, that's why young Jackie was with you, wasn't it? No hacks on your step.'

'Quite – and as far as the hospital and the hacks are concerned she's still Clover Browne. You'll have to talk to Coyn. I can't nobble the coroner, but he can.'

'You really think you can keep it a secret?'

'I'd hate to face Stan if we can't.'

Jack strode to the door, pulling on the handle as he said his last words to Troy.

'I'll try and keep in touch. There'll be a stink of course. Coyn will lose his bottle. But we owe Stan a bit of discretion, I think.'

If this was Jack's way of saying he'd hold the press at arm's length, then Stan would not be the only one thankful for a bit of discretion.

§ 73

Jack sent a detective sergeant to take a full statement from Troy. Troy dictated with all the precision and brevity of a thirty-year copper and the man asked few questions. At the end he gathered up his foolscap sheets and printed forms and said, 'Dreadful business.' And it sounded to Troy like some form of condolence.

The Commissioner, Sir Wilfrid Coyn, telephoned not long afterwards. It was, he said, 'a dreadful business'.

Troy had no respect for Coyn. Indeed, he had come to regard 'respect' as a notion thought up by old men to keep order among the young. It had little or nothing to do with any idea that those so demanding of respect might also have to be deserving of it, that the condition might involve some consideration of worth, either in the disciplines of character or in the soundness of action. It was as meaningless as its oft-invoked adjective 'respectable'. If their positions had been reversed and Coyn were Onions and Onions Coyn, Stan would have called in person, would have assured himself face to face that a matter involving two suspicious deaths, a recently retired policeman of highest rank, and the serving Chief of CID, was wholly above board and wholly without detriment to the force. He'd have raised hell.

The inquest on Clover opened and adjourned. What little Jack had asked of Coyn he appeared to have done. There was not a mention of her real name.

There remained the funeral.

Since Clover had died in the presence of two nurses and a doctor and since a post-mortem had revealed the cause of death in the residue of twenty-eight sleeping pills in her stomach, the coroner saw fit to release the body for burial.

'Tomorrow morning,' Onions said. 'Ten o'clock. Acton Cemetery.'

It was a call Troy had dreaded.

'Stan, I really don't think I should—'

'Be there!' was all Stan said before he hung up.

Troy rode the Central line out to North Acton. It stopped only yards from the cemetery. He could walk from there. It was a morning for the dead, a damp morning, a miasma of autumnal dew.

It was a scene too familiar. He'd been to two other Onions family funerals: Stan's wife Marjorie, dead from cancer in the first weeks of the war, and his son-in-law Kenneth in '56, tortured and murdered by EOKA on Cyprus. He had vivid, etched-in, scorched memories of Valerie Clover, née Onions, clinging for life in the fact of death to her father's arm and weeping copiously – but, as ever, bitterly rather than sadly. Life cheated Val, swindled her at every turn.

There were few mourners. Stan had left his family behind in Rochdale when he moved to the Yard in the 1920s. He was one of the few working-class coppers ever to be Met commissioner – the rank and the title sat uneasily on him, and he'd been given both so close to retirement that the job had proved a disappointment. He could make so little of it in the three years he held it. And it made no friends. A Met commissioner with a Lancashire accent, black boots, belt and braces, was never going to be acceptable in society. He had been a working copper. And when the work had been pulled from under him at retirement he had taken to his allotment in Acton, where the other gardeners would joke about 'Sir Stan', until he told them all to 'bugger off'. Troy stood at the back. The other half-dozen people between him and the upright, pale Onions, the bent, the wilted, weeping Valerie, he took to be neighbours. The dutiful and the decent.

All the same he knew he would not get off lightly.

As they moved off, he wondered if he could just calmly walk back to the Underground without saying anything, but Stan seized him by one elbow and muttered, 'Second car,' to him, and he found himself sharing an old Rolls-Royce with three housewives from Starch Green – who told him they'd been in the Townswomen's Guild with 'Marje', 'Did you know Marje?' – for the ride back to the little house in Tablecloth Terrace and a wake cast in hell.

The small front room was full. Another dozen mourners, mostly women of Stan's age, had appeared from somewhere, and they muttered and munched on crustless sandwiches of tinned salmon and cucumber sliced so thin it was shaved. The Townswomen's Guild must have done the catering, Troy concluded. Stan would never waste the crusts off a loaf of bread. And he'd never known Valerie cook a meal.

Troy watched Stan playing host, commanding the ritual, endlessly thanking all these old women for turning out. Valerie stuck close to him, but stood unaided. Pale, frail, bleached by grief, but at – he guessed – forty-four or five, still good-looking. Her daughter's blowaway blonde hair, the Onions family piercing blue eyes. She had survived the battle with the bottle in a way Charlie would not.

He explained a dozen times that he had worked with Stan up to his retirement and heard a dozen times how interesting that was. Then one of the matrons saw the reality beneath the small talk and told him he needed fattening up. As if to ram home the point, she put a whole plate of sandwiches in his hand, added a couple of cold, crisp sausages, and seemed all set to stand smiling while she personally restored him to good health.

Val crossed the room, seized the plate, slammed it down onto the table and shoved him ahead of her into the back room. 'I want to hear it from you,' she said.

She sat down and waited for him to do the same. They sat a couple of feet apart on straight-back chairs like strangers encountering one another in a dentist's waiting room.

Troy told her. Coming home and finding Jackie. The mad dash to the hospital. The moment the young doctor had come into his cubicle to tell him Jackie had died. It was very matter-of-fact, devoid of emotion. He had long ago learnt not to loose emotion on Val. She would consume all he had and want yet more.

He finished. It seemed stupidly simple in the telling. Val sat silently, her breathing deep and loud, the respectful hubbub of the wake drifting in from the other room.

'There's still one thing,' Val said.

'What's that?' said Troy, with no idea what she'd say next.

'Did you fuck her, Troy?'

Troy said nothing.

'Did you fuck my daughter?'

And when Troy said nothing to this too she said it all the louder.

'Did-You-Fuck-My-Daughter?'

Onions appeared in the doorway, took one look at the two of them and closed the door quietly behind him.

'Do you want everyone to hear you? Keep your voice down, woman!'

He might as well not have spoken. Valerie got to her feet and began to beat Troy about the head with both hands, clenched into fists, raining blows down on him. He rose instinctively, put his hands to his face – the only defence.

'Tell me you didn't fuck her! Tell me you didn't fuck her!'

Onions seemed to freeze. Unless he stepped in she would soon hammer Troy to the floor – he'd no strength to stop her. Over and over, louder and louder. 'Tell me you didn't fuck her! Tell me you didn't fuck her!'

Then it stopped. Onions had put his arms around her and pinned hers to her side.

'For Christ's sake, Freddie, just tell her what she wants to hear!'

Suddenly Valerie was calm. She stopped struggling. Took Troy's silence for answer. 'He can't. Don't you see? He can't.'

'Freddie, for Christ's sake, man!'

He let her go. She took Troy's face in her hands, wiped a streak of blood away from the corner of his mouth with the tip of one thumb. Looked into his eyes, exactly as Troy recalled himself doing with Anna a few months ago.

'He can't say he didn't, because he did. Didn't you, Freddie?'

All he could see was her. Blue eyes, the same shade as her father's, the same shade as Jackie's. And all he could hear was Stan.

'You stupid, stupid bugger. You must be mad. Completely bloody mad. You must have been mad. Mad, mad, mad. Whatever were you thinking of?'

Troy could no more answer Stan's question than he could Valerie's.

§ 74

When he got home he felt dreadful. A nausea akin to seasickness. He looked in the mirror. As a rule he was white as a sheet. He'd got used to that. He thought of it as the colour of the disease – TB was white. Now he was reddish, purple where he was coming up in bruises from Valerie's fists. It was a good job she had beaten him. If she had not, Onions surely would have and he would be a damn sight the worse for it.

He made tea and stretched out on the chaise longue, hoping the world would go away. Sipped tea, tasted blood. With his second cup he felt the need of music. He hadn't played a record in ages. There was one already sitting at the bottom of the pit in the gramophone. He pulled it off the spindle and looked at the label. It was the record Foxx had given him; the one Clover seemed to play at any opportunity; the one she had played every day of that long weekend at Uphill. 'Please, Please Me' by the Beatles. She must have been playing it on the last night of her short life, while he was out with Fitz. And it had sat there ever since.

He read through the song titles, his brain making idle connections and refusing in its present condition to see them as idle. It seemed to him in his madness that they represented coded chapters in the messy saga in which he was now embroiled. He had seen *her standing there* – and of course she was *just seventeen* – he had gone to *Anna*, who had asked him to *please, please her*, then bound him in *chains*, caused his *misery*, and packed him off to the *place*, then the weeks of *secrets*, then his brief *taste of honey* and the final *PS I Love You* . . . Where was the song about the complete fucking idiot he'd been?

He slipped the record back into its sleeve and stuck it in the rack. It had punctuated the spring and summer. He could not yet conceive of the circumstances which would induce him to listen to it again.

§ 75

He found that he could remember the wording of Clover's suicide note. He sat one day, doing nothing, trying to think nothing, and found the words projected in his skull like a silent cinema show from the days of childhood. He could see the words, terse as a caption card, filling in the action one never got to see, substituting for the dialogue one never got to hear.

Just to be certain, he sat at his desk and wrote them down. His fancy, quasi-Russian hand, all flow and loop, replacing her stick-man letters, scarcely joined up at all.

> I'm sorry to do this to you, and I know it's a mess. But it pays to know when it's all pointless. You been great – really you have – but this was always there, always with me, and it was never going to go away. Was it?

Why was it pointless? What was it that was always there and never going to go away? She wrote this as though she thought he knew. Did suicides ever calmly jot anything down beforehand? Didn't death by pills mean that what was written was written as the narcolepsy hit? Why should Clover's words mean a damn thing? Written, as they probably were, through a haze of pills that whacked you sideways, shoved your brains into your loins and then puffed you off to never-never land with a stupid grin of satisfaction on your face?

Clover had her ups and downs. The woman he'd encountered at Uphill was surly, secretive and rude. The child Onions had delivered into his inadequate care was peevish, distraught and rude. He'd seen both personae evaporate in hours. Surly Clover had given way to the self-assured tart who'd strolled across Uphill Park with him wearing only a fur coat and wellies. Peevish Jackie had turned herself around almost as soon as her grandfather had left to become a city girl, professing a greater wisdom of the streets than he pretended to himself. And buried beneath both was a romantic who was touched by *Jules et Jim* and bowled over by his sparse account of Mayerling.

He did not know the woman. Had not known the woman. He had no idea of what she was capable – except change.

If there was one person of whom he knew less than he knew of Clover Browne, it was Frederick Alexeyevitch Troy.

He sat in Embankment Gardens, stranded out of season in the nearest bit of municipal green to his house, on a grey autumnal afternoon, feeling tormented by the sound of seagulls flocking on the Thames, depressed by the optimism of a man who still put out deckchairs at this time of year – and summed up his life.

Not long turned forty-eight, separated but not divorced – unless Fitz was wrong and she had divorced him *in absentia* in some foreign part.

A small man, used to be a looker as Clover herself had put it. Thin as the dying Chatterton in somebody-or-other's famous painting in the Tate, though gaining weight; his bathroom scales told him he was eight stone four now.

Jobless – he never would get back to the Yard. By the time he could muster a clean bill of health, a full year would have passed and a new order come into being. His career was over; he had better accept that. More fuck-ups to his record than he dare count – it seemed to him he was surrounded by the dead. A small mountain of bodies to his name – Diana Brack, Norman Cobb, now Clover Browne. He had killed her with neglect as surely as he had killed the other two with bullets.

No appetite to speak of. No appetite, either, for books or music – he did not read, he did not play, he did not listen.

All in all, it was a good recipe for suicide. Chatterton had topped himself at seventeen. Just like Clover. Except that the recipe simply didn't fit. It was him, not her, who had recognised the pointlessness of it all. Of course, it paid to know when it was all pointless. But that was him talking. His words, written by her, framed by her. But meant for him. What possible reason could she have for dying? He

knew what her grandfather would say – given the chance, Troy
knew he would most certainly say it any day now – she had 'so
much to live for, her whole life ahead of her'. He would wait and say
nothing and nod his agreement when Stan did say it. But he knew –
he had nothing to live for, his life was behind him. Good bloody
grief, had the woman breathed in his despair between his sheets, as
he had breathed in the tubercular bacillus on some crowded Moscow
streetcar? Had this been his protection – to infect her with his own
misery?

The bloke who collected money for deckchairs had finally seen
the light – or seen the lack of it; the sun had not so much as peeped
all day – and was gathering up the chairs with a tuneless clacking of
wood on wood. A bold, a tame, seagull stood near Troy's feet,
ripping the frankfurter from the mustard heart of a day-old hot dog.
If he was quick he could leap on the wretched bird and throttle the
life out of it before it could utter one more of it's ear-splitting
squawks, wrap his hands around its rotten feathery neck and squeeze
until the bugger choked.

§ 76

That night the Demon sat upon his bedpost. Not one he knew. He
knew the Demon of Despair – its eyes were green and it never
stopped talking. He knew the Demon of Madness – its eyes were red
as though lit from within by tiny flames struck over and over again
from flint and tinder.

This Demon said nothing and its eyes were silvered like a
looking-glass. In them he saw his own reflection.

'Which are you?' said Troy.

'Guilt,' said the Demon.

'Don't believe we've met,' said Troy.

'Have now,' said the Demon.

§ 77

'What is this?' said Troy. 'A delegation?'

He had opened the front door to find Jack, Clark and Mary McDiarmuid in the courtyard.

'Yep,' said Jack.

'You'd better come in, then, and don't sit in a row or you'll look like three wise monkeys.'

Jack threw off his coat and said, 'How are you? Are you on the mend?'

It was not idle pleasantry, Troy knew.

'You didn't come here to ask about my health.'

'It matters all the same.'

Jack plonked himself next to Swift Eddie on the sofa. Mary McDiarmuid took a dining chair and Troy stood with his back to the gas fire facing them.

'We want you to come back to the Yard. In fact, it's absolutely vital you come back. I've had a week on the deaths of Paddy Fitz and young Clover. I've made bugger all progress. I've had to fight for forensic resources. I've been swamped by that multiple shooting in Silvertown. By last night I was beginning to think I was being deliberately overworked, diverted, what you will – but then Quint stepped in. Asked for a report, waited while I typed it up, read it and told me it was open and shut, told me I'd had a whole week and turned up nothing – this despite the fact that I'd been handling three other cases for most of the week – pronounced them suicide and told me to wrap it.'

He paused to consult the other two with a silent exchange of glances.

'You have to come back. If you don't, Quint will kill the case.'

'I thought you said he already had?'

Mary McDiarmuid spoke from her place at the table. 'It's protocol.'

'Protocol?'

'Procedure, then.'

This was not a word Troy cared for. The procedural was deadly boring.

'Quint is only overruling Jack because he can.'

'I think that goes with being Assistant Commissioner,' said Troy.

'No, that's what I meant about protocol. Quint does what he does only in your name. He's running CID while you're on sick leave. All you have to do is come back, take a look at the file and decide to reopen it. Perfectly proper procedure.'

'And all Quint has to do is overrule me.'

'And when did that last happen? When did the head of C section last upset the apple cart by telling the chief detective to drop a case?'

She was right. No assistant commissioner would so interfere in a CID investigation at so early a stage. If Troy came back, if he reopened the investigation into the deaths of Clover Browne and Patrick Fitzpatrick, Quint would just bite on the bullet. Later rather than sooner he had every right to ask what result had been achieved, but Troy would have at the least a clear fortnight before that same protocol permitted him to ask much more than a supervisory question, a catch-all put-me-in-the-picture.

'I couldn't investigate and run CID. I'd be dead on my feet within the week.'

'You don't have to. Eddie and I can run it. Or did you think you did it all by yourself anyway? He's had your signature off pat for years. You're damn lucky he's not picking up your pay cheque.'

This was typical Mary McDiarmuid. Blunt as stone on steel. Clark did not react, not so much as a flicker in the face of incontrovertible truth.

'It's not as easy as you might think. Any doctor can sign me off. But only a police surgeon can sign me back on. I haven't a clue whether I could get Anna to pass me fit, but it wouldn't matter if she did, the Yard will only accept a clean bill of health with one of its own as signatory. We'll never get a police surgeon to sign.'

'I've thought of that,' said Jack. 'Only thing is he's late. He was meant to meet us on the doorstep ten minutes ago.'

There was a timely rap at the door. Before Troy could move, Jack had shot from his seat and yanked open the door. 'You're late!' he said to whoever was there.

Then Ladislaw Kolankiewicz, MD, MSc, ARCSc, DIC, FRIC, MBE, Head of the Metropolitan Police Laboratory, pushed him to one side, saying as he did so, 'You want truncheon up arse, copper, you going right way to get it!'

He stuck his homburg on the hatstand, dropped his doctor's bag on the floor and gave a Troy a quick once over.

'You white as snow,' he pronounced in his fractured mode.

Troy got the picture.

'Jack – do you seriously expect this stunt to work?'

'What you mean, stunt? I'm qualified police surgeon – have been since 1934. Qualified enough to know you look like shit and should be in bed with hot-water bottle and back numbers of the *Beano*.'

'Do you see what I mean?' Troy said to Jack.

'Knock it off, the pair of you. This will work. Kolankiewicz is, as he rightly says, a police surgeon. All he has to do is sign one piece of paper.'

'And his patients have one thing in common. They're all dead by the time they get to see him! He hasn't practised on the living in thirty years.'

Kolankiewicz came up close, only inches away, took his wrist and felt for a pulse. 'Hmm,' he said. 'Stick out your tongue.'

Troy shook himself free. 'Stop it. Stop it the lot of you! This isn't going to work.'

Jack moved in, closer, if that were physically possible, than Kolankiewicz himself. 'Freddie. It doesn't have to be real. All we need is the pretence. Once the paperwork's done, who's going to ask any questions?'

'If it's only a pretence then we'll skip the examination. And if he opens his bag I'll throw him out! I'm still alive – being treated by him makes me feel as though I've got one foot in the grave.'

Kolankiewicz looked hurt. Not an expression Troy had ever seen disrupt his countenance before.

'How many times I treat you in the past, smartyarse? How many times you call on me when you in some mess where you don't want the Yard or your regular physician knowing? Troy, I bound up head kickings and knife wounds. For Chrissake I even dug bullets out of you. And what about that time in '55 I treated you for the clap when the last person on earth you wanted finding out was Anna?'

Mary McDiarmuid coughed politely. 'Ladies present,' she said.

All heads turned to her. Silence ensued. Jack retreated to the sofa. Kolankiewicz and Troy stood eye to eye. There was not a hair on

Kolankiewicz's head but for those which sprouted awry in the tiny forests of his ears and nostrils, and the caterpillars which passed for eyebrows. With every year that passed it seemed to Troy that Kolankiewicz got shorter, fatter and uglier, and he invariably smelled of liverwurst. Troy had known him since 1936 or thereabouts. He was quite possibly, defectors to the Soviet Union withstanding, his oldest friend. Bloody of mind and foul of mouth as he was, he deserved better than this.

'I'm sorry. You're right. Of course you're right. And I've been more grateful than I could say on each occasion. The difference is not in you. It is in me. This isn't a kicking or a stabbing. This time I'm ill. This time I haven't bounced. This time, as you so rightly say, I look like shit. This time you can't put Humpty together again with a brown paper bandage and a few Polish curses. I'm sorry. That's all I meant.'

'You want my professional advice?' Kolankiewicz said softly.

Troy nodded.

'You too ill. Tell the coppers go flying fuck.'

'I can't. They need me.'

'Then I sign piece of paper and we say no more about it. All I ask of you is to take care. Remember how weak you are. And if you crack this one do me a favour, Troy, do yourself a favour, and sign off sick again.'

He held out his hand. Jack gave him the medical form and turned his back so Kolankiewicz could scrawl his near-illegible signature across it.

'I put it through system,' Kolankiewicz said, folding the form into three. 'In a month or so maybe it reach Coyn's desk. Maybe not.'

'Tomorrow?' Jack said hopefully.

'Yes,' Troy replied. 'Tomorrow.'

'Good. I've got a squad car waiting. I really must get back to Silvertown.'

Troy wondered, watching Jack, Clark and Mary McDiarmuid file out, just what he had let himself in for. Only a few years ago, it seemed, it was him keeping squad cars waiting, engine running, ready for a dash to some insalubrious nook of the city. Now he was a pen pusher who couldn't even push his own pen – dammit he even had someone to write his name for him.

Kolankiewicz made no move to leave.

'Staying, are you?' Troy asked.

'You got whisky?'

'I'm sure there's a drop in the cupboard somewhere. God knows how old. I haven't drunk Scotch in I don't know when.'

'Be a mensh. Pour a belt for your old pal.'

The cupboard meant under the kitchen sink, where Troy found a twelve-year-old single malt – at least it had been twelve years old when he had put it there in 1952 or '53. He splashed an inch or so into a glass and handed it to Kolankiewicz.

'Not bad,' he said, sipping at it. 'Not bad at all.'

'Just as well,' said Troy. 'I've no vodka.'

'Vodka is for show. Vodka is for being Polish. I drink vodka when I have something to prove.'

'You mean you haven't got something to prove?'

Kolankiewicz shrugged. 'No. Nothing to prove. No Polish points. Just things on my mind.'

The presaging sigh reminded Troy of his Uncle Nikolai, a man given to setting the world – and Troy with it – to rights. It was not the *modus operandi* of the Polish Beast.

'How many corpses you reckon I cut up in my time? How many sternums I hacked through? How many skulls I unscrewed like the top on the pickle jar? How many yards of gut I unravelled like sausage time at the pork butcher's?'

'I've no idea. I couldn't begin to guess.'

'Nor could I. That's my point.'

'I thought you didn't have a point?'

'Indulge me. I'm an old man.'

The next question seemed obligatory. Bad manners not to ask.

'How old are you?'

'I'm sixty-four. I go a year early.'

Troy had often thought the only way the Yard would get rid of Kolankiewicz would be to take him out feet first.

'Why?' he said.

'I'm tired. I'm tired of death. I'm tired of blood. I'm tired of bowels. I'm tired of bones.'

Unexpected as it was, it made sense.

'And I'm tired of the Yard. Tired of Coyn and Quint.'

'When exactly?'

'Fifth of November. Maybe I plant a bomb before I leave.'

He sipped at his whisky. Did not smile at his own joke. Troy stared at his eyebrows. The longest, at his estimate, was getting on for two and a half inches. It waved as his head moved and it was white as snow. Moving wispily across the vast expanse of forehead, itself but a lower slope of the vaster expanse of hairless cranium, it reminded Troy of boyhood nights trying to tune a crystal wireless with a cat's whisker.

'And you?' Kolankiewicz said at last. 'What of you?'

Troy said nothing.

'How many corpses you seen in your time?'

'Dunno.'

'How many you killed in your time? No! Don't answer that. You would only lie. I know you thirty years nearly. You were only boy when we met. You and truth are passing acquaintances at best.'

'What's your point?'

'That we have lived with death too long. We have been living death. Time to stop. Time to quit. When I go you should follow.'

'I'm only forty-eight. I'm fifteen years younger than you.'

'No, my boy. You born old. You older than me. You always have been. You one of those buggers born too many times. Earth-weary from the first day. Take my tip. Time to go now. Use the fifteen years you have on me. Become a mensh while you still can. Leave death behind.'

Troy did not for one moment accept this. He found the touch of pseudo-mysticism out of character for Kolankiewicz.

'And another thing . . .'

That was more like it. That was the real Kolankiewicz. There always was another damn thing with Kolankiewicz.

'And another thing . . .' He waved the medical certificate at Troy. 'This is a work of fiction. The biggest lie of all. As you would do well to remember. You fuck with death one more time you could fall apart like Pinnochio with a bad dose of woodworm!'

When Kolankiewicz had gone, the question rankled. How many had he killed? More than any other copper in the land, that much he knew, and that statistic did not include Inspector Cobb. It was an unenviable reputation. Diana Brack in 1944, who had tried to kill him with a .45, whom he had shot with a .22; Chief Petty Officer May in 1952, who had tried to strangle him, whose neck Troy had broken in the ensuing struggle; and the Ryan brothers, Patrick and Lorcan, in 1959. If he was not infamous before that case, he had been ever since.

The East End gang leaders, always too clever to leave a witness, or too clever to kill in person, had finally gone mad and shot one of their own men in a packed pub in the Mile End Road. The Yard had responded with a full-blown, old-fashioned manhunt. Doors were barred the length and breadth of East London; men who would have suffered torture before they peached had shopped them from every corner of the underworld. And the Ryans had been cornered, cornered in a warehouse on the Isle of Dogs.

Troy had led four armed officers to arrest them. A sergeant and two constables took the back entrance, Troy and one constable the front. The Ryans had come out guns blazing like the heroes of a bad Western. Troy's constable went down in the first volley of shots. But Troy had shot Patrick Ryan dead, and as the man fell his twin had dropped his revolver, cradled Patrick's head and wailed like Hecuba. Troy looked at his constable. The wound was to his leg. The fall had knocked him out. He reached down to drag the man clear. Then Lorcan Ryan spoke.

'You can't leave us like this,' he said.

He was not screaming. He sounded calm. Almost rational.

'You can't leave us like this. Not like this.'

Troy glanced once more at his constable. The man was still out. He let him fall, the gun level with his left thigh, pointing at the ground, finger in the trigger guard, thumb on the hammer.

'Pick it up.'

For a moment he thought Ryan had not heard him. Then he gently laid his brother's head on the cobblestones and lurched for the gun.

Troy blew his brains out.

Seconds later the sergeant had run up to Troy.

'Bloody hell,' was all he could say, and bloody hell it was. A creeping crimson tide seeping out across the stones and vanishing in the cracks.

'He asked for it,' Troy had said simply.

JOHN LAWTON

'Been asking for it for fuckin' years,' said the sergeant with no grasp of what Troy had really meant. And Troy realised that no one would. Whatever it was, murder or mercy, he would get away with it.

Perhaps Kolankiewicz was right. He was tired of blood. Tired of death. Lorcan Ryan had been a death too far. But what had the old man meant by them 'living death'?

§ 78

Troy phoned Anna.

'I need to see you.'

'And I you. In fact I should really see you about once a week. But . . . you know . . . Fitz dying . . . you know.'

He had not called her. It had not occurred to him to call her. Anna and Fitz had been partners – the closest of friends – for more than fifteen years. Some plainclothes copper on Jack Wildeve's squad would have called on her, Troy now thought, to give her the bad news, ask her the bad questions and leave her with the bad things in life. Troy had not tried to imagine her grief.

'I'm going back to work.'

'What?'

'I'm going into the Yard in the morning.'

'Troy, you're mad! You have to be crazy to want to do that.'

She came round to his house. Late in the afternoon. Saddened and concerned. Mistress and physician. Pain had left her pale and quiet, scored the lines about her eyes that bit the deeper.

'I can't sign you off. You know I can't.'

'You don't have to. Kolankiewicz has already done it.'

'Then you're both crazy. You're acting just like you did when I met the pair of you twenty years ago. You're the most unholy alliance I can think of. You've no respect for your own body and he's no respect for anything. The world isn't your oyster, it's your cadaver!'

266

Ah, so this was living death?

'I can't make it alone.'

Anna looked at him, utterly baffled by his last remark. Her black eyes looking into his black eyes in total disbelief.

'I need something to get me through the day. Or I'll be worn out by lunchtime.'

'I can't,' she said, shaking her head. 'I can't.'

'A pill. Something. Anything.'

'I can't.'

'You got me into this. Now get me out of it.'

She said nothing. The muscles in her neck seemed to stiffen with resolution. She knew he was blackmailing her.

'Clover's dead. Jack's been taken off the case. If I don't investigate, no one will.'

He saw tears start up and roll down her cheek.

'When?'

'Same night as Fitz.'

She sat down, put her face in her cupped hands and wept. If the Murder Squad had not told her it was murder, she surely knew now. Troy waited until she looked up. He knelt down and took her hands in his. 'Help me,' he said.

She tore her hands away. Fresh tears spilled out across her reddened face. But these were tears of rage. For a moment he thought she would hit him.

'Damn you, Troy. You complete fucking shit. You've never asked me for anything in your entire life. Don't say "help me" as if you're the fucking victim, the weak one. You've never been the weak one. You've never been the victim. Never. You always get what you want. You always take what you want. Don't start whining at me now! It doesn't ring true. What do you want? Benzedrine? Dexedrine? A nice little upper to go with your nightly downer?'

'Yes,' he said, his voice a whisper in the wake of her anger, 'that's exactly what I want.'

Anna took out her pad and scribbled out a prescription for a hundred Dexedrine tablets.

'I meant what I said, Troy. It's one of the laws of thermodynamics: you cannot get something out of nothing. You know, the myth of perpetual motion and all that. Taking amphetamine doesn't make you superman. All the energy you'll feel comes out of your system. Sooner or later you'll crash. It's nature's way of telling you "no free lunch".'

'I'll be careful.'

She tore the sheet from the pad and pressed it into his hand. She got up, turned her back on him, took out her compact and dabbed at her face.

'Why didn't you tell me about Clover sooner? Did you think I couldn't take one more death after Fitz?'

She glanced at him over her shoulder.

'Clover was Onions' granddaughter. I've told nobody.'

She turned around, swept a lock of hair from her eyes.

'You know, I don't think I can cry three times in five minutes, even for you.'

§ 79

Troy wiped the last flecks of shaving soap from his face and looked deeply into the mirror. He had, as ever, made a hash of it, bristles uncut and soap in the ears, but this did not concern him. Did he look consumptive? Would he pass muster? Or would they walk around him as one best left to his fate? He was embarking on the most preposterous bluff of his life. He did not know what he expected to see, but the worst of what he saw was the stark contrast between the whiteness of his skin and the blackness of his hair and eyes.

He pulled at the mirror to reveal the tiny medicine cupboard buried in the wall behind it. Aspirin; Elastoplast; a ribbed brown bottle of kaolin and morphine mixture that he was pretty certain had been there since before the war, now separated into strata of mud and cement; penicillin left over, and no doubt festering, from the dose of the clap Kolankiewicz had been so indiscreet as to mention. And there were the two bottles of pills side by side. The remaining bottle of Mandrax Clover had not swallowed, and the bottle of Dexedrine he'd got from the all-night chemist's in Piccadilly last night. 'Drink me,' they said. 'Eat me,' they said, regardless of form – one to make you bigger and one to make you small. He unscrewed the cap on the amphetamines and tipped a little yellow pill into his hand.

Walking to work, he knew which one it was. It was the one that made Alice bigger, definitely bigger. The sleeping pill had shrunk him, shrunk the world, nest-wrapped him and Clover to the point where reality had pleasantly blurred. This, the 'upper', as Anna had put it, stretched him, he was taller – well, he felt taller. He filled the space around him, his stride lengthened, his feet left the ground – he grew to fill the world. The world was the world as he thought it. It existed because he thought it. *Cogito, ergo est.* And it was just as pleasant a place as the nest had been.

§ 80

His office felt like the *Marie Celeste*. The outer room was empty, the door to the inner wide open. Clark's Heath Robinson coffee machine bubbled away to itself, pumping best Blue Mountain through a maze of glass tubing. He hung up his coat and looked at the contents of his in-tray: the documents in the case – the case of Patrick Fitzpatrick and Clover Browne. There was pitifully little physical evidence. A buff file in the tray and a cardboard box dumped on his desk. He looked around, tried to remember the last time he had set foot in this room. It had been some time in April. It was now September. The clock ticked away, in synch with the coffee machine. It was typical of Clark to remember the little things. Keeping the clock wound, making fresh coffee, forging his signature on God knew what. Troy was staring out of the window at the Thames. It was filthy. There was talk that the fish were dying or dead. It didn't seem all that long ago that a Labour MP had demonstrated some point or other – the fordability of the Thames? – by trying to walk across the riverbed. Troy wondered how long he'd live. The Thames was not the bright silver ribbon he remembered; it was dirty brown. His thoughts moved laterally. The Thames, he reasoned, was probably much the same. It was he that had changed, the nature and quality of his perception, not the object perceived.

'Good morning, sir.'

It was Clark. Looking at Troy looking out at the river. Two steaming mugs in one hand, a bundle of Scotland Yard standard memos in the other.

'You're bright and early.'

'Bright and lost,' Troy muttered.

'Eh?'

'Nothing, Eddie. Is this the lot?'

'Believe so, sir.'

Mary McDiarmuid put her head round the door.

'Brass alert. Everybody duck!'

Troy dropped the box on the floor and turned over the buff file to the plain side. Clark retreated to his desk just in time to look busy and unconcerned as Assistant Commissioner Quint walked in.

'Freddie! I heard you were back.'

Quint was about the same age as Troy, a little taller, a little broader, a lot rougher at the edges. He was smiling his way through a bluffer's front. He had heard Troy was back because someone had spotted him entering the building and earned a few points by phoning him. He could hardly be pleased to see him or pleased to find out only when it was too late.

'I seem to have made a remarkable recovery,' Troy said flatly, not caring whether this convinced Quint or not.

'Certainly is remarkable. From TB to a clean bill of health in four months.'

'More like six,' Troy lied.

Quint stuck his hands in the pockets of his expensive, grey, single-breasted suit and strolled over to the window. Troy slid the box under his desk with one foot, while pretending to go through the routine memos Clark had dumped on his desk.

'I had an aunt had TB. It was more than a year before she was up and about.'

'Before the war, was it?' Troy asked.

'Oh aye, before the war—'

'Things have improved since then,' Troy said. 'Wonders of modern science and all that.'

'All the same. You're not rushing things are you, Freddie?'

'No. I'm not rushing things.'

Quint strayed closer to the desk. One hand crept out of his pocket and he flicked the edge of the file with a thumbnail in feigned idleness.

'I dare you,' thought Troy, 'I just dare you to turn it over.'

Quint riffled the edge like a dealer shuffling cards. 'You working on anything special?'

Troy dropped half the memos on top of the file. Quint removed his hand.

'No. Just getting my knees under the table. A mountain of routine stuff to catch up on.'

'You'll be at the regular meeting tomorrow, then.'

'Of course,' said Troy.

Troy, Quint and Coyn met twice a week as a matter of course. Whether Troy attended would depend entirely on how far he got with the case.

'Fine,' said Quint. 'Fine. See you then.' And left.

Clark and Mary McDiarmuid stood in the doorway.

'He knows,' said Mary McDiarmuid.

'Of course he knows,' said Troy. 'The question is, what's he going to do about it?'

He sat down, pulled his chair up to the desk, picked up the box and turned over the file. Glanced up at the door. They were still standing there. He waved them away and opened the case file. Stepping back into an old routine, putting on old slippers – and they didn't fit.

He found he could learn so little from material so matter-of-fact. He read it all and felt scarcely the wiser. The only item that made his copper's instinct rise like the fur on a cat's back was the inclusion in the box of two letters from the office of the Leader of the Opposition, Harold Wilson, written to Fitz, standard acknowledgements of correspondence received with no hint of what Fitz had been writing to him about, and one of them so old – October of 1962 – as to be irrelevant. A note in Jack's handwriting was attached with a paperclip: 'Found top LH drawer Fitzpatrick desk.' And nothing in the file pertaining to Clover raised so much as a whisker – the mundane, the obvious – the police 10 × 8s of his own sitting room, and the lab report on the Mandrax pills.

He knew he was rusty. He knew he had to go over it all again with more care. He didn't. This was stage two of any investigation. What he craved was stage one. A good body. And since that was not possible, he took the next best thing. A visit to the scene of the crime. He collected the keys to Fitz's house from Clark and caught a cab to Dreyfus Mews. He could have asked for a car and driver, but that would simply have given one more nark to Quint.

It was obvious that the press had been camped on Fitz's doorstep. The cobblestones of Dreyfus Mews were strewn with more cigarette ends than any passing tramp could have gathered up in a month of Sundays. It was a quiet street. No houses on the opposite side, only garages, a long row of double wooden doors in various peeling colours. Two or three were propped open. The insides of the doors displayed signs, the hung shingles of specialist mechanics, adverts for tyres, the traditional bare-breasted calendar. Here MGs and Jaguars were serviced and repaired by true believers in greasy grey overalls.

The house had not yet achieved the smell of emptiness. It still brought to the nostrils the commingled scents of occupation. It was surprisingly large inside. Looking at the outside, going up the narrow staircase over the garage, he had expected some proportionately small rooms. The living room was vast, stretching away from the street and back towards the big house it had once served as mews. Fitz's living room was thirty-five feet by twelve, hidden completely from the street and overlooking a small, very tidy garden, rather like one of his over-cultivated beds at Uphill – a stone terrace, a square of lawn and a surrounding fringe of miniature roses.

In the centre of the room stood a wing chair in dull green upholstery, the left side wing stained with what Troy knew to be the dried remains of Fitz's blood and brains. Beyond it the worn Persian carpet was blackened by a hundred spots of blood. To the right of the chair, a partner's desk, littered with the paraphernalia of living. A silver letter knife, a green-shaded glass reading lamp, a large piece of white quartz which he presumed Fitz thought to be decorative, a couple of medical journals for the current month, a walrus tooth scrimshanked with the image of Lillie Langtry and inscribed 'New Bedford 1904', a cut-glass inkwell without any ink, a dozen or more ballpoint pens stuffed into a blue-and-white striped coffee mug, a two-week-old copy of the *Observer* folded open at Len Deighton's cookstrip – all bearing the telltale dust of finger-printing powder.

And a book – the last book Fitz had ever read? Troy picked it up. A red, leather-bound copy of the complete works of the Earl of Rochester. It was pure Fitz. Quite the filthiest poet ever to make it into the literary canon. The book fell open, a folded sheet of paper marking the place. Troy found himself reading 'Against Constancy' . . .

> But we, whose hearts do justly swell,
> With no vain-glorious pride,
> Who know how we in love excel,
> Long often to be tried.
>
> Then bring my bath and strew my bed,
> As each kind night returns,
> I'll change a mistress till I'm dead,
> And fate change me for worms.

It had been an unkind night that changed Fitz for worms. But the conceit summed him up neatly: he thought he excelled in love; he cultivated it; he became its connoisseur; it was what the rest of society called perversion.

Troy unfolded the sheet of paper Fitz had used as a bookmark and saw the familiar House of Commons portcullis crest, like the back of a threepenny bit. Another uninformative note from the office of the Leader of the Opposition, this time dating from mid-June. It meant nothing to Troy. It might mean nothing to anyone. Fitz hobnobbed – that was a matter of record. He pocketed it all the same. Jack was thorough. This might well turn out to be the only new item Troy would find.

He scanned the bookshelves. One whole wall was books and records, from floor to ceiling. There were the works of 'Walter', nine hefty volumes sitting just above the gramophone. But it wasn't a gramophone – at least it bore little resemblance to the one Troy had. This was state of the art: a wooden box with lots of knobs to amplify the sound, labelled 'Leak'; what he believed was called a transcription turntable – all weights and counterweights and infinitesimal adjustments, which even then seemed to require a

shilling balanced on the counterweight to ensure maximum performance – and two speakers, spread the width of the room, as big as
dustbins. This was called stereophonic sound. Bores were wont to
demonstrate it to the unwitting guest with a record of steam engines
whizzing past, revealing, as they shot from one speaker to the other,
the Doppler effect. Troy had not 'gone stereo'. Most of the artists he
liked had died before the invention of stereo, and, once heard, the
pleasures of the Doppler effect quickly palled, but sooner or later
he'd have to.

Fitz had liked Mozart. The Jupiter symphony still sat on the
turntable, the Clarinet and Horn concertos lay without covers on the
floor in front of the bookcase. But . . . his *pièce de résistance* was a full-
scale copy of Donatello's *David*, standing in the corner where the
bookshelves joined the wall. No more than five feet tall, it was quite
the sexiest statue Troy had ever seen – the coy tilt of the head, the
outrageous, pagan hat, the slim young body, the girlish waist, the
delicate little prick. Only when you followed the sword down past
the prick to the severed head of Goliath at his feet did any biblical
notion creep into it.

Troy went upstairs. To Fitz's bedroom. There was the much
vaunted ceiling. He had not quite been able to envisage it as Cocket
had conveyed it, as he had solicited it from Moira the prostitute.
Blue with stars and moons did not do it justice. It was Florentine in
its richness of blue, dotted with myriad stars and moons like a
Renaissance room, as though it should look down not on the casual
coupling of Paddy Fitz and Moira Twelvetrees but on Donatello or
Cellini – and God only knew what they had got up to. Fitz's clothes
were still in the wardrobe and the tallboy. A fastidious man. The
socks paired and rolled into balls, the shoes in neat rows, polished to
a shine, the ties on the back of the wardrobe door and an array of his
Harley Street waistcoats all neat on their little hangers. The fastidious
man was not helpful to the detective. The detective thrived on
sloppiness and litter.

He moved onto the next room. Smaller, emptier for far longer.
This must have been Clover's, though there was not a thing in it to
indicate that she had ever been there. The bed was stripped; the
cupboard was bare.

He moved up to the top floor. The Ffitch sisters' room, bright and
beautiful in pale yellow, with skylights let into the roof and large

windows opening out onto a small iron balcony high above the garden. He sat on the bed – what he believed was termed a 'king size' – and he knew that all he was achieving was the confirmation of what he already knew: he was not adding to the sum of his knowledge. He had not lost his powers of observation. The front door had not been jemmied, the desk drawers had not been forced and there were no obvious clear spots in the gathering dust to indicate any theft. He had not thought there would be. There had never been any question in his mind of another motive, of Fitz's killing being incidental to some other crime. Whoever killed him had killed him because of . . . because of what? Because of everything else, because of the scandal of Paddy Fitz and the upsetting of the great English applecart that had ensued. He had seen for himself. The chair in which a man sat, if the wisdom of his superiors was to be believed, to blow out his own brains. It was the old, old method. He had done this so many times – skimmed some poor sod's bookshelves, opened his mail, rifled his bathroom cabinet – and it got him nowhere.

This room was too bare to offer clues. It too had been all but stripped of the presence of its former occupants. All but – one dress hung in the wardrobe. The little black number Tara had worn that first night at Uphill. It prompted one thought in Troy, a thought which would not go away. Jack's file had contained a statement from Pritch-Kemp, who had kept Fitz company in the last days of his life and who had been unfortunate enough to find the body, but he could recall nothing from the Ffitch sisters.

He went back downstairs to Fitz's desk and picked up the telephone. It still worked, although it could hardly be long before the GPO cut Fitz off. Dead men pay no bills – wasn't there a novel of that title? He called the Yard.

'Eddie. There was no report or transcript of any interview with the Ffitch sisters. Could you ask Jack—'

'He's standing right here, sir.'

'Put him on.'

'You're lucky you caught me,' he heard Jack say.

'Jack, did you interview the Ffitch girls?'

'No. They moved out of Fitz's weeks ago. I might well have got around to it. But they'd been putting such obvious distance between each other ever since Fitz's arrest that they could scarcely be my priority. After all, neither one of them could have nipped to the corner shop without some hack spotting them, let alone back to Dreyfus Mews. They're about as far from being suspects as the Home Secretary!'

Troy could not but agree with this last remark, but his feel for the matter was the opposite. The Ffitches were the axis. They might well, indeed almost certainly did, know nothing of the murder of Paddy Fitz, but they had been pivotal to all that had happened. Without them no scandal; without them, no court case; without them, Troy knew, no reason for anyone to want Fitz dead. He wanted to talk to them. Whatever Jack thought, he wanted to talk to them.

'Do you have an address for them?'

'Half a mo'. Right. 19 Melmoth Terrace W2.'

'Thanks, could I have Eddie back?'

Clark came on the line.

'Eddie. It occurs to me. When exactly did Percy Blood get transferred from Special Branch to Vice?'

'Dunno, sir. Do you want me to find out?'

'Yes. Has there been anything I should know about?'

'The Commissioner popped in, sir.'

'And?'

'He seemed a little surprised to find that you'd gone out.'

'Did he ask why? Did he ask what I was working on?'

'No, sir. But he will.'

Troy did not doubt it.

§ 81

Melmoth Terrace was deserted. Parked cars, a prowling cat, the distant sound of the Light Programme. Ten thousand more fag ends ground into the cobblestones outside No. 19 by a dozen more hacks who had hung around for weeks. He knocked but knew before he did that the birds had flown. The house was empty. No one answered and when he stuck his ear to the letterbox all he could hear was the rattle and hum of a badly balanced refrigerator. Across the street he saw curtains twitch. Then a window opened, the sound of the music on the Light surged and a woman's voice yelled, 'Bugger off! Haven't you lazy bastards got proper jobs to go to?' The window slammed shut. He thought better of asking her any questions, whoever she was.

Back at the Yard, Clark said he wasn't surprised. After all, they no longer had any obligation to inform the police of their whereabouts.

Someone knew. Someone had to know.

Troy called Alex.

'Freddie . . .' A breeze in his voice to take the wind out of Troy's sails. 'I was just in the middle of—'

'Don't brush me off, Alex. Stop what you're doing and find time.'

'What do you want?' said Alex, the urgency to be free still audible in his tone.

'The Ffitches have vanished.'

'Can't say I'm surprised.'

'Where are they, Alex?'

'How the hell should I know?'

'Alex, I've two unexplained deaths on my hands. Don't piss me about. Those women were bought and sold like cocoa futures. A quote in this paper, an interview in that, but nobody ran with their story, nobody had their version in full. They knew what it was worth and stored it up for their own future. You made all the running breaking the case. You precipitated everything that followed. You've bought their story, haven't you?'

'Freddie, I—'

'You know where they are!'

'Freddie, you can't ask me to reveal a source. It simply isn't done.'

'The Ffitches aren't a source, Alex. Any way you look at it they're not your source. That journalistic hog won't wash.'

'What are they, then?'

'They're material witnesses. And you're obstructing an investigation.'

Alex's voice dropped to a hoarse whisper. 'Freddie. I can't talk about this matter on this line.'

'Then get to one you can use. And if you don't call me in five minutes, I'll call your editor.'

Troy waited five minutes, then ten, then quarter of an hour. When Alex rang, Troy could hear the roar of traffic in the background.

'Where are you?'

'Far side of Blackfriars Bridge. Had to get a cab across the river. I don't trust any of the call boxes in Fleet Street. You never know who's hooked up to what.'

'A wise precaution, I'm sure.'

'Freddie, I don't care to be bullied.'

'Then tell me where they are and I'll stop.'

There was a pause. He knew Alex was weighing the risk of challenging him one more time.

'OK. OK. Tara's at . . . have you got a pen?'

'Yes.'

'It's a long one. She's at Brick Kiln Cottage, May's Lane, Dedham, near Colchester, in Essex.'

Troy could hardly believe it – the circularity of it. He had thought he had seen the last of Dedham.

'Phone number?'

'Isn't one.'

'And Caro? Are they together?'

'I don't know where Caro is. Honestly, I don't. Tara won't tell me. Says I deal with her or nobody.'

Troy found this perfectly plausible. That was just the way Tara would play it.

'When are you running with their story?'

'As soon as she gets back and spills the beans. She wanted a break from it all. Said it was wearing her sister out. I told her she could have a week. That was three days ago.'

It was perfectly clear to Troy that Alex had his doubts as to Tara ever reappearing to spill the beans.

'Thank you, Alex.'

'Freddie. Just one thing. Please don't fuck this up for me.'

Troy would try not to, but he did not care how much the *Sunday Post* had paid for the Ffitch version or whether they got to run with it or not.

§ 82

In the middle of the afternoon he set off for Dedham, the first long drive he had attempted in many months. He was surprised how good it felt.

Two hours later he stopped outside a pub on the edge of the village, an old thatched pub called The Lamb. He did not recall that he had ever seen it before, but it was a landmark on his map and according to his map he should turn left to get to The Glebe and right to find May's Lane.

It could scarcely be more than an hour to dusk – the sun sat reddening on the skyline. He found May's Lane, less than a mile away. A long, unmade track lined with unleaving elm and oak, a small forest of wild horseradish lining the banks of the deep drainage ditches to either side. Half a mile on, a mud-spattered white Mini Cooper was pulled up in front of a skew-whiff redbrick cottage, one of those ancient houses built before the discovery of the right angle, a crumbling anachronism in powder red and green-mossed tile.

He parked the car. No one came out to see, but then a Bentley hardly made any noise, purred rather than roared for all its power. He rounded the corner to the back of the house. A mousey-haired woman in blue jeans and a grubby crêpe-de-chine blouse was snipping away at the straggling limbs of a climbing tree.

She turned at the sound of his shoes on the twigs and pebbles of the big back yard. It was Tara. Tara without a hint of surprise.

'I don't suppose you know anything about figs, do you, Troy?'

'Not much. I'm a bit of a gardener, but I run more to spuds and leeks than to figs.'

'It's a Brown Turkey.'

'You're asking the wrong person.'

'I know. That's the trouble with the dead. You can always think of one more damn thing you want to ask them.'

'I hardly recognised you,' he said lamely.

'I couldn't wait for the blonde to grow out. Takes for ever. This is near enough my natural colour. I say "near" – can you imagine going into Boots and asking for hair colour in a shade of "mouse"? They don't do it. Now, shall we go in and have a drink? And you can tell me what brings you all this way, as if I couldn't guess.'

The kitchen floor made him seasick just looking at it. Old yellow-white bricks undulated across a large, dusty farmhouse kitchen, worn shallow in the tracks of several hundred years of shuffling feet. Cobwebs clung to every beam and spiders scuttled in the corners of the windows. A single brass tap on the end of a lead pipe stuck out of the wall above a dirty porcelain sink; a bright-blue bottled gas cylinder under the draining board fed a two-ring cooker. It was basic; it was primitive; it was the raw, unscrubbed reality Fitz had copied in his hi-tech farmhouse kitchen at Uphill, but it was the way it was not because it been planned or designed but because it had been neglected. Neglect, he thought, was the missing principle in Darwinism.

'It was my mother's,' Tara said as though reading his mind. 'Been in the family for years. She left it to us, to me and Caro. Wanted us to have something the old man couldn't touch. I've never really had need of it till now . . .'

She opened the door of the larder. It was painted that very familiar shade of washed-out, flat green that had been so prevalent when Troy was a boy. There were times when it seemed that what the Victorians had not painted black they had painted this pale pea-green.

He heard the clunk of a gin bottle on the tabletop.

'You OK?'

'Sorry, I was miles away.'

Or was it years?

She handed him a gin and tonic. 'Don't ask for ice,' she said. 'There's no fridge, because there's no electricity. I can barely manage the cooker.'

The wastebin overflowed with empty baked-bean tins. This was Tara's idea of cooking. The only beans she'd spilled.

'You know,' Tara said. 'I was surprised, really very surprised at you taking Clover in.'

Not half as surprised as Troy was at the question.

'How did you know?'

'Clover called me from your house a couple of times. Never said why. Why did you do it?'

'She . . . she just turned up.'

'What? Knocked on your door and said, "Take me in"?'

'More or less.'

'OK. Fine. You're not going to tell me. But – I wonder – was that where she died?'

'Who told you she was dead? You'd have to have read the coroner's reports to know that.'

'Young Alex. You may have killed the story. But he knows an awful lot. You going to answer me?'

'She died in the Charing Cross Hospital. But yes . . . she overdosed in my sitting room.'

'And that's why you're here?'

'I can't believe in the coincidence of two suicides, those two suicides.'

'Right under your own nose, eh?'

'I'd just left Fitz at Leoni's.'

'I'd only seen him from the witness box, you know. Been weeks since we met face to face.'

'I know, but I can't think where else to start.'

'You could try asking me why I lied in court.'

'Well . . . it did make me wonder.'

'That copper from the Yard. Blood. He interviewed most of Fitz's friends. He had me and Caro in there at least a dozen times. After the second time he split us up. Very clever. He'd get nothing out of her with me there, and he'd get nothing out of me but the truth. I never gave Fitz so much as a farthing. I think Caro has better manners. She bought a pair of oven gloves and occasionally came home with a packet of coffee beans; but I'm a pig. I was happy to live off Fitz and most of the time Fitz was happy to let me. All this stuff about Pritch-Kemp giving us money which we then passed to Fitz is just that – stuff and nonsense, as my mother would have said. I gave the Yard Pritch-Kemp. They were idiots. I wouldn't name him, but it was obvious who I meant. They thought I'd handed them a loaded gun, but I'd given them a time bomb. They were idiots to think Pritch was the kind of man who'd hide from it. They thought he'd bury his head in the sand like Tim. I knew damn well he'd stand up for the defence. But I seemed to be the only person who did.

'I think it must have been the last time but two, or thereabouts, that we'd been to the Yard. I met up with Caro on the

Embankment. She was in floods of tears. Blood had played his trump card. He'd found out about the baby.'

'What baby?'

'Caro's daughter. She's two now. Vivienne Elizabeth. Caro's had a nanny for her for the last year. We lead the life of working women in reverse – Caro sees the child midweek, the nanny has her weekends. Fitz never needed to have a baby and wet nappies around the place, and life goes on as . . . as normal. Shocking word isn't it, "normal"? Our dear father doesn't even know. But Blood found out. Told Caro if she didn't co-operate he'd have the child put in care. She was quite resolute. Got guts, my little sister. She told Blood to go to hell. I'm more of a realist. I knew he could do just what he threatened. The next time he got us in I changed my story. Caro never would, but I couldn't let her do that to herself. I nagged her and I nagged her until eventually she signed a statement. I suppose it was naive of me to think she'd stick to it in court, once she had to face poor old Fitz across a courtroom. I've been wondering ever since what it must have looked like. I knew what she'd done, but by the time she could tell me she was all over the place. I thought she'd go mad. I still don't know what Blood said to her before she signed. She won't tell me. But if he wants to exact his vengeance, he's got to find her first.'

'So have I,' Troy said simply.

Tara said nothing. Troy decided to tack off and come back to the point at a better moment.

'When did you and Fitz meet?'

She swigged gin. Seemed to muse on the question.

'Can you remember?' he prompted.

'Oh yes, I can remember all right. I met him late in the summer of 1959. A Saturday. One of those Indian summer days when they stick tables outside the London cafés and try to pretend it's Rome or Paris or anywhere but London. It was in Endell Street, near Covent Garden. I was with Caro. Fitz was sipping his cappuccino at another table. Saturday is a mufti day for men like Fitz. Wore his linen suit and this preposterous hat – a Stetson I think you'd call it. Anyway, it was his affectation at that time. Did the trick. Made people notice him. As he was leaving he came over and said, "I'm having a party at my house tonight. It would be so nice if you could come." Then he picked up the menu, jotted down the mews address and a phone number and went. We'd neither of us spoken. Then we debated whether or not we'd go to a party given by a man we'd never met before and it sort of resolved itself down into I-will-if-you-will-so-will-I. So we did. Two days later we moved in. We were there four years. He only moved us out when the police came. Said it would be better for all of us. Said it was strictly pro tem. He was much quicker with Clover. Stuck her in a bedsit as soon as young Alex started his campaign in the *Post*. He wasn't taking any chances with her.'

'How did they meet? Fitz and Clover, I mean.'

'Same way. Almost to the letter. Another summer. Last year's. Another café. Old Compton Street this time. Except she was working as a waitress. He even used the same line. Told her we were having a party. Which we were not. But we were by the time she arrived. Fitz drummed up a drunken quorum between four in the afternoon and eight in the evening. He was a bit more hesitant about moving her in than he was with us. I think she dropped a few hints. She'd seen how we lived. She knew Caro and I only needed the one room between us, so I think in the end he just gave in to her.'

'What did he see in her? She wasn't your age. She was scarcely more than a child.'

'She was fifteen, Troy. We both know that. I can see no need to hide it now they're both dead.'

She paused, thought through something and picked up her thread very decisively.

'He made people. Or rather remade them. It was a sort of hobby of his, remaking people.'

Hobby? More like a colossal vanity, Troy thought. He had never understood it – the Pygmalion syndrome. His father had a touch of it, but surely a man was entitled to some share in the making of his own sons? And if Alex Troy made Frederick Troy with an excess of zeal, it was in part due to the vicissitudes of Troy's health, in that he was around, always around, and in part due to the age his father had reached – sixtyish and bored by his own success. His father's old rival Lord Beaverbrook had indulged this vanity in spades, remaking mistresses and protégés. Rod's brief rebellion against his father had been to go and work for Beaverbrook's *Daily Express* for a year. Lord B had seen not only the potential in Rod, but the potential rage to which he could provoke Old Troy. It did no one any good. Rod had the makings of a good journalist, but he did not have the makings of a good Tory — simply rearranging the letters was not enough — and there the relationship foundered. It showed in Rod to this day. If he read a book he liked he would go back to the shop buy three or four copies and give them to friends or family — it was remaking reduced to its most basic components of knowledge and influence. Take it or leave it. It worked or it didn't. Troy still had somewhere a copy of *Lucky Jim* by Kingsley Amis, received one day nine or ten years ago when Rod had rushed in, dishing out copies saying it was funniest thing he had read since Evelyn Waugh stopped being funny. It wasn't. Troy's bookmark stuck where he had placed it after twenty-odd yawnsome pages. Somewhere in his house now was Clover's cookery book — 'New girls begin here' — the testament of Fitz's Pygmalion game with the child.

'There were others?' he said.

'Two at least that I know of. Frances. No surname that I ever heard. I've no idea what became of her. Simply vanished about a year before I met Fitz. But I've seen the photographs. The before and after shots, as it were. The before have her looking more waifish than Clover ever did. The afters have her looking like a duchess. The end result of the Fitz method. And then there was Tanya Hennessey. I knew Tanya. She didn't vanish. She lived the dream so well she fulfilled it and in its fulfilment there wasn't a deal of room for Fitz. She married one of Tommy's nephews in the spring of 1960. In fact, she married the heir. So I suppose, now that Tommy's gone to the great nightclub in the sky, she's Lady Athelnay. Everything Fitz could have wanted for her. And he isn't here to see it, and if he was I doubt she'd give him houseroom. If you ask me he did a better job on Clover. Didn't run against the grain. Found her an unsophisticated little tart and left her a sophisticated little tart. No elocution lessons, no class pretension, simply told her what she needed to know. Much the better way. You see, once he'd remade himself he thought it was easy to remake others. He was soft for me and Caro, but we didn't much need what he had to offer. We learnt from Fitz, without doubt, but we were not recast in his image. Tanya did need him, Clover did. They were his Elizas; they were his Gigis.'

Troy was not entirely sure he believed her disavowal. It was probably what Frances, wherever she was, and Tanya, Lady Athelnay, said — if they spoke of Fitz at all. He knew there was truth in Rebecca West's damning assessment – Fitz had packaged the Ffitches.

'Tell me, Troy, did Clover show off her cooking?'

'Yes. Was that the obvious thing?'

'Oh yes, her *pièce de résistance*. Did not wait to be asked. Fitz lesson No. 1. I do hope you enjoyed it. I can't cook for toffee.'

Troy looked at his watch, remembered the pile of empty bean tins spilling out of the wastebin. 'I can,' he said.

She showed him the larder. It was bare enough for the age of rationing. The sight of few and sorry vegetables put him in mind of the austerity of war and the long, stark years that followed. A meal out of this would be a small miracle. Three eggs, two potatoes, a rare red pepper wrinkling with age, an onion green with mould at the outer skin . . . but in his war he had produced little miracles on a regular basis, helped by the fact that his mother had used her huge Hertfordshire garden to produce vegetables and eggs aplenty. It called for a Spanish omelette. He had seemed to make them quite a lot during the war.

Tara's contribution was to light three candles on the kitchen table, candles undignified by candelabra, stuck into enamel Wee Willie Winkie candleholders. Troy thought for a moment how romantic and how absurd this was, and then remembered that there was no electricity and that she was coping with necessity, not setting a mood.

They ate in near silence. For the moment she seemed to have nothing to say. The most he got out of her was a 'not bad'. Then à propos of nothing she said, 'What was Clover's real name? Did she ever tell you?'

'I thought it was Clover,' he said, telling truth as lies.

'Nobody's christened Clover. At least nobody born to a couple of cockneys at the end of the war. Surely she was a Pauline or a Susan?'

'Never said.'

'I bet Fitz knew.'

Tara stacked the plates in the sink and left them, reached for the gin bottle again, poured two huge measures and flavoured them lightly with a splash of tonic.

'Shall we sit outside?' she said. 'I think there's about fifteen minutes of a rather spectacular sunset left.'

She stuck two kitchen chairs in the yard, and they sat looking westward either side of the door. The last slice of sun was glowing burnt orange and sinking beneath the horizon.

'It is beautiful, isn't it?' she said. 'Makes me think I don't get out of London often enough.'

'I do,' said Troy. 'I have to get out of the fray. I have to get out of the fray, because I have to be in it. You could stay out of it. You don't have to go back.'

He was not looking at her as he spoke, he was looking at the sun, but he was sure her non-word amounted to 'hrrummph', and turned to find her looking hard at him.

'You took a shine to me at Uphill? Am I right?'

'A shine?'

'Coyness doesn't suit you, Troy.'

'OK. A shine it is.'

'Glad we can agree. But . . . Troy . . . do not mistake me. Do not think me one of the good girls. I'm not. Forget the whore with the heart of gold. T'ain't me. I am in what I am in for what is in it for me.'

'Aha?'

'Now – I know a little bit about you. Fitz seemed to think you were the best thing at a piano since Russ Conway, and Anna used to talk about this eccentric copper who bred pigs and won prizes for his leeks. I rather think she loved your rural idyll, and you were a bastard not to let her see more of it than you did. You can tell me it's bliss to be out of the fray – you can tell me till the cows come home and God knows there's enough of the four-footed fuckers around here. But . . . big big but . . . I am a child of the fray. Going back? Of course I'm going back. Did you think I meant to stay here for ever? I can't fulfil your rural idyll for you, Troy. I'm going back. More than that, I'm taking the money. I've already sold Fitz. I want my thirty pieces of silver. My father cut me off in 1955. I've torn away ever since, since I was seventeen. There've always been other "daddies". Although right now there's really a shortage of daddies, at least of daddies I'd ever want. So I'm taking the money. I'd never have done it if Fitz had lived – but he didn't, so nothing I can say will hurt him.'

'You'll be notorious.'

'I'm already notorious.'

'How much are they offering?'

'Thousands. Believe me, thousands. I'll give Fleet Street what they want, every last damn scrap of it. And if it isn't enough I'll make it up. But I'll nail Chief Inspector Blood. And I don't care if he sues. I'll tell Britain what the bastard did and I'll take the consequences.'

'When?' said Troy.

'Any day now. As soon as I can screw up the courage.'

'Can you give me more time?'

'You? I don't understand.'

'I can nail Blood. But Blood's a dim bugger. It's possible he set out to convict Fitz at any price. There's a kind of policeman in every force whose idea of good coppering is to convict at any price. And they don't think they're dishonest. They think they're making up for all the loopholes in the law. He might have thought this up on his own. But I'd be very surprised. And I cannot nail him and whoever pulls his strings in a couple of days.'

'How long?'

'A fortnight. Give me a fortnight.'

Tara sipped gin and thought. Tapped against the leg of his chair with the toe of her plimsoll.

'OK. A fortnight it is. But you must the one to talk to Alex. I don't want to do it. In fact, I don't want to see the little shit until you're through.'

'Is he a little shit?'

Tara thought about this too.

'I don't have your family loyalties. Perhaps it's fairer to say he's ambitious and he knows he's pulled off a real coup this time, and that has consequences upon his character. He's just not like you or your brother.'

'You've met my brother?'

'Tommy took me to lunch at the Lords a few times. Your brother was there once. I think it was just about passable for a socialist to be seen dining with a cross-bencher. Your brother's a sweet man. Your nephew isn't. It's about as simple as that.'

'I don't think Rod remembers meeting you.'

'He wouldn't, would he? I wore National Health specs, put my hair up and tried to look like a secretary. Tommy did that a lot, you know. Primmed and primped me and took me out to meet the respectable and the boring. I think it gave him enormous pleasure. "This is Miss Jones, doing a little research for me." It was his idea of

JOHN LAWTON

sailing close to the wind, but as most of the people he introduced me to would have been none the wiser if he'd told them my real name and left me looking, as he used to put it, "like a scarlet beauty", I don't think there was really any risk at all. That was just silly old Tommy. Fitz, now Fitz did take risks. But then Tommy was an insider, wasn't he? He could flirt harmlessly because he belonged. Fitz was an outsider. He wanted to belong and to destroy in equal measure. So he took real risks. He used to fuck in St James's Park, in the bushes – who hasn't after all? – but as close as he could get to people passing by, as close as he could get to public sex without it being public. Flirting with the outrageous, wanting to outrage, which of course he never quite did. The man who wanted to belong always in some sort of bizarre equilibrium with the man who wanted to destroy. Poor Fitz, he finally did outrage the public, and what a price he paid.

'Tommy untarting me was his rather tame version of the same flirtation. He introduced me to your brother as Miss Brown, I think. Rod asked if I was any relation to George Brown. Tommy stepped on my foot to stop me laughing out loud and then your brother tried to talk Tommy into supporting a Labour vote in the Lords. Rod was sweetness itself, but I doubt I figured much in his thoughts. Some men never look twice at another woman. They still exist, much to my surprise, and he's one of them. But there you and your brother differ – don't you, Troy?'

Troy said nothing. The sun winked out.

'Am I shocking you, Troy?'

'No,' he said. And she wasn't.

'But all this, all this sort of thing isn't you is it? Isn't your thing.'

'No. It's not me.' He found he could not utter the phrase 'my thing' without mentally adding inverted commas. 'Not "my thing".'

'Are you staying the night?'

'Dunno. What time is it?'

'Dunno. But it's dark. Do you really want to drive back in the pitch dark?'

§ 83

In the morning he found there was nothing in the cupboard but bread, butter, a splash of milk and half a packet of maggoty old flour – and there was no water in the tap. Hot or cold. Then he saw the shiny new galvanised steel bucket below the kitchen sink and realised that drawning water from a well probably went with cooking on bottled gas and pissing in an earth closet.

He went into the yard and prised up the wooden lid of the well. He'd done nothing like this since before the war. A gardener's cottage on his father's estate. An old boy who refused all the new-fangled gadgetry that his father would have installed in 1930 – water in taps, a bog that flushed, electricity. The old boy had lived all his life thirty-odd miles from London and never been there. In his retirement he had raised the lushest garden Troy had ever seen, so rich, so colour-crammed, Fitz would have been chlorophyll green with envy – head-high delphiniums in palest blue, tiny tulips in darkest black, and the mottled, browning greens of foul, fug-making homegrown tobacco, strung out in late summer to dry – and he knew the proper names of none of his blooms, no more than he knew the real names of half the creatures of the garden. One word had lodged in Troy's mind for ever: the old boy had called snails 'hodmandods', a word peculiar to the dialects of eastern England. 'Hodmandod,' thought Troy, as he saw one of the creatures slide up the inner wall of the well.

Perhaps Tara was right. Perhaps he laboured under an habitual fancy of being a rustic. Even as he thought the mundane thought he heard the crash of conkers in their spiky shells hitting the ground, looked up to see crows conspiratorially perched on the barn ridge, and a fighter formation of Canada geese, gently flapping southward, watched a black-stained, mildewed sycamore leaf float slowly down, and smelt the unmistakable cheesy, rotten smell of *Phallus impudicus* – the stinkhorn toadstool. Autumn in all her fruitfulness, and yet again a new season spelt out to him how much of the year had gone, how much of it he had passed in the dream.

He rested the full bucket on the lip of the well. It was definitely autumn, the last pretence of summer dropped, too cold to be out before eight in the morning in his shirtsleeves. Half a mile in the distance he could see the slate gables of a big house, and he realised he was staring at the back of The Glebe, that the meadow that rolled down into the valley from Tara Ffitch's yard was the same one he had looked into for the best part of twenty weeks from The Glebe. If he found the time, he'd look in on Catesby before he drove to London.

He followed the scent of stinkhorn. Only a fool would eat the stinking prick, but if it was close by, so might be the highly edible *Boletus edulis* or the more common *Agaricus campestris*, and a day without much in the way of breakfast might suddenly have the best of beginnings.

Half an hour later he woke Tara. She was buried in a rough mountain of sheets and blankets. One arm, one foot and a few strands of mousy hair showed where she was.

'Good God, Troy. I don't do mornings. Never have. What time is it?'

'About half past eight.'

'Troy, just fuck off will you!'

'I need to talk to you. Besides I've made breakfast.'

'Out of what? Fresh air and toadstools?'

'More or less.'

She sat at the kitchen table wearing the eiderdown, held in place by a firm grip from her armpits. The look on her face said 'so surprise me'. He did. She took one bite and gasped.

'Good grief. It's bloody marvellous! Whatever is it?'

'Toast.'

'I can see that.'

'With creamed *cèpes*, a touch of parsley I found in what remains of your garden, and a dash of garlic I found growing wild. The rest I improvised from the contents of your larder.'

He did not tell her that he had picked the maggots from the flour. She wolfed the slice, the eiderdown slipped, a nipple escaped and she did not care to retrieve it.

'Any more?'

'Toast takes a while over a gas ring, but yes, there's more.'

He stuck a slice of bread on the end of the toasting fork and lit the gas ring. He dangled the bread, a visible temptation.

'You were saying last night that Blood gave the worst of his interrogation to Caro.'

'Bastard. He'd have never have got the better of her with me there.'

'I'll need to talk to Caro.'

'Nothing doing, Troy.'

He lit a flame under the mushroom sauce, hoping the aroma would waft her way.

'I have to know everything. If I thought you'd seen it all, believe me, I wouldn't ask to see her. Where is she, by the way?'

Tara said nothing.

Troy said nothing. Turned the toast, stirred the sauce.

'If I were to tell you . . .'

Troy was not about to finish this or any other sentence for her.

'It would be off the record, wouldn't it?'

'I'm investigating a murder. Nothing's off the record. If, along the way, I have to investigate Percy Blood because he's conducted his investigation with scant regard for the rules, then I will. But nothing's off the record.'

'We lied. Both of us in our statements. Me in court. That's perjury, isn't it?'

'Yes. But I wouldn't worry about it. If Blood did what you say he did, no one is going to charge you with perjury. No one is going to take Caro's baby. Trust me, I'm a very important policeman. All I want to do is get Caro's version. That means notes. If as a result of that Blood is reprimanded, or God knows perhaps charged, I'll need it in writing.'

'With the two of us as witnesses?'

'Yes.'

'Then the answer's no. Caro's been a witness once too often. We can't put her through that again. Now, are you going to give me seconds or are we going play temptation all morning?'

'I do have one last question.'

'Fire away,' she said.

'Do you know of anyone who might want Fitz dead?'

'No one and everyone,' she replied. 'No one who knew him, and almost everyone who didn't.'

After breakfast Tara yawned, kissed him on the cheek and went back to bed. He was in the lane starting the Bentley when she stuck her head out of her bedroom window.

'Troy,' she yelled, 'I meant what I said. You have to talk to Alex. I don't want to hear a peep out of him for two weeks. Capiche?'

§ 84

At the turn-off for the London road, just before the pub, he braked and paused, and only when someone honked behind him was the decision made for him, and he drove on, down the hill and into the driveway of The Glebe.

Nurse appeared at the sound of his tyres on the gravel, almost as though she had been listening out for him.

'Well, Frederick, we didn't expect to see you so soon. How long is it now?'

'About six weeks, I suppose. I was hoping to see some of the others.'

'Our Geoffrey left when you did.'

'No,' said Troy. 'He left weeks before me. It was Alfie left when I did. The day before, in fact. I suppose I was wondering about the General.'

'We lost the General.'

'I'm sorry?'

'He didn't make it.'

The almost military style of the euphemism startled him.

'When?'

'This morning. About six thirty. He was not responding to treatment. His heart and kidneys were weak . . .'

'Is he still here?'

'Yes. We don't have a morgue. He's laid out in one of the single wards.'

'Can I see him?'

She thought for a second. Another of her little battles with her sense of authority.

'I don't know. Some people are shocked by the fact of death. Have you ever seen a dead person?'

'I've seen more corpses than I can count. I'm a policeman.'

The mask slipped just a fraction. 'You kept pretty quiet about that. OK. Follow me.'

His sparse hair was neatly brushed and combed, his moustaches trimmed, his hands crossed on his belly, his skin waxen, all but translucent. His eyelids looked older than parchment, beaten thin by time. Only the rims and lobes of his elephantine ears showed colour where the blood had pooled blue at extremity. It was corny but it was the only thing that occurred. The old man looked as though he were sleeping.

Troy had thought this and moved on to nothing more profound than the residue of his own affection for the old man. Nurse peeked over.

'It's the passing of an era, isn't it?' she said. 'When one of them goes.'

It was as blithely trite, as barren of thought as anything he'd ever heard her utter, but it was accurate. As unerringly accurate as she'd be when she said the same thing at the passing of General Eisenhower or Field Marshal Montgomery or Churchill. In their passing, passed the era. And God alone knew what kept Churchill alive.

§ 85

He thought Jack was saying something very like 'I told you so.'

'Yes,' said Troy. 'I have got somewhere, as you put it. But I was trying to say that I think it's a digression. And that's not the same thing as a waste of time. Blood intimidated witnesses. He seems to have been hell-bent on convicting Fitz at any price.'

'But that's hardly murder, is it? It's hardly rare either.'

'No, Jack, I'd like to think it's rare, I'd like to think . . .'

'I know what you'd like to think, but I'm thinking of a time in 1944 when you dragged a corpse out of the mortuary cold cupboard and shoved it in front of your witness!'

Troy was thinking of it too. Sergeant Miller's body, his face shot to pieces, the back of his head smashed like a conker. He'd done exactly what Jack was saying he'd done. He'd intimidated a witness with a brutality that had shocked even Onions. But there was one vital difference.

'Not a witness, Jack, the killer. Diana Brack had killed that man.'

'I know, but we neither of us knew that at the time. And to get back to the point, Blood bullied witnesses. I have little difficulty believing that. But he'd have to be mad to want to shoot one!'

Clark was waving at them from the other side of the room.

'Eddie?' said Troy.

'I've been trying to show you this. I came across it yesterday.'

He shoved a single sheet of paper in front of Troy. 'Came across' – a Swift Eddie euphemism for whatever method he had really used to obtain it. It was a medical report from the Chief Police Surgeon, Scotland Yard. It was signed in a scrawl that Troy took to be the man's signature, and it was addressed to Quint with the initials FYEO – For Your Eyes Only – and dated 19/9/63.

Subject: *Blood, Perceval Albert*
          Detective Chief Inspector, Vice Squad

I saw DCI Blood after repeated and insistent calls from his wife. He was reluctant, but once ordered to report did so. Mrs Blood had been complaining to me of his violent – and I use that word literally – mood swings. After examining Blood over a period of two days, I found no physical complaint worse than dyspepsia and flatulence. However I consider that he is suffering in extremis from the strain of work – the minor physical discomforts I hold to be symptomatic of a larger mental problem – and have placed him on sick leave, with the strong recommendation to his GP that he be referred for psychiatric consultation. If Blood declines this course of voluntary action, I will consider imposing it. Initial period of sick leave – 1 (one) month minimum.

Troy passed it to Jack.

'Oh bugger. Oh bugger.'

'You were saying . . . he'd have to be mad.'

'I wasn't aware I was being literal.'

'Beggin' your joint pardon, sirs,' Clark said. 'But if the two of you sat in the staff canteen a bit more often you'd know that most of Percy's colleagues think he's a bit mad.'

Troy said, 'I know. Blood's mad, I'm wild and Jack's a flash bastard. Eddie, this is beyond gossip.'

'So,' Jack concluded, 'it could be out of our hands altogether.'

'How so?'

'Procedure, Freddie. It's A10's job investigating coppers' misdeeds, not ours.'

A10 was Scotland Yard's internal investigations arm.

'A10?' said Troy. 'I'm not letting A10 within a mile of Blood! Blood is in this so steeped—'

Jack leant forward in his chair. Fixed Troy with his gaze. 'Freddie. Tell me truthfully. Do you in your wildest dreams think DCI Blood murdered Paddy Fitz?'

Troy pulled back a little. Jack was that bit too close.

'No,' he said. 'Of course not. But don't tell me I'm clutching at straws. I'm not. Right now, Blood's all I've got.'

Jack lowered, softened his voice, 'Right now, Freddie, you've got irises as big as saucers. Whatever you're on, don't overdo it.'

When he had gone Clark remained.

'Spit it out, Eddie.'

Clark handed him another sheet of paper.

It was a transfer order, signed by Quint, moving Blood from Special Branch to Vice, dated at the end of May.

'You did ask,' said Clark.

For the moment Troy could not remember that he had asked.

'The date, sir,' said Clark.

'I was in the wilderness in May. You'll have to remind me.'

'It was the morning after Timothy Woodbridge made his denial in the House of Commons, sir.'

'Surely you mean the morning after his admission?'

'No. I mean what I said. Percy was transferred between Woodbridge's statement of denial and his letter admitting the lot five days later. There was no Commons admission. This is Westminster. You stand firm in public, you capitulate quietly.'

Jack's words came precisely to mind. 'Oh bugger, oh bugger.'

'I rather think I'll want a word or two with Chief Inspector Blood before the day's out.'

'Exactly what I was thinking, sir. A word with our Percy. I've already checked. He's taking it easy at home. And he lives south of the water. In Camberwell. I've jotted the address down for you.'

Clark handed Troy a third piece of paper. It was his day for pieces of paper. He handed them out as though rationed. Released them judiciously for full effect. Troy glanced at it and pocketed it. He held up the second, Quint's memo.

'Eddie?'

'Yes sir.'

'Firstly, you're a smug bastard, and secondly, we never saw this.'

Clark smiled a smile as smug as he could muster and went to answer the phone.

'For you, sir. A woman. Won't give her name.'

'I want to see Blood. Put her off.'

'Asked for you as "Troy", sir. No rank.'

Troy took the telephone from him.

'Troy? It's Tara. Don't talk. I'm in a phone box feeding in coppers at a rate of knots. Just jot this down. 44 St Simon Square, W11. Flat 1. And if you upset her or hurt her I'll never, never, never forgive you. Capiche? And if we end up in court again, I'll tell young Alex you spent the night here and rogered me rigid.'

'Truth or dare?' said Troy, but the pennies shot through the gate and the dialling tone was all he heard by way of answer.

§ 86

Troy caught a cab to Notting Hill. He thought better of parking a Bentley anywhere in the vicinity of St Simon Square. It was the heart of what had lately become known as Rachman country, after the infamous slum landlord who had died the previous year. St Simon Square looked typical of the poorly maintained London houses that had formed the backbone of his property empire. Tall, once-elegant, terraced houses, surrounding a square, once green with grass and shrubs, now grey with cinders and cordoned off by chainlink fencing. Paint peeled from high windows, rubbish piled up in porticoed doorways. Ironically, two or three houses on either side of the square were boarded up – ironically, as those houses that were not would undoubtedly be bursting at the seams with human life. Rachman had had a simple policy, and he had not been its only practitioner. Buy cheap – and the Church of England in the fifties had been only too willing to sell – mortgage to the hilt, boot out the existing tenants and then fill up with West Indian immigrants – Jamaicans, Barbadians and Trinidadians – and charge them the earth whilst pointing out that the rest of London did not 'take coloured'. And, of course, this was true. Troy could recall seeing signs in the windows of London lodging houses, when he was a beat bobby before the war, that read, 'No Coloured, No Irish, No Dogs.' It was a policy of playing upon the prejudices of the English in order to make it pay. By the late fifties there had been race riots on the streets of West London.

Some time this winter, the door of No. 44 had had a fresh coat of paint. Deep, glossy green. Troy knocked. Heard feet bounding upstairs.

The door swung sharply back. A black face peered out at Troy.

'Man, when you told us you were the heat you weren't joking, were you?'

It was Philly the sax player from the Cool in the Shade Club.

'No,' he said. 'I told you the truth.' Troy had never felt the need to apologise for his profession.

'An' now I s'pose you tellin' me you lookin' for Caro?'

'Is she at home?'

Philly said nothing and kept his hand firmly gripped on the edge of the door.

'I'm not investigating Caro. I'm investigating the death of Paddy Fitz.'

'She still upset about that.'

Aren't we all? thought Troy. Philly pulled the door wide and admitted Troy.

'Right to the back, and down the stairs. She's in the kitchen.'

Troy descended a rickety, uncarpeted staircase to the basement.

Caro was standing by the gas stove, hair up in a headscarf, no make-up, blue jeans and a dark, billowing, chequered blue shirt many sizes too big. She was stirring a pan with one hand, holding and gently rocking a coffee-coloured infant with the other.

'Troy,' she said with the merest hint of surprise. 'Phil. Take Vivienne will you. I'm sure Troy just wants a quiet word.'

Philly reached over and hefted the two-year-old into his arms. 'No,' said the child.

'Yes,' said Philly, and he disappeared back up the stairs.

Caro turned off the gas, swept an errant lock of blonde hair back under the headscarf and sat down at the kitchen table. 'He's very good with children,' she said. 'Loves them.'

It occurred to Troy that nature was somewhat awry if fathers did not, but it seemed as though she had read his mind.

'Vivienne isn't Philly's. She's Cliff's. Cliff's all right in his way. But he's never got any money.'

She seemed disinclined to push the line she had opened. Troy pulled out a chair and sat opposite her.

'Tara told you I'd be coming?'

'Yes. I don't mind. Really I don't. But I suppose I did think Fitz might have shot himself until . . .'

'Until I told Tara otherwise?'

She nodded.

'I need to know what happened between you and Chief Inspector Blood.'

'I know.'

'I've heard what happened with Tara. I need to know what happened when you were alone with him.'

'We weren't alone at first. He split us up as a way of getting at me. He was never easy on me, never pleasant, but after Tara was gone he became horrible. She has a way of deflecting other people's anger away from me and onto herself. She's done it since we were children. I was lost without her. Blood sensed this. He'd asked us about men we slept with and Fitz. He wanted us to say we were tarts and we paid Fitz as our pimp. We wouldn't.

'That changed when he got me alone. He stopped asking me the same questions over and over again. Of course he'd always come back to them. But there was something else eating away at him. He had a real bee in his bonnet. He got angrier and angrier. I couldn't understand it. It was as though I'd done something to him personally, offended him personally. It was like nothing quite so much as talking to my own father. I came home one day, I'd been shopping, I'd bought one of those flared ya-ya underskirts that made your skirt stick out like you were Sandra Dee. He went apoplectic. Before I could even try it on he'd torn it out of my hands and stuffed it on the fire. He stood there, ramming the poker into it, boiling with rage. Like it was a personal insult. Blood was like that. "Do you know what you've done?" he kept saying. "Do you know what you've done?" I said nothing. What could I say? At first I didn't even know what he was talking about. Then it got clearer. He was talking about Vivienne. Or to be precise, he was talking about sex with black men. Nig-nogs as he called them. "You've tainted some very important people," he said. I still didn't know what he meant. Tainted? A white woman sharing her body with black men and white men. Decent people, tainted by me. Through me. "What do you think that disgusting little twat of yours is?" he said. "A melting pot? I'll tell you what it is, a cesspit chock-full of nig-nog come. You taint decent men. You spread your filth across decent men. Important men." Well, I knew now, didn't I? I was a cesspit.'

'Who do you think he meant by important men?'

'Woodbridge, I suppose. I don't suppose for one moment he meant Tony. And I don't suppose he even knew about old Tommy. I was very fond of Tommy. He was the one man we never shared. Tara thought he was fun, but nothing more. I used to give Tommy one from time to time. Kept him happy. Now – I do sound like a whore don't I?'

Troy said nothing.

'Then it got really weird. I think Blood lost sight of me. Almost literally. It was as though he couldn't see me. It was though he saw some kind of composite whore made up of me and Tara and Clover.'

'He asked about Clover?'

'Oh boy, did he ask about Clover. You'd think his life depended on it. I didn't know where she was. There was nothing I could tell him. But it seems as though I was responsible for her. I'd taught her how to fuck black men. I've no idea whether she did or not. Absolutely no idea. And I shouldn't think she needed lessons. But I was responsible. I'd spread my filth, to her and to whoever she was fucking. Then he said it again. I'd tainted very important, very decent men. Only this time I'd done it through Clover. I'd no idea I'd so much power. I didn't understand any of this. He was just ranting. Bonkers, Troy. Truly bonkers.'

It paid to see the world through other men's eyes from time to time, he knew. To Percy Blood the Ffitch sisters and Clover must seem like uncontrollable forces, bending and breaking the lines of race and class precisely where they should hold firm. Blood had not mingled the ethos of the two squads he had served; he had merely brought the solidity of one to meet the insubstantiality of the other – the political certainties of Special Branch met the sexual uncertainties of Vice. In women such as these, to a man such as Blood, race, class, politics and sex mixed. Those which should be kept apart flowed into one another, dissolved in the wetness of women. No wonder he was apoplectic.

'That was when he started on Vivienne. My piccaninny as he called her. He asked me to imagine how my life would look to a magistrate trying to determine her well-being. I was a slut. I was the most notorious whore in the country. I had no husband; I had one man after another – didn't seem to occur to him that I might have two at once – I had nig-nogs; Vivienne's father was a nig-nog who paid nothing for her keep. Worse, he was a jazz musician. I don't know how he knew that. And I knew what jazz musicians were, didn't I? Drug addicts. All of them. He painted a bleak picture. Said he could have her put into care just like that. He snapped his fingers. I remember that. Horrible big hands and flat, ugly fingernails. Right in front of my eyes. He wanted me to brand myself a whore and Fitz a pimp. I still wouldn't do it.

'I met Tara afterwards, when he'd finished with her. She dragged me into a pub. Everybody gawping at us. She stared them down. Told me Blood had said the same thing to her. That he'd take Vivienne away from me. Said she'd made a statement and signed it. Then she said I had to do the same. I said I wouldn't. She squeezed my hand and told me I was being stupid. Then she was bullying me too, telling me I was always the baby sister – "b'ister" she used to call me – that she was the one with the brains. "Trust me," she said. "I know what I'm doing."

'Blood got me in the next day. He must have known I still wasn't going to make a statement. He had one typed out. Set it on the table as soon as I walked in the door, before I could sit down. I just shook my head. He slipped behind me, and he hit me so hard I thought I'd throw up. I didn't, though.'

'Where?' said Troy. 'Where did he hit you?'

Caro twisted her torso, pointed to her back above the hip. A kidney punch.

'I tried saying no. All I could do was whisper. He hit me again. Other side this time. I signed. I didn't read a word of it, but I signed. Tara was waiting when he was through with me. I had a smudgy carbon of what I'd signed clenched in my fist. I couldn't read it. I asked her what I'd signed. When she told me, I wept. It seemed like we'd damned Fitz. I never wanted to do that. Fitz had been good to me. I loved Fitz.'

'And you determined to tell the truth at the trial?'

'Troy, please don't ask me about the trial. I don't want to talk about the trial. I really don't.'

He could press for more — he'd get more, but at a price. He did not think her distress a price worth paying. He asked Caro the same question he had asked her sister.

'Do you know of anyone who would want Fitz dead?'

'I loved Fitz,' she said again. 'Until all this blew up I rather thought everyone else did too.'

Passing the sitting-room door, Troy saw the child playing on the carpet, a noisy game with a wooden hammer, board and blocks. It looked to him to be a game of square pegs in round holes. Philly sat restringing an old guitar.

'Well, piano man — she OK?'

'I think so,' said Troy. 'And you? Is your band still together?'

'Yeah, we giggin' Friday and Saturday. Still one step ahead of the man.'

Troy took out one of his calling cards, the personal ones with the Goodwin's Court address and his home telephone number.

'You might call me if the Home Office try to deport you. My brother will be Home Secretary in a few months' time.'

Philly pulled a face. Mock astonishment. 'You got to be the best-connected piano player I ever had.'

'That's me,' said Troy.

He had no idea what he might say to Rod if push came to shove. He could try telling him that to break up a working band would be to put half its members on the dole — God knows, it might work.

JOHN LAWTON

§ 87

Blood, Perceval Albert. Chief Inspector (9/9/58)
b. 3/8/07 Manchester

Educated St Thomas's School, Manchester. No Matric.
Left 27/6/21
Apprentice butcher 1921–6
Butcher in family business 1926–7
Enrolled Special Constable 1926
Applied Lancs. Constabulary 23/10/26. Failed literacy
Volunteered British Palestine Police 1927
2 Commendations from Insp-General for bravery
Requested transfer to Royal Navy June 1941 – refused
Requested transfer to Royal Air Force Aug. 1941 – refused
Requested transfer to Army Sept. 1941 – accepted
Enrolled Military Police, Camberley 5/11/41
Served Hamburg and Berlin 1945–6
Transferred Metropolitan Police 1/8/46 with rank of Sgt.
CID from 14/10/48
Flying Squad 14/10/48
Promoted Inspector 1/2/51
Special Branch 1/6/53
Promoted Chief Inspector 1/9/58

Clark's summary of the career of Percy Blood was a bald set of dates and ranks, but it told a story. Blood had rescued himself from the boredom of working for his father by volunteering as a Special, an unpaid, part-time constable – and the date was a giveaway. He had come forward on the side of law and order at the age of nineteen, during the General Strike. The first taste of power had been unforgettable. He had tried to join the regular police force, but he could not spell, or his lips moved when he read and they'd turned him down. Troy could guess what happened next. He'd studied hard, overcome his disability and made it into one of the colonial forces – Palestine. And he had served with distinction. Palestine had become a battleground, even before the Second World War – first the Arabs and then the Jewish guerrillas, Stern and Irgun. Troy had no doubt that he'd earned his commendations. And then the war had broken out in Europe. Good God, how Blood had wanted to be in it – he'd volunteered for every arm of our fighting forces until one accepted him. It was probably only his age that had barred him from the navy and the RAF – he was thirty-four; it would be a long time before men of that age were called up – and when he got into the army it must have disappointed him deeply that all they wanted of him was more police work. He'd have seen no combat as a Redcap stuck in Camberley and then in the occupied cities of Germany. He'd drawn the short straw with his war. Not a good war – that line which every Englishman yearned to be able to utter – not a bad one, but a dull one, busting petrol thieves, sobering the habitual drunks, and stamping his feet at Courts Martial. Then he got lucky. The Met – the London Metropolitan Police Force – accepted him. He went from a life on the periphery to the heart of the matter, straight in at Scotland Yard. His promotion had been slow, and it was now almost certainly stuck. He'd never make superintendent. And there the record stuck. It was not up to date. There was no mention of his transfer from the Branch to Vice. There was also no mention of last year's investigation into allegations of brutality in his handling of Ban-the-Bombers at one of those interminable Trafalgar Square demonstrations. He'd been cleared. But, as Troy recalled, it had been touch and go. Troy tended to pay scant attention to the operations of the political police – they did not answer to him – but if the last word had been Troy's he might not have been quite so inclined to give Blood the benefit of the doubt. All in all, the record bore out the Blood he had thought he knew. This was the making of a disappointed man, a bitterly disappointed man.

He turned to page two – medical history. Percy Blood had never taken a day off sick since the day he joined the Met seventeen years ago. Until now.

§ 88

Seventy-one Marsh Lane was an Edwardian villa. Red and white tiles in diamond formation led up a short path from a rickety, rotten garden gate, past a ragged blue hydrangea to a maroon front door with a leaded stained-glass window depicting a square-rigger in full sail set in its upper half. It was the sort of door to make John Betjeman lyrical or tearful or both. It was the sort of house, the sort of street, to cheer the heart of nostalgic man. Hardly a parked car, not a twitter from a trannie, only the roosting H-shaped television aerials on the chimney stacks told you it was the seventh decade of the century rather than the first. That and the hideous 1950s fill-in where half the terrace had succumbed to a bomb in 1940. The fifties had put up flats between terraced houses with no regard for architectural style in much the same way Troy's brother put on socks. Nothing ever matched. It had been an era in which nothing matched. Troy would always think of it as the odd-socks age.

He banged the brass knocker across the top of the letterbox.

A small rodent of a woman opened the door. A woman in her mid-fifties, he thought. The spiralling remnants of a home perm. Not a trace of make-up. A nylon housecoat in pink and pale blue, its sleeves stopping far short of the sleeves of the woollen dress she wore beneath it. She looked to Troy to be the kind of houseproud woman who might well spend all her time in such a housecoat, never far from a duster. There was a yellow duster in her hand as she spoke to him.

'Yes.'

'Good morning, Mrs Blood. Is your husband at home?'

She scrutinised him, put one hand to her eyes to shield them from the sun slanting across his shoulder. 'It's Mr Troy, isn't it?'

'Yes. Is the Chief Inspector at home?'

'He's not expecting you.'

'I was passing.'

She let the obvious lie go by, pulled the door wide to admit him, quickly shook her duster in the open air and pushed the door to.

'He's in there. I'll tell him you're here.'

She crossed the hall and opened the door opposite. Troy could see Blood beyond her, sitting on the far side of a green-baize table, head bent over something, hands poised on a puzzle or a kit of some sort.

'Percy,' she said.

Blood did not seem to hear her.

'Percy!' she said the louder, and Blood looked up, looked from her, with annoyance in his eyes, to Troy, with evident surprise.

He stood up, put down the model ship he'd been working on, still clutching an odd-shaped piece of the kit in his other hand.

'Mr Troy.'

'Mr Blood.'

Blood looked at his wife.

'All right, Peggy. It's all right, you can leave us now.'

He dismissed her as readily as any servant. As Troy approached the table, Blood pointed at the chair opposite him, but glared at his wife, hovering in the doorway.

'Later, Peggy, later,' he said.

Still she did not move, then Blood waved his hand. Troy heard the soft click of the door behind him.

Blood put down the sheet of extruded plastic he had been holding.

'I won't shake hands, sir. The glue, d'ye see?'

He picked up a rag, poured a drop of thinner onto it and began to rub at his hands, working the solvent down the side of his fingernails, looking at his hands, not at Troy.

The room seemed to Troy to be a shrine to the navy, a personal museum of ships and sailing. Everywhere he looked there were models of ships in balsa and plastic, or passepartout-mounted prints of ships. Tall ships, steamships, ships in bottles. Even the lamp by which Blood worked was a familiar, unlovesome object from the 1930s – a lamp in the shape of a galleon, a Maltese cross upon the foresail, an English leopard on the mizzen, looking as though they'd been cut from dried skin. The room was so very thirties, so very suburbia. No sign of television; a large wireless, still tuneable to lost stations such as Droitwich and Hilversum, topped by a large goldfish bowl, home to a pair of orbiting goldfish; the disused fireplace, neatly, absurdly ornamented by a fan of folded paper; a brass holder for tongs, poker and brush; the rising sun patterned rug, its beams radiating outward from the hearth; the ashtrays precarious on the chair arms; the hand-embroidered antimacassars creaseless upon the backs. It was lost in time – perhaps many English homes now were. Would someone come upon his home in ten or twenty years' time and think it all so quaintly dated?

Troy looked at the box lid in front of him. This was the quick version of model-making. Warships by numbers, available in every Woolworth's the length and breadth of the land. Aimed at children, but then he'd once whiled away a wet Saturday himself making a model of a Spitfire. This specimen was huge.

'May I?' said Troy, and turned the lid towards him.

'The *Hood*,' said Blood simply.

Troy doubted there was anyone in his generation – and Blood's – who would not have recognised the silhouette of this ship. HMS *Hood*. Launched when Troy had been five or six years old. At 42,000 tons the largest battleship afloat. The pride of the Royal Navy for twenty-one years, until its successor – the next ship to be the largest ship afloat, the *Bismarck* – had sent it to the bottom of the Atlantic in less than two minutes. Troy knew the death roll – they all did – 1,400. He knew the survivors – they all did – three out of 1,400.

Blood put down the rag. The smell of polystyrene thinner pervaded the air. Ever after Troy would associate that smell with Blood.

'My brother was on the *Hood*. Chief Petty Officer. Thirty-five years old. Married. Three kids.'

Blood paused. He was looking straight at Troy without, it seemed, seeing him.

'Not one . . .' Troy said.

'No,' Blood said. 'Not one of the survivors.'

Troy saw the pattern beneath the curriculum vitae. May 1941. Blood had volunteered so keenly, so persistently, in the wake of his brother's death. That was why his first choice had been the navy. That was why his hobby was model ships, if something so obviously total, so obviously obsessive, could be as simple as a hobby. He had probably bought the house for the pattern on its front door.

Blood threw down the rag, sniffed at his fingers and, satisfied with the smell, straightened the ragged sleeves of his cardigan. Perhaps, too, there would come a time in Troy's life when the unexpected visitor would come across him in such a cosseting garment, darned at the elbows, frayed at the cuffs, taking his private comfort from a public world?

'Tell me, Mr Troy. What brings you my way?'

Hit him hard, Troy thought.

'It's really very simple. Did you tell Caroline Ffitch you'd have her child taken away?'

'I explored that possibility.'

Troy was gobsmacked. The precision of the man's evasion. A perfect sentence in the art of understatement. It was almost the last thing he'd expected of him. Round one to Blood, and Blood had the second punch in before Troy could draw breath.

''Scuse me asking, sir, but exactly what case are you investigating?'

'Just answer me, Percy. Humour me.'

'Did I threaten the Ffitch woman? Is that what you're asking?'

'Yes.'

'Then that's my answer. Yes. I threatened her. I told her I'd put the council onto her, onto the way she cared for her kid. And there was nothing illegal about that. I did no more than you'd have done in the same situation. I had a witness I knew in me bones was lying to me. Call it copper's instinct, sir. Find me a copper who says he doesn't believe in copper's instinct and I'll show you a poor copper. Tell me you don't believe in such a thing as copper's instinct and I'll call you a liar. All I did was use what I had to get her to tell me the truth.'

'She says you hit her.'

'Well, she would, wouldn't she? Did she show you any bruises? Did she show anyone any bruises?'

Troy knew that one of the talents Blood would have learnt in ten years in Special Branch was how not to leave marks when he hit a suspect.

'I'd have done it too,' Blood said. 'And the courts would've backed me. A single woman, with a bastard child, seeing the kid when it suits her, keeping the company of nig-nogs and reefer addicts, and earning her keep by parading her fanny. If I'd shopped her, the kid would have been taken into care and the magistrate would have backed it with a court order. I threatened her with nothing I couldn't follow through. It wasn't idle, it wasn't malicious and it wasn't illegal. It was horsetrading. She had something I wanted and I had something on her. We came to an arrangement. And if that strikes you as odd or bent, then, sir, I don't think we've been serving in the same force these last twenty years.'

Blood was red with the tinge of anger. He bought himself a moment of time. Got up from his chair. Put the lid on the box and set it down on a side table. It seemed to Troy that he had symbolically cleared the space between them.

'You interviewed her more than a dozen times. Bit excessive, isn't it?'

Blood stood gripping the back of the chair – his hands locked onto it like big, boiled crabs – broad palms and stubby red fingers.

'Seventeen times to be precise. And the answer's no. I did what my duty required of me. If I'd had to have her in twenty times I'd have done it.'

'Why do you think she changed her mind in court?'

'Did she, sir? I wasn't in court. I was a witness myself, if you recall.'

'She retracted her statement.'

'And her sister didn't. If you ask me the two of them had been rowing before the case came up. I think they fell out among themselves. According to the papers I read, the woman was hysterical, and when the prosecuting brief asked her why she'd signed a false statement she couldn't tell him. I doubt the jury would have been taken in by it.'

'We'll never know,' said Troy.

'No sir, we'll never know.'

Blood crossed the room. He'd seized the upper hand, the minute he'd stood up, and now he was showing Troy the door.

'It was good of you to call, sir.'

He opened the door to the hall. Troy rolled with it and let himself be steered to the front door.

'I wasn't aware you were back at the Yard, sir.'

'And I', said Troy, 'was not aware that you weren't.'

'Sick leave, sir. Happens to the best of us one time or another.'

Blood took on the colours of the rainbow as he stood for a moment behind the stained-glass door, with the noon sun shining through the sailing ship. Then he twisted the doorknob, and white light washed in. There could be but one sentence left in him before he ushered Troy across the threshold.

'It was good of you to call, sir. But I don't answer to you, and if you call again I'd be grateful of a bit of notice. I'll have a rep from the Police Association, and you'll have an officer from A10 with you, won't you, sir?'

One small thing was still nagging at Troy. At the best of times it was hard to believe in coincidence, even though this so obviously was one. He asked all the same.

'You saw the medical officer on the 19th? Is that right?'

'I don't recall.'

'You should. It was the day Fitzpatrick died.'

Blood roared. 'Peggy!!!'

And the mouse-woman scurried to his side.

'Mr Troy would like a word. He's a question he wants to ask you. He'd like to know where I was on the night of the 19th. Tell 'im, Peggy.'

'Percy was here with me. We had our tea and we listened to the wireless. There was a concert on the Light. Dance band. We went to bed about half past ten,' she said.

Blood slammed the door on him. It was all very pat and precise. But then, Blood was a career copper and precision was his business. He had not even asked what day of the week the 19th was – nor had his wife – and Troy was not at all sure that this meant anything. He could hammer on the door and ask Percy Blood what dance band had been playing, but he would know – Joe Loss, Ted Heath – he'd know.

§ 89

'The Commissioner's been in again,' said Clark.

'No problem,' Troy replied.

'And Mr Wiggins.'

Troy had had so little to do with Superintendent Wiggins. He ran Vice. A shady bunch of nogoodniks for whom Troy was very happy to have no responsibility. Wiggins was no problem either. He'd have stuck in his two penn'orth sooner or later. Offended by Troy's disregard of procedural courtesies. Troy would smooth ruffled feathers and give it to him straight. The occasion arose sooner than he had expected.

Troy was sipping at a cup of nut-brown, stewed and scummy Scotland Yard tea in the canteen. It was late in the afternoon, and he felt fairly safe from attention. Then he saw the dark blur above him and looked up to see Dudley Wiggins, a man in the fierce grip of five o'clock shadow.

'Mind if join you, sir?'

Troy showed an open hand and beckoned him. Wiggins sat down and plonked his cup and saucer on the yellow-spotted Formica tabletop. Half an inch of tea slopped over into the saucer. Troy looked at his face – a man ten years older than he, grey and lined and worn out by the job – and realised why moustaches such as Wiggins sported were called tea-strainers.

Wiggins poured back the spillage and slurped. 'I hear you've had a chat with Percy Blood.'

If Wiggins knew it was now pretty certain most of the Yard knew. It had taken a mere five hours to be common knowledge. Troy saw no reason to lie to the man. He could like it or he could lump it.

'I have,' said Troy. 'I know I should have told you first, but I acted quickly and I wanted to be certain Percy got no hint of my arrival. There wasn't a lot of time for the protocol.'

And that was as near an apology as the man was going to get.

'Oh, I don't mind about that. Blood's not one of mine.'

'But he's on your squad?'

'I got stuck wi' Percy Blood. That's what I've been trying to tell you. I never asked for him. I got stuck with him. The AC just called me one day last May and told me I'd got Blood as DCI. What I thought didn't matter Sweet Fanny Adams. I didn't want the bugger on my squad. I didn't want a career Special Branch copper trained in all the dirty tricks running my lads in Soho.'

Troy could believe this. Wiggins didn't want a member of the political police working in the Vice Squad and being privy to the countless little fiddles that Wiggins's men ran from day to day.

'I'm an old-school copper. I don't hold wi' people like Percy Blood.'

This was fatuous, conceited, arrogant to the point of banality. Wiggins had probably served the best part of forty years, Troy had served twenty-seven and Blood had served at least thirty-five. They were all old-school coppers. That was the thing about the old school. Sooner or later everybody turned out to have been there. You just didn't know it at the time. And simply to have been to the old school didn't mean you'd sat at the same form as Dudley Wiggins while he carved 'I love Ethel Bloggs' in the desktop – and it sure as hell didn't mean you shared the same values. Wiggins's old school was one that nodded to all his fiddles, one that turned Soho into his private fiefdom. Of course he didn't want Percy Blood muscling in.

'He was never part of the team, y'know.'

'I don't follow,' said Troy.

'I mean he didn't account to me or to Mr Tattershall. He accounted direct to Mr Quint.'

It occurred to Troy that Wiggins's first reaction must have been to think that Blood had been brought in to spy on him.

'And another thing – it cut us out of the juiciest case this side of Kitty O'Shea!'

Ah – so his vanity was singed?

'You think you could have made a case against Fitzpatrick, do you?'

'Made it? Made it? I'd've put the twisted bugger away for life!'

And it seemed to Troy that Fitz was a mirror to the nation, in which none could recognise their own image, save as dogs do, barking at their own reflection in a rock pool.

§ 90

That evening as he walked down Goodwin's Court, he heard boots clattering after him, and turned to see Onions. He'd been sitting in the Salisbury, waiting. It was the way people Troy knew found to find him. Onions was pretty close to being the last person Troy expected to be waiting for him.

'I was waiting.'

'I know,' said Troy, paused with the key in the lock not knowing what came next. There'd been rows between them – they'd known each other the best part of thirty years – but nothing like the last. Troy had left Tablecloth Terrace concluding that Onions would not speak to him again.

'Are we going in?' Onions asked, and Troy pushed the door open.

Troy tried letting routine carry them. He put the kettle on. Onions sat on the sofa and did not take off his mac. So far a typical Stan and Troy meeting, except that Stan usually had a bit more colour to his cheeks, and rarely, hardly looked his age. Grey before he was forty, and built like docker, he had scarcely seemed to Troy to change. He was nearing seventy now. Perhaps Jackie's death had been the one thing that could let time catch up with him? Perhaps Jackie's death would be his death?

'I hear you got something,' he said.

Troy said nothing.

'I hear you've been to see Percy Blood.'

Troy did not need to ask how he knew, although he was surprised at the speed with which he had been told. Blood would have complained to his cronies in Special Branch, and someone in the Branch would have been an old Onions protégé and would have called him at home. He thought of putting a small ad in *The Times*. 'Commander Troy has been to see Percy Blood.'

'What have you got on him?'

'Not much. He's crossed the line. Bullied the statements out of the Ffitch girls. He's passing it off as routine – "We all do it, don't we?" – but it wasn't. I'm afraid it's all I've got to go on. And it doesn't connect with Jackie at all. I'm sorry.'

'Doesn't connect?'

'I meant . . . well he didn't interview her, did he?'

'Of course he didn't. I told him not to.'

'What?'

'I told that bugger Blood. I may be retired, but if he drags our Jackie into this I'll see his career on the rocks.'

'Blood knew?'

'O' course he bloody knew! I got word he was asking, so I met him in the Dog and Truss in Maiden Lane, and I told him. He left her alone or I'd sink him! I didn't give the best years of my life to the Met to have my own grandchildren pestered by buggers like Percy

Blood. The job owes me one favour. That's it. I told him she knew nowt about owt – she's wayward and she's silly, but she's not bent – and if I heard one more time that he was asking questions about her, I'd have 'im.'

That Clover Browne was Jackie Clover was the best-kept secret of the whole affair. The Ffitch sisters did not know – Fitz might have known – the press did not know; Rebecca West did not know; the prosecution had dropped the charge of procurement because they did not know, because they could not find Clover Browne, and they could not find her because her real name was so well concealed. But Blood knew. Blood knew? How did Blood know? Troy knew only because Stan had told him. All the efforts of young bloods like Alex Troy had failed to find her, but Percy Blood knew?

Suddenly Blood had moved from the periphery to the centre, simply because he knew. Troy was no further on, had not a scrap of new evidence – but Blood knew. It didn't fit. Quite simply, it didn't fit.

He had not been listening to Stan. He tuned back in and tried to pick up the thread.

'She had so much to live for, her whole life ahead of her,' Stan was saying.

Troy said nothing, and nodded his agreement.

§ 91

He knew what he ought to do. He had been wrong to put it off in the first place. He needed a quiet spot, somewhere in the Yard where no one would think of looking for him, somewhere where he could go over all the evidence Jack had dumped on his desk.

He went down to Forensics. Through the glass wall he could see Kolankiewicz eviscerating some poor sod. His office would be empty. Perfect. Most policemen were far more squeamish than Troy and tended to avoid Forensics, and few would beard the Polish Beast in his lair.

He cleared a space on Kolankiewicz's desk and dipped into the cardboard box. There wasn't much. The empty pill jar with his own name on the label, the Webley .38 revolver that had killed Paddy Fitz, four bullets and a spent cartridge. The folder contained Jack's hastily written report, a Forensics report from one of Kolankiewicz's assistants, photographs of his own sitting room, and photographs of Fitz's. The latter were messy. The bullet had taken off a large part of Fitz's skull. There were also statements from some of the hacks outside Fitz's house, from Pritch-Kemp on the finding of Fitz's body and from himself on the finding of Clover's. It was not promising material. He was searching for something new. He was deeply uncertain of finding it.

He read it all, and felt blank. 'Rusty,' he thought to himself, 'I'm rusty. I've just been out of things a bit too long.'

He read it all again – and the first sore thumb reared up.

A dozen hacks, his own nephew included, had signed statements to say that they had been on Fitz's doorstep all night, as they had been for many weeks, and had seen no one come or go except Pritch-Kemp.

Then why had no one heard the shot?

He phoned Alex.

Alex said, 'Did you see Tara?'

'Yes.'

'Well?'

'It's confidential, Alex. And it's not why I'm calling. I'm calling about your statement.'

'Statement?'

'The one you made to Jack Wildeve's murder team on the morning of the twentieth.'

Alex sighed audibly. This, clearly, interested him not one jot. Troy knew he would be looking at his watch, wondering how quickly he could get rid of his uncle.

'You say you were there all night.'

'Yes. We were. We ended up pissing into milk bottles.'

'But you don't report hearing the shot.'

'I *didn't* hear it.'

'Why not? A Webley is not a sophisticated weapon. In the dead of night, it would sound like a cannon going off.'

'Fitz lived at the back of the house, Freddie. Largely to get away from us, I should think.'

'You'd still have heard it if you'd been there all night.'

'Of course we were there all night. It was routine. So routine I thought it was a waste of time. Fitz would get home. Give us a smiley "Goodnight, gentlemen." Then Pritch-Kemp would show up about midnight. And then there'd be nothing until the beat bobby moved us on about—'

'What?'

'It was routine, Freddie. We were moved on between eleven and about half past twelve every night. We just walked round the block, came in the other end of the mews. We were still there all night – it took less than five minutes!'

'You don't think that's long enough for a murder?'

'The last time you called me it was an "unexplained death"!'

'Things have moved on. What time did the beat bobby move you on?'

'I don't know. I told you it was routine. No one gave it any thought.'

'Try.'

'I dunno – eleven, eleven fifteen. I doubt it was much later than that. I suppose Pritch-Kemp came in about an hour later. Sometimes he came in before we were moved on, sometimes after. That night it was after.'

'You're sure?'

'Yes, I'm sure.'

Troy hung up and checked Pritch-Kemp's statement.

The press were outside as usual. Joky, a bit loud for the time of night. I asked them to keep down the noise.

Troy flicked forward a page.

Fitz was half in, half out of the armchair. I went to the bog and puked. It was several minutes before I could go back in - and I certainly could not have spoken, so I wasn't yelling 'Help! Help!' or any-thing. When I did go back it was so quiet. Then this scraping cut through. I couldn't place it

```
and it started to fill up the room. I got very agitated.
Irrational, but I did. It turned out to be the
turntable on Fitz's hi-fi. The needle was stuck in the
final groove. Just repeating it endlessly - scrape,
scrape, scrape.
```

So Fitz had died to the sound of Mozart's Jupiter symphony. It did not strike Troy as music to commit suicide to. But what was? There was a radio show that could beat the hell out of *Desert Island Discs*. He would never have chosen the Jupiter – it was not other-worldly, it was so much of this world. It had . . . it had . . . pomp. It seemed to him that there was no other word for it. Heavy on the combined force of brass and strings – at least it was on the one recording he knew, the one Von Karajan had made in Italy during the war. It had oomph. He supposed that a man unfamiliar with the report of a gunshot might have presumed that a louder passage might drown it out. It wouldn't, but if suicides' minds worked so rationally, why not the 1812? – which Troy recalled seeing in Fitz's collection of long-playing records, and which at full volume would drown out the Blitz.

He called Paddington Green police station and asked for the station sergeant.

'Did you instruct the foot patrol in Dreyfus Mews to move on the press?'

'I did, sir. I thought we should show the force. Not a lot we could do, and I don't have the men to leave anyone outside the door day and night, but the blokes on the beat were told to make our presence felt from time to time. We run the streets of London, not the gentlemen of the press.'

Troy understood the logic. Men like this thought like soldiers. It was their turf, their territory. He doubted very much whether it had occurred to the man to give Fitz a bit of peace. He had done it because he believed in the thin blue line.

'Was this common knowledge?'

'I've no idea, sir. It certainly wasn't a secret.'

Anyone who cared to watch Dreyfus Mews, and, God knows, there were enough dark corners from which to watch, would have no difficulty working out the copper's routine. Ninety minutes was hardly a long time. Two or three nights of observation and they'd know. On the other hand, a Chief Inspector of Vice could simply find an excuse to visit Paddington Green and sneak a look at the duty roster and the accompanying standing orders. No one would question his presence; no one would much remember seeing him.

'Has Chief Inspector Blood been in lately, do you know?'

The man thought for a minute and then proved Troy right.

'Not so's I can recall, sir.'

The second thing to strike him was in a photograph of his living room. The chair in which he had found Clover, slumped and dying, stood between the gas fire and the coffee table. On the coffee table the Mandrax jar lay on its side, the cap and the little swab of cotton wool next to it. But beneath the table, a foot or so nearer the other armchair than Clover's, was a white blob. He had no recollection of seeing this – and whatever it was it received no mention in Jack's report or the findings of the forensic officer.

He called the Scene of Crime man, a sergeant named Hopkins.

'It was cotton wool, sir.'

'And what did you do with it.'

'I stuffed it back in the jar when I cleared up, sir.'

Troy had taken a pill from that jar every day for a fortnight. The piece of cotton wool had been a devil to remove the first time – he'd got his little finger stuck in the neck of the jar trying. And each night he had stuffed it back thinking that it surely served some purpose. But there had been just the one piece, of this he was certain.

He opened the jar. Two pieces. The two together far larger than the one he remembered. He checked the Forensics report. The jar had still had one pill left in when it reached the lab. Cameron, Kolankiewicz's assistant, had analysed it and confirmed it as Mandrax. He had not analysed the cotton wool. This was far from sloppy work, but it wasn't top notch either. He had made assumptions. Hopkins had made assumptions. They were not necessarily facts.

He read the fingerprint report. The only prints on the jar belonged to Clover and to himself.

The door to the office opened quietly. Troy looked up to find Kolankiewicz looking back at him.

'Refuge?' said Kolankiewicz.

'Sort of. I began needing a place to hide. Now I rather think I need you.'

Kolankiewicz crossed to the corner of the room and plugged in the kettle.

'You want doughnut with your tea?'

'Is it that time of day?'

'Be dark soon. Of course it's that time of day.'

'I didn't realise. I've been in here since lunchtime. Yes, I'll take a doughnut.'

Kolankiewicz inched him aside, tugged open a drawer in his desk and took out a box from a Viennese patisserie in Golder's Green, a beautifully square box, pea-green lettering on white cardboard, held shut with golden thread.

'I like the Viennese. You plonk them down anywhere on earth they do three civilised things. They found a university, they form a string quartet and they open a patisserie. You will appreciate I use the word doughnut lightly.'

Indeed he did. Such was the array of cream and pastry that it brought back the appetite of a man who had presumed it had left him for ever.

Over a custard slice Troy said, 'Can you analyse these?' And held up the two pieces of cotton wool.

'Piece of cake,' said Kolankiewicz.

'And why would your man Cameron not have analysed them?'

'Cameron is a good man, Troy. He was rushed by Jack. Jack was rushed by Quint. That said, if the cotton wool was in the jar . . . ?'

Kolankiewicz did not finish the sentence.

'There've been too many ready conclusions drawn in this case,' said Troy. 'Jack's man put it in the jar, assuming it had come from there. Your man didn't ask any questions. And none of my people thought to check whether there was a beat bobby around.'

'I repeat. He's a good man. What you are saying is that he didn't ask the right questions.'

Kolankiewicz shoved the box of cakes towards him, a 'help-yourself' gesture. Troy went back to reading the reports.

It took a while. He must have read it half a dozen times and not seen what it meant.

Cameron: one shot fired. Four unused .38 cartridges in the chamber. Manufacturer's standard load. No modifications. Gun in all prob. untraceable.

To this Jack had added a scrawl saying, 'No other firearms in house – no bullets – no box.'

'If you were hell-bent on suicide, would you load five chambers in a revolver or would you presume to kill yourself with the first shot?'

Kolankiewicz peered over his shoulder at the report.

'Eh?'

'All he needed was one bullet. Why would he put in more?'

'Suicides aren't usually that rational.'

Troy ignored this.

'If you loaded a gun without really thinking you'd fill six chambers. If you were hell-bent on suicide and a part of your mind was still rational, and, after all, suicide requires a certain practicality – I've known them to pay all their bills first, empty the ashtrays and flush the lavatory – then you'd load one. But a trained a man setting out to use a gun leaves one chamber empty to avoid accidents. Standard procedure. You do it on auto. A thug with a gun fills all six and doesn't care if he blows his foot off drawing the damn thing. A trained man always leaves the hammer on an empty chamber.'

'Any old soldier would know that. Any officer. And Fitz did his bit. You told me so yourself.'

'No, not soldiers. Coppers. It's a copper's thing. Soldiers are blasé – wear a gun all the time and it becomes as routine as tying your shoelaces. And Fitz wasn't in the infantry, he was in the Army Medical Corps – he refused weapons training. Even defied them to court-martial him. He wouldn't know the ropes. The only gun Fitz ever had was made of wood.'

But the only prints on the Webley were Fitz's.

He went back to the report.

Pritch-Kemp: Fitz's head, what was left of it, was lolling over the left arm of the chair. His right hand was over the right arm, still holding the gun. I've never known why this happens. It's the stuff of a twopenny mystery. Why does the dead hand grip so? Why doesn't the weight just pull the gun out of the hand? I got my breath back and phoned Scotland Yard. I told them I had found Dr Fitzpatrick dead. Then I sat and waited. I

couldn't leave the room, I couldn't leave him –
but I couldn't look at him either. I sat still. I
didn't touch anything, except the arm of the hi-fi.
The scraping would have driven me mad. I suppose
it took less than ten minutes for the police to
arrive. I knew they'd got here when I heard the
hubbub in the street.

Few people ever so speculated in police statements. It looked to
Troy as though Jack had simply decided to let him rip and tell it in
his own words. It contrasted sharply with his own matter-of-fact
account.

Wildeve: The deceased was still holding a .38 Webley
in his right hand when I arrived S-O-C. There were
severe powder burns to the right side of the head
approx. one inch above and one inch in front of
right ear.

This figured. The gun pressed to the skull. The instinctive turning
of the head away from the barrel. No matter whether you were
aiming the gun yourself or someone else was.

Wildeve: I took the gun from his hand. On opening the
chamber I found one spent round under the hammer
and four live bullets.

Bullets. Bullets. Bullets.
Then it hit him. He almost dropped the file. 'Bullets!' he said.
'We just did bullets,' said Kolankiewicz.
'There's no fingerprint report on the bullets! Only on the gun.'
Kolankiewicz tore the file from his fingers.
'Shit, shit, shit and lots more shit!'
'You going to tell me he's a good man one more time?'
But Kolankiewicz wasn't listening. He had a jeweller's glass in one
eye and was holding one of the bullets under his desk lamp.
'There's a partial on this one. Pass me another – and pick it up by
the lead end.'
One by one, Troy handed him the remaining live bullets, and
then the spent shell on the end of a ballpoint pen.
Kolankiewicz pulled out his eyepiece.

'I need to dust them and photograph them. The sides are badly smudged. The percussion ends all have partials, and I think they are all thumbprints.'

'Figures,' said Troy. 'You palm the bullets and shove them into the chamber with your thumb.'

'I make no promises, Troy. But I say this. If I photograph all five I may be able to reconstruct a single print with a little cut and paste.'

'When?' said Troy.

'Tomorrow morning. First thing.'

§ 92

Kolankiewicz had one wall of his office lined in cork. He had cleared it of pins and paper and by the time Troy and Mary McDiarmuid arrived the next morning he had it covered in 10 × 8 blow-ups of thumbprints. They looked on this scale like contour maps of some mountainous country – central Italy or Transylvania or Idaho. The middle of thumb – spiralling whorls vanishing into obdiplostemonous vortices – the outer edges of thumb – formidable Apennine ridges running north to south and east to west. Across half of them he had drawn blue lines with a setsquare, and from the copies now littering the floor he had cut and pasted to assemble in the centre of the board a composite thumbprint, as neat as the face of Frankenstein's monster, but complete. Next to it he had pinned a thumbprint marked up in red crayon as 'Fitzpatrick'.

Even with them blown up to the size of dinner plates, he was peering from one to the other through a magnifying glass.

'Well?' said Troy.

Kolankiewicz did not turn. He roved across his masterpiece, reached out blindly with one hand and adjusted the anglepoise lamp to give more light. 'Even if I have to say so myself, this is bloody good,' he said. 'The print is not Fitzpatrick's.'

Even Troy could see that.

'You never thought it was, did you?' Kolankiewicz said.

He put his glass down and faced them.

'There is, as we surmised, just the one digit, but in five different sections. They overlap considerably, and I think we got lucky. Your man did not set out a row of bullets on a desktop and pick them up one by one. He did what you said you would do. Palmed the lot and fed them in. This is what smudged prints on the sides of the cartridge – we have only blurs – but it also caused much twisting of the right hand, and consequently brought the thumb down at a different angle and area of surface each time. Essentially five different actions rather than the same action repeated five times. Hence the variations in pressure, density of latent image and area of print.'

'Hence our picture.'

'Indeed. Behold. Am I not magnificent? Am I not the Leonardo of the Yard?'

'Did he work in Kodak and cow-gum, then?' said Mary McDiarmuid.

Kolankiewicz smiled. Sarcasm he could handle. What he hated was 'the great English po-face', as he called it. And Mary McDiarmuid had none of it.

'Believe me, Scottish person, if Leonardo had known about Kodak and cow-gum he would have used them. Now, see for yourself.'

He handed Troy the magnifying glass. Troy agreed silently that the print was pretty well complete, but beyond that he had no idea what to make of it.

'Can you', he asked, 'get enough points of similarity to take into court?'

'Similarity with what? You given me nothing to match it with!'

'Sorry, I was getting ahead of myself. Mary, would you call Chief Inspector Blood and ask him to come in this afternoon? Say about two o'clock?'

Mary McDiarmuid seized Troy by the arm, dragged him into the corridor and banged the door behind them.

'Are you out of your mind? I thought you thought Blood was a link, a connection. At worst guilty of bullying the witnesses. Are you saying now that you think he killed Paddy Fitz?'

'Yes. In fact I'm almost certain he did.'

'Why?'

'He knew too much.'

Mary McDiarmuid tilted her head, screwed up one eye and squinted at him.

'Cliché, Troy.'

'Nonetheless it's true.'

'Percy Blood knew too much? You expect me to drag a serving member of the force off the street on the strength of that? Can you imagine the row? As things are I have a table to myself in the canteen. None of the other women want to sit with me 'cos you're giving one of our own a hard time. Now you want to accuse him of murder?'

'Not accuse. I just want to ask him a few questions. And to ask for a set of his prints.'

'They may well be on record.'

'They may, but they'll be with the Branch and the minute we ask for them someone will accidentally put a match to them. Get the bugger in, Mary.'

She was still looking awry at him. 'You don't think it's time to call in A10?'

'It's murder, Mary, not a protection racket squeezing a few quid out of the clubs and restaurants.'

'Your office at two?'

'No, an interview room at two. Let's see how Percy likes being on the receiving end.'

§ 93

Troy was standing on one of the many half-landings on the south staircase, in front of one of Norman Shaw's vast windows, watching the river flow. He saw Coyn reflected in the glass – the dark mass of his uniform, dotted with the brightness of buttons and his insignia of rank – as he came up the staircase towards him. This was one more reason why he'd never be Commissioner – he did not much want a title, but he certainly did not want to wear the uniform again. He could never be a chocolate-creme soldier. He could never be that neat in blue and silver. Sir Wilfrid Coyn never had a hair out of place. He was the sort of man whose moustache could be measured with a micrometer, whose fingertips were little arcs of perfection, buffed nicotine-clean with lemon juice and pumice stone, the sort of man whose wife regularly trimmed the hairs in his nose and ears. They stood side by side. The briefest exchange of looks and then Coyn too stared at the river.

'Do you not think you're a bit close to this one, Freddie?'

The best lies are always couched in the vocabulary of the lied to.

'It's because I'm close to it that I can handle it. It's not just any crime. It's a matter of Met pride. Onions will be unrelenting if we don't handle this properly.'

'Mr Quint considered it wrapped, I believe.'

'No disrespect to Mr Quint, but I've spent my entire career in murder. I deemed this worth a second look.'

'Should you be out in the field so soon? Couldn't one of your chaps handle it?'

'After five months away I need a practical case to work on. This was simply the top of the pile.'

He could believe this if he liked.

'But you won't overdo it, will you?'

Troy said nothing. What was it Jack had said? Eyes as big as saucers? Every cell in his body was overdoing it.

§ 94

Troy met with Blood alone in a stark, windowless room at the Yard. Three chairs, a table and an ashtray. He lumbered in. The old school of men like Wiggins and Blood had its uniform. A heavy brown macintosh, a grey chalk-stripe suit that had seen better days, a row of biros peeping out from the breast pocket, a trilby, police-issue black boots that did not quite meet the turn-ups of his trousers, and five o'clock shadow at any o'clock of the day. On formal occasions he probably wore a bowler and looked like a plainclothes copper from a Giles cartoon in the *Daily Express*.

'Do I need to ask what this is about? Or have the Ffitch sisters been complaining about me again?'

'Take a seat, Percy.'

Blood sat opposite Troy, placed his hat on one corner of the table, and made no move to take off his mac. Symbolic of his belief that he'd not be here long.

'It's not about the Ffitch sisters. It's about Patrick Fitzpatrick.'

'Matter of record, sir. All in my notes. I had a case.'

'I've read your notes. You don't record striking Caroline Ffitch.'

'I thought this wasn't about the Ffitches, sir.'

'And you don't record your search for Clover Browne.'

'Suspicions, sir. Hunches. We don't record 'em all or our files would be as thick as the London phone directory. All I had on Clover Browne was a hunch and a whisper.'

He was lying, and Troy knew it, but to chase him down this path would be a waste of time.

'Tell me where you were on the 19th.'

'At 'ome with the wife.'

'Except when you saw the chief police surgeon here?'

'That was in the morning. I went home for me dinner. We listened to the afternoon play on the wireless. I had a nap. Peggy washed up. I worked on one of me ships and when our tea was ready Peggy called me into the dining room.'

'What did you have for tea?'

'Potted meat, slice or two of haslet. Nothing grand.'

Indeed it wasn't – the offal-based fare of a working-class English family. But since it wasn't, why would one remember? It seemed to Troy that Percy had put some effort and planning into what he would and would not choose to remember.

Blood had stopped. There did not seem to be any reason, he had just stopped.

'And?' said Troy.

'My wife told you, sir. Or had you forgotten? I'll go over it again if you can't recall. We had our tea, I went back to me ship. We listened to a dance band on the wireless and we went up about half past ten.'

'You didn't go to Dreyfus Mews?'

'No, I didn't.'

'When were you last in Dreyfus Mews?'

'The day after I arrested Fitzpatrick. I obtained a search warrant and I looked for evidence in the case against him.'

'Evidence of what?'

'I had a case to make for pimping, if you recall, sir. I was looking for ready cash; I was looking for bank statements.'

'And?'

'I found neither. That's in my notes too. But that proved nothing. In the end Fitzpatrick's solicitor agreed to give us the bank statements. It was neither here nor there in the end. Didn't need to prove he dealt a lot in cash to prove he was pimping.'

'What else did you find?'

'It's all in my notes.'

'You've just told me your notes are selective. What else might you have found?'

It was a small miracle he hadn't found Fitz's letters from Wilson. Or maybe he had and thought nothing of them?

'Such as?'

'Such as a gun?'

'No, sir. I didn't find a gun.'

Mary McDiarmuid shoved the door open with her backside and set down a tray of tea for three. She took the third chair, said nothing, poured and passed a mug to each of them. Stuck a bowl of sugar in front of Blood.

'Do you think Fitzpatrick went out and bought the gun when he decided to end it all?'

'I don't know, sir. I haven't given the matter a lot of thought.'

Blood was giving nothing away. The strength of his hostility to Troy buried any other response. Blood spooned in sugar and sipped at his tea. Troy followed suit and decided to backtrack.

'You listened to the radio. What programme?'

'A dance band. Like my wife told you the other day. A dance band.'

'Whose?'

'Whose?'

'Whose band?'

'Joe Loss. Joe Loss at the Hammersmith Palais.'

'What did he play?'

'"In the Mood".'

This wasn't good enough. Joe Loss played an awful, staccato, chunka-chunka version of 'In the Mood' the way Bob Hope sang 'Thanks for the Memory' — it was his theme tune.

'And what else?'

'I don't know, Mr Troy. I'm not musical. I never had the training. I didn't have the benefits of your education, sir. One tune's pretty much the same as another to me. It's the wife as likes music. I've got tin ears. I just got on with me ship.'

'And you were home all night?'

'I was.'

'Do you know what time Fitzpatrick died?'

"Round midnight, according to the papers.'

'And around midnight you were tucked up in bed?'

'Fast asleep.'

'Did you know the beat bobby moved the press on at about eleven fifteen?'

'No. Should I?'

'No. But I thought you might have known that they did that every night. It wouldn't have been difficult to find out. Anyone who wanted to nip in and shoot Fitzpatrick would only have needed to hang around one of the alleys to learn the routine. Did you know about it? Did you know Paddington Green moved the press on every night?'

'Knew about it? Of course I knew about it. And I didn't have to stand in dark alleyways at midnight to find out. Chief inspectors of the Branch don't—'

'Vice, Percy. You're in Vice now.'

It occurred to Troy that Blood resented being in Vice as much as Wiggins resented having him.

'I didn't need to do that! DDI Harrop at Paddington Green called me when the trial started. Said what did I want done about security at Dreyfus Mews. I said there was no security problem, but that we shouldn't let the press think they own the streets of London. He suggested showing the torch and truncheon, see the beat bobby looked in once a night. I agreed with him. Wasn't my decision. It was just good manners on his part to consult the arresting officer. Wasn't for me to tell him how to do his job.'

It was a brilliant answer. Far, far better than a denial. He had paraded his knowledge and given chapter and verse on it as good, professional police work. And implicit in the answer was that he thought Troy unprofessional.

Blood swigged at his tea, inwardly smirking, pleased with himself, giving nothing away.

'You didn't find a gun at Dreyfus Mews?'

'I've already said. No. I didn't.'

'You don't think that perhaps an old World War Two Webley might have been sitting in a desk drawer since 1945?'

'No sir. I don't. You might recall we had a firearms amnesty a couple of years back. Most decent folks handed their weapons in then.'

Troy hoped he wasn't smiling. This was the first thing Blood had given him. He knew now how Blood had obtained the gun. Thousands of old buffers had turned in their Webleys – Troy had vivid memories of one bloke staggering into Scotland Yard with a fully loaded Bren gun. Blood had simply helped himself from the pile when no one was looking. So had Troy.

Once more up the garden path with Percy.

'So you didn't find a gun at Dreyfus Mews?'

'I've said – no.'

'Would it surprise you to learn that I have a print off the gun that killed Fitzpatrick that does not match his fingerprints?'

'Nothing about this case would surprise me, and nothing wouldn't surprise me. My involvement in it ended when I stepped down from the witness box. I've not been privy to the details of your investigation, sir.'

'I have reason to believe that this fingerprint is the fingerprint of the man who murdered Fitzpatrick.'

'I'm sure you have.'

And Troy was equally sure that Blood's slow-but-sly brain was now reviewing his last denial, telling himself once more that he *had* wiped down the gun first, that he *had* worn gloves, and wondering whether he should not have invented the finding of a gun. A gun he had somehow neglected to confiscate and forgotten to mention in his notes. A plausible explanation of how his fingerprints came to be on the gun. God knows, Troy had given him ample opportunity to dig that grave if he was not happy with this one – no lie the man could come up with would explain why his prints might be on the bullets inside the gun.

'I'd like to request that you allow us to take your fingerprints.'

Mary stuck a voluminous handbag on the table and took out an ink pad and fingerprint form.

'Here?' said Blood. 'Now?'

'Why not?' said Troy.

'I don't have to.'

Troy was not certain whether this was question or statement. Blood showed none of the nervousness of obvious guilt, but he was close to outrage, his copper's pride severely insulted.

'No, you don't, but it would help us enormously if you would.'

'You mean like eliminate me from further enquiry?'

'No. That's not what I meant.'

'Well,' Percy said through gritted teeth. 'I decline to give 'em. I'm not a villain you've dragged in from Watney Street, I'm a serving copper. I deserve to be treated a bit better than that. You want my prints – you want *me*, Mr Troy! – then you'll have to charge me. But I don't think you're ready for that, are you, sir? So I'll say this to you. Charge me or I walk.'

It seemed to Troy that he should at least pretend to give this some thought.

'You may leave whenever you choose.'

'Then I choose now,' said Blood in a rasping, angry whisper. He pushed his chair across the tiles with a scrape fit to crack tooth enamel, yanked open the door and left. They heard his boots ringing on the stone steps all the way to the next floor.

Mary McDiarmuid opened her handbag once more, took out a dust puffer and, holding Blood's tea mug by the rim, blew powder over it.

'Oh dear Percy, where were you when God gave out the brains? He must be part sealion to swallow so many red herrings. I'm amazed you didn't ask him his collar size.'

'At least there was poetry in his answers. Potted meat and haslet,' said Troy, shaking his head gently. 'I ask you . . . potted meat and haslet.'

'Eh?'

'Never mind.'

She puffed again. A cloud of white powder settled on the body of the mug. She pursed her lips, blew off the surplus and looked closely.

'Two clear thumbs and a partial,' she said. 'Nae problem.'

§ 95

Late in the afternoon Kolankiewicz came in dressed ready for the street. He was clutching a large brown envelope. He took out two 10 × 8s, pinned them to the back of the door and slapped the flat of his hand across them.

'They're identical,' he said. 'I have all sixteen points. Enough to hang this Blood.'

'I'm not out to hang him,' Troy said.

'What you have set out to do is of no matter. This case is now cast in iron. Blood would be a fool to plead anything but guilty. You may not want to hang him. Equally he may well hang. The choice is not yours.'

Troy looked at him, in his homburg and macintosh, already pulling his gloves out of his pocket, anxious to leave.

'Why so ratty? What's the hurry?'

'Cribbage night at the Brickie's Arms. Or had you forgotten?'

Troy had forgotten. Twice a week a group of old men sat in the Bricklayer's Arms on Stepney Green and played cribbage. Among them Kolankiewicz and Troy's old station sergeant from his first posting at Leman Street nick – George Bonham. Like Onions, George was now nearing seventy. A giant of a man unbent by age, thirty years ago he had taught Troy all he knew about the law and police work, 'coppering', as he called it. Troy had long ago outstripped his teacher. He had not seen George in how long?

'I haven't seen George in ages,' he said aloud. 'Not since . . .'

'Not since you caught the plague,' said Kolankiewicz bluntly. 'Be a mensh and drop in some time. He always asks after you.'

'Be a mensh' was getting to be Kolankiewicz's catchphrase. But he was right. When all this was over he would 'drop in'.

Kolankiewicz left. Troy found himself staring at the prints. It was unmistakable. A small scar in the shape of a crescent moon slicing across the ridges on each one.

He could feel Mary McDiarmuid sneaking up next to him. 'What now?' she said, arms folded across her bosom, that steely look in her eye.

'I'm going to arrest Chief Inspector Blood.'

She kicked the door to with the toe of her shoe. The rest of her body did not seem to move. Her arms remained symbolically folded, some Berlin Wall Troy had to cross to get what he wanted.

'Bad idea,' she said.

'Bad idea?'

'He's still one of us. Bad idea. Bad form.'

'He's not one of us any longer.'

'He's a copper, Troy. I can't say I think we owe him. In fact I can't bring myself to say I think we owe Percy Blood a damn thing – but we owe something to the force. Troy, don't go tearing down to Camberwell in a squad car to bring Blood back in cuffs. In his mad way Percy was right when he said he deserved better than that, if only because we all deserve better than that.'

'What do you suggest?'

'Go and see him. Off the record. Absolutely off the record. Tell him what you know and give him twenty-four hours to turn himself in. If he does that we can always say we didn't get Kolankiewicz's report till tomorrow. We can sit on it for the good of the force. When Blood turns himself in we charge him and let the record state that he came in voluntarily.'

Troy looked at his watch. It was almost five thirty.

'Eighteen hours,' he said. 'If he doesn't turn himself in by noon tomorrow I'll go down there with the cavalry.'

'You're doing the right thing. Believe me, you're doing the right thing.'

§ 96

Peggy Blood came to the door. It opened only a matter of inches and she said soft as a whisper, 'He doesn't want to see you.'

It had been a long time since he'd put his foot in a door. It was something he thought best left to uniformed coppers in black boots. A big bugger could break the toes of a man in ordinary shoes.

Mrs Blood retreated at the intrusive foot and Troy pushed past her. The first blow caught him just behind the ear, the second on the back of the neck — so hard he found himself ducking and wrapping his arms around his head. Then they fell on him like hailstones.

'Haven't you done enough? Haven't you done enough? Haven't you done enough?'

She caught him a stinger on the right cheek. A tiny fist with the whole weight of her back and shoulder behind it.

'Go away. Just go away and let us alone!'

Then a voice like thunder said, 'Leave go, woman!'

She stopped. Troy took down his hands and saw Blood standing in the doorway of the sitting room. Frayed cardigan and carpet slippers. Peggy and Blood stood stock still, staring at one another for a moment as though Troy were invisible. Then she fled, running between them in the direction of the kitchen. Blood turned around without another word and disappeared through the doorway.

Troy could hear a pulse beating loudly in his head. His own breath in audible rasps. He straightened up, gulped air and followed Blood.

He was at the green-baize table once more. Lit by the galleon lamp. The muted mumble of the six o'clock news on the wireless. The fish circling frantically. A single-bar electric fire glowing dully on the sunburst hearthrug. Another model in his great crab hands. A ship to be fitted into a bottle, its hull slender as an eel, its tiny, fragile masts folded down to be threaded through the neck of the bottle.

Troy sat opposite Blood, hoping he did not sound as pathetic as he felt. Blood tinkered, took up a wire hook and made invisible readjustments to the lie of the masts.

'Percy.'

Blood did not look up. Not the faintest acknowledgement that Troy was in the room.

'Percy. Things have moved on.'

Blood did not look up.

'I've no more questions. I've all the evidence I need. Your prints match.'

Blood slotted the stern of the sailing ship into the neck of the bottle.

'This visit is off the record.'

The ship slid to the belly of the bottle and keeled over.

'If I arrest you now you'll do the full stretch for murder.'

Troy thought it unlikely in the extreme that Blood would hang. He might not be as mad as jokes and gossip would have him, but somewhere, somewhere in the legal process of blind drunk justice, something would mitigate.

Blood took a longer wire hook and righted the vessel.

'If you come to the Yard and give yourself up, I will add to my report the fact that you co-operated and I'll see the judge knows this.'

The masts flicked upright, filling the bottle – as delicate and beautiful as the spread of a butterfly's wings. As instant as the blossom of frame-stop filming.

'You have until noon tomorrow. You have eighteen hours to come to your senses. After that I'll issue a warrant for your arrest. Do you understand me, Percy?'

Blood set the bottle on its blocks. In profile Troy saw the ship for what it was – the *Cutty Sark*. He left without Blood having looked at him. Once he had called off his wife it was as though Troy had not existed for him.

§ 97

He was exhausted. It was still early in the evening, but he was spent. He sat at his desk, still in his overcoat, hands sunk in his pockets. He tried to count the days since he had come back to work. Four? Five? Or was it six? Perhaps his body was caving in only because it could? Blood would turn himself in tomorrow and the case would be wrapped as soon as he had made his statement. The huge 'but' lurking at the end of this sliced into his tiredness. He felt his eyes must be shining like beacons in the paleness of his wasted body. He felt his mind wrenching itself free of the weight of flesh. Blood had killed Fitz – but he had not killed Clover. He might have been party to it, but he had not committed the act. And what was the act? How did anyone compel a woman to write suicide notes, how did he force-feed her sleeping pills without leaving a mark?

'Come on.'

Mary McDiarmuid was standing in the doorway.

'You look dead beat. I'll drive you home. And then Eddie here will cook us a meal. When did you last have a decent meal, Troy?'

He could not recall and he could not argue. He quite fancied potted meat. Blood had stirred a childhood memory of it as nursery food – like toast and dripping, and jam roly-poly. He'd not had that in years either. Fat chance. Clark was into the gourmet stuff. He'd probably get ratatouille or moules marinières, followed by Calvados pomme tarte.

It seemed to please Mary enormously to be at the wheel of a seventeen-foot 1952 Bentley Continental. Troy got in the back and closed his eyes. Clark took the passenger seat and directed Mary to Bedfordbury and the back entrance to Goodwin's Court. It took a matter of minutes. All the same, Troy nodded off, and Clark shook him to wake him. He saw Mary turn her head and smile with pleasure. If she enjoyed it this much he must let her drive more often. The two of them pushed their doors open; Clark bent down to gather up his shopping.

Troy never saw the man who shot him. He stood in the black shadow of the alley and fired his revolver at point-blank range. He was a lousy shot. Five bullets, and only the last hit Troy, grazing the back of his left hand with a crimson tear.

The first four killed Mary McDiarmuid.

Troy found himself on the ground, one leg bent under him, his shoulder against the car door, the bleeding hand shielding his eyes in a stupidly instinctive reaction. What you cannot see cannot hurt you. He lowered the hand. Heard the sound of the hammer falling on empty chambers, heard the slow, seemingly methodical, unhurried steps as his would-be-assassin walked back down the alley, into the courtyard, out into St Martin's Lane.

Clark appeared from the other side of the car. Troy could not find Mary McDiarmuid's pulse. His hand was bleeding all over hers. Her wrist seemed to him as thin and slippery as an eel. Her chest leaked blood like a squeezed sponge. Clark put his fingers to her neck and shook his head.

'She's dead, sir.'

He took off his macintosh and draped it over Mary McDiarmuid.

'Stay with her,' Troy said. 'I'm going in to call the Yard.'

'Careful, he might—'

'No,' Troy said. 'He's gone. He's said his piece. He won't be back.'

Troy called the Yard. And then he called an ambulance. He bound up the wound on his hand as best he could. It bled copiously, but he found he could still move his fingers without great pain, found he could still grip the butt of the old World War Two-issue Webley .38 he disinterred from beneath the loose floorboard by the hatstand.

When he got back to Bedfordbury a patrol car had already arrived, the back end blocking the way from New Row, headlights full on, the beam flooding the street. Mary McDiarmuid still lay in the open door of the Bentley, head back, legs bent, the shoe twisted from one foot, Clark's macintosh preserving decency.

A uniformed sergeant was holding one edge. Peering at her face. 'Jesus Christ,' he said softly.

'I need your car,' said Troy as he walked past.

'My man'll drive you,' said the sergeant to Troy's retreating back. But Troy simply told the driver to leave the keys and get out. There was sharp stab of pain as he put the car in gear. Then he headed south for Waterloo Bridge and Camberwell, wondering who would get there first.

§ 98

There were no lights on in 71 Marsh Lane, Camberwell. Troy knelt down, pushed the letterbox inwards and pressed an ear to it. Among the myriad creaks and hums of a silent house he thought he could hear the uncontrollable rhythm of someone sobbing.

He stuck his hand through the letterbox to see if there was a latchkey hanging by a string on the inside. In so many English homes there would be. There wasn't. He gripped his revolver by the barrel and tapped out the pane of stained glass nearest the lock. The shards fell with a soft tinkle like chimes in a breeze onto the doormat. He stepped in, pointing the gun ahead of him. Something inside told him Blood had shot his bolt, that he was harmless now. He could hear Blood's gun firing on an empty chamber, the ratchet sound as the chamber spun, then the futile slam of the hammer falling. It would have been a matter of seconds for Blood to reload and blow Troy away, and he hadn't done it. The hand had kept on squeezing the trigger until the brain noticed it was all over – as though the man himself could not hear the firing.

Troy followed his nose. He could see the sitting room by the light of a street lamp streaking in through the open curtains. Before he saw it he could smell it. Dinner was set for two. The all-pervasive steamy reek of bad cooking, dinner canteen-style, the glory that was grease. One plate of meat and two veg was half eaten, the knife and fork crossed on the edge. The other was covered with an upturned plate to keep it warm. A sauce bottle stood sentry duty by it. A cut-glass bowl of tinned fruit salad sat on the sideboard next to an unopened can of condensed milk. Mrs Blood had made the effort to wait for her husband, and given up. It looked like the routine of a million British marriages, a thousand spoilt dinners.

A whimper came from the corner by the fireplace, darker than he could see. He stared, levelled the gun and let his eyes resolve the darkness. A small woman was huddled between the wall and a glass-fronted display cabinet. Pieces of broken china and shattered plaster of Paris lay scattered around the shuddering figure of Mrs Blood. She moaned. Troy bent down and took her hands from her face. She screamed, eyes wide, staring into his. A bruise the size of a half-crown coin across her cheek and eye, a streak of blood snaking from one split nostril. She snatched her hands back and began to whimper again. Blood had come in, found her halfway through dinner and batted her sideways with all the force of his right hand.

'Where's Percy?'

She sobbed and would not look at him.

'Where's Percy?'

It seemed to Troy that she did not really know he was there, that she could hear the sound of his words and not their meaning.

Blood was not on the ground floor. Troy went up the stairs. Every creak seemed louder than a gunshot.

Every door opened onto the same landing, and every door except the one at the top of the stairs stood open. He tried the handle. The door was locked. He bent down and peered through the keyhole. The key had been turned from the inside. He bent lower, and found a split panel in the door. The interior was lit by the street lamp. With his eyes no more than two or three feet off the ground he found himself staring at the feet of Percy Blood as they swayed slowly back and forth. The lamplight glinted off his shoes, buffed to a military shine, and a dripping stream of excrement ran off one shoe to puddle on the carpet below.

He kicked in the door with a single blow. It crashed back against the wall, stirred up a new current of air and set Blood swinging all the more. Troy looked up. The eyes popped, the tongue protruded and the smell of shit began to fill the room. The man had prised open the trapdoor to the attic, looped a tow-rope around the main beam of the house and kicked away the stepladder. The room was half stripped, half newly papered. Pots of paint lay dotted around the floor, a dustsheet across the bed. Chief Inspector Blood had whiled away his sick leave redecorating the front bedroom, and when his mind had finally flipped, simply ascended the same ladder to his death. A scaffold for the D-I-Y.

Blood had had the foresight, or perhaps merely the anger, to rip the phone from the wall. Troy did something he had not done in years. He stood in the middle of the street and blew his police whistle. It had lain so long in his coat pocket that his first blast produced nothing but a cloud of fluff and dust. His second brought forth the unmistakable contralto honk of the Metropolitan Police Force Emergency Whistle. He blew and blew until he heard the clatter of police boots on paving stones.

A stout constable lumbered into sight at the street corner, running for Troy for all he was worth and scarcely touching five miles an hour. He stopped so suddenly that his boots skidded on the pavement and the studs in the soles showered sparks like striking flint. Troy stood, warrant card in his right hand, the gun in his left hanging loosely at his side. The man stared at the gun and did not speak. Troy moved under the lamp, held out his warrant card, and let the man get a good look at him.

'Do you know who I am?' he said.

'Yessir.'

'Then knock up the neighbours, find one with a telephone and call the Yard. Superintendent Wildeve, Murder Squad. We have one body and one injured. Then dial 999 and get an ambulance. I'll be in number 71.'

It would be ten minutes or more before anyone else arrived. Mrs Blood had not moved from the safety of her corner. He went back into the bedroom, threw the dustcover off a chair and sat down with the carcass of the late Chief Inspector Blood still swaying gently to and fro. He had fucked up and he knew it. His 'eighteen hours to come to your senses' had been uttered to a man who had long ago lost his senses. It had cost Mary McDiarmuid her life, and cost him the only lead he had. It crossed his mind that he should cut Blood down, but he didn't. As his ears grew accustomed to the house, the sound of sobbing crept up the stairs to him. There might still be something he could do for her, but he didn't. He sat and he listened to her cry until the sound of a police siren coming down the street drowned out her sobs.

§ 99

Dawn was coming up over Sir Wilfrid Coyn's shoulder. Not that he saw it. He had his face in his hands, the base of his palms buttressing his cheekbones, eyes down, staring at the top of his desk. Quint could see it, but Quint was far too busy pacing and shouting. Only Troy saw the weak glow of autumn sunlight straining to break free over Bermondsey. He sat facing the two of them in silence.

'I don't bloody believe this. I just don't believe it. Two coppers dead in a single evening. It's the worst we've had since I don't know when. Why in God's name didn't you send a squad car to Camberwell?'

'They would not have got there any quicker than I did,' Troy said softly.

'At least you'd have had back-up; you wouldn't have been steaming in on your own!'

'Blood was already dead. Mary was already dead.'

'Jesus Christ. Jesus Christ!'

Quint fumbled in his pocket for a cigarette. His lighter would not strike and he slammed both down onto Coyn's desk.

'Cowboys,' he was saying. 'Complete bloody cowboys!'

This seemed to jolt Coyn to life. He took away his hands and stared at Troy. 'It's a mess, Freddie,' he said simply.

'Cowboys!' Quint repeated.

Coyn shot him a look. He retreated to the window, found another cigarette and matches and lit up.

'Daniel has a point,' said Coyn.

'Cowboys?' Troy echoed as though the term meant nothing to him.

'You do seem to have displayed a somewhat cavalier attitude, Freddie.'

'Blood killed Fitzpatrick. I had enough evidence to convict him of that. Then he shot Mary in front of me and Clark. He ceased to be a copper at that moment. I pursued him as I would pursue any murderer. You can call it what you like, I call it my duty.'

Quint could not stay silent. 'Call it what we like – you arrogant bugger! It's what the press'll call it that bothers me. Two dead coppers, Troy. Two dead coppers on a single night! Just think about that!'

Coyn picked up a handwritten sheet of foolscap from his desk. Pushed aside the five-page report Clark had spent the last hour typing up for Troy.

'I've read Constable Selwyn's report. He's the beat bobby you summoned. He says he thinks you were carrying a gun when he got to you.'

Quint snatched the cigarette from his lips long enough to say, 'What?'

'He's mistaken,' said Troy.

The Webley now lay in the middle drawer of his desk.

'He's confident enough to have put it in writing.'

'In that light, at that time of night? He's rash to be confident of anything.'

Quint exploded. 'You're lying! You're a lying son of a bitch! You went there armed to the teeth to tackle Blood. You're as mad as he was. What did you think you were going to do? Shoot him? Jesus Christ, Troy, it's not ten minutes since the Ryan brothers! Or did you think we didn't hear about that up in Birmingham. Troy, everybody knows you shot the Ryan brothers!'

'Constable Selwyn made an understandable mistake,' said Troy.

'And is this an understandable mistake?'

Coyn picked up a second sheet and pushed it across the desk to Troy. It was a standard Scotland Yard medical certificate.

'The chief surgeon passed it onto me. The signature seems to baffle him. Said he cannot make head nor tail of it. I can. It says Kolankiewicz.'

Troy said nothing.

'Freddie, you've been unlucky. You've lost a good colleague, you've lost a suspect and you've taken a bullet yourself. Go home and take a week's sick leave.'

Troy covered his left hand with his right, felt the crisp and bloody bandage beneath his fingers.

'It's just a scratch.'

'Go home, man!' Coyn stood up and put every ounce of energy into three short words. His voice boomed far louder than the rantings of Quint. He went borscht red in the face. He roared.

Troy left. It was the first time he had felt the slightest twinge of respect for the man.

§ 100

When he got back to his own office, Jack and Clark were waiting. Clark quietly getting on with his paperwork, oblivious to the time of night or day, Jack sitting on Mary McDiarmuid's desk yawning and rubbing at his eyes in a desperate effort to stay awake.

'Well?' he said.

Troy closed the door, beckoned them into the inner office and closed the door on that too.

'I've given them my report – and I'm back on sick leave.'

'They've shut down the case. After a night like this?'

'I didn't say that. It's me they've shut down. For a week. Until I heal.'

Troy held up his bandaged left hand.

'However, I don't know what difference it'll make. Percy Blood was all we had.'

'And you still don't think he killed Clover?'

'I know damn well he didn't.'

Troy opened his briefcase and swept the contents of his desktop into it.

'Do you have anything relevant to the case? Either of you?'

'Papers,' said Eddie. 'Lots of papers.'

'Nothing,' said Jack. 'I gave it all to you.'

'Take it all home with you,' Troy said to Clark. 'Don't leave anything lying round.'

Troy pulled open the middle drawer of his desk and stuck his gun into his briefcase. Jack tossed a polythene bag onto Troy's desk. It banged down heavily. It was a gun, an army-issue Webley. Just like Troy's. Just like the one that killed Fitz.

'Blood's?' said Troy.

'He must have collected them. It was on the hallstand. Next to his hat and gloves. All in a row, ship-shape and Bristol fashion.'

'He wore gloves?'

'Doesn't matter. He didn't wipe it down first. There are prints all over it. It's empty and it's been fired. Absolutely reeks of it.'

'Good. Because I never got so much as a glimpse of Blood. Eddie?'

'Dark side of the street, sir. Perfect cover.'

'I don't know what happens next. Coyn or Quint or both of them never wanted us to catch Blood. My guess is that at the end of the week, once the press interest in two dead coppers has given place to the latest teenage heart-throb or the biggest tits on the Golden Mile, Coyn will pronounce. He'll let us go on or he'll wrap up the case. It would help enormously to know which of them wants it wrapped, but all the same it won't stop us.'

'I do find myself asking why they would want it stopped,' said Jack.

'I shouldn't think either of them would relish a Scotland Yard scandal.'

'That presumes they knew it was Blood when they first told me to drop it. You're not saying they knew it was Blood, are you?'

'No. No, I'm not. But I do think that somewhere in the collective mind of our masters the notion was formed that to look too closely into the death of Paddy Fitz would win no favour.'

'That sounds just a bit shy of conspiracy,' Jack said.

'Then it's as precise as I would want it to be.'

Jack insisted on walking home with him. It was as clear as day – it was day – but Troy did not object. He shoved the gun back under the loose floorboard by the hatstand, popped a Mandrax and fell into bed hoping for dreamless sleep and if not dreamless, then not to dream of Mary.

§ 101

He dreamt of Tosca. It came back to him as he sat in the bath after peeling the bandage off his hand. It had stuck like glue, and he soaked it in the water until it softened and he could strip it from the wound. The cut was not deep. He had been lucky. It had missed the fine bones in the back of his hand. But it was broad and ragged. He took nail scissors to the dead tissue and trimmed it. It would leave a scar, one of the worst of his many. And then he remembered Tosca counting up his scars. One night in 1944, when there were fewer than he had now – playing this little piggy. Not the clean, clinical touch of the young woman who had diagnosed his TB, a lingering, playful touch, circling his wounds as though each were some sensory, erogenous organ unique to him. And then he remembered his dream.

She had come to him last night. Still aged thirty-odd, still in her

WAC's uniform – Master Sergeant Larissa Tosca, United States Army. He was forty-eight, as he was now, pale, battered.

'Does it hurt, baby?'

'Not as much as you'd think,' he heard himself say, watching the two of them from some inside/outside stance, part and not part of his own dream.

'I know what you need,' she said. 'And I got what you want.'

And she had performed a slow striptease, something she had never done in life, shedding her army uniform, piece by piece. The olive-green blouse – kicking off her shoes – the non-regulation skirt – unhooking the silk stockings from the suspenders – the joint-defying backward/upward swing of both hands to unclip the bra, the slow slide of a shoulder strap down her right arm as she stood in profile, head back, tits out. Turning frontward, white knickers her only garment – vanished, yanked down in a single movement. Then she pulled back the bedclothes, and he found himself looking down the length of his own body, a thinness exaggerated into bone geometry by the power of dream, a pitiful wreck of a body.

'Anything I should know about? Any new piggies?'

He raised his left hand. Feebly. Like Lazarus. Trailing a bandage that stretched down to the floor, out of the door and down the stairs to the room below, weaving in and out and around the furniture, Ariadne's thread.

She lay across him, her toes touching his toes. He felt her nipples brush his chest, tits landing on him, a hand playing with the lock of hair across his forehead. He closed his eyes, felt himself come up, stiff as a pikestaff. Opened his eyes. Tosca had become Clover. Brown eyes turned metallic blue. He screamed. Woke up and screamed the more.

§ 102

Morning.

The little yellow pill.

The hypodermic jab to the backside.
The dog with eyes as big as millwheels.

§ 103

Later in the day Kolankiewicz called.

'Coyn sent for me this morning.'

'And?'

'He stuck your medical certificate under my nose. "So? What's up?" I said. He said, "It's a standard Scotland Yard medical form type 006/C." "So?" I said. "Read the signature," he said. "Ladislaw Kolankiewicz," I said. "You think I so dumb I don't know my own name?" "And you see nothing wrong in this?" he said. So I said, "Quite right." Took out a Biro and added MD after my name. He was still staring at it when I walked out.'

'You're shoving your retirement up his bum, aren't you?'

'I should care. However, that is not my reason for calling. I have the chemical analysis of your bits of fluff. The smaller bears the dust of your sleeping pills. The larger is, I presume, the one you're interested in. I got lucky — there was a fairly large fragment of pill embedded in it. You ready? In descending order — Ascorbic Acid, Potassium, Sodium, Calcium, Magnesium, Manganese, Zinc, Carotene, Thiamine, Riboflavin, Niacin, Pyridoxine, Tocopherol, Cobalamine and minor quantities of stuff we will sum up with an et cetera. Now smartyarse — you tell me what that lot adds up to.'

It made no sense.

'Ascorbic Acid. In what proportion?'

'Granted even distribution over a pill I calculate at five-eighths of an inch diameter . . . I'd say about eight times the RDA.'

'It's a vitamin pill. Nothing more than a proprietary vitamin pill. Vitamin C, Vitamin A, the Vitamin B complex, Vitamin E, and a sprinkling of minerals on a chalk base. A shilling a packet at any branch of Boots.'

'Congratulations. You win a major prize.'
'I don't get it.'
'Nor I. Do you keep such stuff in the house?'
'No . . . no, I don't.'
'Well, we know how it got into death's jar. How did it get onto your carpet?'
'Just what I was thinking,' said Troy.

§ 104

Night again.
The fat white pill.
Flipped like a coin.
M_x – heads.
Single scored line – tails.
Do not dream.
Do not dare to dream.

§ 105

The best part of a week had passed in tiredness and enforced idleness. He sat in front of the gas fire and reread the copy of Graham Greene's *Our Man in Havana* that Woodbridge had given him months ago, the funny-sad tale of Wormold the vacuum cleaner salesman out of his depth, playing with the spooks.

It crossed his mind to ignore the phone when it rang. It was too late in the day for it to be Clark, who was, likely as not, going to be the only person to call him with anything that mattered. He didn't. 'You never know' passed quickly through his mind.

'Troy,' said a voice he knew well but had not heard in a while – Tom Driberg, an old friend since the war, and the utterly maverick MP for Maldon in Essex. 'I hear you've been in the wars?'

'You heard right. An absolute stinker. I've had TB.'

'Are you mending? Fit for human consumption?'

Troy wondered if this were a bad joke or just Freud speaking.

'I'm OK. I was back at work until a few days ago,' he lied.

'Fancy a night out?'

Troy thought about it. When a man like Driberg uttered these words it was a fool who did not for a moment entertain some of the bizarre possibilities they might imply.

'What did you have in mind?'

'The Establishment in Greek Street. The satire boys – a drink or two – perhaps a dash of music . . .'

Troy knew the Establishment Club. It was part of the satire boom – damn, that word again – and it had its origins in an irreverent production at the 1960 Edinburgh Festival called *Beyond the Fringe*. When the show had transferred to a West End theatre, Rod had dragged Troy to see it, to see sacred cows eviscerated. Not a sacred stone of England left unturned, dug up and flung at the Establishment – hence the club's name.

Rod had laughed fit to die as a slim, dark, impossibly tall young man named Peter Cook had impersonated the Prime Minister, alone on a bare stage, wrapped in a plaid blanket, tucked into an armchair, a Scottish old age pensioner answering the letters of other old age pensioners. It was daring and it was funny – though probably not as funny as Rod thought it was – and it had never been done before. A line had been crossed: the hitherto time-honoured entitlement to respect-regardless-of-worth ditched. It was impossible to imagine Winston having the piss taken out of him in this way, and the only way to take the piss out of Eden was to have it surgically removed. Rod concluded, wrongly, that Troy had missed the joke.

'You don't get it, do you?' he said as they walked home.

'No, Rod. It's you who doesn't get it. I'm all in favour of it. Take the piss out of the bastards at every turn. But in a couple of years' time it'll be you. If you haven't worked out that they'll be just as hard on you, that in year or two it'll be you or Hugh or Mittiavelli being sent up, then you really don't get it.'

Rod looked just a little hurt. Troy knew what he was thinking, and was not uttering for fear Troy would turn more savage than Peter Cook – 'But we're the good guys!'

Believe it if you will, thought Troy.

The Establishment was Cook's club. Stark and black and clinically chic, in amongst the nochic tit-and-bum bars of Greek Street. Right now, as Troy and Driberg took their seats, a short stout chap was up on the stage at the end of the room doing his impression of Wilson. Very dull. Very Yorkshire. Very Wilson. Troy doubted whether he could ever get Rod to witness such a sight with him. He still wouldn't get it. For all he took the mickey out of Wilson behind his back, for all that he had nicknamed him Mittiavelli, some unerring instinct for party loyalty would surely take over if he saw someone doing the same thing on the stage.

Troy was hoping for music. Satire – or was it just language? – required more concentration than he seemed to be able to muster. He had heard that Cook's partner led a three-piece jazz group and sometimes played in the club. But as successive comics took to the stage, he rather thought that this was not one of their nights.

'Do Dudley Moore's trio still play here?' he asked.

'So I'm told,' said Driberg. 'Not tonight, though. He's on Broadway in the American version of the *Fringe*. All the *Fringe* boys are on Broadway.'

The short stout bloke reappeared and was joined by a tall thin bloke. They stood with their backs to the audience and appeared to have their hands at their flies. They had gagged their way through half a dozen lines before Troy twigged that they were playing the roles of Woodbridge and Tereshkov, comparing notes on Tara and Caro Ffitch like a couple of old rakes meeting side by side in a urinal and discussing the kinky merits of their sexual partners while pissing. Only they weren't. This wasn't, 'You get a better blow job with Tara', or 'Caro is a spanker.' It was the quality of the secrets they revealed; it was what their women knew about the inner workings of the Foreign Office or our nuclear deterrent that these two were swapping like dirty details.

A man at the next table – late fifties, Troy thought, thick grey hair, bushy beard turning white – laughed so loudly the actors paused to let him rip before the punch line.

'Of course,' said the short stout one. 'If you really want the hard stuff . . .'

'The hard stuff?'

'You know, the *hard* stuff.'

'Oh, I see, the *hard* stuff. You mean our negotiations for Common Market entry?'

'. . . Then you want Miss Whiplash in Wardour Street.'

They turned sideways to the audience, mimed shaking their pricks and zipping up. This brought the house down, and brought them to an interval.

Troy said, 'Tom, why did you get me here?'

As if cued, Driberg got to his feet. 'See a man about a dog,' he said, and walked off to the gents'.

Thanks, Tom.

Suddenly Troy felt a hand on his shoulder. He looked up and the chap at the next table, who had been laughing so loudly, was standing over him.

'Troy,' he said.

'Yes,' said Troy. 'Have we . . . er . . .'

And he looked beneath the beard, beneath the dyed hair and, finding the man, realised it was Tereshkov.

He spoke in Russian, softly and quickly. 'There are things you don't know about the case. And if you don't know them you will blunder in the dark for ever. Know this, Troy. It was a honeytrap. It was me they were after, not Woodbridge, and they snared the wrong bird. The man you want is Wallace Curran.'

And with that he strolled off towards the stairs and was halfway up it before Troy could even rise from his seat. Troy collided with a man carrying a cello down the staircase. A panel opened up in the soundbox – a squeaky Punch and Judy voice began to intone 'You've never had it so good, so good, so good' – and the Prime Minister's head shot out, propelled by a length of pantographic trellis, and jammed Troy and cello into the narrow staircase. By the time he had struggled past the contraption and its inventor, Tereshkov had vanished. He rushed out into Greek Street, but there was no sign of him. Troy did not even know which way he had turned. The chase was pointless.

'So good, so good, so good,' squawked the voice on the stairs.

'Shit, shit, shit,' said Troy.

'Trouble?'

He turned around. Driberg had come up silently behind him.

Tom had set him up, for the best of reasons, but still set him up. He was in on the conspiracy, if that were not becoming too hackneyed a term. He, an elected Member of Parliament, had thought little or nothing of arranging a clandestine meeting between a Russian spy and Scotland Yard's chief detective. The press would have a field day, if they but knew. The least he could have done was dropped a hint. He owed Troy the price of the deceit. There was nothing to lose by asking.

'What's a honeytrap?'

'Pussy,' said Tom. 'Twat, cunt – quim, if you're feeling poetic. I believe Chaucer has a variant on the word as queynte – *Miller's Tale*, I shouldn't wonder. Something so sweet it's irresistible. God knows why they should apply such a term to women but they do – and your guess at the truth of it would be better informed than mine, I should think.'

Tom was married. Married, Troy knew, these ten years or more. He doubted very much that the union had ever been consummated, and he had no idea why Driberg had felt the need of a fig leaf for his unflaggingly queer propensity – he who could sing hymns to the joys of blowing a nice bit of rough trade. He found it hard to believe that it was just a political ploy, a crowd and constituency pleaser. That Troy's own marriage, seven years old, seven years neglected, went also unconsummated he did not impart to anyone. Driberg could guess if he liked, but he wasn't guessing. He was simply disdaining heterosexual practices with a flip, all-encompassing remark. The look on his face told Troy that.

'Common practice, is it?' Troy asked.

'Virtually standard among the spooks,' Driberg opined. 'They seem to think most men are fools for cunt.'

He shrugged off an issue less than distasteful, of simply no interest to him. 'And I suppose they're right. By and large,' he concluded.

Troy had fallen asleep, he remembered, not long after taking off from Moscow. He had awoken over eastern Austria to the realisation that he'd been had. He had laughed out loud. The man sitting next to him had looked at him as though he thought he was crazy. And if he'd known the word honeytrap he would have laughed the louder. He had spent a pleasured night, a delicious night, with Valentina Vassilievna – call me Vivi – Asimova and it had only then, half an hour away from landing in Zurich, occurred to him that if Charlie's room was bugged – which it surely was – then it was more than likely his was too and if he knew it, then she knew it the better. If she slept with him, and she had, she had done so in the full knowledge that their every sigh and intimate whisper was being recorded. She had slept with him simply because she had been told to. Her inept act of following him had been just that, an act. She had thrown herself in his way to gain his attention and his sympathy – one copper to another in a world of spies. Her appearing at his bedroom door had not been a secret plea for understanding, but an open seduction by the Russian rule book. He'd been had, by the book, down to the last delicious, dirty moan, the last whispered 'otchi tchernye'. He could not believe they'd learnt a thing – he was beyond blackmail and what secrets did he know? – but he'd been, as Tom put it, a fool for cunt, and if that was a honeytrap, then he understood the concept very well.

'And I don't suppose you know anyone called Curran, do you? Wallace Curran?'

Driberg mused a moment. 'Only Curran I know is old Egg Curran.'

'Egg?'

'Edward George Gilbert, hence Egg. He's one of the Soho boozing lot. You can find him most afternoons in the Colony, or the French pub of an evening.'

'I rather think the bloke I want is MI5.'

'Then it's not Egg. He drinks professionally. No other known skills.'

§ 106

Clover came up the stairs from the bathroom. He could not hear the treads creak, nor the silent step of shoeless, sockless feet. He could smell the floral mixture of her talcum powder. He could see the dappled texture of her skin, here dusted, here damp, the pattern of camouflage. He could see the wet footprints she left across the floorboards of his bedroom. Watched them vanish into air, heel to toe, like will o' the wisp.

> I dreamed it last night
> That my dead love came in
> So softly she came, that her feet made no din
> She laid her hand on me
> And this she did say
> It will not be long love, till our wedding day.

She stretched out next to him, her lips touching his ear, both hands gripping his upper arm, one leg slipped over his, the foot slowly easing his legs apart, the rough skin on her heel scraping against his thigh and raising goose pimples on his skin. He woke calm and curious. No screams. He could still feel the imagined touch of her dead hand on him. What was it Pritch-Kemp had said? Why does the dead hand grip so? Ripped from its context, pushed into the man's own field of literary symbols, rather than literal truths, Troy knew exactly why. The demon/dead lover comes back from the dead – to claim you for death. 'Our wedding day' was death. Consummation was death. Sex was death. The dead hand gripped simply to remind him of this.

Time for the little yellow friend.

§ 107

Troy called Clark first. Took the risk of mentioning Curran's name on a Scotland Yard line.

'You couldn't try and find out a bit more, could you? Sit in the canteen and pick up a bit of Special Branch gossip. Curran must be known to some of them. Dammit, the name's familiar to me – I just can't place it. I've heard it somewhere . . .'

He found himself with a stronger mental image.

'. . . I've *seen* it somewhere.'

Clark sighed. 'It won't work, sir. Not this time. We're *persona non grata* with the Branch. All of us, you, me, Mr Wildeve, virtually anyone who's ever served in the Murder Squad.'

'They've sent you to Coventry?'

'Worse. I couldn't come up with a metaphor strong enough. It's like the mid-fifties all over again, sir. Only worse. You'll remember, sir, the reputation you had when you got me down from Birmingham in 1956. Not to put too fine a point on it, sir, you were known as trouble. The last few years have been good. You put a lot behind you. It was unfortunate that the line of duty occasionally put you in the line of fire – but you came through. Even with the Ryan affair there wasn't a man jack in the Yard didn't think you deserved to run CID. You'd earned it. Everybody said so. Right now it's as though the good years never happened. Right now, as far as the Branch is concerned, you might just as well have put the noose around Percy Blood's neck yourself. Half of 'em think you went down to Camberwell to shoot him anyway. They're not going to give us the time of day. So there's no point in me asking.'

'And Mary? What about Mary? What are these instant moralists saying about murdering coppers on the streets of London?'

'Nothing, sir. She wasn't one of theirs. Honestly, sir, I don't know who to ask. Even some of the ordinary coppers are saying you're as mad as Percy.'

This struck home.

'That's what Quint said to me.'

'I wouldn't take it personally, if I were you. He's not exactly Sigmund Freud, is he?'

'I'm not. It was what he said about Blood that concerned me.'

'I don't follow.'

'Gossip is one thing. "So and so is crazy." Doesn't mean much at the best of times. But Quint was blazing with anger. I've never subscribed to the idea that what people say in anger is something you dismiss as an aberration. More often than not it's the lifting of the inhibitions. It says what they really think. Quint really thought Blood was nuts. And I don't mean just because of that medical report you pinched. I think he thought Blood was nuts as long ago as last year when Percy came close to getting disciplined over that CND business. And I think he transferred him from the Branch to Vice because he needed the doggedness, the sheer tenacity of a good nutter.'

'You're edging a bit nearer conspiracy, aren't you, sir?'

'My speciality,' said Troy. 'But if Quint didn't want me looking for conspiracies, he should never have told me.'

§ 108

Troy felt he had little choice. He called young Alex at the *Sunday Post*.

'What have I done now?'

'Nothing. I need a favour.'

'Freddie, your favours are proving rather costly.'

'Meaning?'

'After your visit to Tara her fortnight off became a month. I don't know what you said to her, but she's still out in the sticks. If she doesn't sit down and write the story with me soon it'll lose momentum altogether.'

'I doubt the saga of the Ffitch sisters will ever go cold.'

'I didn't mean cold. I mean it'll be eclipsed by the next scandal.'

'You mean there's more!'

'Of course there's more, Freddie. Don't be naive. They're going to roll out for the rest of our days. We have unleashed the flood, opened whatsername's box. There'll never be an end to it. This is the shape of things to come. And the shape is priapic.'

Troy wondered if he was shocked by this. He was not accustomed to being shocked. 'Can you meet me after work?' he said.

'I suppose so. The Scandalmonger's Arms. About six thirty?'

§ 109

'In the course of your investigations have you—'

'Freddie, don't you think that's a bit hi'falutin? I'm a reporter, not Plodder of the Yard.'

'Are you going to be serious?'

'Sorry.'

'Does the name Wallace Curran mean anything to you?'

'No. What's the context?'

'MI5.'

Suddenly the ingenue was wiped from Alex's expression. He looked hammily around to see who in a roomful of deafening noise might hear their whispers, nudged his glass nearer Troy's and put his weight on one elbow.

'You mean Paddy Fitz and MI5?'

'Yes. Have you heard this?'

'No. I've not heard it. I've thought it, my God I've thought it, but truth to tell I'd dismissed it as pretty well preposterous. But it does rather explain one thing that's had me puzzled.'

'Just tell me what you know, Alex.'

'Official, is it?'

'How official do you like your murders to be?'

'There've been deals done.'

'Deals?' said Troy, sounding and feeling rather ignorant.

'In the House.'

'The Commons?'

'Of course the Commons. Does anyone give a fuck what happens in the Lords? Contrary to popular definition, there's more to being a good parliamentarian than remembering to call your opponent honourable as you shout the bugger down. It covers some very shady cross-party deals. For example, I know for a fact that Wilson agreed not to press for a debate when Charles Leigh-Hunt defected. He even argued against the idea in the House. Didn't it surprise you to find another Burgess and Maclean scandal spread across the papers and no real reaction from the Opposition? They did a deal. To keep

Macmillan in power. If there's one thing Wilson is scared of it's facing one of the younger Tories in the next election. He wants Macmillan to lead the Tories till the flesh falls off his bones. They did a similar deal over Fitz and Woodbridge. There'd be only the pretence of a debate. I think the way they handled Charlie set the pattern, and if they hadn't I might not have been so suspicious this time. They sold Fitz out, for the same reason they did a deal over old Charlie. Complete waste of time of course – Woodbridge has done for Macmillan. Only a matter of time. The smart money says Supermac will go before the year's out. But . . . and what a but it is . . . I've been mightily puzzled to know quite what Wilson had on the Tories, but if it's this, if you've got it right, then it explains everything.'

'I don't believe this.'

'Freddie, I know you and my father have nothing but contempt for Wilson. In fact, he seems to be the butt of most of your jokes when the two of you get together, but believe me, he's the most devious operator in the Commons. His mother's false teeth are not safe in their tumbler!

'Think about what you're telling me. If MI5 ran the Tereshkov business, then there was no security issue. Labour agreed not to make an issue of Tim Woodbridge's morals, simply because it was a shot in the dark; it could rebound anywhere. We're a nation in rut. There are illicit couplings in every layby of every highway; there are orgies twice nightly with matinées on Wednesdays in half the houses of Belgravia. The aristocracy seem to be going mad with Polaroid cameras and blow jobs. There are more nymphs and satyrs in Richmond Park than frolicked in ancient Greece. Who knows who is fucking who? Who really wants that question answered? So they kicked around the non-issue of security instead, knowing it was nonsense. They had a lot of fun, but that's all it was. However, there still had to be a national scapegoat. And since it couldn't be Woodbridge, it had to be Fitz. He was a dead duck the minute Macmillan and Wilson put their heads together – and if I knew for certain that that was the literal truth and not just a metaphor, I'd have the story of a lifetime. Now, if I had a name – if in fact you have just given me a name—'

'Don't even think about it, Alex. If Fitz was a spook, then this is a mess and a half. You may never get to print it.'

'So Wallace Curran is between you and me?'

'Yes.'

'How did you find out about him?'

'I can't tell you.'

'You know, Uncle mine, there are times when the family act seems singularly less effective than the old pals' act. Whatever happened to you scratch my back and I'll scratch yours?'

Troy said nothing. Alex changed tack. 'How do you think Wilson found out about it?'

'I've no idea,' Troy lied, with copies of Wilson's replies to Fitz tucked away in his wallet. 'Have you spoken to your father?'

'No,' said Alex. 'I don't know how to. How does one discuss such a thing with one's own father? I can't think of a way to raise it with him.'

'I can,' said Troy.

§ 110

'How long have you known Fitz was MI5?'

Rod hung up on him.

Troy walked round to the Commons, through the tunnel that linked the Palace of Westminster to the Underground and the Thames Embankment. He found Rod already coming down the staircase, briefcase in hand, hell-bent on avoiding him.

'I can't talk to you, Freddie,' Rod said and bustled past him and out into the courtyard. 'Not now, not ever.'

Troy followed closely, feeling more than a little winded by the haste, but casting around him for the makings of an embarrassing confrontation. All he needed was string, sealing wax and eye of newt.

He grabbed Rod by the sleeve.

'Rod, you talk to me and you tell me what you know or I ask you all the questions you don't want to hear right now and at the top of my voice.'

It worked. Out of term it may have been, but enough nobs and names seemed to be hanging about the corridors of blather to impress a sense of privacy on Rod. Troy recognised the lean, dog-like figure of George Wigg stalking the cloister, received a fleeting if friendly wave of hello from George Brown, and fended off an anxious-looking Driberg with a killer look. Whatever Tom wanted, it would have to wait. He'd got Rod by the trouser buttons and he was not about to let him go.

'For Christ's sake, Freddie. Not here. I'll meet you in the park in an hour. Downing Street entrance.'

The old routine. How often had he met someone for the purposes of indiscretion in St James's Park? The nearest bit of open space to Whitehall, Westminster and Scotland Yard. Here permanent secretaries heard secrets from private secretaries, ministers dallied with the kind of secretaries who typed and took shorthand, and Murder Squad detectives swapped information they didn't want to hear whistling down the corridors at the Yard. He and Jack had stood in the park a thousand times and thrashed out matters that never saw pen and paper – Clark, even now, was in the habit of ostentatiously picking up his plastic bag of sandwiches and his Boots' thermos flask and saying none too convincingly that he was 'just off to feed the ducks'. If the secret intelligence services had any intelligence they'd have had a microphone in every tree, up every damn duck, years ago. At the very least they'd have hours of tapes of Fitz fucking in the bushes.

An hour later Troy stood by the pedestrian entrance to the park on Horse Guards Parade opposite the narrow back end of Downing Street. He had no doubts that Rod would show up, he was, after all an honourable man all but crippled by his sense of honour – and ten minutes past the hour he saw him coming down the steps by the whips' office.

He walked a few feet past Troy, stopped and turned.

'Well,' he said. 'Are you coming or not? You do want your pound of flesh, don't you?'

Troy followed. Rod could not cow him now. No one could.

Rod picked a spot on the north side of the water, opposite a couple of preening pelicans. Unless Troy was very much mistaken, it was the same spot at which he and Jack had stood nearly twenty years ago, in the last year of the war, at a time when secret services were just that, secret – and Troy had set Jack to follow one of MI5's section heads, Muriel Edge. And if she were alive now he might not be buttonholing his own brother. Troy dearly missed having a nark on the inside of the not-so-secret-service.

Rod was hurt. Troy could see that – could hear that. He could not afford to care.

'Ask me again, Freddie, and be very careful how you phrase it.'

'Fitz was MI5. I have no doubts about it. I know that he wrote to Wilson, at least twice. I have Wilson's replies. It took me an age to figure out why Fitz had bothered to write to him but I know now. It's my opinion, my professional opinion, that Fitz was covering his back. Letting the powers that be know that he was one of them and that he expected them to get him out of the mess they had made. I also think that everyone concerned sold him up the river. I think Wilson knew Fitz was MI5 because Fitz told him so. I think Macmillan knew because if he didn't it was an appalling dereliction of duty. And I think that they put their heads together and, far from covering Fitz's back for services rendered, decided to let him go hang. Your party conspired with the government to handle the Tereshkov affair in such a way as to preserve the status quo. Fitz was framed. Your lot knew this and let it happen. My question is simple, and I will alter not one syllable of it. How long have you known?'

'For Christ's sake, Freddie, I am not one of Wilson's inner circle – there're hacks on the *Daily Mirror* know more about the goings-on in the Shadow Cabinet than I do!'

Rod gathered himself. Something in Troy's tirade had struck home.

'You say you've got Wilson's letters to Fitz?'

Troy took the copies from his inside pocket and opened them out for Rod. He held onto the third, left it folded in the palm of his hand and waited while Rod skimmed the first two.

'They're standard replies, Freddie. I send out over a hundred a week just like these. The second one isn't even signed by Wilson. They're . . . they're nothing. Fitz wrote to a lot of people. He tried to ward off prosecution by threatening to tell the truth about Woodbridge. Of course he wrote letters to Wilson. Wilson even brought them up in the debate about Woodbridge in June. The first letter was about Cuba, he said that quite openly. The second was about . . . well it was about Woodbridge . . . wasn't it?'

'I know, I've read Hansard. I've spent most of the morning at the British Museum. It's what Wilson doesn't say that bothers me.'

'Meaning . . . ?'

'All he does is quote the first letter, Fitz saying, "I was an intermediary." Wilson inserts the word Soviet, as though Fitz had never used it, but we are meant to believe that he did. In either letter he could have told Wilson everything about his MI5 connection. And Wilson is careful not to quote directly from the second at all.'

'Could have, Freddie, could have?'

'I haven't seen Fitz's letters to Wilson. Only Wilson's answers. But I have read Hansard in its entirety for the day of the Woodbridge debate. Wilson avoids quoting anything from Fitz wherever possible. There was parliamentary hay to be made by reading those letters out loud. He could have brought the House down, and I am very curious to know why he didn't simply cash in and do just that. And I think there's only one reason why he didn't.'

Troy paused.

Rod said, 'Do you want me to guess?' As though he could not.

Troy held the third letter up between the largest fingers of his left hand, like a ticket tout hawking his wares. Rod took it from him, looking deeply puzzled.

'What's this?'

'Look at the date.'

Rod peered.

'I don't get it.'

'Wilson must have got Fitz's letter that day. Three days before the Woodbridge debate. He doesn't mention it at all in the course of that debate. Reading Hansard you'd end up thinking Fitz had written to him twice; you'd get no hint that Fitz had written to him three times and the third that recently. Fitz was in jail on that day and for quite a few before it. Took him a while to get bail. The Yard had been round bullying most of his friends, after all. Unless Wilson took a fortnight to answer, Fitz was writing to Wilson from prison. And I'll bet you a penny to a pound Wilson's reply went out within twenty-four hours. That would make it June 13th. Why would Fitz write to Wilson about Woodbridge then? He couldn't threaten to expose him. The man had already resigned. There was only one card left to play. Fitz told him about Tereshkov and the plan to turn Tereshkov, told him he was MI5, and if Fitz was working for MI5 there was, there could be, no security issue, only an unholy cock-up. Wilson could have wiped the floor with the government, but he didn't do it. Instead he pushed at a security issue which did not exist, when what there was beneath it was an operational issue, and that's not the same thing. Not the same thing at all. There's a world of difference between secrets of the security services and secrets of state. There's loyalty to the country and there's plain old watching your arse. Wilson played a colossal red herring. He knew there had been no leak; he knew Fitz was working for the British not the Russians; even as he speculated on Fitz's loyalties, he knew Tereshkov was the object not the instigator. And after what he said it was inevitable there'd be a scapegoat – and it was never going to be Woodbridge, was it?'

Rod sighed. Troy could hear the truth surface like bubbles breaking the meniscus on water.

'I don't know for sure. I know nothing with the certainty you seem to desire so. We are stuck with a colossal "if". But Fitz did talk to one of Wilson's narks – George Wigg. That's common knowledge, after all. And Wigg talked to Wilson and Brown. Brown said, "Drop it," but as you rightly surmise Wilson talked to Macmillan. But *what* was told by Fitz to anyone else, and by anyone else to whomsoever, and what of the whatsoever Wilson passed to Macmillan, you cannot prove. Without Fitz's letters you have no proof – but you are, as ever, Freddie, trying to prove something to just one person. Me!'

'Tell me you didn't *know*.'

'I didn't. Not in the sense you mean. Wilson doesn't tell me a damn thing. The only confirmation I've received came from you about an hour and a half ago. I'd heard that Fitz met with people in the PM's office, Macmillan eventually admitted that, and it was no secret that Fitz had had a meeting with Wigg. But it's anybody's guess what he told him. I worked it out for myself. Much as you did. I do not think the front bench as a whole knew or knows now. I think it's confined to Wilson's kitchen cabinet – to the narks, to George fucking Wigg and the likes of George fucking Wigg. I was told to keep out of it. I think George Brown was too. God knows, he said bugger all, and that's rare enough for George. I think I first knew when I realised we were pussyfooting through it. A nice show of bluster from Wilson – 'in glorious Technicolor' as the bastard put it – the predictable tub-thumping from backbenchers who can't be silenced, but all of it hollow, short of the mark, leaving the big stones unturned. And people like me who might have asked the awkward questions told to shut up. There wasn't a damn thing I could do about it. To be honest, I think the last thing Wilson wanted was a public row with the security services. We'll be in power any minute – why would he risk their enmity? He's paranoid enough on the subject of the spooks as it is. If Fitz told him he was a spook then it would be purest Wilson not to want to know. And when Fitz killed himself that was an end of it – neat, nasty, but an end. I could never see the man accepting prison. It was the only way out. They had him trussed up like a turkey.'

'You could have spoken. The Yard answers to the Home Office. The Home Secretary's the highest court of appeal within the Metropolitan Police Force. It's your brief to challenge the Home Office. You could have defied Wilson. You'd have had no difficulty catching the Speaker's eye.'

'In an election year? How do you think it would look if we fell out among ourselves? We've only just got over the last row about nuclear disarmament. The Labour Party has an infinite capacity for shooting itself in the foot. We're weeks away from an election. This is no time to do it. I had to stand with the party.'

'So you built your garden wall and let Rome burn.'

'Freddie, so help me, I'll thump you—'

'Anything for power? Has that become the ethos of the Labour Party?'

'For God's sake Freddie—'

'And Fitz?'

'One can never accept responsibility for another man's suicide. It was his life and hence his choice and his death. In a sane society, it would be his right.'

Troy spoke softly. 'His right?'

'Yes – his right to kill himself if life had become so . . . so . . . intolerable.'

'How very fashionable. How very liberal. A pink at the edges sentiment if ever I heard one.'

'Freddie, I don't—'

'He was murdered!'

The blood drained from Rod's face.

'Murdered by those fuckers in MI5!'

'Oh Jesus.'

'Murdered by MI5 while you and your fat-arsed cronies were playing power politics with the striped ties of the Conservative Party. Fitz didn't kill himself. He was murdered, and he was murdered because no one in Opposition had the guts or the brains to ask the right questions in the one forum this country has that can't be silenced.'

'How?'

'He was shot by a Special Branch officer who was probably, even if indirectly, working for the spooks. I can prove he did it, and no one in the Yard is arguing with me about it, but I can't make the connection to the spooks. I knew Fitz. He would never have touched a gun. He went through the whole of the war without touching a gun. I have a fingerprint from the inside of the gun that killed him matching that of Chief Inspector Blood. Fitz was run for Five by a bloke called Wallace Curran. Maybe Blood was too, maybe not – but I need to know who he is and where to find him.'

'I'm sorry, Freddie, I don't know the name.'

'D Branch. MI5. He must be D Branch. D1, the Soviet watchers.'

'Still don't know him.'

'I need to know what he's up to and how they got to Fitz.'

'You say that as though you think I'll know.'

'No – I don't, but you did know Tommy Athelnay during the war, didn't you?'

'Not well, but yes I knew him. We sat on a few Joint Services committees together. Bored me rigid.'

'And what was his unit?'

'Naval Intelligence.'

Rod looked at Troy – disbelief in his eyes. 'But you're not telling me you think MI5 were stupid enough to use Tommy to recruit Fitz, are you? The war was one thing – *the* thing, nothing else like it – no one, not even MI5, would be stupid enough to keep an agent like Tommy Athelnay in peacetime. He couldn't keep a secret from the cat!'

'There are daft buggers in the dungeons of Whitehall who haven't noticed the war is over. Somebody recruited Fitz. Tommy had a good war record; he was known to the spooks; he was one of them. Why wouldn't they use him? Tommy took money wherever he could find it. Anything was better than the indignity of work. And as for stupidity, your party was stupid enough to do a deal with the government, so nothing the spooks do should surprise you. Whatever this is, it goes back quite a while. They picked up on Fitz when Tereshkov became a patient of his. Then they set old Tommy to recruit him. And when Woodbridge fell into the trap too they didn't call it off. Now, how stupid can you get? They should have dropped the whole thing then. But they didn't and it blew up in their faces. Then they got lucky. Poor old Tommy died. So whatever Fitz said, and he said nothing, he could never call on Tommy; he could never prove the link. MI5 got instant deniability. An almighty mess suddenly began to look containable. Killing Fitz, faking his suicide, tied up all the loose ends. They got their trial, their scapegoat and then they got the long silence. What more could a good secret service ask?'

Rod sucked in air as though he was drowning and almost lost what voice he had.

'You're certain it was murder.'

'Rod! Please!'

'And the girl? Young Clover?'

'Murdered too, but not by Percy Blood. He had the time but he could not have committed both murders. It was beyond his ability to think them through. He didn't have the brains to devise two murders in one day. They were so utterly different in execution. The spooks did that one personally. I know it in my bones.'

'This Wallace Curran chap?'

'Yes.'

'Why, Freddie? What did they gain by killing her?'

'I don't know, but they did. Something she knew and Fitz knew and the sisters didn't.'

'How did they get Fitz to say nothing at his own trial? He didn't even take the stand. How did they get him to agree not to call Woodbridge as a witness?'

'I don't know that either. He expected something of them. He'd been promised something. Right up to the end, when I tried to tell him he'd go down, he still expected something, some *deus ex machina*, to whisk him to freedom and safety – and for all I knew, gratitude too. They convinced him he was one them. For Christ's sake, he convinced himself. He was the unlikeliest Bohemian there ever was. All he wanted was to have gone to a good school and to belong to the right club. If he could have chosen, he'd have been you, not Paddy Fitz. It's likely he didn't know Curran by his real name. If he had named him, without Tommy to back him up, he might well have looked simply foolish – adding fantasy to fetish. And there was a good chance the prosecutor could get it laughed out of court. But then foolishness was inherent from the start. Fitz was a fool. A harmless, charming, garrulous fool, who shut up just when he should have told everything. And the buggers crushed him as though he were no more than a beetle.'

Rod sagged, an oppressive weariness written in his face. Troy began to feel he had all but annihilated his brother.

'Have you thought of asking Nikolai?'

'I've thought about it. Ten years ago I'd've asked him before anyone else, but what would be the point now? He's been out of it for so long. Buried in his book. He's over eighty, for Christ's sake.'

'What now? What will you do now?'

'Now? I'll knock on every door in London till I find Curran. That's what I'll do now.'

'I was afraid you'd say something like that. The power of metaphor notwithstanding, whatever you do, you know I can't knock on any doors for you, don't you, Freddie?'

It was the odd, familiar moment – so many of them in the life they had led together. Hostility resolved into common purpose, lies boiled down to a frankness Troy seemed to achieve with few people, then the line too far, the rout, the retreat, the withdrawal, and they edged their way back to the perimeter, strangers and brothers once more.

§ III

It was a pointless boast. There was no door on which Troy could knock. It was the knock upon his door that mattered. Driberg, standing in the courtyard, hesitant, startled, his arm outstretched to the knocker, so quickly had Troy snatched back the door.

'Not a bad time, I hope? Did try to catch you this morning, but it looked to me as though you and your brother were knee deep in something.'

'We were. Are you coming in?'

'Yes.' He followed Troy back into the house. 'But then, if you've time we should nip out pretty sharpish.'

'Why's that?'

'Curran.'

'What?'

'Spoke too soon about old Egg. Appears there's something he has to say to you. I left him in the Coach and Horses not ten minutes ago.'

§ 112

Troy had spent much of the year gazing upon the lean and hungry. Men, like himself, sapped skeletal by ill-health, the ullage of all that was vital. Edward George Gilbert Curran was a robust, rotund slob of a man and looked by far to be the unhealthiest specimen he had seen all year. Even Charlie on his self-imposed drunkard's ride to bloated death by cirrhosis looked better than this dandruffed, walrus-jowled, purple-faced, reeking wreck of humanity. Imagine, thought Troy, if Dante Gabriel Rossetti had gone to pot, not just to fat as he did, but utterly, irretrievably to pot, boozed out of brain and body – he would look something like the unfortunate Egg.

Egg was drinking the drinking man's version of beer and a shot – beer and a triple shot. Like most habitual drunks he had a way of communicating through any amount of booze and seemed, for all his inebriation, to have an immaculate portion of his mind that remained untouched – virgin for speech, even if that speech only amounted to 'Don't mind if I do', which were his first words once Driberg had introduced them.

'He hasn't finished what he's got,' Troy whispered.

'No matter,' said Tom. 'He's a pro. Bring him a large one. Show willing. Look on it as a peace offering, glass beads to the natives.'

'You mean another triple?'

'I mean a sextuple. Get them to fill a tumbler.'

When Troy returned from the bar with a pint for Tom, a ginger-beer shandy for himself, and a quarter pint of Scotch for Egg, the two of them were rocking with laughter at something Driberg had said.

'Stop it, stop it,' Egg was saying. 'Or I'll wet meself.'

Judging by the state of his trousers this was not an uncommon occurrence. Troy waited for the laughter to die down, waited while he knocked back his pint and triple and started on the tumblerful of Scotch.

'Your very good health, sir,' he said to Troy. 'Now are you the chap was going to ask me about that bugger Wig?'

Wigg. No. He'd got it wrong. He'd talked to Rod about Wigg. He wanted to talk to this bloke about Curran.

'That's right,' said Driberg, elbowing Troy out of interrupting.

'Shit,' said Egg.

And for the best part of a minute shit was all he said.

'Tell me, er . . .'

'Troy,' said Troy.

'Troy, tell me. D'ye have a brother?'

'Yes,' said Troy. 'I do.'

'Younger'n you?'

'Older.'

'Shit is he?'

'Sometimes,' said Troy.

'All brothers are shits,' Egg went on. 'Still, could be worse I suppose. With your name you could have that shit in the Commons for a brother.'

Egg roared, spluttered and choked on his own joke. Tom smiled falsely. Troy had no idea what to do, and regretted bitterly that he'd fallen for another of Tom's wild goose chases.

'Ingratitude. That's what it all comes down to. Ingratitude. All the things I've done for young Wig in his time . . . sheer fucking ingratitude.'

'Who's Wigg?' Troy asked, thinking that perhaps he could cut through this mess, that perhaps they were not talking about the same Wigg, and not getting the elbow from Driberg.

'Wig? Wig? He's me little brother, the little shit. Our Wig – Wallace Irving Gordon . . . *ergo* Wig!'

At last. The bastard was Wallace Curran's brother. Driberg winked at him across the top of his pint.

'You wouldn't by any chance know how I could get in touch with young Wig, would you?'

Egg leant in, his gut wedged against the table, his breath foul upon the tap-room air.

'Cross me palm with silver.'

'Simple as that, eh?' said Troy.

'Man's gotta eat.'

'You mean a man's gotta drink,' said Troy.

'Don't mind if I do,' said Egg before Troy could even blink.

Troy whispered to Driberg. 'Agree a price with the fool, while I go to the bar. I don't want to find myself haggling with him when I get back.'

Troy returned with another glass of liver rot. Egg was grinning the grin of self-satisfaction.

'Twenty-five should see us right,' said Tom.

Twenty-five pounds was outrageous. The last round had all but cleaned Troy out. He was down to a fiver.

'It'll have to be a cheque,' he said.

Egg shook his head slowly. Driberg nodded. Egg shook. Driberg nodded and won. Egg nodded and said, 'Made out to "Cash", of course.'

Troy whipped out his cheque book and dashed off a cheque for twenty-five pounds before the rogue upped the ante on him.

'Now,' he said, holding up the cheque in one hand and the whisky in the other.

'Albert Hall Mansions. Back of the hall. Lived there for years.'

The whisky was downed, the cheque trousered with the speed of a magician palming pigeons.

Troy remembered telling Clark he had heard the name Wallace Curran before when what he had meant was that he had seen it. His Uncle Nikolai lived in Albert Hall Mansions, between the eponymous hall and his old college, Imperial. Long, long ago, in the days of lower crime rates and more bobbies on the beat, the flats in the mansion block had had an in/out nameboard rather like a Cambridge college. Burglary had put paid to its use, but the board remained, the gold leaf lettering fading on the names, minus its little wooden shutters across the in/out part – and above the name Troitsky, N.R. Troy could now see in his mind's eye the name Curran, W.I.G. All this time wondering and he could not pull the name from his unconscious to recognise that he had seen it a hundred times over the years.

§ 113

It had crossed his mind to talk to Nikolai – Rod had suggested it too – and he had dismissed the notion. The last time he and Nikolai had talked at length had been before dinner, the day he had been discharged from the sanatorium. Troy had uttered a few words to the old man, and while he would readily concede that he was softly spoken, he had not thought himself inaudible.

'Ah, dear boy,' Nikolai had said. 'I think perhaps you haff become a two-hearing-aid man.'

He was already wearing a hearing aid, the bulky batteries stretching his cardigan pocket out of shape, the black plastic receiver pinned to his waistcoat, a snaky, cream cable curling up his chest, around and into his right ear. He produced a second set from his jacket pocket. Stuck an earpiece in his left ear, fiddled with the volume and pinned a second receiver symmetrically to his waistcoat.

'Proceed, dear boy. We haff stereo.'

When he opened the door to Troy at Albert Hall Mansions the following morning, he was still wearing two sets. The idea had taken root.

'What brings you here, nephew? Am I dying and has no one told me?'

There was no answer Troy could or would make standing on the threshold. Nikolai ushered him in.

It had changed much since the last time he was here. The room was now dominated by a huge desk, strewn with books and papers, and where the desk ended they overflowed onto lesser tables, onto chairs and cascaded down to the floor. The magnum opus, whatever it was, and he never said, had become his life. It seemed to Troy that he lived at the desk. The remains of bacon and egg congealed upon a plate perched high on a batch of manuscripts. His false teeth grinned from a tumbler between the inkwells. The living part of the living room was reduced to a chaise longue wedged between the desk and the wall and two small chairs either side of a roaring gas fire. This, plus the central heating, made for the typically stifling, overheated flat of an old person.

Nikolai resumed his seat at his desk, turned down the deafening blast of Mahler on the Third Programme. Troy stood. The only chairs not littered were the two by the fire. He'd roast if he sat there.

'Thank God for Mahler, say I. Loud enough to get through to the deafest ear.'

'I wanted to ask you about one of your neighbours.'

'Which one? As if I could not guess from the look of the conspirator you wear so raggedly.'

'Curran.'

'Third floor back,' said Nikolai. 'Now, ask me your question.'

Nikolai began to shuffle papers. Troy was not at all sure he had the old man's full attention.

'You do know him?'

'So, so . . .'

'Professionally?'

'I met him in the corridors of power from time to time.'

'What exactly is it he does for Five?'

'He was D1, as I recall. A good Russian speaker.'

'Is he still D1? What do you think he does for them?'

'Since Sir Roger Hollis saw fit to put me out to grass I have learnt nothing new, nor have I cared to. But when I knew Curran in the old days, he was many things – pimp, blackmailer, a purveyor of lies and misinformation, a rumourmonger, a . . . a . . .'

'It's OK. I get the picture.'

'Do you, Freddie, do you? I cannot but think that if you did you would want nothing to do with the man. But he has crossed your path in some way, hasn't he? What has he done?'

'All the things you just listed.'

'And?'

'And murder.'

Nikolai stopped playing with his manuscript. The word did that. It was in the nature of 'murder' to eclipse other words and actions. He leant back in his chair, ran his fingers through the spirals of white hair that coiled out like a haircut from the *Bride of Frankenstein*.

'Ach,' he said as he was often wont. 'Ach, ach!'

Troy pushed a sheaf of papers aside and sat on the chaise longue, a wayward spring grazing his backside. Whatever was passing through his uncle's mind was taking its time arriving at language, any language.

'No,' he said at last.

'No?'

'Not Curran. I could fancify it by saying it is not his "style" but it is more . . . it is not . . . not his . . . not his "function". He does not kill. They haff plenty who can kill. What skill does it take?'

Nikolai cocked his right hand and took aim at Troy, the thumb arced in lieu of a hammer, the long finger coiled round an imagined trigger.

'You point a gun, you pull the trigger. Pouf! Blackmail takes talent. Good blackmailers are not trained, well . . . not trained by MI5 anyway. They are made; they are shaped in their playpens, in their nurseries . . . families make blackmailers. To an organisation like ours they are priceless. They would never waste a man like Wallace Curran on the crudity of killing.'

'Then he sent someone.'

This was to Troy the most plausible of arguments – Blood as a serving officer of Special Branch had spent much of his career at the beck and call of MI5. It was odd, very odd, for them to have sent a Branch man to carry out a hit, but it was, nonetheless, what had happened. What Troy would not believe was that they had sent Blood to carry out both murders. Therefore Curran had someone else at his beck and call, someone more subtle, less clumsy, less crazy than Percy Blood.

'Do you propose to ask Curran yourself?'

'Of course,' said Troy.

'Then now is your chance. I heard his door close not five seconds ago.'

'I thought you were deaf?'

'The vibrations, dear boy, the vibrations. I can feel this building as though I lived in the belly of a long-case clock. Every tick vibrates in the inner ear. He will pass the door any second. You have only to follow. But . . . I warn you. I would not. If I were you I would not want to mix my life with that of Wallace Curran. I would prefer it if our paths did not cross.'

'As you said,' said Troy, 'they have already crossed.'

Feet were dashing down the staircase below as he left Nikolai's flat, the old man's voice ringing out behind him, 'You don't need an excuse to come and see me, you know!'

Out in the street a small man in a blue coat had his back to him, opening the door of a Riley Pathfinder.

'Mr Curran?' Troy said.

The man turned, hands resting on the open door of the car. He was short, as short as Troy, in heavy, black-rimmed, thick-lensed spectacles. All the same, he was recognisable. The thin, controlled version of Egg. Egg leaked and spilled. This man was contained.

Troy held up his warrant card.

'Put it away, Commander. You may not know me, but I most certainly know you. Put it away and walk away. There is nothing you can discuss with me.'

His gaze was intense. Beyond the intimidation of words. He looked like a weasel. He did not act like one. He really did expect Troy to be stared down and walk away.

'I have reason to believe you can help me with my enquiries.'

'Why so formal? Why not just ask me who killed her? That is why you're here, isn't it? To expiate your own guilt by asking me who killed her?'

Troy kicked the car door shut on his hands. Curran moved quickly, but not quickly enough. One hand trapped in the gap, and held him by broken fingers. He screamed. Troy kept his foot against the door and pressed slowly. Curran sank to the ground, almost suspended by his fingers.

'Fine,' said Troy. 'Tell me who killed her.'

'I don't know!'

Troy put all his weight on the car door. Curran no longer screamed; he gurgled from deep within his throat.

'Who killed Clover Browne?'

'I don't bloody know. And if I did, I wouldn't tell you!'

'Who killed Clover Browne?'

'You'll regret this, Troy. Believe me, you'll regret it.'

Troy eased back, pulled the door open and let Curran roll into the gutter. He turned onto his side, nursing his damaged hand up one armpit.

'It wasn't Blood. Who was it?'

It took a few seconds before Troy realised that the rasping, wheezing noise that Curran made was laughter.

'Blood?' he was saying. 'Blood? Blood? You're a fool, Troy. A complete bloody fool. If you think you've got a thing on me – a single damn thing – then arrest me. Go on, arrest me! Don't expect me to make it easy for you. I won't string myself up for your convenience. Go on, arrest me!'

Curran shoved down his throat what he had avoided thinking for days now. He had not a thing on him. The bastard was right. There was nothing they could discuss. Troy had but one question. All important and pointless. Who killed Clover Browne?

Troy kicked him once and walked on.

§ 114

Troy weighed his options. He could go back to the Yard tomorrow. The week Coyn had ordered him to rest was up. Once at the Yard he could then go back to Albert Hall Mansions mob-handed and bring Curran in for questioning. But what was the question? He already knew the answer. The spooks had killed Fitz and Clover to cover up the honeytrap. If he got Curran to the Yard his brief would have him on habeas corpus before the day was out.

He could ask Rod to put a question in the House, force the government to retreat into not answering for reasons of national security. But, from all he had said, Rod's own people would come down on him like a ton of bricks if he rocked the boat between now and the next election.

Or he could disinter the Webley, go round and shoot the little sod. How many killings could London take in a single week, and all with the same type of gun? Besides, that moment had passed. He would willingly have shot him as he taunted him in the street this morning, but not now. It was too much like cold blood. As Nikolai had said, anyone can point a gun and pull the trigger.

He had blown it. He should not have approached Curran. He should not have lost his temper. He should have looked on from a safe distance.

He was still contemplating this mess of inaction when the phone rang.

'Right, y'bugger!'

Angus. Angus Pakenham. Anna's errant husband. He who had gone walkabout, as she put it, some time last winter.

'Where are you, Angus?'

'I'm in London. In a pub.'

Troy could have guessed that.

'Are you going to see Anna?'

'Can't old boy, simply can't. Got to see you though. Right away. Very urgent. Matter of life and death. Can you pop out?'

To a pub? To a pub with Angus Pakenham? A drunk with a genuine hollow leg? It might stop the grinding process that left Troy thinking he was trapped between two millstones. Take the wind out of the sails. Better someone else's problems than his own. Even better Angus's problems, and they were legion, than his own. Whatever it was, it was hardly likely to be a matter of life and death – that was just Angus-speak. Everything, without exception, was a matter of life and death to Angus. Besides, Angus was a raree. Miserable drunks like Egg Curran were ten a penny. Every pub in London had them. But Angus was a daring, exquisite original.

'Which pub are you in?'

'Pig Heaven. See you in half an hour.'

He rang off before Troy could ask more.

Now, which pub was Pig Heaven? Angus's habit was to rechristen every pub he frequented. His names were usually the more apt, but since their purpose was concealment – from Anna if no one else – you had to remember what was what. Pig Heaven, Troy was pretty sure, was a free house called The Eight Bells, down past Waterloo station, not two hundred yards from the Old Vic theatre. What he could not recall was why Angus called it Pig Heaven.

He knew as soon as he pushed open the door. It was a drizzling early autumnal night – dammit, he had thought, the clocks go back in three weeks, and had wrapped up in overcoat and scarf – and the public bar was miasmic with wet wool and cloth caps, a brown fug of steam and tobacco smoke, and strewn its length and breadth with sawdust. He dared not think about the spit. It was filthy hole of a pub, a veritable Pig Heaven. Cissie would love it, plenty of grot to nose around in, and he was immediately reminded of Angus's definition of a truly bad pub – 'Spit and sawdust, if you bring your own sawdust.' He would chortle every time he cracked that one. Pig Heaven at least supplied its own, and in the middle of it all, alone at a corner table, head bent over a vast sheaf of papers, a large malt whisky next to him, sat Angus. It seemed for the moment as though in the course of one day Troy had traded the old Russian for the mad Celt, men living by the word, lost in paper.

Troy watched him, scribbling furiously on a foolscap sheet. His reddish hair was trimmed within its usual wayward limits, and there wasn't really much of it left. Just a few brandy snaps curling off above the ears. And he was shaved, as Troy could tell from the abundance of foam in one ear. But his suit was on its last legs, its last elbows and its last cuffs. His shoes looked as though they leaked, and on a pisser of a night like this he'd be lucky not to get trench foot. He'd soak up half the puddles in London as though he were made of blotting paper.

'Won't be a mo',' he said without looking up.

Troy had not even thought the man had noticed him. He sat next to him and waited.

'I'm on the last page now.'

'Last page of what?'

'Me memoirs.'

Troy's heart sank. He was barking again. Poor, crazy, shell-shocked, one-legged Angus – the poet-philosopher of half the pubs in central London, over the edge again.

Troy peeked. He could not read Angus's handwriting. It seemed to him to meander across the page without achieving the definition that might enable him to perceive a single character. He would not get a second chance. Angus wrote 'The End' in large capitals and turned the page face down onto the pile.

'Cheers!'

He reached for his malt.

'You're not drinking!'

'Er . . .'

Angus's hand shot up for the barman before he could think of an excuse.

'Tommy! Right, Troy, what are you on?'

'Ginger beer,' he bleated, knowing he had just solicited a lecture on the joys of grain and grape. But Angus ordered the drink without comment.

'Long time no thingy,' he said.

'Quite,' said Troy, waiting for the bang.

'Seen anything of the old girl?'

This meant his wife, Anna.

'As a matter of fact I have.'

'Been giving her one, have you?'

'What?'

'I do hope you have. I haven't been around for months. I was hoping she'd hook up with you again. Keep her off the streets and all that. Needs a good shag from time to time.'

Troy said nothing.

'Any chance you'll be seeing her in the near future?'

'It's possible,' said Troy, with no idea where all this was leading.

'Good. I want you to give her this.'

Angus banged his fist down on the manuscript.

'Your . . . memoirs?'

'Me memoirs. Everything from when I first looked around the nursery to meeting you in this boozer tonight. The thirties, that time I knocked six of Mosley's blackshirts out cold in a pub in Wapping, the war, my old man blowing his brains out when he heard Chamberlain's speech, the RAF, fucking Colditz, that glider we built in the attic to fly over the walls, the time I thought fuckit and jumped, sawing off me leg, that nice little chap in the village who made the tin leg for me, all the benders, that time I got arrested outside Downing Street for challenging Eden to come out and fight like a man, all the time I've spent in the wilderness contemplating me belly button. In short, the meaning of life! Free, free, I'm free of all of it now!'

Troy began to wish he'd asked for something stronger, like Polish vodka.

'Tell her to start with Weidenfeld and Nicolson, always liked their stuff. Then there's Olympia in Paris. Always liked their stuff too. And if those buggers say no find out who published Monty's memoirs and send 'em there.'

Britain was awash in war memoirs. They'd all done them: Churchill, Monty, Horrocks . . . everyone, it seemed, but Auchinleck had set down a war memoir. P.R. Reid had told his *Colditz Story*, Romilly and Alexander had had their *Privileged Nightmare* . . . Britain didn't much need Angus Pakenham's.

Troy sipped a ginger beer he didn't want and let Angus prattle as he wrapped his masterpiece up in polythene carrier bags.

'Do you remember that time we took on all those damn patriots during Suez? We knocked 'em into next week before they slung us out of the Two Dogs At It.'

This was not how Troy remembered it. He hadn't hit anyone. It was all Angus.

He wondered how many layers there were going to be. Not one polythene bag, but six, or seven or . . . the last one Troy estimated to be number twelve. The package was now bulky and puffy.

'Don't want it getting wet on the way home,' Angus said. 'Troy, I want you to promise me faithfully you will deliver this safely to Anna.'

'Do I have any choice?'

'Good man!'

Angus clapped him on the shoulder with enough force to part body and spirit.

'Right. Chop, chop. Can't sit here all night.'

He downed his malt, Troy left his ginger beer, and they stepped out into a wet London night. The package had no handle by which to grip it. Troy undid his overcoat, loose upon his frame since TB, and buttoned the bundle to his chest.

They walked on, north, in the direction of the Thames, and at the south end of the Hungerford Footbridge, fifty yards from the Royal Festival Hall, they went their ways.

Troy was halfway up the steps when Angus called out to him.

'Free, free, as that black bloke said in Washington, Lord almighty free at last!'

'Free of what?' said Troy.

'The war, dammit, the war!'

He walked on a few steps, then he turned back to Troy.

'Of course I knew it would get me in the end.'

'What? What would get you?' said Troy.

Angus just swivelled, both arms on him juddering back and forth like the muzzles on Browning machine guns and said, 'Takkatakka-takkatakkatakka!'

And then he walked off in silence, the tin leg swinging out at its inhuman angle, as ever setting himself a cracking pace few two-legs could ever match. Troy watched him out of sight and then ascended to the bridge. He had reached the centre bay, a train rumbled out of Charing Cross and set the whole bridge shaking. He never heard the soft splash of shoes on wet tarmac as the man leapt from the steel girders of the bridge. The blow to the head turned the world green. He vaguely, dreamily, had a sense of his right hand being laid flat on the parapet and seeing the butt of a gun come down on it. But he felt no pain, and the green enveloped him.

When he awoke he found himself floating on his back in midstream. Unless he was very much mistaken he had just passed under Blackfriars Railway Bridge. He found himself wondering how many bridges there were and in what order. He'd missed Waterloo — never one of his favourites; Blackfriars was far prettier, all neat in cast iron. Southwark was next. He glided under like a man doing the most effortless backstroke the world had ever seen. Only when he'd shot by London Bridge and could see, by putting his head back, Tower Bridge looming towards him, upside down, did he begin to think that he might be in a bit of a pickle. After Tower Bridge, no more bridges. Only the pool of London, the wider reaches of the Thames, then out into the estuary, into the North Sea, past Chatham dockyard, the oil refineries on the Isle of Sheppey, Broadstairs, Ramsgate, the South Goodwins lightship, the Channel and next stop South Africa. Yes — it was a bit of a pickle. High time he did something about it.

A motor boat appeared to be coming upriver straight for him. He rolled onto his belly and dived, only to find that as soon as it had passed he bobbed to the surface as surely as a cork. He was stuck, on his back again. It was almost impossible to swim. Another gut-wrenching effort and he rolled over again, tore off his overcoat, and bobbed to the surface once more. There was something, some wet and clammy creature clinging limpet-like to his chest. He tore at it furiously, digging into its puffy skin with his fingernails. It was tough as old boots. It seemed like minutes before he cut through it, then in one great white rush it shot upwards to scatter down in a kaleidoscope of giant confetti on the water, soft as shrapnel. What the fuck was it? Whatever it was, without it he was sinking. He rolled onto his belly once more, kicked off his shoes, sloughed off his jacket, found he could achieve a passable breaststroke and began to strike out for the shore.

Both hands hurt, but he couldn't work out why. Not crippling pain, but sharpening pain, a pain that seemed slowly to be growing. He struck land. A Thames mudflat. He hauled himself upright and took two steps into the mud. It sucked a sock clean off his foot. He stepped again and lost the other sock, but he was standing. He looked around. Lights glinting on the other side of the river. But which side of the river was he on? Wapping? Or Rotherhithe – Injun country?

He turned to find an old stone wall, a rusty, weed-strewn iron ladder leading up to street level. He hauled himself up it. His right hand was bleeding badly, the left less so, but the week-old wound had opened up. He found himself facing a blitzed warehouse, not a door or window intact, but from somewhere within it the glow of light, of fire. He staggered on. Into the warehouse, his bare feet crunching over broken glass, leaving a trail of blood. The light was a bonfire, blazing on the stone floor of the warehouse, tended by two ragged children, a boy and a girl, of about nine or ten years of age. They crouched by the fire. The boy fished out a charred potato with a stick and juggled it from hand to hand; the girl noticed Troy and stood up as he approached.

'Who are you?' she asked.

'I fell,' said Troy.

'Fell?'

'Into the . . . river.'

'You fell in the river!'

'Yes . . . that is, I think so.'

'Where from?'

He didn't know. He could only point upwards with one of his broken hands. Upwards. Up there. Somewhere.

'From the sky? You fell from the sky?'

Troy nodded, fell on his face and lost consciousness.

When he came to it was light. He was lying under several foul-smelling blankets on top of a couple of wooden pallets. He could smell smoke. He craned his head, and a few feet to his left he could see the remains of a bonfire. He could see his feet sticking out from the blanket. They were black and mud-encrusted, and bloody. He wiggled his toes to see if he could, and tried to move his legs. He could move them, but the effort was exhausting so he lay where he was and waited. When he had waited an age he fell asleep, and when he awoke it was dark again. The bonfire was lit, and a small boy was hacking the top off a tin of baked beans with a bayonet.

'I bet yer 'ungry, in't yer?'

'Yes,' Troy said softly. 'I am.'

He paused, gathered breath.

'Where am I?'

'Eng-land,' replied the boy enunciating clearly. 'You-are-in-Eng-land. Lon-don. A big city in Eng-land.'

'Could you be a bit more precise?'

Accent and fluency did not impress the child. He spoke as before.

'Lime-house. You-are-in-Lime-house.'

'How did I get here?'

'Yer fell from the sky!'

So he had.

The boy brought him the tin of beans, jagged-edged and leaking ketchup everywhere. He pulled a spoon from his pocket and began to feed Troy cold baked beans straight from the tin. They were remarkably good. Troy made a mental note never to heat up beans in a saucepan again.

When he had finished, Troy noticed that the girl had returned and with her an even smaller girl, clutching a yellow teddy bear with button-glass eyes.

'Go on,' said girl the larger to girl the lesser. 'Give it to 'im.'

The child laid the bear on top of the blankets within reach of Troy's bloody left hand, still bearing the sodden remains of its bandage.

It was a good-looking bear. Troy almost wished he could keep it. But, more than a bear, he wanted a drink.

'Did you bring water?'

The boy rummaged in his satchel and brought out a half-empty bottle of Tizer. Much to his disappointment, Troy drained it.

'Could you tell someone?' he said to the three of them.

All heads shook.

'Just tell someone I'm here. Ask someone to come and get me? A grown-up?'

This seemed to be the last straw. At these final syllables they fled. He'd said the wrong thing, he knew.

He slept. The bonfire was warm. When he awoke it was cold. The day was sunny and he knew from the angle of the sun slanting in through the broken windows that it was way past noon.

An hour or so later the boy reappeared and gave him a Mars Bar and a Sherbert Fountain to eat. Afterwards, Troy decided to try his legs. They weren't exactly steady, but they got him upright. He leant on the boy, who seemed both frightened and delighted by this action. They hobbled round the floor of the warehouse together, and Troy realised sharply that he had glass embedded in his feet. He had the boy lower him onto the pallets, and swung his foot upward to inspect the damage. He couldn't see anything for dirt, but then he couldn't walk either. Something had to be done.

'Is that where they went?' the boy asked suddenly.

'Where what went?'

'The nails.'

'Nails?'

'He thinks you're Jesus,' said a familiar voice from the doorway. 'They've all been to see that film *Whistle Down the Wind* at the Troxy down the Commercial Road. And when you told 'em you'd fallen from the sky . . . what with the blood on your hands and feet.'

It was George Bonham, retired Station Sergeant Bonham, his old boss from his days as a constable. The man Kolankiewicz had as good as told him he neglected. A man seven foot tall in the blue pointy hat, now looming large and hatless over him.

'What have you been up to, Freddie?'

'Wish I knew, George, wish I knew. How did you find me?'

'Betty Spenser. The little girl as give you her teddy. She cried to her mum that their Julie had made her give her Teddy to Jesus. It all came out then. Their mum came to see me. No point in retiring from the force 'round 'ere. You're still a copper as far as everybody else is concerned. Sort of village headman. O' course I'd already heard from Kolankiewicz that you'd gone missing, so I put two and two together. It would be typical of you to fall from the sky after all.'

'Have I been here long?'

''Bout two days I reckon.'

'Can you get me out of here?'

Bonham hauled him to his feet as though he weighed no more than a couple of pounds. Tucked him under one arm, Teddy under the other.

'All arranged,' he said. 'Your carriage is waiting.'

They emerged onto the street. There was the Fat Man, waiting, almost smiling and tut-tutting at the same time.

'No,' said Troy. 'Not that fucking motorbike again!'

'Language, Freddie. There's kids about.'

Indeed there were. The three kids of yesterday had been joined on the pavement by half a dozen others.

'I meant I'll rattle to pieces.'

'Nah,' said the Fat Man. 'When Sergeant Bonham explained the mess you were in, I went and got the Bentley. You'll be snug as a bug in a rug.'

The car was parked around the corner. Bonham stuck him in the passenger seat. He did not feel like Jesus; he felt like a scarecrow. He must look like a scarecrow. He had no jacket, just a filthy white shirt and his trousers. His wallet had gone with his jacket in the Thames.

'George. Could you give them something? I've no money. I rather think they may have saved my life.'

Bonham fished in his pocket, found half a dozen half-crowns and a few florins.

'Jesus would like to give you something,' he said as he dished out the boodle. He turned back to Troy, winked and beckoned the Fat Man to drive on. The little girl made a dash for him and retrieved her Teddy.

Jesus, thought Troy. Jesus. 'Get me home,' he said to the Fat Man.

'Home,' said the Fat Man. 'Home be buggered. You're going to the nearest hospital.'

Shit, thought Troy.

The Fat Man swung the car up onto The Highway and seemed to

be heading for the London Hospital. Troy could see no point in trying to stop him. The Fat Man was bigger than he was.

'Did you fall from the sky?' the Fat Man asked.

'No I was pushed. Knocked senseless and pushed off the Hungerford Bridge to drown.'

It was as well the Fat Man had asked. It had forced Troy to remember.

§ 115

The London Hospital X-rayed his head and pronounced it whole. A bone in his right hand was broken. They bandaged it up with a wooden splint like a lollipop stick. Told him he was lucky it was just the one bone. His left hand had ceased to bleed. They cleaned the wound and bandaged that too. They picked the glass out of his feet with tweezers and stuck Elastoplast over the cuts.

Washed and clean, in hospital-loaned pyjamas, he lay in a single room, in peace and quiet, watching the evening sky turn black. He had not asked for the room; the Fat Man must have arranged VIP treatment for him. It was the same room he had lain in in 1944 after Diana Brack had shot him and blown away half a kidney. He had lain here and watched the big windows blown to crystal by a doodlebug. And Onions had stormed in and all but read the riot act to him.

Onions' days were over. Just when he needed Onions he got Coyn. All buttons and bows in his Commissioner's uniform, with a look of deep concern – how neutral concern was, how devoid of any specifiable feeling – where Onions would have blazed with rage.

He came in quietly and drew a chair up to the bedside.

'This is most unfortunate,' he said. 'The South Bank is become a robber's haven. Something will have to be done.'

'I wasn't robbed. You know I wasn't robbed.'

Coyn did not look at him, ignored what he said. He would say what he had come to say regardless of Troy.

'Make a statement when you're up to it. Describe him if you can. We'll catch this villain, Freddie.'

'I can give you his name. Wallace Curran.'

Coyn ignored this too. Looked at a spot on the wall rather than catch Troy's eye.

'I've had time to think while you were away. We received a report from the psychiatrist Blood was seeing. It seems that Percy was a deeply disturbed man. The coroner will likely as not record a verdict of suicide while the balance of his mind was disturbed. You'll have to give evidence of course, but it should be little more than a formality now we have the medical report. Blood was mad. It explained a lot of things. Why he killed himself, why he killed poor Mary and why he killed Fitzpatrick. It wraps up a lot of loose ends. We none of us suspected Blood. It was excellent police work on your part. First rate.'

No it wasn't – it was obvious police work. Blood was a blunderer.

'And of course it also explains why he killed young Jackie Clover. He'd become obsessed with finding her. I shall have to talk to her grandfather.'

If Coyn was waiting for Troy to volunteer for that task, he would wait for ever. He muttered platitudes about a speedy recovery, get back to work as soon as you can, if there's anything, anything at all, just call me, I'll look in on you later in the week, and then he put his chair back neatly where he had found it, forced a smile and headed for the door.

'Don't you want to know who Wallace Curran is?' Troy said.

'I didn't hear that, Freddie.'

'Don't you want to know who Wallace Curran is?' Troy yelled.

'The case is closed, Freddie. That's final. That's an order.'

Troy yelled it all the louder. Coyn closed the door behind him. Troy yelled at the closed door until a nurse came in and firmly and politely told him to shut up.

Five seconds after she closed the door on him it opened again. Jack came in, clutching a small suitcase. It was an oh-so-familiar moment.

'Clean shirt, new suit, socks, shoes, the lot. The Bentley's in the car park. Coyn never saw me.'

Troy threw back the covers and swung his feet to the floor. He'd never in his life been quite so glad to see Jack. And he'd lost track of the number of times Jack had shown up in a hospital ward to bail him out.

'Am I going to spend the rest of my life getting you out of scrapes, Freddie?'

They made it out to the car park, Troy still buttoning his shirt, the nurse trailing after them in protest until Troy firmly and politely told her to fuck off.

'Where to?' said Jack.

'Hampstead. I have to see Rod.'

'Rod?'

'Coyn closed the case on me. I have to go over his head. Through Rod to the Home Secretary.'

'Playing with the big boys, eh?'

'If you like.'

Jack steered with one hand and fished in his pocket with the other.

'Then I think you'll find these a useful combination.'

He handed Troy his warrant card and the bottle of Dexedrine.

'I went in to pick up your clothes after the Fat Man phoned me. I found these on the kitchen table. I rather thought you wouldn't want to be without either.'

Troy pocketed the warrant card – felt armed again, like the gunslinger in the western holstering his gun – and swallowed two Dexedrine. He held the bottle out to Jack.

'Don't mind if I do,' said Jack.

Jack's metabolism worked quicker than Troy's. Roaring up Rosslyn Hill, he said, 'Thar she blows,' and grinned at Troy like an idiot.

§ 116

Rod seemed so beaming smiley – elated.

'Isn't it marvellous?'

Jack and Troy stood on the doorstep of Rod's house in Church Row, wondering if he'd tell them what was so marvellous or let them in.

'What?' said Troy.

'He's gone. The old bugger's finally gone.'

'Who?'

'Macmillan. The Prime Minister! He's said he'll resign as soon as the Tories can select a new leader.'

'I thought Tory leaders fell from heaven,' said Troy. 'Now, are you going to let us in?'

'Eh? What? Of course.'

Rod stepped aside. Jack plonked down Troy's suitcase and his briefcase containing the "documents in the case", and said, 'I can't stop.'

'Nonsense. Come and have a snifter. It's been ages since we—'

'Sorry, Rod. The job calls. Freddie, you will phone me? As soon as there's anything?'

'Of course,' said Troy.

Rod shifted quickly from beaming to babbling. 'I mean – ideally one would want him there till the last minute, but it's always such a buzz when one of them finally goes. He says it's his prostate trouble, but it's just as much the Woodbridge business. You've only just caught me, you know. I only got back from our Party Conference tonight. It was a cracker.'

In the living room Troy slumped on the sofa and wondered if he could be bothered to listen to any of this. Rod perched on the edge of his chair – absurdly animated.

'For the first time it actually felt as though we were on the verge of power. Hatchets buried. United. It was great. Wilson even made a good speech. An absolute rouser. "The white heat of the technological revolution".'

Troy had closed his eyes. He opened one at this.

'Meaning?'

'Well . . . not meaning anything actually. After all, I should think the nearest Wilson has ever come to grasping technology is playing with his blasted Meccano kit. But that's hardly the point is it? It's catchy, it's new! It'll appeal to the punters.'

'Is that the ethos of the new Labour Party? Anything for power? Tell the voters any old twaddle? After all, they aren't so much voters as punters?'

'Freddie – so help me I'll thump you!'

Troy held up his white-wrapped hands.

'Ready when you are, Cassius.'

Rod seemed to notice him for the first time, took in the broken hands, the whopping great bruise on his forehead, the washed-up, washed-out colour of his skin.

'Fucking hell. What happened to you? You look like something the cat dragged in!'

Troy told him.

Rod heard him out and then said, 'Why have you come to me, Freddie?'

'I can't let it drop now. Coyn is an ass. I have to bypass him. I have to talk to the Home Secretary.'

'So?'

'I want you to arrange a meeting with Nick Travis.'

'You'll have to be quick. Their Party Conference starts this week. With Mac out the way it'll be a free-for-all.'

'That's why I'm asking you.'

Rod thought about this.

'Of course you could just go and knock on his door.'

'I don't follow,' said Troy.

'He lives on the other side of the Row. The house due opposite.'

'Good Lord. How long's he been there?'

'About a year. He's not in now. There's no lights on, and his wife seems to spend as little time there as possible. I get the impression they fight like cat and dog.'

'Do you see much of him?'

'What? You mean do I nip over and ask to borrow a cup of sugar? He's a Tory, for crying out loud.'

'I just thought. You work in the same place. Travel the same route . . .'

'We don't share a cab, if that's what you mean. He has a Home Office chauffeured car and I take the bloody Northern line. You can't socialise with the fuckers, Freddie, really you can't. Cid tried. Popped over to introduce herself to Jane Travis the day after they moved in. Won't make that mistake again. If there's one thing Tory wives hate more than Labour wives, its Labour wives with titles. I bet she spat feathers when Cid said "call me Lucinda" after the first utterance of "Lady Troy" – must have choked the bitch to have to utter those two words.'

'Is she a bitch?'

'One of the worst. I think the marriage only holds together because he wants a crack at the leadership. Well – now's his chance.'

Troy pulled Rod back to the point.

'No – I can't just walk across and ring on his bell, this is official.'

'If it's official, why have you come to me?'

'You're the Shadow Home Secretary.'

'No – I'm your brother. In coming to me you want a favour. You're pulling a string. So it isn't official.'

'Yes it is. If I go through channels, as I've every right to do, it'll take days maybe even a couple of weeks to get to Travis. I need to talk to him tomorrow. The favour you do me is that you create the access – a hotline if you like. Once we get there, it's official.'

'You'll have to give me something in writing.'

Troy held up his hands again.

'I can't type.'

'I can. You're looking at the fastest two-fingered typist in Westminster.'

'You mean you'll do it? You'll make the call?'

'Yes. I'll call him first thing in the morning. And I'll drop off whatever we bash out tonight. But I'll warn you now. If you're going to bang on about the spooks and this Curran chap, forget it. The shutters will come down like closing time at the fishmonger's. Travis won't even consider seeing you.'

'Curran is my suspect. More than that, he did it. He had Clover killed. He had me sapped on the head and dumped in the Thames.'

'Take my advice. If you mention MI5 to Travis you'll get nothing but silence.'

'OK,' said Troy reluctantly. 'If that's the way it has to be.'

They moved upstairs to a box room Rod laughingly called his study. He had a prewar manual Corona typewriter set up on a tiny writing desk, a beautiful machine, bright with chipped green paint and gold lettering, the sort that still dealt in guineas rather than pounds. It had belonged to their father. He had personally typed up an account of Lawrence's entry into Damascus on it more than forty years ago. There was probably sand in the works to this day. In amongst the parliamentary bumf there was just enough room for Rod and Troy.

Troy thought, spoke, Rod typed; Troy thought, spoke, Rod argued.

'Keep it simple, Freddie. Travis is going to give this about five minutes flat. Just stick to the facts. Stop speculating.'

Troy dictated again. Rod was right. He was the fastest two-fingered typist in the West. All the same, they had taken an age to get through three pages, and they weren't done yet.

Rod's wife, Cid, brought in beef sandwiches and beer. She kissed Troy on the forehead. Told him he'd used up eight of his nine lives.

Troy realised he had scarcely eaten in more than three days. He wolfed the sandwiches and left Rod the beer. When they had finished it ran to five typed pages, and struck Troy as over-simplified, but Rod pronounced himself pleased with it.

'It gets to the point. And above all you won't trigger his alarm bells. When you're writing to a politician that's the first thing to remember. Political man is wired like Fort Knox, designed to go off at the slightest sign of trouble. Now—'

He looked at his watch.

'You're staying the night.'

'No I'm not.'

'Yes you are. You look like shit. And as my wife so rightly says, you've only the one life left. Time you took better care of it. Sleep in in the morning. I'll call home as soon as I get any word from Travis.'

Troy stopped arguing. Clean sheets could be such a joy.

§ 117

The phone went around ten fifteen the next morning. Cid woke Troy and told him Rod wanted him.

'He'll see us. Straight after lunch. Two thirty.'

Troy pondered the 'us', but accepted it. That was the price he paid for dragging Rod into this.

He rose slowly, accepting everything Cid set in front of him. Fresh, strong coffee. Porridge. He could not remember when he'd last had porridge. He never made it for himself. The washing-up afterwards always seemed like too much trouble. He walked around the kitchen. What was it L.P. Hartley had written? "Only a cad eats his porridge sitting down"? Looked at the shelves of cookery books. Cid had the same one Clover had used; Troy had never thought of Cid as ever having lived in a bedsit. Said hello to the family tom who hissed and lashed out at him and retreated under the stove. Then he got stuck into bacon and eggs and fried bread. All in all, it was bliss.

At ten to three, he sat in the Home Secretary's outer office listening to two typists rattle away. Every so often the shift arms would be pushed at the same moment and the banality of synchronicity would ring forth. Somewhere in the civil service hereafter, the great typing pool in the sky, a shorthand angel got her wings. When he got bored with this, he thought, he'd try seeing faces in the wallpaper. But there was no wallpaper, only an off-white paint, sort of eggy-creamy. Why did these bastards always keep you waiting? Why was Rod late?

Rod bustled in. 'Not late, am I?'

'No,' said Troy.

'Good, good. Has he been out?'

'No,' said Troy.

'Tell me, you have met him?'

'Of course. One of the disadvantages of rank is having to attend meetings and sit on damn committees. I've known every Home Sec since Churchill's last government.'

'Good, good,' said Rod, and it dawned on Troy that Rod was not much looking forward to this meeting. He'd put Rod in a bit of an awkward spot. But he didn't care.

A Parliamentary Under Secretary of State, a species of minister so low down on the life chain that they were acronymed to PUSS and probably lived under the gas stove too, emerged from Travis's office.

'The Home Secretary will see you now.'

He flung the door wide to admit them. Travis was emerging from behind his desk. He was a big man, as tall as Rod and about the same age, Troy thought, late fifties. Not as good-looking. Conk too big, Troy had always thought. The sort of bloke who favoured a striped shirt with red braces, so that when he took off his jacket as he had done for this meeting, or the one before, he could look like a hard-working, hard-drinking, truth-chasing national newspaper editor rather than just a clapped-out lawyer with a parliamentary sinecure. There were times when Troy was not sure whom he loathed the more, spooks or pols.

'Rod,' Travis said heartily. 'Good to see you without a dispatch box in-between.'

'Nick,' said Rod. 'I believe you know my brother, Freddie.'

'Of course, of course, Commander Troy. Scotland Yard's finest.'

Rod smiled at this, happy to pretend to anything that took out the tension. Troy didn't, but then Troy silently agreed with it anyway.

A quick handshake. Travis looked at Troy's bandaged hands without comment, sat at his desk, back to the window, and picked up Troy's letter. Rod and Troy sat and waited while he flicked through it. Then he said exactly what Coyn had said.

'Excellent piece of detection. First class, absolutely first class.'

'First class' never impressed Troy as a compliment. It was too Oxonian. It was part of the vocabulary of excuseology, whereby an upper-class fool who had pissed away three years at university drinking yards of ale and rowing boats was saved from the justice of his innate stupidity by having 'a first-class mind'. Half the prats on the front benches of both parties had 'first-class minds'. It meant nothing.

'Without your diligence and persistence it would appear that Chief Inspector Blood would have got away with murder.'

Odd, thought Troy. Blood had got away with murder. Justice was hardly served by his suicide.

'Assistant Commissioner Quint was clearly wrong, and thanks to you the murder of Fitzpatrick was solved. I am also inclined to agree with you that Sir Wilfrid Coyn is wrong. At least wrong in terms of the blanket solution he seems to believe in. I'm satisfied from the report you've given me, and the forensic reports you enclosed, that Blood killed Fitzpatrick and Detective Sergeant McDiarmuid, and I can see nothing that points to him having killed young Jackie Clover. But . . .'

Troy was waiting for the but. There had to be one. There always was.

'You can't have it both ways, Commander. If Blood did not kill Miss Clover and the evidence you offer is the difference in *modus operandi*, and that evidence in turn invokes the apparent lack of violence in her death, then it simply begs the next question. If Blood could not force pills down a young girl's throat without leaving marks – and you're insistent on the medical report's finding that there were none – surely no one else could? I agree with you. There is no evidence to support Sir Wilfrid's belief that Blood committed all three murders, but there's none to show that anyone else killed Miss Clover either. I've thought about this. Perhaps, for once, first impressions are the most plausible? The most obvious cause seems to me to be the real one. She died by her own hand. Consider her circumstances: you were out; she was bored and lonely; she'd been under all the pressure of a court case happening around her with no power to influence it; she'd experienced the wrath of her grandfather, and been entrusted to the care of a man more than twice her age with whom she could have little in common. She stole your sleeping pills. She swallowed a handful, dashed off a couple of suicide notes and then she was . . .'

Neither Troy nor Travis cared to finish that sentence.

Rod said, 'Dead,' looking from one to the other, wondering at their silence in the face of the word.

'I can endorse your view. I can write to the Commissioner and tell him I consider it unwise to attribute the death of Jackie Clover to Blood – but what would it achieve? A different coroner's verdict? A lightening of Blood's load from three murders to two? But I can't go back to him and tell him to let you carry on investigating it as murder. After all . . .'

Travis glanced quickly at the last two pages of Troy's letter and put the whole document down on his desk.

'After all, you haven't even got a suspect in the picture, have you?'

Troy felt Rod's foot tap against his, telling him to say nothing.

'I'm sorry, Commander, I really am.'

Troy got up. Rod seemed a little surprised to find it was all over so soon. But it suited Troy and it suited Travis.

He showed them out.

'Forgive me, but I'm due at the conference at noon tomorrow and I've at least three boxes of government papers to get through before then.'

It seemed to Troy that he was rubbing it in, just a little. Reminding Rod that it had been years and years since he had last got his hands on a government red box.

Traipsing down the interminable Whitehall corridor, Troy suddenly felt weak, and stopped to rest a while on a wooden bench. Rod sat next to him.

'Well?' he said.

'I was wrong,' said Troy.

Troy wondered if Rod might be relieved to hear this. He was not.

'Wrong? Wrong? After all you've said to me? You mean you're telling me you think Travis is right?'

Troy had not and would not say that.

'I meant . . . there was no conspiracy . . . no MI5 hit. I was wrong.'

'No conspiracy? God, you're amazing. You know, Freddie, you almost had me believing it that day in St James's Park.'

Almost? No, Rod had been only too willing to believe him. Had believed him before he even spoke. But if he was now backtracking, then that was fine by Troy. The less he knew the better. If it meant undoing what was true, retreating into what was safe, then the less he knew the better. Troy had a case to pursue. A criminal to catch, not, it would seem, the criminal he had thought, but the hunt was far from over.

'I'm sorry,' he lied. 'I was wrong.'

Rod could not stay seated. When he was angry he stamped or he paced or, as now, just moved. He stood across the corridor, his back to Troy, one hand pressed to his skull as though preventing its imminent explosion.

'Freddie, I cannot begin to tell you how angry this makes me. All your life, you've had a devious, oblique, perhaps even an interesting mind, a terrier tenacity I have grown to admire, a relentlessness I find unforgiving and frequently pointless, and for the last twenty years you've seen conspiracies around every corner. Where is it all leading?'

He turned to face Troy.

'When is it all going to end?'

Troy said nothing.

'Are you going you go on making a fool of yourself?'

Troy said nothing.

'Are you going to make fools of us all?'

'No. I'm not. It's over. There was no conspiracy. I was wrong. Who knows, perhaps I went back to work too soon? Perhaps I need a rest.'

'You're lying to me. You've been a liar all your life. You think I don't know when you're lying!'

It's for your own good, thought Troy. What I know you'd rather not.

§ 118

Troy phoned Kolankiewicz. And when he had talked to him he knew how Clover Browne came to be murdered.

'That compound analysis you did for me . . . ?'

'The piece of cotton wool?'

'Yes. What would happen if one were to take a large quantity of it?'

'In what form?'

'Pills. Pills corresponding in their make-up to the residue you found. Like the bit you found.'

'Such a pill would be a large-dose vitamin pill. You would take one at a time. Sort of thing you might do if you have the flu.'

'Supposing you took twenty-eight or thirty.'

'Well . . . Vitamin A cannot be processed in excess. It ends up stored in the liver and as such becomes toxic. But a single overdose would hardly have a dramatic effect – you'd do yourself damage only if you took too much every day for weeks. We know very little about the effects of Vitamin E or Vitamin K, of which there was a trace in the et ceteras – but Vitamin C, by far the largest factor in the residue, the body will not store. It uses what it wants and pisses out the rest.'

'So what ill-effects would you feel after such a dose.'

'You'd buzz all night. I doubt you'd get a deal of sleep and your piss would turn an alarming shade of green.'

'And that's all?'

'That's all.'

§ 119

It had occurred to Troy not to tell Jack, not to involve him, to let him escape into ignorance. It seemed like a violation. Jack was not his brother. Jack was his partner. Thrust together by necessity. Twenty-two years could not count for nothing. So he told him. Told him how Clover Browne came to die. Sitting at Goodwin's Court, he laid the case out as clearly as he could. Even so he faltered, he lost his thread and took the best part of half an hour to get through it. Jack had said nothing. Then he put the same questions Troy would have put if he'd been Jack.

'You're certain?'

'Yes.'

'So what's the crime?'

'Suicide pact.'

'I've never encountered one. Is it murder?'

'I don't know. I'm waiting to find out.'

On cue, Clark let himself in the front door, one arm wrapped around law books, stuffed with bookmarks. He dumped them on the dining table. Turned to Troy.

'It's better than you'd think.'

'Better?'

'Clearer. It seems the powers that be have given the matter more attention than I thought, and at that a damn sight more recently.'

'You have the floor, Eddie.'

Clark was in his element. Jack stretched, locked his hands behind his head and tried not to yawn.

'Prior to 1957 it would have been clear as mud. To enter into a suicide pact and simply to survive, whether by accident or design, ought to have been murder as the law stood at the time. However, we had a Royal Commission on Capital Punishment sitting between '49 and '53 just to muddy the waters . . .'

Jack and Troy exchanged looks. They'd both given evidence to the Commission. As far as Troy was concerned it might as well have happened in another lifetime. Clark flipped open a volume.

'. . . "There are cases in which the survivor alleges that he and the deceased had agreed to die together, but it is doubtful whether there was a genuine agreement or a genuine attempt or intention to commit suicide on his part. Such cases are considered on their merits . . ." and what that amounts to is the exercise of the Royal Prerogative, which naturally falls to the Home Secretary. He decided who hanged and who didn't depending on whether or not he believed the story. The Commission goes on . . . "It may be less easy for the Home Secretary to satisfy himself that the parties have agreed to die, especially if the survivor does not appear to have made a very determined attempt on his own life." The Commission then recommended a change in the law to the effect that if the other party in a suicide pact takes their own life, the survivor is guilty only of aiding and abetting a suicide; but if the pact was tit for tat – you do me as I do you – then it's murder.'

'Sounds a bit bloody mechanical to me.' said Jack. 'Means not motives. Eddie, have we got this bastard or not?'

'Bear with me, sir.'

He opened a second fat book and ran a finger down the margin.

'The 1957 Homicide Act did not implement the recommendation. Instead it made participation in such a pact manslaughter, and dropped the active/passive distinction. "A suicide pact is defined as a common agreement between two or more persons having for its object the death of all of them, whether or not each is to take his own life . . . but nothing done by a person who enters into a suicide pact shall be treated as done by him in pursuance of the pact unless it is done while he has the settled intention of dying in pursuance of the pact."'

'God give me strength. Eddie, have we got the bugger or not?'

Troy intervened.

'Yes. We have. It's murder. Murder. Plain and simple. The act ironed out the ambiguities. It's murder. Premeditated murder. Just imagine it. They'd been lovers. Forced apart by the Tereshkov rumpus and by Stan dumping Jackie on me. He came to see her. He knew how susceptible she was to romantic rubbish. She even thought *Jules et Jim* was romantic. He spun her a line, conned her into thinking a joint suicide was the only escape for both of them. He sat there while she swallowed Mandrax by the handful and fed himself plain white pills. When it was all over for Clover he packed up and left. But he missed the cotton wool out of the top of his jar of pills. Kolankiewicz analysed the residue as nothing stronger than vitamins. You can't enter into a suicide pact and expect to kill yourself with a jar of vitamin pills.'

'At last. At last. Now, can we prove it?'

That was the one question Troy would not have asked.

§ 120

'To what do I owe this pleasure?' Rod said. 'Twice in two days. Have you spent so much time in this house since the old man died?'

'Time to kill.'

Rod took his coat and hung it up. The house was wonderfully warm. There was music playing softly. Pablo Casals, the Bach solo cello suites – designed, Rod had once told him, to make you stoic. Troy was stoic. What he needed was to be brave. Rod was in evening work mode, sleeves rolled up, tie at half-mast and the least sexy pair of tartan slippers Troy had ever seen.

'Time to kill. I do hope that's a metaphor,' Rod said, and before Troy could say anything added, 'I'm sorry, Freddie. That was absolutely tasteless.'

Always the decency, that all-pervading, all-English decency that Troy could never muster with a thousand pounds of torque. Less than twelve hours ago Rod had been spitting fury. Now, as always, it was as though it had never happened. When would the man learn to hate properly?

Troy said a quick 'never mind' and let Rod bustle him into a fireside chair in front of the roaring heat of a smokeless fire. Most Londoners had boarded up their fireplaces years ago when the city went smokeless in an effort to stop the killer smogs that had swamped the city in the early fifties. Rod had not given up. He had discovered a man-made fuel that looked like black sponge cake and stuck by his one practical skill in life – lighting the fire. Rod in front of a cheery fire, obligatory red tie dangling, was the man in his element − relaxed, self-contained, affable. From where he sat Troy could see right through the window, across Church Row to Travis's front door.

Troy was wrong. It was not a work evening. There were no parliamentary papers scattered on the carpet. Just a book. Face down on the threadbare Bakhtiar − *The Last Days of Socrates.*

'Would you like a drink? Scotch perhaps?'

Troy said yes. He'd just broken his dry spell at a house around the corner, and with Mandies, speed and two glasses of Margaux swimming in his blood, what did a drop of malt matter? Alcohol did not seem to get him pissed; it combined with the drugs into a sensation he could not name. Not drunk. Not drugged. High, in a lucid, crystalline way. He felt focused, very focused.

'Miserable stuff for a quiet evening in,' he said, pointing at the book.

Rod handed him a large malt. They sat opposite each other and sniffed the peaty smell of malt whisky.

'I read it again once in a while. Usually after a brush with death.'

'You've had a brush with death?'

'I meant you. You have. Or did you think it was just a bout of flu? It was the book the old man asked me to read aloud to him while he was dying.'

Alexei Troy's last illness had been sudden and brief. Fine one day, dying the next and dead within the week. It had been the middle of the Second World War. Troy had been at the Yard, Rod on an RAF base in mid-Essex. They each got a week's leave. The old man had taken to his bed and, in death as in life, he had talked and talked and talked. There was, Troy thought, structure to his reminiscence. He did not ramble. Even if Troy could not see the connections, he could not think of it as rambling − a visit to Paris in 1909 to hear the famous Russian bass Fyodor Chaliapin sing, and two months later standing on the coast of France to watch Louis Blériot take wing for England. A meeting with H.H. Asquith in 1915, a blazing row with Beaverbrook in 1920, an audience − was that the word he had used? − with Hitler in 1930. And when his voice began to fail, what he wanted of his sons was that they should read aloud to him. He asked Troy to read him the *Last Poems* of W.B. Yeats. If, as it turned out, he had had Rod read Plato to him, then it made sense. Troy had

read him the regrets, the miserable haunting might-have-beens of life
– *Why Should Not Old Men Be Mad?* – and Rod had read him the
optimism, the bravura stoicism, of Socrates under sentence of death,
the philosopher's sense of impending freedom in death. Troy had no
idea which notion had gone with him to the grave. All he
remembered was the old man's last words to him as he had read him
High Talk for the umpteenth time: 'Barnacle goose? What the fuck's
a barnacle goose? I've never even seen a bloody barnacle goose.' And
he had died before Troy could answer. As famous last words went, it
almost ranked with 'Bugger Bognor.'

It prompted Troy to think of the last mystery. The riddle he had
asked Charlie to solve. He had never heard from Charlie again, and
he doubted now that he ever would.

Travis's house was dark. Not a light to be seen.

They said nothing for a while. Troy was thinking nothing more
than that synthetic coal didn't crackle or split or smell of anything.
Then Rod spoke.

'It's like that time we sat in the cellar and toasted the old man in
Veuve Clicquot.'

'January,' said Troy. 'This year.'

'Seems like longer.'

'Seems like a bloody lifetime to me.'

'Been a long year. Britain feels to me like someone just ripped out
its giblets. And after all that's happened I still never thought I'd see
Macmillan go. But he's gone.'

'Does it matter?'

'Oh, it matters all right.'

'Doesn't get you an election, though, does it?'

'No. There'll be no election this year. The Tories will run to the
limit now. A week from now we'll have Travis, or Butler, or
Hailsham.'

'I've never known you not place a bet on something like that.'

'If Mac had called it quits before May this year I'd've backed
Woodbridge. However, I'll stick twenty-five nicker on Travis.'

'Win or place?'

Rod laughed.

'No such thing as coming second in politics. It's called losing.'

A Humber pulled up on the other side of the street. A figure in a
black overcoat got out. A few words with a flunkie on the

pavement, the flunkie got back in, the car drove off, the policeman on the door saluted and Travis went inside.

Troy put down his glass and stood up.

'Don't back Travis,' he said. 'You'll lose.'

Troy went for his coat. Rod followed with *that* look on his face.

'What do you mean? Freddie, what are you up to?'

Troy opened the door, stepped into the street and turned up his collar against the rain.

'Freddie, for Christ's sake—'

But Troy no longer heard him. He heard his shoes on the wet tarmac, then that too drowned out to the narco-rhythm in his head, the roaring in his veins he had felt so often at times like this.

The duty copper watched him cross the street, a puzzled look on his face. He let Troy get right up to him and then he saluted. Troy knew the man, an old-timer with twenty-five years of service under his belt.

'Take a tea break, Reg,' Troy said.

'I'm not really supposed to . . .'

'Mr Travis will be quite safe with me. Come back in an hour.'

Reg sloped off, inasmuch as a uniformed constable can slope. If he could he would have put his hands in pockets, but he couldn't.

Troy let him reach the end of the street and then he yanked on the bell pull.

Travis answered. Just like Rod, shirtsleeves and half-mast tie, but without the rotten taste in slippers. He had a bottle of wine in one hand, the corkscrew sticking out of the top, the cork waiting to be pulled. He did not in the least seem surprised.

'Was it something I said?' he said.

'Of course,' Troy replied.

'Then you'd better come in. We don't want Big Brother watching, now do we?'

He led the way into the front room, the dining room as this version of a Church Row house was laid out, set the bottle down unopened and pulled the curtains to. Troy caught a glimpse of Rod, lit up in his own front window, staring out at them. Then he was gone and it was just Troy and Travis alone on opposite sides of a vast table, in the light and shade of a single lamp.

'I'm not going to help you, Commander Troy. Whatever's on your mind, just spit it out.'

'I know you killed Clover Browne. I know how you killed Clover Browne.'

Travis said nothing. He stuck the bottle, still with its corkscrew sticking out, on a silver tray on the sideboard, and from somewhere produced a packet of cork-tipped cigarettes and lit up. He did not offer one to Troy. The table lamp cut off Troy's view as he took the first drag – all he could see was the tilt of his chin, the glowing tip of the cigarette beneath the haze of smoke. Then a glass ashtray appeared on the table. Travis leant in, flicked ash and Troy could just see his eyes, disappearing into darkness, unexpressive.

'You've got ten minutes. After that I may well take you by the scruff of the neck and throw you out.'

Travis looked at his watch. Troy looked at his.

'I spent Easter at Uphill, as I'm sure you know. You were there too, keeping a pretty low profile. Woodbridge didn't, but then he had so much less to lose. When I found out Woodbridge and Tereshkov were sharing the Ffitch girls I tried very hard to warn Fitz that he was playing with fire. Wouldn't listen. Just kept saying, "Ace in the hole." He was drunk but he knew what he was saying. For long time I didn't. And I've spent the best part of the last week thinking he meant his MI5 connections. But he didn't. He wisely did not trust MI5 and he certainly didn't rely on them to get him out of the hole he'd dug for himself. But he did trust you. You were his ace in the hole, not MI5. I could scarcely have been more wrong.

'That same night, after Fitz fell into a drunken stupor, I walked across the Park with young Clover Browne. She was on her way to meet someone in the North Lodge. She was wearing nothing but an operetta mask and high-heeled shoes. "Lucky Tommy," I said. And for a long time I made nothing of her reply – indeed I gave it no thought. What she said was "Tommy? I should cocoa." A bit of cockney slang. Took me an age to hear the question mark in there. She wasn't telling me who she was tripping through the darkness to fuck, but she was telling me it wasn't Tommy. It was you. I know that now. I looked up your constituency. Winchelsea and Rye. You go to Winchelsea every weekend on constituency business. It's five miles from Uphill. You were probably a regular guest of Tommy's, and through him you met Fitz and you met Clover. It's common knowledge around the House that your marriage is a bickering mess.

A young mistress in discreet surroundings was probably exactly what you wanted.

'But then Woodbridge and Fitz became the object of a furious press enquiry, a great national nosiness, and then a scandal and then a messy resignation. You must have been worried, but compared to Woodbridge, you'd been very discreet. So few people knew. But, things got worse. Scotland Yard decided someone had to be punished and they began a case against Fitz. I should think it was the last thing you wanted. But Coyn and Quint thought the opposite. They didn't even wait for Woodbridge to resign – they moved against Fitz as soon as Woodbridge tried to deny it all. They thought they were serving you, the Party, the House and their duty all in one action. This is the way the establishment works after all, not on the level of a contrived conspiracy, but like a machine on automatic. Everyone doing what they think is expected of them. Mirkeyn did the same. It's probably never crossed Mirkeyn's mind that he's a bad judge or a bent judge. He simply did what was expected. Didn't even need a nod or a wink. It's probably never crossed Wilfrid Coyn's mind that he's a poor excuse for a copper. In his book, the law demanded justice and justice demanded a scapegoat – a sacrificial victim. And, since the victim could not be Woodbridge, it had to be Fitz. Coyn and Quint moved Blood from Special Branch just to make sure they had someone who understood the machine a bit better than those plodding fools in Vice.

'It must have crossed your mind a thousand times to stop the prosecution, but you didn't. The risk was too great. You would then be the centre of attention; your own motives would be held up to scrutiny. You must have prayed for the Director of Public Prosecutions to throw it out, but he didn't – he too did what he thought the system required of him. So you did the only thing you could. You looked at the evidence, and you did a deal with Fitz. You told him the case would likely as not fall apart in court, and but for an old bugger like Mirkeyn it would have, and if it didn't he would get off on appeal. I don't know what else you promised him by way of compensation, but the two of you had a deal. Somehow you bought his silence. Somehow you got him to agree not even to testify in his own defence.

'Then, Blood turned out to be a bit too good at his job. He couldn't find Clover, but he rightly deduced that a charge of procurement would be far more damaging to Fitz than one of immoral earnings. Half of England thought Fitz was some sort of pervert, a bounder at the very least, but the other half of England admired Fitz as a lucky blighter for having a couple of women like the Ffitch sisters. No one would admire him for being involved with a girl who'd been under age for most of the time he knew her. When Blood could not find Clover, the Yard took a risk. They named her in the submission anyway. I can imagine the conversation with Blood. "Just give me more time," he'd've said. "I can find her. By the time it gets to court I can find her." Because the truth is that Blood knew who Clover really was. I even think he knew about you and thought he was serving you by tracking her down, enacting some sort of bizarre vengeance on your behalf. He kept that knowledge to himself. He looked for her personally. He kept no notes of where he looked or to whom he talked. This must have been dreadful for you. If Blood found her there would be no way to keep your name out of it. There'd be a scandal to put Fitz and Woodbridge and Tereshkov in the shade. But then Onions stepped in. Told Blood to drop it. Or else. Now, Onions can think he still has that kind of power if it flatters his vanity. He's an old man, after all. But I doubt that Blood would have given up on Clover just because Onions said so. God knows, I wouldn't have. Blood did exactly what I'd have done in his position. He passed the buck upwards. Told Coyn and Quint that he knew the girl's real name and that Onions had warned him off. He must have thought they'd back him, but they didn't – they panicked. Blood may not have had enough imagination to see that it had now become an issue of loyalty to the Yard, but they did. They knew damn well that the Yard would come very badly out of a scandal involving Sir Stanley Onions' family, and they wanted to drop it.

'By now it's day one of the trial. I checked the court reports. David Cocket approached the bench and there was a long, unrecorded three-way discussion in chambers between the judge, the prosecution and the defence. It's not hard to guess what Cocket said. That there was no statement accompanying the name of Clover Browne as witness, and that if they attempted to introduce her as a witness at a later date without a prior statement he would ask for her evidence to be ruled inadmissible. Mirkeyn would have loved to say no, but he couldn't. He probably told Furbelow to produce a police statement from Clover by day two or withdraw the charge. Furbelow got on to the Yard and they all agreed to drop it. The procurement charge wouldn't stick. For you this was little short of a miracle. The Yard had dropped the charge out of sheer self-interest and you'd come so far without having to step in yourself and risk giving any reasons. You were where you wanted to be – out of it.

'Then, Clover vanished. She was still at large, knowing enough to destroy you, and you'd lost her. I don't think you worked out that Onions had dumped her on me. But then she phoned you from my house. I know she phoned the Ffitch girls, and I think she phoned you too. I was late back from the court one day towards the end of the trial and I found her still in the bath. But she'd bathed that morning. It occurs to me now that she was washing you off. She'd heard my key in the door, and dashed for bathroom to rinse off an afternoon of sex. And when she emerged, smelling of soap and talc and scent instead of man, she fell into my bed like an apple from a tree. I flattered myself I'd made all the running. Indeed, I cursed myself I'd made all the running. But giving in to me had just been her way of settling my suspicions. She threw a sexual cloud over me to mask all trace of you. A man who's getting fucked silly doesn't much wonder who the woman was with a couple of hours before, or even *if* she was with another man a couple of hours before.

'I don't know when you decided to kill her, but you couldn't let her roam around knowing what she did. You thought that sooner or later she'd tell someone. On the last morning of the trial, you talked to Fitz. After all, you still had your arrangement with Fitz; he still trusted you to get him out of the mess. And you told him you needed me out of the way for an evening. So the two of us ate at Leoni's. And while we did you turned up at my house. Clover had already told you her ludicrous fantasy of a lovers' suicide pact, just as she'd told it to me. And she'd probably told you I was taking sleeping pills. So you turned up armed with a jar of plain white vitamin pills. You told her it was all up for the two of you. That there was only one way out. And as she swallowed my sleeping pills, you matched her pill for pill with nothing more harmful than Vitamin C. And when she was just a bit gaga you told her to write a suicide note. She wrote two. One to her grandfather and one to me. And when she was comatose, beyond any hope of recovery, you washed your glass, packed way your pills, wiped away your fingerprints and left. Fitz and I went our separate ways. When he got home, Percy Blood blew his brains out, and when I got home I found Clover dying. You'd rounded everything up in a single evening. All the people who knew you were having an affair with a girl a third your age were dead. Your career was safe; what was left of your marriage was safe, and with Macmillan ailing fast, you were in with a shot at Number 10.

'Of course it was something you said. You should never have let her write two notes. I never told anyone about the note for Onions except Onions himself. It isn't mentioned in any report I made to the Yard. It wasn't in the account I wrote for you. You were damned the minute you told me she'd written two notes. The only way you could have known that was if you had been there when she wrote them. Really, you should never have agreed to see me. I was the only person you had to fear. You'd almost got away with it.'

Travis had finished his cigarette, and lit up another tip to tail.

'I do so admire neatness in a policeman,' he said. 'It makes me almost proud of my job. An excellent analysis of method, very good on the legal procedure, but a shot in the dark at motive. It all hinges on who knew about me and Clover, and, as you so rightly say, Tommy is dead, Fitz is dead and Clover is dead. Without them you have the perfect *modus operandi* without a motive or a murderer.'

'Not quite,' said Troy.

'Not quite?'

'There has to be one person left who knew. One person from whom you could not conceal the affair.'

Travis smiled. Inhaled deeply and shook his head. Disembodied in the part-light like the grinning head of the Cheshire cat.

'No, no, no, Commander Troy, it's not going to wash.'

Troy wondered at the beauty of the timing. The purity of coincidence that led the doorbell to ring out now as if a demented Quasimodo had swung on the bell pull with all his might.

Travis stared at Troy. The smile fading fast.

'Well,' Troy said. 'It won't be for me, will it?'

Travis got up. He had looked at Troy unresponsively throughout, saying nothing with lips and eyes, the hand reaching out to tap on the ashtray his only movement. Now he looked with something like suspicion turning to hatred in his eyes. Could he not guess? Troy thought. Did he not know what was coming? He walked into the hallway just as Quasimodo swung on the bell again. Troy heard the door creak on its hinges. A muted exchange. No words, just the tones of incredulity in Travis's voice. He came back, sweeping his fingers though his hair, stood a moment with his back to Troy. Troy heard the scraping of the parquet as the chair next to him was pulled back, but he did not turn. He looked sideways from the corners of his eyes. Until he saw with his own eyes, he still might not dare to believe. He had been so aware of the amount of time he had allowed him for second thoughts. But there he was, sitting next to him, fair hair damp with rain, buttoned to the chin against the night, eyes fixed on Travis's back. Woodbridge.

§ 121

Troy had called on Woodbridge an hour or so before he had called on Rod. Without Woodbridge, his meeting with Travis would be a colossal bluff. Even afterwards, as he made his way to Rod's, he could not be wholly sure what agreement the two of them had reached – but before he tackled Travis he had had to talk to Woodbridge.

Woodbridge had a largish early-Victorian house he called his 'cottage' in Flask Walk, less than quarter of a mile from Church Row. Troy stood on the opposite side of the street. Every light in the cottage blazed. Several of the windows seemed to have been stripped of their curtains. There wasn't a reporter in sight. It looked as though Woodbridge's moment of fame had finally passed.

'Long time no see,' he said as he opened the door to Troy. He stood a moment on the doorstep. This was not the man Troy had seen before. It was the mufti version, not the politician, the former politician. Troy had never seen anyone of his age in American blue jeans before, the incongruous, ironed white shirt flapping loose over the waistband of the blue denim, the shiny black shoes at odds with the rolled turn-ups at the ankle. He hadn't quite got the hang of it, Troy thought, but he'd learn. You needed the figure for them at forty-eight. Woodbridge looked good in them. Long legs helped, no beer belly helped. He'd learn.

He motioned Troy in. Troy shut the door behind him and followed the sound of Woodbridge's footsteps, the unmistakable echo of an empty house where noise is unmuffled by furniture or curtains or flesh and seems to bounce from wall to wall and room to room. The drawing room contained nothing but three hefty tea-chests standing on the bare floorboards amid the disturbed dust of absent furniture, lit only by a single, naked overhead bulb. Woodbridge rummaged in the middle chest, the only one not yet nailed down. He pulled out a bottle and two glasses wrapped in yesterday's newspaper. As he peeled away the paper he turned the label towards Troy.

'Chateau Margaux '56,' he said. 'It'd only be coals to Newcastle. We might as well open it now and drink a toast to Mother England.'

Troy sort of knew what he meant, but did not ask any questions. He would be happy if a glass of Margaux proved to be his only distraction.

They each took a tea-chest. Bon viveurs at a moveable feast.

'You're looking better,' said Woodbridge as he poured. Then he raised his glass, 'Cheers,' he said, and Troy took a swig of the finest claret he'd had in quite a while. Then he said, 'You know Clover's dead?'

'I heard it on the grapevine.'

'You mean Anna told you?'

'Yes. You did a good job keeping it out of the papers. Same night as Fitz, wasn't it? Must have been awful for you. Dreadful coincidence.'

'I'm a policeman. I have difficulty with coincidence.'

'Is that what you've come to tell me?'

Troy told him everything he had told himself in the course of what already seemed to be an unending day, everything he had told Eddie, everything he had told Jack. He knew the lines by heart now. The sad, confusing story of the death of Clover Browne. Sadder with every repetition.

Woodbridge heard him out as Jack had done – in silence, without question – then he said, 'Are you seriously telling me you think the Home Secretary murdered Clover Browne?'

'Yes.'

'On the strength of one ill-phrased remark?'

'It said what he thought and what he knew. "She swallowed a handful of sleeping pills, then dashed off a couple of suicide notes." I know you think the phrase is vague and casual, but it remains. I never told anyone that Clover left two suicide notes. I thought I owed that to her grandfather.'

'Who did the old boy turn out to be? Who is Sir Somebody Something?'

'Stanley Onions.'

'My God, Fitz played with fire, didn't he?'

'If there had been anything material in the note Clover left him he would have told me. And I would have told the Yard. As he didn't, I let him have the last of his granddaughter in privacy. Only three people knew she left two notes: Stan, me and the man who killed her. "A couple of suicide notes" is not a casual imprecision. It was Freud speaking. Travis said what he knew to be true even as he tried to lie to me. And he knew it to be true because he was there when Clover wrote them.'

He was not all sure that he had convinced Woodbridge. It all depended on what Woodbridge said next.

'What do you want from me, Troy? What is it you want me to say?'

'You knew Travis was staying at Tommy Athelnay's. You're the one person who had to know. He could not have spent that Sunday at the north lodge and not bumped into you – he'd have had to hide in his room all day. He was a friend of yours. You have adjoining constituencies. You stood in for him at surgeries from time to time. Of course you knew he was there – the two of you turned up together.'

'Fine. He was there.'

It seemed to Troy to be a strangely confrontational answer, an unspoken but plain 'so what?'

'And Clover too.'

'If you say so.'

'No. I want you to say so.'

Woodbridge tipped his head back and stared at the ceiling. Troy could hear the rasp of his breath, could almost feel the inner debate within the man.

'Supposing . . . supposing I were to say that she was. Suppose I

407

were to say that she and Travis had been having an affair since Christmas. Suppose that. What then?'

'Then I would ask you to back me. To back me when I confront Travis.'

'Oh God, Troy. I can't do that. I don't want to do that. Give me one good reason why I would ever do that?'

'Clover's dead. Fitz is dead.'

'Neither you nor I can bring them back. And I don't see that exposing Nick will do her one jot of good.'

'He killed her.'

'So it's justice?'

'In as much as we can wield it, yes.'

Woodbridge sighed again.

'I still cannot do what you ask. If I thought it would do anything for Clover or Fitz then . . . but I can't . . . I can't see the reason in it. He's got away with it.'

'One good reason, you said. One good reason to back me.'

Woodbridge said nothing.

'In 1957 you got up and lied to the House about Charlie Leigh-Hunt.'

'Old news, Troy. We were all wrong about Charlie.'

'And at the end of January this year you got up and lied to the House again when you told them Charlie had now been exposed as a spy by his defection to the Soviet Union. The Government and the Opposition cut a deal not to debate the matter. Your version was accepted by both sides. And it was as big a lie as any you've told lately.'

'Lies? Troy, it's common knowledge the bugger's in Moscow. He scarpered there from Beirut.'

'He fled Beirut only after you'd been to see him at our embassy there. You spent a whole afternoon with Charlie before he got on that Russian freighter.'

'What? What? Troy, are you trying to blackmail me?'

'Charlie told me himself. He told me you came out to see him and told him it was all over for him and he should cut and run. But if that was all there was to it, why not just bump him off? He could vanish without trace. Or why not simply send a junior intelligence officer. If the message was simply, "Bugger off", why did it take the time and effort of a Minister of State? Why did it go to the highest level?

Tim, when you told the House Charlie was not a Russian agent, you lied. When you told the House he was a Russian agent, you lied. Because the truth is Charlie Leigh-Hunt is a triple agent. You went to Beirut to tell him it was time to go to Moscow. Sometime in '57 SIS learnt what Charlie was and turned him. Charlie was a believer. You people turned him into your whore. And he accepted it because it was marginally preferable to death. You let my brother think that Charlie was nothing more than a thoroughly discredited, clapped-out old spy. You let Rod believe his career as a spook was over. The messy years between your endorsement and your exposure of Charlie were nothing more than an elaborate cover to fool the Russians and keep him out of harm's way. You put Charlie in the wilderness until they had no suspicions left, and at the right moment you placed him where you wanted him. Charlie is our new man in Moscow. He whores for Britain. He whores for Russia, and he whores for Britain again. Right now I should think he's about as sore as the junior bumboy in an English public school. Charlie's getting fucked up every orifice for Queen and Country. And if you do not help me now, I'll blow the whistle.'

For a moment Troy thought he had blasted Woodbridge off his tea-chest, but when he spoke his words were calm, his voice devoid of the anger Troy felt in spades.

'Troy — be sensible. If you leak this you could do irreparable damage to the country.'

'I don't care.'

'You'd be signing Charlie's death warrant.'

'I don't care. I'd probably be doing him a favour.'

'The Government would slap a D notice on it at the first whiff of a leak.'

'Could you stop my nephew when you wanted to? Do you think Alex won't find ways of letting the truth be known? Do you think you could stop Rod? If I tell Rod what I know, he'll bung in a standard, "What are the Prime Minister's plans for the day?" at question time, and his follow-up will be, "Why was Tim Wood-bridge in Beirut the day Charles Leigh-Hunt defected?" Try slapping a D notice on that.'

'You think Labour will not recognise the national interest? Do you think Rod has no loyalty?'

'Oh Rod's got bags of the stuff. But how do you think Wilson's going to react when he finds out you conned him? He's a vain, pompous little prick. You didn't see fit to tell him the truth when you invoked the national interest. He's priding himself on his ability to horse-trade, flattered that you took him into your confidence over a matter of national security, pleased as punch to play hard-ball with the big boys, and suddenly he finds you worked a fast one on him? He'll be furious. Labour will be furious. All deals will be off. They'll probably agree to keep it secret – they'll still turn the Commons into open warfare. But Rod – Rod's a believer in Love and Justice and Democracy. He hates lies. Whatever new deals the Commons can cut in the national interest, Rod will brand you a liar in public all over again. You'll be front-page news just when you thought your fifteen minutes of infamy had passed.'

They passed an age in silence. It seemed to Troy that what Woodbridge had to say cost him dearly in the effort of expression.

'You're wrong. I know you're wrong. You're underestimating the way things hang together and you're underestimating your own brother. But if you kick up any fuss, there'll be a scandal. That I will not deny. I don't want another scandal, Troy. I don't want to be dragged back. I want simply to leave. If you do this I'll be tied and bound all over again. Can I not just go in peace? Is that too much to ask? If you can't do this for me, could you at least think of the international implications and do it for England?'

'Bugger England,' said Troy. 'Do this for Paddy Fitz and Clover Browne!'

§ 122

Travis still stood with his back to them, one hand pressed to his forehead, the elbow crooked, as though fighting to contain what cerebrally could no longer be contained. He said nothing. Troy counted the stripes on his shirt.

'What now?' he said at last, without turning. 'What do the two of you have in mind?'

Troy looked at Woodbridge to find Woodbridge looking at him.

'Let's have some light on the subject, shall we?'

Woodbridge got up, flicked the light switch by the door. A chandelier bearing two dozen electric candles flashed on, and he parked his backside on a radiator beneath the window. Travis lowered his hand, sat facing Troy once more, the comfort of darkness stripped from him, every line in his face visible, the blankness in his eyes, and the bags beneath them. He put his palms flat on the polished surface of the table as though steadying his whole body with the slightest pressure.

'You resign,' said Troy.

It seemed to him that Travis nodded.

'You stand down at the next election. You do not accept a peerage. You leave public life.'

Again the merest nod of the head.

'Coyn retires at Christmas.'

He nodded again, eyes down, not looking at Troy, staring at the spread of his own fingers on the table top.

'Quint is fired.'

'All of us?' said Travis simply.

Troy heard the words come to him from some distant schoolbook history. Words he could not have said he knew.

'"You have sat too long for any good you might have been doing. In the name of God go."'

This remark seemed to galvanise Travis. The fingers closed, the hands locked, his eyes met Troy's.

'How very convenient for you, Commander Troy. Everyone out of the way. Leaving you a clear field. A quick bit of Shakespearian blank verse, and you sweep us all away and run Scotland Yard yourself.'

Troy was sure he heard it. Ricocheting between earth and sky. Sure he saw it. Him, the boy Troy, running up the aisle of that long-forgotten theatre in Le Touquet. His father's voice ringing in his ears. A sound like breaking string. He heard it snap, over his head somewhere, deep within him somewhere. Something snapped. Something snapped in Mr Charlie. Something snapped in Troy. Then he could hear Woodbridge speaking from the edge of the room.

'You're an ignorant bugger, Nick. It isn't blank verse and it isn't Shakespeare. It's Cromwell dismissing the Long Parliament.'

And then all he could hear was the sound like breaking string. 'A distant sound, as though coming from the sky, like the breaking of a string.'

'No,' he said. 'We all go. I'll resign too. We all go.'

A quarter of an hour later, ash white with burnt-out rage, Travis showed them to the door.

'One last thing,' Troy said in the open doorway, buttoning up his coat. 'How did you get Percy Blood to shoot Fitz?'

Travis didn't even think about it, as though he had expected the question all along, an ironic smile twisting his thin lips.

'If I'd wanted Fitz killed, do you seriously think I'd've sent a lunatic to do it?'

'How were you going to do it?'

'Do you know, I never worked that out. As you said, I had my arrangement with Fitz. I took one thing at a time. And then . . . then I didn't have to. The problem had sorted itself.'

The door closed. Troy and Woodbridge found themselves alone in the stillness of a wet, deserted street. They walked to the end of Church Row and stood on the corner.

'Thank you,' said Troy. It seemed to him that it needed to be said.

'Had to be done,' said Woodbridge. 'It had to be done for Fitz and for Clover. I won't deny I gave it some thought after you'd gone. And I don't much care for blackmail. But you were right. We do it for Fitz and for Clover. They neither of them deserved what was done to them. She didn't deserve to be dead at seventeen. Fitz never deserved to be publicly pilloried in that way. He didn't deserve to be hounded and he didn't deserve to be in their line of fire. As you said to me not so long ago – aim too low and you never know who you might hit.'

'All the same, I'm grateful to you. I'd've hated signing Charlie's death warrant.'

'But you'd've done it?'

Troy shrugged.

'Answer me one question, Troy. Why aren't you bringing down the government? First Profumo and Keeler, then me and the Ffitch sisters. After a year like this it will only take one more scandal to finish us. You arrest Travis and we're finished.'

'You're finished whatever I do. Macmillan's already said he'll go. You and Fitz have done for Macmillan as surely as if you'd put a gun to his head. You lot aren't going to have a party conference this week; it's a beauty contest. Perhaps Rab Butler will lead you into the next election. He's never struck me as a winner. Or, since one can now resign a peerage, perhaps some Tory in the Lords will decide to throw in his cap. Who knows, you might end up led by a fool like Hailsham, and that's a losing ticket if ever I saw one. No – I'm not using this to bring down a government because I don't have to and I don't think it's my job to. The next election is Labour's for the asking. Besides, Travis is a bigger fool than even you think. We've evidence of his infidelities, but I've nothing that would stand up in court and convict him of murder. If he thinks he's getting away with murder, then let him. Just so long as he goes.'

'Do you know how that piece of Cromwell you quoted him ends?'

'No. I shot my bolt in quoting as much as I did.'

'It ends, "You shall now give place to better men." Do you really think the other lot will be better men?'

'Family loyalties apart, probably not. But at least give them a chance to fuck up in their own way. Harold Wilson is about as dry as a cream cracker and scarcely more witty. I doubt he's the imagination to compete with you or Travis – I should think he has few thoughts below the collar stud let alone below the waist. George Brown is genial enough but a complete liability with two drinks inside him. I doubt very much whether the party has ever forgiven him for telling Khrushchev where he got off. I think it's asking too much that politicians should not be bent, but at least let's have some new kinks and curves.'

'And I alas shall not be here to see them. I'm going to live in France. Turn the summer place into a permanent home. I was packing when you called. And you? Will you really resign?'

'Yes. I meant it. We . . . I mean our generation . . . has made a hash of it. Let's see if the new lot can do any better.'

'The new generation? Wilson and Brown? New Britain?'

Troy's memory told him he had heard such incredulity recently, expressed in pretty much the same terms. Only then it had been Troy himself uttering them. Woodbridge was laughing. In the same way, in the same words Troy had laughed at Rod months ago. This was the dawn of the 'New Britain', and they neither of them believed in the validity of the 'new' any more than Rebecca West had done . . . New Woman, New Britain – but where were the New Men? There were only old men. At best, old men in new trousers. Now, there was a phrase. 'New Britain, New Trousers.' It had all the catchiness of a good political slogan. Let Rod put that to his 'punters'.

'I don't think I meant Wilson and Brown. I meant . . .'

He was not sure how this sentence ended, but since names came in handy couples . . .

'I meant Lennon and McCartney. And for that matter Tara and Caro Ffitch.'

'I'll be leaving in the morning. If you fancy a week in the Cevennes next spring, give me a call.'

Woodbridge crossed the empty street, heading for the alley that cut across to Hampstead High Street. He stopped and called back to Troy. 'And you? Where will you go?'

'I don't know,' said Troy. 'I really don't.'

It occurred to him that he could still call Woodbridge back while he was still within earshot, and tell him the truth, that his career had been destroyed by a trap, not of the Russians' making, but of his own side's. A trap they had been too stupid or too cowardly to stop. But if Woodbridge felt that another scandal and his own guilt would bind him, how would he be not be bound by the force of his own anger?

§ 123

Troy had that feeling. The Demon would come tonight. Squat on his bedpost. Green. Guilty.

He slept with the old Webley loaded and tucked between the sheets. Sure enough, the Demon appeared, silvered eyes flashing back his own image.

'Well now,' said the Demon. 'You have been busy.'

Troy blew its green brains out and went back to sleep.

In the morning he could recall the strangest dream. More vivid than any he could remember before it. Then he saw the Webley on the bedside table. He flipped the chamber open and counted only four bullets where he usually kept five. He saw the hole in the plaster of his bedroom wall, the size of a side-plate.

He went into the bathroom, tipped all his pills down the bog and pulled the chain.

§ 124

Troy asked himself why. He wanted the neatness of an answer. The last piece banged into the puzzle. The last square peg hammered into its round hole. Why did Percy Blood kill Paddy Fitz?

Blood was mad to begin with. Almost the only person who did not know this was Percy himself. When the chief police surgeon called him in on 19 September he had put Blood on sick leave. This was a body blow, the second such in a matter of months. First leaving the bosom of the Branch, then ordered to rest. Perhaps Quint had promised him a transfer back to the Branch when it was all over. Now, that was unlikely to happen soon enough. He was on sick leave. Worse he had been told to see a psychiatrist. Blood would bridle at this. The idea of psychiatry meant next to nothing to him. All he would know was the army use of the term as 'trick-cyclist', and only malingerers ever saw the 'trick-cyclist'. His life was effectively in ruins. He was either mad or he was a malingerer and he did not care to be called either. Someone had to be to blame. It could not be Peggy Blood. Troy would bet a penny to a pound that she'd called the chief surgeon only in confidence, in fear of another beating. Blood looked at the coincidence of dates. The last day of the Fitz trial – his biggest case and it had not gone well – was the first day of his 'madness'. There were too many things about this case he did not understand. Why had the Yard stopped him bringing in the girl Clover? Why had that bastard Troy suddenly turned up at the Old Bailey? It was obvious who was to blame. If he'd never got mixed up with that disgusting ponce Patrick Fitzpatrick he wouldn't be in this mess now. Worse, it looked to Percy as though Fitz might get off. Justice and vengeance met in Percy's mind. He shot Paddy Fitz for Percy Blood and blind drunk justice.

§ 125

He found the newspaper headlines gave him no pleasure. 'SCOT-LAND YARD ROCKED BY RESIGNATIONS.' But it worked like clockwork. After a lacklustre speech to his party conference, Travis had not put in his bid for the leadership, and when the resignations hit – first Quint (men in jobs like his never get fired, they merely accept that they have resigned, like it or not) – then Coyn's request for early retirement, and finally Troy – no one could be in any way surprised that the Home Secretary thought fit to follow. He tendered his resignation to the new Prime Minster, Sir Alec Douglas-(lately Lord)Home, and was accepted. Half the newspapers in the land implied or openly said that he must be to blame. The bolder even suggested another scandal, to round off the year of scandals, that was being buried in this rapid tumble of the Titans.

Kolankiewicz, Quint and Troy all left the Yard on the same day. The press paid no heed to Kolankiewicz – they had never heard of him. Troy, when pressed by the *Sunday Post*, merely pointed to the state of his health. Quint seethed in silence. The front, since it mattered, was maintained to the point of the Commissioner holding a leaving party for the three of them. Troy thought that he had never attended a drearier, more joyless gathering of human beings. After Coyn's brief speech he could have sworn he heard the sound of one hand clapping.

The man clearly thought he should make a toast. He looked from Quint to Troy and back to Troy again, and Troy saved him from the 'umms' and 'ers' by raising his glass and giving the detectives of Scotland Yard an unambiguous toast.

'Mary McDiarmuid,' he said, and the room echoed his cry. It was, he thought, the one toast that would not have them thumping each other between the filing cabinets.

He went to the bogs and relieved himself of two glasses of lukewarm, flat beer. He did not hear a sound behind him. The first he knew was an excruciating blow to the kidneys that sucked the air out of his lungs and left him pissing down his trouser leg. Halfway to the floor, an elbow wedged in the trough, he saw the foot aiming at his face and braced himself for the blow. Then foot and man went flying and Jack reached out to help him to his feet. He looked down at Quint stretched full length on the lavatory floor. Jack had knocked him out cold.

'Am I going to spend the rest of my life getting you out of scrapes, Freddie?'

It was not the rest of Jack's life that concerned Troy, it was the rest of his own. If this was the limit of Quint's idea of vengeance then he would not waste one second of it worrying about him.

Out in the corridor a posse of the short and stout waited for them. Kolankiewicz in his ancient homburg, a copy of the *Daily Herald* sticking out of his macintosh pocket, and Clark, identical in girth, stature and macintosh, but favouring *Private Eye* and a trilby. Kolankiewicz dangled what looked very much like a hatbox at the end of one arm.

'Come,' he said, 'let us wash the dust of thirty years from our throats.'

He led the way, out of the south entrance and round the corner to St Stephen's Tavern, watering hole of the odd copper and the even odder MP, being, as it was, almost directly opposite the Houses of Parliament. They pushed in past a noisy horde of backbenchers. Troy even recognised a few of them, part of the new intake of 1959, one or two of them disciples of Rod's. Most of them could bore for Britain. He picked up fragments as Jack and Eddie went to the bar and bought for the four of them.

'We've got the bastards on the run this time,' a red-faced Yorkshireman was saying. 'Travis is the straw that'll break the camel's back.'

And from another corner of the room, 'Twelve years in power. Twelve miserable bloody years! Do you know there are kids out campaigning in my constituency who can't remember any other government?'

And Troy turned off to it. They could say nothing he wanted to hear. Nothing he had not heard before. Nothing he had not himself said to Woodbridge a month or so ago in the wet streets of Hampstead. Nineteen-sixty-three would end as it had begun, with futile speculation along the lines of imminent election. Rod was right: build your wall. While the glue that held us together dissolved

– if there was now a generation that could not remember life before the Tories, there was most assuredly one and a half which could not remember the war – build your wall high.

'What will you do?' Jack said to Kolankiewicz.

'I have my allotment. I have raised most of my own veg since the war. The contrast between slicing into a carrot grown on your own plot and slicing into the skull of some poor bugger you've never met in life cannot be overstated. I might go so far as to say that it has kept me sane these many years.'

There were, thought Troy, many who might disagree. If this was Kolankiewicz the sane version, he never wanted to see the nutter who lurked within.

'And', he went on, 'my particular delight in my small front garden has been the cultivation of the flag iris, on which I now propose to write a book.'

Jack looked gobsmacked. Looked at Troy.

'Don't ask,' said Troy.

'Ask what?'

'Don't ask me what I'm going to do. Because I don't know.'

A hour or more later they had toasted freedom, cursed the Yard, voiced regret, pledged eternal friendship, reminisced at random and were ready to leave. Troy asked the question that had nagged at him most of the evening.

'What's in the hatbox?'

Kolankiewicz opened it up and removed what appeared to be a leather football, a casey, painted black, with a short length of fuse sticking out of the seam, and the word 'Bomb' neatly stencilled on the side.

'Is November 5th,' he said. 'Gunpowder, treason and to hell with those fuckers over the road.'

Jack roared with laughter. Troy knew Kolankiewicz better and while he saw the joke he was more puzzled than amused. The more so when Kolankiewicz carried the 'bomb' head high past a mob of cheering, half-pissed backbenchers. Troy would not have thought they were capable of taking themselves and their dubious trade lightly enough to find this funny.

Outside the pub, they reached the parting of ways. Jack, the only one of them in any way sentimental, hugged a startled Kolankiewicz, hugged a less startled Troy and was about to hug Clark when Clark said, 'But I'll be seeing you at work tomorrow, sir.'

'So you will,' said Jack, 'so you will.'

Jack and Eddie went south, Troy and Kolankiewicz north.

'Look over your shoulder,' Kolankiewicz said. 'Are they looking back at us?'

No,' said Troy. 'They're going over Westminster Bridge. Jack's a bit unsteady on his feet. Eddie's holding him up.'

'Good.'

Kolankiewicz crossed the street, just north of Big Ben. Troy followed. A beat bobby, big as a barn door, passed them on the pavement. Troy was not sure whether he recognised either of them or not. But he looked at Kolankiewicz's 'bomb', laughed out loud and walked on chuckling, hands clasped behind his back, plodding into Lambeth in best copper fashion. The great English cliché, the laughing policeman. Troy could still hear the sound of his laughter as Kolankiewicz put a match to the fuse and lobbed the 'bomb' over the railings and into New Palace Yard.

'We got three minutes,' he said.

'Three minutes for what?'

Troy hurried after him. They had just rounded the corner into Horse Guards Parade when Kolankiewicz stopped, took out his pocket watch and began to count off the seconds on his fingers. On the count of three a dull whumphff was just audible behind them.

'Not bad,' said Kolankiewicz. 'Out by only three seconds.'

He walked on. Troy stood rooted to the spot, all but openmouthed. Then he tore after Kolankiewicz.

'You don't mean that bomb was real?'

'Very small, but, yes, very real. Call it a parting gesture.'

They went their separate ways at the Strand Underground station, where Kolankiewicz could catch the Northern Line home to Hampstead Garden Suburb.

'A book on flag irises?' said Troy.

'Why not?' said Kolankiewicz.

Troy walked home. Across the Strand, past the Charing Cross Hospital, up Bedfordbury, retracing at a slow walk the exact route he had taken the night he had run down the street with the dying Clover in his arms. In the back way, down the courtyard to his front door, and into the rest of his life.

§ 126

The rest of his life was proving to be a bit of a bore. The first morning he had plucked the *Morning Herald* off the doormat, made coffee and toast and gone back to bed. One item amused him – a group of confused MPs reported how they had emerged from St Stephen's Tavern to find themselves suddenly showered with scraps of old leather and smothered in the smell of what could only be described as the world's biggest banger, that firework so favoured by aggressive pre-adolescent boys. The report did not mention that these guardians of liberty were probably pissed out of their skulls at the time. If they weren't, why hadn't they given Kolankiewicz's description to the Yard? The Yard. How odd it seemed to use the words and not have them mean himself.

Kolankiewicz phoned. 'Damn,' he said. 'Missed the bastards!'

He passed the rest of the day without quite seeming to do anything. And by the third day he was restless. The pleasures of toast and coffee in bed while the rest of London slogged to work on buses and tube trains were beginning to seem distinctly limited. He had choices. So many choices. He could go home, home, that is to Mimram, where Sasha would be waiting to adopt him. He'd get to see his pig. He was already envious of Kolankiewicz having his book to write. Perhaps he could write a handbook of pig husbandry? But he'd be stuck with his sister. Or he could go out.

He went to one of the music shops in the Charing Cross Road and bought the sheet music of the Well-Tempered Clavier Book One. He liked it less than the Goldbergs or the French Suites, but he had never in his life attempted to play it. It was 'new'. And the 'new' soon palled.

Within ten days – ten days in which he had banged his way badly through bits of Bach – he knew what the restlessness was telling him. Not that he had planned badly. He had not planned at all. He knew that. What it told him was to get out of England, to ignore home, homes, any of his homes, and just go. What it told him was the opposite of what it had told him when they had finally let him out of

The Glebe. The last thing he had wanted was women. Now he wanted women. Or, to be precise, woman.

He seemed to recall a vague invitation to visit a shop in Carnaby Street. So he went in search of Foxx.

He crossed Soho Square, cut through Great Chapel Street, along Great Marlborough Street and came into Carnaby Street via the top end, next to Liberty's store. The shop was not where she had told him it would be. That shop was boarded up. He walked further down the street, towards the Beak Street end, to where a pile of old lath and plaster was piled on the pavement, to where a shiny, new, white Lambretta motor scooter was parked. The windows of this shop were whitewashed to let in daylight and keep out prying eyes, but there was a light on and the door was not locked. He pushed it open, and stepped into what had once been the front room of a small Georgian house, and for years since had probably been a tailor's premises. The room had been gutted, stripped of most of its plasterwork, its cornices and its wooden fittings. Dust lay everywhere, pieces of wallpaper many layers thick lay across the floor stiff as hardboard. The dividing wall to the back room had been removed and a sheet of heavy transparent plastic cordoned it off.

A hand, then an arm, emerged through a gap in the plastic, followed by a torso. Foxx appeared like a large blonde butterfly from its chrysalis. Vintage Foxx, the Foxx he had first tumbled for – T-shirt, blue jeans and frayed baseball boots. Plaster in her hair, the powdery residue of ancient paints dusting her cheeks.

'What are you doing here?'

She kissed him, hugged him, before he could answer.

'How did you find it? I got outbid for the last shop at the last minute. Had to move halfway down the street. I'm weeks behind with the reopening.'

'I'm sure London can do without its blue jeans for a week or two.'

'Oh, this won't be just blue jeans and sneakers. I'm designing now. And I'm importing direct from Italy. I'll have a range of new clothes. A little revolution – my personal mission to get the Englishwoman out of potato sacks and her man out of Charlie Chaplin pants. All I need is a name. You couldn't come up with a good name for the shop, could you? I've been racking my brains.'

A piece of paper detached itself from high up on the wall to fall on

Troy's head. He plucked it off, looked at the layers, the generations, overlapping like the pages in a book.

'You've taken on quite a task,' he said.

'Nothing I can't handle. It's great fun.'

She twirled to the centre of the room, arms outstretched, eyes bright with pleasure.

'You won't believe the dirt that was here. I don't think anything had been done to this place since some time in the last century. Dickens was a boy when this place last got a spring clean.'

He was still holding the paper. He'd counted eleven different layers in it. The last wasn't even Victorian, he thought. It was probably put up in the reign of George III.

'England was like that,' he said. 'There always seemed to be corners that gathered dust. Some cranny where things you thought you'd never see again lingered generations after they'd gone from everyplace else. I was forever finding time compressed into the corners of Mimram when I was a boy.'

'Well you won't find it here in a fortnight's time. I'm clearing the whole lot out.'

'Off with the old and on with new? I rather think that's becoming the philosophy of our times.'

'I don't know what we've been witnessing lately – the death throes of the old or the birth pangs of the new, but I know this. In a couple of years' time it won't matter a damn. England is going to go boom!'

She reinforced her words with her hands, arms swinging upward to simulate the explosion, cheeks blowing out as she 'boomed'.

'I know,' said Troy. 'People keep telling me that.'

'By 1965 or '66 you won't recognise the place. It'll be a . . . a . . .'

'A new world?' Troy ventured.

'Yes. That's exactly what it'll be. A new world.'

'Then there's the name for your shop.'

'What? "New World"?'

'I was thinking more of "Terra Nova".'

'That would be a bit beyond the grasp of most of my customers.'

'Everyone's heard of Captain Scott.'

'Wanna bet?'

'Doesn't matter as long as they can pronounce it.'

'How about just "Nova"?'

'Sounds fine. For your customers, I mean. Personally I have heard "new" to the point of tedium this year. It's part of the vocabulary of advertising. Advertising has only three adjectives: more, real and new. I have grown suspicious of the new.'

'Get used to it, Troy. It's here to stay.'

'On the contrary, it's here only until the next "new" comes along.'

'The king is dead,' she said. 'Long live the king.'

He threw down the piece of paper. It had set him musing now, musing out loud. But she was used to that.

'When I was five or six – and I suppose that would make it about 1920 – my father took me for tea at the old Midland Hotel, you know, the one that stands in front of St Pancras Station. Most people think it is St Pancras I'm sure, but it's newer than the station and designed by a different bloke. George Gilbert Scott, the most lavish of the Victorian gothics. I suppose the old man had taken me there many times as a toddler, but this is the only occasion I was old enough to remember, and it was the last. The war had been over just a couple of years. Looking back I think the nation was desperately trying to create a sense of light and air and carefreeness. And what they did was to look at the preceding age – the Victorian – and see that it had lingered those dozen or so years after the old Queen's death, associate it with bloody mess that followed almost as cause and effect, and decide to whitewash it. Almost literally. The Midland Hotel was a staggeringly beautiful creation, a myriad of hardwood grains, marble from Ireland streaked with lime-green swirls, stencil-work that ran for miles, iron fine as filigree and murals fifteen feet high. It was, for want of a better word, a masterpiece. And in 1920 they painted it all over. They were putting on the coat of white in the corridors as we took tea. And white became dull nothing, and dull nothing became brown. And we have lived with the shades of brown ever since. Seeking out light and air, carving out our clean lines, we brushed away colours we had ceased to perceive.'

'What's your point, Troy?'

'Are we now painting out the Britain we knew, twenty years after that in its turn ended? Ended, in a bloody war, much the same, and we have lived with its vestiges far too long, but . . . are we now to be walled up alive in Pegboard, suffused in a sea of Magicoat, bound

423

and gagged in strips of Fablon? . . . The last whitewash turned out to be philistinism on the grand scale.'

'If the only way to defeat the new philistinism is to defend all that is without discrimination, then philistinism wins – cannot lose, in fact.'

It was a shrewd answer, shrewder by far than his analysis.

'Might we not come to regret the "boom"? Might we not come to regret the 1960s?'

'Why not just roll with 'em' Troy? It's the only way we'll find out. You've kicked against the pricks as long as I've known you. You've staged a personal vendetta against the Britain that raised us. One more roll and we might well have seen the last of her.'

'Come away with me.'

He had changed tack so suddenly she was visibly startled.

'What? I mean where?'

'I don't know. Pick a country. Let's just get away for a while.'

'Troy, I can't.'

'Let your builders get on with it for a couple of weeks.'

'No. It isn't that. That would be fine. It's . . . it's just that I've already arranged to go away while the work's done. I'm leaving tomorrow as a matter of fact.'

'Where?'

'France. I'm spending ten days in the Cevennes.'

'Woodbridge,' Troy said simply.

'How did you know?'

'He was wearing blue jeans the last time I saw him. You're starting your fashion revolution in the most unlikely places.'

'Well,' said Foxx. 'Well, he did ask first. Troy, I'm so sorry. I'd love to go somewhere, but I'd be letting him down. Why didn't you ask me a fortnight ago? I'd've jumped at the chance. We could have gone somewhere warm. The Cevennes in November won't exactly be April in Paris, will it?'

She hugged him. Kissed him once. Her way with apology.

'It doesn't matter,' he lied. 'Really it doesn't.'

§ 127

Troy phoned Anna. He waited almost a whole day after Foxx turned him down and then he called Anna. He could not remember when he had last called her.

'I've been trying to reach you for two days,' she said.

He thought she sounded tearful, an immense sadness in her voice.

'I've been out a lot,' he said lamely. 'Just walking around.'

'Could you come over right away?'

'What's up?'

'Angus is dead. They've found his body. It appears he jumped in the river and drowned himself about a month back. Now the body's washed up on the Essex coast by Jacob's Reach. The police came to see me two days ago.'

Tumbling through his mind, the kaleidoscopic explosion of paper as he had torn Angus's manuscript free from his chest, the manuscript he had faithfully promised Angus he would deliver safely to Anna, the last words he had spoken, 'I knew it would get me in the end.' Had he jumped before or after Troy had been pushed? Then the indelible words Charlie had uttered to him – Jacob's Reach, the muddy promontory on the Essex coast where the body of Norman Cobb had finally broken surface. Anna's voice cut into his reverie.

'Oh God, Troy. I can't take any more. Just get over here pronto, will you?'

He listened to the buzz of the dialling tone, put down the phone and, wondering how long he'd be gone, packed a toothbrush and a clean shirt. Then he collected the Bentley, parked in Bedfordbury almost exactly where it had stood the night Percy Blood had riddled it with bullets, and drove to Unbearable Bassington Street.

'They asked me to identify him,' she said. 'I didn't want to. I didn't want to see my husband dead. I didn't want the memory of him looking like a half-decayed corpse. I spend my working life with the dead and dying. I wanted to remember Angus alive. I wanted him vital, I wanted him to be the man I married. I called you. You could have gone instead. But I had to go. And I couldn't swear that it was him. He was unrecognisable. The water, the fish, God knows. The eyes were gone. Troy! He had no eyes! A one-legged man with Angus's wallet in his coat pocket. And I wished they hadn't made me look. So I asked for the leg. And there it was, that old tin leg with all the repairs he'd had made to it over twenty years. And on the back of the calf a maker's stamp. I'll remember it till the day I die: 'A. Futscher, Colditz, fecit. MCMXLII.' So it was him, I said. Him or some other one-legged RAF ace with a tin leg made by the same little man in the same little German town. God, Troy, where were you when I needed you?'

Angus was buried the following day. Troy had spent the night in Anna's guest room, heard her cry till dawn and watched her emerge in black, decline his offer of breakfast, hiding her grief beneath a layer or more of make-up.

A damp November day, ten thousand leaves waiting to be swept up, soggy underfoot, clinging to the soles of the shoes. No one came. Angus had few friends, no siblings, and his parents were long dead. Troy stood with Anna on his arm while a priest, two gravediggers and an old lady who seemed to be a professional mourner watched Angus's vast coffin lowered into the grave. He found thoughts so idle, so pointless he could never utter them – had they buried his tin leg in the coffin with him?

They walked back to his car as the thud of earth hitting the coffin lid boomed out. He did not know how Anna felt, but he could not bear to hear this sound.

They stopped under a leafless chestnut tree. She slipped her arm from his.

'Well?' he said.

'Well?' she said. 'Well? You bastard, you complete and utter fucking bastard.'

Her arms flailed and the blows of small clenched fists caught him on the chest, the cheeks, the ears. She laid into Troy just as Peggy Blood and Valerie Clover had done.

Troy held her fast, her arms with his, stilled the rain of blows and her head sank onto his chest and her tears rolled forth in flood.

'Oh Troy, just hold me, will you?'

Minutes passed. He could not have guessed how many. The furious pounding of her heart slowed, the tectonic heaving of her breast calmed. At last she spoke again, her voiced muffled by the tear-wet wool of his winter overcoat.

'Oh Troy, just fuck off, will you?'

§ 128

Troy resorted to cleaning up. The house was a mess. He'd done nothing to it since the end of August. He started with his own wardrobe. There hung the suit he had been wearing the night Fitz and Clover had died. He hadn't worn it since. Superstition? Fortuity. It was a good suit; too good be written off as he'd had to do with the remains of the one he had been wearing the night – as things turned out – that wandering Angus had died.

He decided to send it to the cleaner's, and turned out the pockets. The left-hand pocket yielded a folded piece of notepaper. It was the letter from Tosca that Fitz had given him. 'Come up and see me some time.' He had completely forgotten that he had it.

He called Rod's secretary. She booked all Rod's foreign travel and had always offered to do the same for him if he ever again took to travelling. Half an hour later she phoned him back and told him he was booked on the next afternoon's Pan Am to Idlewild.

'. . . And Rod had me book a car to take you to the airport.'

'I'm quite happy with the coach,' said Troy.

'He insisted. His treat.'

At lunchtime the following day, he was packed and stuck in that expectant phase of the journey when all is ready, but the clock tells you 'too soon'. He was sitting in his house, in his topcoat, doing no more than listen to the clock tick.

Someone knocked at the door. His sister Sasha. Bright, busy and nosy.

'I wondered if you were free for lunch?'

'I'm not.'

She noticed the suitcase, upright by the hatstand, bound up with a stout leather strap, plastered with long-defunct hotel labels from the days when his father had globetrotted with it half a century ago.

'Where are you going?'

'New York.'

'New York?'

'Why not?'

'Perhaps a wee drinkie, then, before you leave, a little something to steady your nerves?'

It seemed to Troy that he might have to open the door and push her out. She wanted something. Probably, simply the doubtful pleasure of his company, and she wasn't going to get it. Another knock at the door spared him this. It was Tara Ffitch – defying the November weather in a simple, startling red Chanel two-piece. Her hair was still brown – perhaps she had renounced the sins of the blonde? – and she was clutching a smudgy, inky newspaper galley.

'I've not called at a bad time?'

'None better,' said Troy seeing relief from his sister in her presence. 'Do come in.'

He made the introductions. Sasha beamed, seemed genuinely pleased to be meeting a 'celebrity'.

'I brought you the last instalment,' said Tara. 'This will run in the *Post* next Sunday. I don't suppose you followed the story, did you?'

'I'm afraid I didn't. I suppose I should have. The moral tale for our times?'

He had not meant to say this. It slipped out. He liked the woman. He had no wish to offend her.

'If you like,' she said, using one of his favourite phrases. 'You know what morality is? It's the great sideshow, beats bloody hell out of wireless and the telly, and before wireless and the telly were invented it was all they had. It's wonderfully simple. You set up your morality, your moral code that the dull, the lazy and the unimaginative will have no difficulty with, and then when the rest of us, you and I, the few, break it – since it is not in our nature to do otherwise – the many – that is the unimaginative, the lazy and the dull – have hours of endless fun tut-tutting and condemning, the vicarious fun of who fucks who and who does worse. And if we did not fuck and if we did not fuck up, then what would they have to talk about? You see, they need us far more than we need them. In fact, we don't need them at all. So, I'll give them what they want. Or, since in this day and age everything has its price, to be precise I'll sell them what they want.'

'Precisely,' said Sasha. 'Fuck 'em.'

'Quite,' said Tara. 'Fuck 'em.'

It was a dreadful moment. Generations met, years rolled away. Troy knew from the twinkling hagshine in her black eyes that his sister had found her dark soulmate, realised that he had been the unwitting midwife to a friendship cast in hell. That each had lost their twin – whether real or pretend – Masha lost to continuing marriage and motherhood, Caro to the joys and struggles of illegitimacy and miscegenation – and had simply realigned, struck new liaisons, the elective affinity, the coven, the twindom wreathed in sulphur.

'My dear,' said Sasha, 'we appear to be manless. May I buy you lunch?'

'That's just what I came to ask Troy. But he's not coming out to play, is he?'

Troy watched them down the alley, Fox and Cat arm in arm, almost to the kink in the way that led under the buildings on St Martin's Lane. Then Tara was running back to him. Her arms around his neck, a smacking kiss.

'Thanks for not giving me away.'

'What?' he said.

'You know. You always knew.'

'Knew what?'

'Caro never testified in court. I couldn't put her through that. Don't you think I deserve an Oscar for my performance?'

Another smackeroo, and she ran to catch up with Sasha. It was, he had to admit, little short of brilliant, and it had almost worked. She'd seen that Blood meant to charge Fitz come what may, felt first hand his mania to subvert justice and suborn witnesses and, knowing if it were not her it would be someone, she had set him up. Good girl, bad girl – and she had played both parts. She'd pushed Mirkeyn almost to the limit with her 'hysterical' performance; she'd risked contempt and perjury and got away with both. She'd clouded his judgement and but for his ultimately sharing Blood's mania to convict, she could so easily have destroyed the case against Fitz. Troy sincerely hoped that she had just had the last word on the case of Paddy Fitz. There was no more he wanted to hear.

He went back for his suitcase. It felt oddly light. He'd no idea how much to pack. No idea how long he'd be there. Five minutes later he followed the women, down Goodwin's Court, under the arch, out into St Martin's Lane to wait for the hire car. A deep blue, wire-wheeled Morgan shot past him and braked just down the lane, between the Court and the Coliseum. A woman opened the silly toy door and climbed out. It was just like Tereshkov's car. For a moment he looked in double-take. They weren't so common as to be unremarkable. The woman straightened her black winter coat and came up the street towards him, smiling and waving. He did not recognise her. She was in her fifties, he thought. A looker for her age, but all the same he did not know her. An open car in November meant hats and gloves and headscarves. She could see much more of him than he could of her. Only when she stopped less than five feet away and spoke his name did he know her. It was Judy Leigh-Hunt, mother of the errant Charlie. And she wasn't fifty, she was sixty-five or more – a looker all the same.

'I thought I'd missed you.'

'You almost have. I'm on my way to Heathrow.'

'Then I'll be quick. I've had a letter from Charlie. He's written three or four times since February. Usually childish whinges about life in Russia, but by the last letter I finally twigged. When he was a little boy he loved all those *Boy's Own* and *Magnet* thingies, and he'd write me coded letters from school, pretending he was Richard Hannay or Bulldog Thingie or somebody like that, until he got too big to want to bother. I realised he was using it again. I won't bore you with the details, but there was a message for you buried in his last complaint about borscht and fried tripe.'

She opened her handbag and fished out a piece of paper.

'Haven't a clue what it means, but when I got through the nursery code this is what he says: "Tell Freddie his old man was kosher, the real McCoy, the dog's"' . . . herrum . . . oh dear . . . "the dog's bollocks. No need to worry." Now does that mean anything?'

'Yes,' said Troy, wondering if it mattered any more. 'Yes, it's quite clear.'

Over her shoulder he could see the man in the driving seat of the blue Morgan twisting his neck to look at Judy. One of the blue-blazered RAF types. He leant on the horn.

'Who's your friend?'

'Oh, Barry, you mean.'

She coloured almost imperceptibly. Her right hand flapped once, sweeping away something invisible to the eye.

'Well. Bloody hell I thought, when that Woodbridge thing blew up – all these blokes and all those young women – sauce for the goose, I thought. Young Barry – I say young, he's your age if he's a day, darling – well, he'd been hanging around for weeks, and I thought, bugger the family, bugger the neighbours, bugger the village. You're only old once. Well, must dash. Toodle-oo.'

She took a few steps then turned back to him. Sizing him up.

'Freddie. You shouldn't, you know.'

'Shouldn't what?'

'Worry about Charlie. He's not worth it. Men like Charlie, men like Woodbridge, Fitzpatrick – they're none of them worth a damn.'

The Morgan vanished into the snarl of traffic waiting to enter Trafalgar Square. Behind him a horn pipped. He turned and saw a Rolls-Royce at the kerb, a peak-capped driver waving at him. Trust Rod to overdo it. To Heathrow in a Roller? Why not?

He got in the back. The driver looked at him and said, ''Eaffrow, guv'nor?' And whipped off his cap. It was Alfie. Alfie from The Glebe Sanatorium.

'Yes,' said Troy, feeling he should explain, somewhat nonplussed to see the man again. 'Yes. I'm on my way to New York.'

'New York, Fred?' Then he cackled like Tommy Trinder. 'You lucky people!'

Epilogue
November 1963
New York

It was a fortress of a building, dwarfed now by the larger, vulgar developments of the post-war years, but still dominant on its site halfway up Central Park West. It was easy to imagine it as it once was, standing alone on the edge of a virtually treeless Central Park, a mock-gothic castle in a sea of mud so far from the heart of fashionable Manhattan, at a time when rich New Yorkers lived no further north than Union Square, that they said you might just as well live in the Dakotas as live at One West Seventy-Second Street.

It was remarkably like his father's old town house in Moscow, the same pale brick, black with dirt, the same extravagant use of copper, weathered to a startling powder-green, the same tiny turrets and dormers, islands in the sky. But this was the town house writ large, the town house on a monumental scale, ten or eleven storeys, the building running the length of a city block all the way to Seventy-Third.

Troy walked along from the corner – a row of black Neptunes peered at him from the ironwork – and stopped by a blue-uniformed, peak-capped porter, who had just stepped from his sentry box. The man pointed the way to the office. For a moment the fortress became a cathedral as he passed under a high vaulted ceiling, then up a flight of steps and into a small room to face another man in uniform, perched in front of the massed spaghetti of an ancient telephone exchange. Whatever this place was it could not be cheap. Either Tosca had landed on her feet or . . . but there was no end to the sentence, no speculation worth the thought.

432

'Number 66, please,' he said.

'Mrs Troy?'

'Yes.'

The man dialled. Troy could hear the phone ring and ring.

'Nobody home.'

It was pointless asking to be let in. The look on the doorman's face told him that this was not the sort of place that let you in on a bluff or a whim.

'I'm her husband,' he said, knowing how lame the line sounded. The man nodded. 'Sure, sure,' said the look.

'She could be gone a day or two, you know. Tends to do that.'

Troy checked into a hotel and killed two days walking the streets of the city. A wet, misty late November. It seemed to him that with the closing year he had reached the year's antithesis. Twelve months ago or thereabouts he had been in Moscow, the city without. Now New York, the city with.

His sense of the place, based on a single visit in 1928, was that they'd got round to finishing it. In 1928 it had struck him as being a construction site on an unimaginable scale. The Chrysler Building at Lexington and Forty-Second almost built, 40 Wall Street, almost as high and almost as built – and the Empire State Building, webbed with scaffolding, half-built, like the younger brother growing so fast it was all too evident he would soon outgrow his siblings. Troy searched for a metaphor. If Beirut had been London in the war, all black market and fiddles; if Moscow had been London in the bleak years, all want and worry . . . what, then, was New York? At dusk on the second day he found himself at Radio City, on Sixth Avenue, the cross-street led directly into the Rockefeller Center, rising topless from the concrete to vanish in the rain and mist, lit in lurid lilac by the floodlights. It looked hellish, supernatural, futuristic. A backdrop for The Shape of Things to Come. That was it. New York was London in the future. He was not at all sure it was a future he wanted.

He headed back to the Upper West Side, a maverick route up Ninth Avenue until it became Columbus, past the bulldozed tenements of the Jets and the Sharks, a voice inside Troy singing, 'I like to be in Ameeerrriiika!'

At West Seventy-Second the same man said simply, 'You can go up. She's expecting you.'

He was admitted through the second gate, into the courtyard. The walls rose up around him like a keep. More than ever it resembled a castle. And right in front of him was a fountain. Little fishes spouted water, arched their backs and spread their fins around the base of huge conch shells from which rose the same yellowy-white lilies that graced the iron gates of his father's house, spouting still more water. He began to wonder. All those years she had spent in Moscow. Had she made the same visit he had? A quick look at the closed gates of the Ministry of Agriculture, Subdivision of Planning & Production, Wheat & Barley, then on to the guided tour of the Tolstoy house. Is that what attracted her to this Victorian monstrosity? Its very Russianness, its seeming un-Americanness?

Yet another porter, a young woman in blue, wearing a pillbox hat, took him up in the lift, a marvel in mahogany, a plush confessional for the unrepentant, with its Neptunes now in brass, a brass so shiny it must be polished every day.

The door of apartment 66 stood ajar. Darkness within. He pushed gently. A very fat tabby cat, a good eighteen pounds of furry beast, lay on its back on the carpet, barring the threshold, legs in the air, head raised slightly so it could see who was coming in. He took a step forward, expecting the cat to bolt. It didn't.

'He won't let you in 'less you tickle his belly,' said a voice from the darkness.

The floor beneath his feet began to float; the walls took wing. He'd heard that voice in a thousand dreams. Damn romance – of late he'd heard it in a dozen nightmares.

'Where are you? I can't see you.'

'In the dark. One of us always seems to be.'

He scrunched his eyes. Willed his irises to widen to the light. A short figure assumed shape at the edge of vision. The cat rolled onto his feet and took flight. A barefoot Tosca padded slowly towards him.

'What kept ya?'

She pecked him on the cheek, pushed the door to and walked on into the sitting room without waiting for his answer.

He looked around. Books from floor to ceiling, books in piles on the floor, books three layers deep adding six inches to the height of the coffee table. The Tosca he had known had read *Huck Finn* over and over again. In the mid-fifties, when they'd married, he had tried to broaden her taste. He'd no idea he had succeeded on quite such a scale. It was more a Troy household than a Tosca one. Troy Nation new-built in the New World. But then, as Fitz had said, she was Mrs Troy.

She was dressed of old. A blouse and slacks. He could not recall that he had ever seen her in a dress. He looked at her. She bloomed. She was older than he, fifty-two, but she had kept her figure. The starched white blouse, a cotton sculpture over big breasts, the black slacks clinging to the curve of her backside. Her neck had not gone, but that it would was inevitable with women. The neck went before the tits. The eyes shone, nut-brown, fleckless and cat healthy. She was looking back at him, smiling, so obviously glad to see him. He wondered what she saw when she looked at him.

And he knew at once that everything had changed.

Troy woke. A post-coital wakefulness, the kind that used to drive her nuts. She could sleep like death, and if he woke her she would complain. But she was awake first. He realised almost at once that she could see him in the half-darkness, the reflected light of the building opposite cutting through the curtains of the bedroom.

She threw off the sheets and disappeared down the corridor. A few minutes later she returned, a plate of warm pizza in her hand. Still naked. Tanned, trim. Tits up, arse firm. She took some form of regular exercise, he concluded. Cared for herself in a way he'd never found possible or practical. The job had blown him apart, time and Kolankiewicz had sewn him back together. Until now.

'Figured you'd be hungry. You used to eat like a horse after. Ah, the joys of a Toast'R'Oven.'

He'd not eaten pizza in years. It had never caught on in England. Probably never would. His first taste of it from the PX during the war had struck him as exotically un-English. Now it seemed too rich, too greasy; it merely filled a space in his belly.

She ate more than he. A rolling tear of oil coursed from the corner of her mouth, down her neck and across her left breast. He dammed it just short of the nipple with the tip of a finger and traced its route back to her lips.

'Why did you want me back?' he asked.

'Well . . . the sex was always good . . .'

She was grinning as she said it. But she also meant it, he knew. As though his inhibitions were smothered by her lack.

He was astounded. The idea that there could be such a thing as 'good' sex. All sex was bad sex. It drew you and it bound you and it spent you. It took all your unspecified desire and then it tossed you aside with your desire still unsatisfied. But that was less than half her answer.

'I love you. Took an age for me to accept it, but I do. Or to be precise, it took a world for me to accept it.'

Troy said nothing. She had not ducked her own words, had looked at him through every syllable.

'Could you live here? I mean. Being practical. Could you live here?'

'I don't know,' he lied, knowing damn well he couldn't. He did like to be in Ameeerrriiika; he just didn't want to live there. 'Could you live in England?'

'No. It's an uptight—'

He knew the lyrics to this one and cut her off.

'—Tight-assed little nation.'

'You've noticed?'

'It's changing. Everybody tells me its changing.'

'Believe that when I see it.'

The pause, the deep intake of breath, told him more was coming – that what followed would not be so flippant.

'I had to do this my own way. You understand? I had . . . I had a world to make.'

This was her considered word on an absence of seven years. This was what his father had told him. This was what he had told Charlie. A world of difference, the one between the world as you find it and the world as you make it.

'I mean. Who am I? Took me a while to know.'

This was the question she had posed over and over again when she had fled Russia in '56. It was a reasonable question after a life of deceit and disguise. A war spent the US Army, a cold war spent with the KGB and the years since 1956 spent, if not hiding from, then avoiding, both. It seemed to Troy that she had fled one way almost as Charlie had fled the other. My friend the spy, my wife the spy. The pity of it was he hated spooks.

Now, he was startled by the combination of personalities she was displaying to him. The wise-cracking Lower East Side she-huckster who had seduced him effortlessly in 1944, now overlain by the Manhattan sophisticate – two styles of competence and confidence. And the broken-winged bird he had married in 1956 – endlessly pushing him out to arm's length – was nowhere to be seen. It was he whose wings flapped hopelessly, he who had looked in the mirror and failed to recognise his own body.

'Who am I?' he said back to her, and departed from the script. He had never asked her that before. It was not a question he would ever have put to anyone.

Out in the corridor the cat struck up a wail. Only when Tosca got out of bed and opened the door to him did the beast shut up. All Troy saw was a flash of tabby fur as he shot into the room. A couple of minutes later he appeared on Troy's pillow, silent, looking into Troy's black eyes with his own merely slits of emerald green. He could not help the feeling that he'd seen this look before.

That night he dreamt of Clover again. Wet-footed, softly to his bed. The dead hand upon him. He felt no pain.

He woke to the brightness of day and a fit of coughing. He'd not hacked so badly in quite a while. He grabbed a handkerchief and spat blood into it. He'd never done that before. Maybe it was a mistake to have flushed all his pills down the bog, the TB tablets along with the uppers and downers.

He looked sideways. Tosca was on the floor. On the other side of the room, by the window. The cat next to her, eyes flashing. They were both staring at him.

'Y'OK?'

'I'll be fine. What are you doing?'

She turned back to the window. Put a knuckle and a diamond ring to the glass.

'You remember that window in the Blue Room at Mimram, where your sister scratched the date of her engagement and their initials in the glass. I kinda thought I'd do the same. Mark the date we got it back together in glass. Otherwise we'll neither of us remember it. It was way after midnight, so it'll be today's date.'

She was right. He would not remember. He could remember nothing save that which tumbled headlong through his dreams.

Nothing. Nothing lasted. Everything changed. Everything passed. The brightest tent, its shining yards hung in tatters from the rail for moth and mouse to feed upon.

> Why should not middle-aged men be mad?
> She
> who never knew a word of
> Dante, who half-remembered
> Oscar Wilde, and once,
> long ago,
> had heard
> Dylan Thomas on the wireless . . .
> who cares what the old books said?
> who cares why middle-aged men should be
> mad . . .

She had made her world, as she rightly, proudly put it. There was no place for him in it, though she did not know it – and there was no place in it that he wanted. He had lived so long without – without wife, without family, without feeling – without the value scheme, the moral scheme that life builds on reciprocal emotion. These were things he did not know and did not wish to know and would never know.

He had learnt a lesson too late in life – that other people's emotions do not matter.

Her 'I love you' was meaningless to him.

She might just as well have said, 'Your flies are undone.'

Once acknowledged, instantly forgotten.

Other people's emotions are out there somewhere beyond, beyond the bubble. The glass bubble. He had come to think of the glass bubble as the condition of tuberculosis, the White Death – but it was the human condition, the Living Death.

A fire engine roared up Central Park West, full siren song. He found himself gazing at her spine, bent over her etching. Naked but for knickers. She pulled back from the windowpane.

'There,' she said. 'That should do it.'

He saw his initials entwined in hers, and the date diamond deep. 'November 22nd 1963.'

She was right. No one would ever remember that.

Historical Note

There is an obvious source for some of what precedes. The Profumo
Affair of 1963 gave me some of the plot and a few of the details of
the second quarter of this book. Equally, there are other, perhaps less
obvious sources – the case of Detective Sergeant Challenor of 1962,
the defection of Kim Philby, also in 1963, and the resignation of
Lord Lambton some ten years later. I was also influenced by, among
others, Ian Fleming's *Goldfinger*, V. C. Fishwick's *Pigs: Their Breeding
and Management* (rev. edn, 1956), the poetry of Brian Patten and the
Diaries of Alan Clark.

This is not a roman à clef. It does not help to presume that
Woodbridge is Profumo or to presume that Charlie is Philby.
Equally, Fitz is not Ward and Tara, Caro and Clover are neither
Mandy nor Christine. The 'real' people are the minor characters –
Driberg, Rebecca West – or background figures who do not appear
– Wilson, Kennedy *et al.* I made the rest up. Only two 'speeches'
made by anyone in 1963 are used in this book, the first uttered by
Stephen Ward at his trial is given, slightly amended, to Marty Pritch-
Kemp on p. 231, and the second, uttered, perhaps apocryphally, by
Rebecca West is on p. 188.

I've bent history as little as possible, but for reasons of plot I sent
Troy and Driberg to the Establishment Club after the real
Establishment had folded, and I'm well aware that a 1952 Bentley
Continental was a two-door car, and that I gave it four.

If a novel can have a single starting point, it was this. Several years
ago I interviewed a reporter who had covered the Stephen Ward

JOHN LAWTON

case in 1963, and had known Ward well. 'Any idea that he was bumped off is fantasy,' I was told. 'He killed himself.' And I started to think of a plot whose premise was 'supposing he didn't?' Once I'd gone down that road, since I'd no doubts that Ward did kill himself, the resemblances to what really happened in 1963 became those of mood, as in 'national mood', and tone rather than of incident and character. I stuck with the axis of the plot being a sex scandal because no other plot would be authentically as axiomatic of the times. As Rebecca West put it: 'The state of mind of England in 1963 was itself a historic event . . .'